The Blackened Threshold

By

David Ben Efraim

Acknowledgements

This book is dedicated to my parents, Yakov and Evgenia Ben Efraim, as well as my grandmother, Natalia Bebeher, for their enduring love, unwavering support of my ambitions, and belief in my abilities.

Special thanks to Laurie Bech from Nihil Art for her patient work on the cover art, and the breathtaking results she produced.

This is a work of fiction. Names, characters, places, and incidents either are the product of the author's imagination or are used in a fictitious manner. Any resemblance to actual persons, living or dead, events, or locales is merely coincidental.

THE BLACKENED THRESHOLD
ISBN: 978-1-7778619-0-2

Chapter 0

The General sat in his childhood cottage surrounded by an oppressive swathe of trees, coddling his need for an illusion of safety he had grown accustomed to since a forgettable adolescence. He didn't believe himself to be a fool, and knew anyone who wanted to find him only had to look hard enough; he simply had no reason to fear. On the contrary, his years of honourable service left him with many honestly-earned medals and a list of exploits long enough for a few poorly-selling memoirs. As a matter of fact, he had already written two self-indulgent autobiographies, and there was even discussion of naming a town in his honour. Nobody, of course, knew where the town was. For a man with a conscience supposedly clean as a whistle, the General was quite nervous on this night, sucking on his pipe incessantly while tapping his unusually large foot on the hard wooden floor. He opened his private journal, slowly and carefully, so as to avoid triggering the attached mechanism designed to strike with poisoned blades the hands of anyone attempting to meddle with it. He dipped his feather in ink, licked it at the tip, a guilty pleasure of his, and began to write: *"July 19th, 1945, My secret cottage, no formal address. Dear diary, this is your General speaking. You know as well as anyone I've been more than virtuous my whole life: I served the ideals of those above me without doubt nor question. Today, my resolve is tested beyond all imaginable limits, as I am, dear Diary, for the first time experiencing a smidgen of doubt about the country's plans, and my place in them. Two days ago, on July 17th, 1945, I was assigned to a secret subdivision, smuggled fifty kilometres north of the Canadian border at specific coordinates which I've now forgotten as ordered, with our journey having begun at Knife Lake. My sole direction was to supervise my comrades and ensure they would comply with their orders, which I was to learn on-site, but never did. Whence we arrived on-site, we received a conspicuous signal via a gas lamp, which led us to an offensively unfurnished bunker set up by Command. Soon as we entered, the doors locked behind us, and I heard the countdown over the radio. From ten to one. With all the other numbers in-between. The ground, walls, and ceiling shook. I was then handed a strange full-body suit which, as I was told, was lined with special protective material which might or might not keep me safe. I was informed via radio my mission had been accomplished, and it was time to return. I put the suit on, and left the bunker at a leisurely pace, to instill the idea I had accomplished something important, whatever it might have been. The men followed suit. The walk from the bunker back to our vehicle was less than a minute long, and during this minute I observed a strange pulsating light not far from our bunker, and a miniature cloud hanging approximately twenty-three point eight meters from the ground. It might have been taller, or shorter; I omitted to bring my ruler. I observed how beautiful of a sight it was, and the men nodded in agreement. Good boys. They'll get far, but not farther than me. So, where does my guilt lay, you might ask of me, dear Diary? I cannot bear the thought I was simply sent as a fixture, to pad my service record with yet another completed mission. It is not fair I should be recognized for this service, and I will take it up with the President personally. Maybe I'll even ask him what it was all about. Your General, signing off."*

Upon closing the diary, the General began to hastily caress it, absorbed in thought, and the coiled viper of a defense mechanism sprang into action, sliced his hands with the poisoned blades and fulfilled its destiny. This set in motion the second mechanism, which crushed two hidden ampules and mixed their contents, potassium permanganate and glycerine, starting an ineffective fire which only partially burnt the cover in approximately the same amount of time it took for the General to leave this world of wars and medals. His greatest regret in his last moment was never having been able to take it up with the President personally. These things happen.

Chapter 1

For as long as Jeremiah Baxter had lived, which was about thirty-four years now since his quiet birth in December of 1975, he never left his tiny little hometown of Hollow Crest in search of a greater life elsewhere, a concept he never did know how to define. He managed the unfathomable exploit of growing up into a perfectly-healthy, dark-haired and slightly-taller-than-average man, only blemished by a few wrinkles which settled in before their time. His forehead and chin were strong and prominent, but not enough to make them truly remarkable, and his dark-brown eyes only reinforced his unassuming nature. Why would he ever need to leave the confines of the seemingly self-sustaining and eternal town-wide fortress which catered to his every need since birth, and where he was accepted as an extremely unremarkable member of society? Neither he nor his family had ever asked themselves how they would pay the month's rent, nor did they ever know the existential terror which comes with a rising stack of utility bills. There was always food on the table, presents at Christmas, and most importantly, constant access to the internet. What greater life could there be?

The Hollow Crest Formal Public Academy of Knowledge and Education was the unnecessarily lengthy name given to the local school upon its inception in times none seemed to actually remember. It doubled both as the town's elementary and high-school. Year after year it swallowed new young students it could bore to death while spitting out the old ones into a confusing illusion of freedom. A flawless system. For the most part, they were unleashed into the great wide world of working at the local cow milking and dairy processing plant. It was affectionately and creatively referred to as the Big Cow by the locals for its giant, cow-depicting logo visible across town. The bovine sentinel of Hollow Crest. Unlike many of his classmates who would have rather been anywhere than painfully well-sanitized and blindingly-bright classrooms, Jeremiah was only bored half the time in school, enjoying the subjects which let his imagination travel a bit, namely literature and history. He never put much of it to good use though, sharing the lack of enthusiasm his teachers had for education, already knowing the career paths the overwhelming majority of their students would end up taking… not to speak of their life paths. Thankfully, his twelve years of mild suffering were rewarded with two people he could, if thinking long and hard about it, call his friends: Roger Silver and Naomi Wolfe.

After having spent a very safe and unmemorable childhood together, the trio took the habit of meeting for drinks once a month at the Amber Goblet, the less noisy of the two pubs in town. As much as all three of them were disinterested with the rest of the world, they found some comfort in each other's like-mindedness, and most of their conversations devolved into a drunken derision of the reality they would be forced to endure on the following day. To those with the observational skills to be aware of them, they became a bit of an inside joke, the town's very own three stooges. If they had been aware of it, it probably wouldn't have made a difference.

The Baxters had never wanted for money, and just like his father Patrick before him – God rest his soul lost at sea on a tragic leisure boating accident – Jeremiah found his calling in life at the Big Cow, the heart and blood of the town's livelihood. The monolith towering over a history none cared to learn anymore, above the pathetic lives of all beneath it, had acquired a sacred character over the years. However, unlike his father – a high-ranking manager who tore his way through the politics and into his colleagues' hearts – Jeremiah found peace and comfort in being the trusty and essential nighttime security guard. The job title was a bit of a joke in and of itself; only a few of the oldest of old-timers could remember a day when a crime more serious than loitering or noise pollution graced the town; most of them couldn't remember much of anything at all. Nevertheless, he kept up his tireless duty of watching movies on the little television set his predecessor had left, reading novels, and making about half the rounds he was supposed to. At times, he wondered if anyone at work even knew of his existence, only to promptly remind himself he didn't really care enough to find out.

Jeremiah's weeks were largely the same, save for the monthly Amber Goblet reunion. The days were spent sleeping off the night of hard work from before, Saturdays were spent shopping and watching movies, while on Sundays he spent the day with his mother, Annabelle. As much as he loved her, he could never forget the glint of relief in her eyes when the news came of her husband's demise. She kept insisting he was a "brainless moron" for wanting to take a trip to the ocean in his old age while battling with both emphysema and arthritis, and frankly-speaking, so did Jeremiah. Ultimately for Annabelle though, her the grief of losing her moderately-beloved Patrick was more than compensated for by the elation of the most powerful joy known to mankind: being right. From that day forth, whenever she got into any type of argument, an activity which made up roughly ninety percent of her daily routine, she would inevitably bring up her prophetic powers, at which point most people would lose what little interest they had left in having anything to do with her. Thus, Annabelle emerged from every argument victorious. If anything, she appreciated Patrick more in his death: "He does more for me dead than alive.", Annabelle once confided to Jeremiah. He learned quickly not to press her on the matter of Patrick any further, and imagined she too would turn senile one day; it runs in the family. Part of him was glad the Sunday visits came to an end when she suddenly decided to immigrate to the Bahamas to open a beauty salon. He only wished her luck and didn't try to stop her. The guilt from it did tug at his conscience from time to time, until he reminded himself nobody alive can always make the correct decisions. The occasional drink also helped.

How Patrick and Annabelle Baxter came to be was always a mystery to him. The only bit of information he had on the matter was a vague memory of his grandfather claiming Patrick met Annabelle when he helped her flee Morocco as a fugitive, alongside her other husband back then. One day, after watching *Casablanca*, Jeremiah decided this was a dead end. He never had the mind to ask his father during his lifetime, and knew better than to bring up the dead man's name in front of his potentially-crazy mother. The mystery would remain unsolved for evermore, and Jeremiah was grateful he wouldn't have to deal with the disappointment of a completely predictable and mundane resolution.

Jeremiah himself had a few girlfriends along the way, but none who stuck for long or whom he got serious with. They were mostly distractions to fill up his spare time, and sooner or later even the most hopeful ones understood his wavering interest in them was the glorious pinnacle of their relationship. He didn't mind seeing them leave, and as the years went by he grew increasingly tired of letting them in through the unkempt revolving door of his romantic life. If anything, he believed marriage made his parents loathe each other, or at least drove them both to the brink of insanity... a mistake he proudly promised to himself he wouldn't repeat. Or so he kept telling himself.

Thus, Jeremiah Baxter had forged for himself an existence he could keep up until the end of all time if need be; it was simple, comfortable, and predictable to both a relaxing and nauseating extent. The questions which tugged at him from time to time were forgotten as quickly and suddenly as they appeared, and through many years of finding few answers to life's great mysteries he learned to simply accept it all as it was, is, and will be. Nothing could possibly shatter Jeremiah's completely solid existence. Nothing at all.

Chapter 2

If they ever had the opportunity to look back on it, the citizens of Hollow Crest would have pegged the morning of March 16th, 2007, as the day when the strangeness began to seep into their reality, carefully sterilized through generations of hard work. The day itself wasn't exactly impressive, beginning like any other Tuesday in the town's history. For most people, it meant either going to school, opening their shops, or clocking in at the Big Cow to fulfill the same duties as the day before. It was all the price of safety. For Jeremiah Baxter, this meant crashing in bed after yet another night of work so easy it bordered on being illegal. With the impending arrival of spring, the town's morale was ever so slightly more joyful than usual, and an air of certitude established itself... certitude in the existence of the days yet to come.

By pure coincidence, Roger Silver was the very first person to unknowingly witness the beginning of the transformation no one knew had begun. Fair-haired, early riser and an avid smoker, he had a habit of waking up earlier because he believed in an article which declared tobacco was less harmful the earlier it was consumed in the day, and could even help develop an immunity to itself. Roger never did realize it was a satirical article, and nobody cared enough to correct him… a separate challenge in itself. His heavy-set body was accompanied by an equally-rotund face which had the habit of turning red all too easily. His nose was more akin to a potato than any other vegetable, and his small eyes were made to look even more sunk in thanks to the plump cheeks they were resting on. On the early morning of March 16th, while adjusting his massive frame on the balcony and enjoying the pleasure of smoking with none of the harm, he saw near the edge of town a dark, slender figure approaching from a distance. A lonesome visitor the crack of dawn? This qualified as newsworthy in Hollow Crest. After shaking off the shock of potentially witnessing something new happening in his life, he ran back inside, cigarette in his mouth, smoke streaming into his eyes, and fetched his nautical spyglass, a misguided gift once sent to him by an uncle he never actually met. The roof was only one floor above his own apartment, but he still decided he needed to reach the highest ground for the best view. After finding a way to trip over the stairs in his excitement and humiliating himself in front of all the germs and spiders in the building, his long voyage to the roof was finally complete. Impatiently, he began scanning the horizon in search of the lonely newcomer, but it was all in vain; the figure seemed to have vanished as suddenly as it had appeared. After roughly thirty seconds of intense peering through the spyglass, the cigarette Roger forgot about burnt all the way to the tip, and the searing pain on his lips brought him out his trance along with a short and sharp yelp. Ending this adventure much more disappointed in himself than he had started it, he couldn't shake the feeling things would no longer be the same. "Man... I'm hungry." he boldly enunciated for his own benefit, retreated back into his modern cave, and got to work on his lone breakfast tomato.

Energized and ready for the day to come, Roger always recognized himself superior to most of his fellow citizens, by simple virtue he wasn't working at the Big Cow, but was running his own business: the sole meditation centre for hundreds of miles around. Consistently bouncing back and forth between different names, on this specific day it was still registered as the "Loose Brain Dojo", a name Roger had stuck with for a few months now, by far his longest streak in this regard. He considered his endeavours to be essential to the town, to the point where he began filing demands to have his centre legally classified as such. Faced with his tremendous relentlessness and lack of logical thinking, the city council eventually relented and granted him his wish, if only so they could half the daily number of phone calls they had to sit through. Contrary to everyone's expectations, even Roger's, the business bloomed and grew from the moment its doors opened, to the point where he had to set up projects to expand his large rented room into something resembling an actual studio. As much as he would have wanted to open a second centre, there was nobody in the world bar himself he could trust with such complex and crucial classes.

His clientele mainly consisted of retired old ladies, mixed in with a few curious youngsters eager to learn the transcendental ways of the hippie, and a few self-professed adults suffering a rudimentary mid-life crisis. Deep inside, Roger truly believed it was his calling to teach people how to find peace within themselves and gain a better understanding of the magnificent and mysterious world around them. Deep inside, the old ladies just wanted to spend their time outside the house and eventually came to see him as a grandchild they could all care for. He demonstrated breathing exercises, and the hippies were too stoned to understand him. The mid-life crisis practitioners did listen to him for a class or two, but like many in their situation, they didn't stick with one thing for very long. Nevertheless, a certain balance was achieved, with everyone being happy with what they were doing, even if it was for all the wrong reasons.

Every morning when he came in to teach the first class, his four most loyal meditators were always eagerly awaiting his arrival: Betty, Lisa, Amanda and Marge. All four of them widowed and in their seventies, they formed his royal guard and so long as he would have his "adorable" round face, reminiscent of a misshaped tomato, they would follow him to the end of the world. Today was, once again, the same as any other day, and after greeting them with a smile which he assumed exuded wisdom, he opened the doors to the Loose Brain Dojo and began the half-hour countdown to give more potential students a chance to join in before embarking on the road to self-realization, whatever it meant. Thirty minutes later, after a few more old ladies and a couple of lost souls stumbled in, he was finally ready to begin his work. After a few minutes of reminding everyone the basics of human breathing and extolling the "absolutely phenomenal" virtues of our species' ability to keep our eyes closed at will, he ordered everyone to begin meditating. This meant they would spend the next hour and a half breathing, occasionally opening their eyes not to fall asleep, while Roger droned out wise and ancient instructions in a hushed tone from time to time.

After spending a few minutes with his eyes closed, Roger suddenly experienced something he wasn't quite familiar with: an involuntary rupture of his inner meditative silence. Before his mind's eye flashed the dark figure he saw earlier from his rooftop, and he could feel it slowly marching its way towards him as he stood unable to open his eyes and escape unreality. Frozen in near-total darkness, he could only watch as the figure stopped a few steps short of him, the outlines of its visage barely visible. It seemed to Roger he was standing face-to-face with an elderly man, appearing almost too old and decrepit to even be of this world and exuding a foul, unnatural smell. The old man showed the faintest trace of a smile, relaxed his jaw and let his mouth droop ever so slightly. What followed eclipsed anything Roger had experienced during the psychedelic journeys of his misspent youth, as a prismatic wave of colours across the entire spectrum began to pour out from the old man's eyes and mouth, accompanied by a monstrous cacophony echoing every sound both known and unknown to mankind; the symphony of annihilation. At last, Roger found the power of will to free himself from the trance, accidentally letting out his second high-pitched girlish scream of the day to the befuddled dismay of his students. This certainly wasn't the norm.

"Classes are cancelled for today. BLAM, meet me in my office." Spoke Roger with an air of gravity to him, cold sweat on his forehead.

"...What?" wisely asked the first hippie.

"Are you feeling ill dear?" interjected the concerned Betty.

"First of all, it means no more classes for today. Second of all, nobody's ill. Third of all, Betty, Lisa, Amanda and Marge, meet me in my office." Roger mercifully clarified.

"Okay man, but we want like, a refund, cause we paid for a full class, you know?" the second lost soul made his presence known.

"I have something better than a refund for you, gentlemen." Roger paused for dramatic effect "Your next time here I will allow you to stay for two sessions at the price of one. Now for the love of all that is holy, please leave. This is important." Roger walked to the glass door and held it open without breaking eye contact.

After nodding at each other for what felt like an eternity, they declared in perfectly synchronized tandem: "Okay man." With their most pressing issue of the day resolved, they began the laborious process of getting up from the floor and leaving the establishment, which only took a couple of minutes. The other students followed their example and slowly piled onto the sidewalk, still positively shocked by the idea of something unusual happening in their routine. For the rest of the day they would try to divine what Roger was getting up to with his faithful guards, and by the end of it sporadic rumours would be going around about strange happenings at the Loose Brain Dojo. The absence of facts naturally didn't stop people from drawing conclusions. Naturally, the hippies were the exception to the rule as they tend to be, and largely forgot about the whole ordeal within a few hours, including the compensation they agreed to. Roger predicted this.

With the door locked behind him, the master of the dojo gathered his army of four and sat them down on the floor like school children. He stood straight up, gathered his arms behind his back, and waited in perfect stillness for a few moments, trying to buy himself some time to figure out how to actually explain the situation to them, which was as he believed, quite dire. The four ladies waited with bated breath, as if preparing themselves to fulfill the great destiny they were born for. The silence lasted an uncomfortably long time, but finally it was broken.

Thus spoke Roger Silver:

"Ladies, there are only two people in this life I trust more than you, and they're both hard to reach most of the time, so I'll have to make due with you for now. As you're aware, I've been meditating for a much longer time than any of you have, meaning my connection with the forces beyond this world are much stronger than yours. It's nothing to be ashamed of, ladies, I simply lucked out in... being who I am? Yes. Now, today I believe you witnessed me making contact with those forces when I screamed..." An interruption was inevitable.

"Like a little bitch." added Amanda through her smoker's cough. Her throat had essentially turned into a chimney.

"...Yes, Amanda, thank you for the input." eyes closed and hands on his temples, Roger regained his composure. "When I screamed today, I saw something... that I can't describe. Well, I can, but it wouldn't make much sense to the uninitiated, so I think it's best I don't tell you *all* the details. Besides, it's not important. I'm convinced of one thing: we're getting invaded." He gave the thought a good, long pause to let it sink in.

"You mean like the Germans?" asked Lisa with complete honesty.

"Hmm... No, I don't think the Germans have anything to do with this..." Roger replied, with an equal level of honesty.

"Oh dear, this doesn't sound too good. Can we do anything for you darling?" Betty reminded the others she too, was in the room.

"Listen carefully, ladies. I need you to spread the word around town about the coming invasion. By nightfall, I want every man, woman, child, cat and dog to be armed and ready. Make posters, I'll bring you a megaphone, and get to work on spreading the word. Hollow Crest will have to defend itself ladies, and you'll be our... uhm... vanguard. The spearhead of our collective strike force." Hope and passion began to radiate from Roger's enthusiasm.

"My arthritis is acting up, I'm out." Marge seemed keen on killing those feelings though.

"Here we go again... sissy Marge... your arthritis... is always actin' up." Amanda managed to squeeze out between taxing gulps of air. "I'm dead inside out... and I'll help 'im"

"Yea, well, you don't have arthritis bad as I do... and what you have is called being a dumbass." Marge's wit was proving unusually quick on this day.

"I hope you die soon!" Amanda's reserves of creativity had been exhausted long ago in this conversation.

"LADIES! LADIES! Now is not the time!" Roger's sudden moment of concern was thankfully enough to bring the argument which was going nowhere to a halt "This is obviously the invader's plan. A tale as old as time. Make us fight between ourselves, while we should be spreading the warning. Quick, start making the posters, I'll run to the store and get us what we need." The big plan was ready to be set in motion.

"Can't we just use those things the kids do, like the internet?" Marge's creativity knew no bounds.

"Um, I guess that works too, actually." Roger's disappointment was painfully real.

"So... how do we do it? And what do we tell people?" Marge pressed on.

"Well, let's see, I'll make dummy accounts for all of you, and you're going to spend the day sending out a message of warning to every person from Hollow Crest you can find on there. The library should have a few computers we can use..." Roger's eagerness took little time to be reborn.

"Actually, that's too far for me." interrupted Marge once again. "I'll just go home and tell my neighbours about the invasion."

"... and the message we will send:" it took Roger every ounce of his willpower to ignore her and stay on track, "WARNING TO EVERYONE! HOLLOW CREST IS IN DANGER! WE ARE BEING INVADED! KEEP YOUR EYES OPEN... AND YOUR MINDS CLOSED!" after a moment's pause lost in deep thought, he added: "SEND MORE GUNS." proud of his ability to think ahead, he concluded the message with a satisfied smile "THE END."

Having sent off his valiant knights to spread word of the doom coming to Hollow Crest, he gauged the chances they would forget everything he just told them upon leaving his studio. About fifty-fifty, he figured. Roger then set his sights on the other important task for today: making sure his two best friends and the only people he almost considered equals were warned of the situation. Jeremiah was in a deep sleep at this time of day, and likely dreamless Roger assumed, since he could never remember his friend sharing any dreams with him. This made him safe for the time being. Naomi, on the other hand, was a different story...

Chapter 3

Naomi Wolfe underwent fewer physical changes in her life than most people, her tall stature, pitch-black hair, and long-lost but slightly apparent Asian genetics being constants worthy of serving as basis for mathematical formulae. Her green eyes stood out like large globes in a slender and vertically-impressive face, which her remaining features followed quite accurately. More importantly, she was, simply put, born with a silver spoon in her mouth the size of a ladle. First entering the world in a private clinic, the Wolfe family had set up inside their opulent mansion a few minutes outside of town, Naomi scarcely saw her parents during a childhood spent changing between one snobbish nanny and the next. Her parents took pride in every aristocratic way in which they could distinguish themselves from the regular townsfolk, leading to the logical decision of adding yet another wing to their mansion, serving as a private school of the highest calibre for their daughter's benefit. At first the plan was coming along smoothly, but there was one factor they hadn't really considered: there couldn't possibly be another child in this town whose family matched their own in stature. Week after week they would interview five, six, and then seven-year-old girls in their downtown office. This lasted until the night of Naomi's eighth birthday, when she burnt the cherished school wing down as a sign of protest and declaration of love for pyrotechnics. After inviting multiple child psychologists, therapists, and eventually mystics to help talk Naomi down from her crazy idea of going to public school, they relented and only hoped she would see the error of her ways soon enough.

She would never admit to it even with a gun pointed to her head, but for the next eight years of her life Naomi regretted the decision of leaving the comfort of her sometimes-insane, but nevertheless familiar home school in favour of The Hollow Crest Formal Public Academy of Knowledge and Education. She soon began to take note of the harsh reality life was punishing her with for a coddled existence: other people can't always be trusted, and as a matter of fact, they can be extremely unpleasant. Her upbringing and social status had already, unbeknownst to her, been the talk of the town for the last couple of years before she entered society, and were reignited more recently by her pyromaniac escapades. Marked as a pariah before she ever had a chance to introduce herself, Naomi was largely avoided by most people, and the few who did deign speak to her usually did so for the irreplaceable exhilaration of mocking her. Nevertheless, she trudged onward, and her suffering more or less paid off when she managed to find the other two generally-ignored outcasts, Roger and Jeremiah. Roger took it as his calling to impart the accumulated wisdom of his life to an uninitiated member of society, which even then was already somewhat significant by his own appraisal. Jeremiah, on the other hand, was mostly glad to finally have someone else to speak with, and more importantly, he was happy Roger would finally also have someone else to talk to. Together, they tentatively discovered the world during lunch breaks and sometimes after school, and though Naomi's time with her friends wasn't objectively remarkable, it gave her a sense of belonging in the world and acceptance she had never truly known before. Also, it was they who first taught her the definition of the word "cult".

She never did have a clear picture of what sort of career her parents were in, her questions mostly rebutted with vague job titles. "Law consultant" was the one she got the most often out of them, and so it was the one she settled on when people would inevitably ask her about it. The summer of her fourteenth year marked the beginning of the end for her little world she always considered invulnerable... it marked the first time some of the more distasteful rumours about her family found their way into her ears. According to the tales of Eric Boozebeard the Trustworthy

– the local drunk famous for legally changing his name to suit his personality – "The Wolfe family "arr avin' demselfs ah cult in der manshun, basterds". She didn't pay much attention to it at the time, but the seed of unravelling destruction had already been planted.

Three years later, with her high-school graduation and life out of the way, she decided to leave the world of peasants behind and enter the family business, whatever it might be. To her dismay and mild surprise, her parents were completely opposed to the idea, and wouldn't even let her into their downtown office. More than suspicious, she began to grow curious, slowly taking a liking to exposing herself to her parents' business specifically because it was against their wishes. With the summer off and little else to do, she decided it would be her mission to break into the coveted office no matter the cost. In the end, she didn't need nearly this long. She found the spare key right on the desk of her father's main home office, and had it copied during the day while they were off doing whatever it was they did. By the time they came home, the key was back in its exact position, atom to atom. When the sun set and her parents retired, she put on her best jogging outfit, and satisfied with her disguise as a highly-driven nighttime sportswoman, made her way to the object of her current obsession.

It took her about half an hour of leisurely jogging to find her way to the target, and she approached the lobby door of the imposing twelve-story tall marble shrine in the middle of the city. It was unlocked. Sweat beads of uncertainty rolling down her forehead, she awkwardly crossed the threshold and began walking to the elevator of a simple lobby decked out in cherry wood and marble. Suddenly, a voice calls out to her and makes her freeze in her tracks: "Oi!". She turned to her left: a British Cerberus guarded to the Wolfe underworld.

"Ya can't go in there ah'm afraid, place is closed." the guard's disarming tone caught Naomi off-guard.

"Hi. I'm Naomi. Wolfe. Here, hold on." her heart racing, she reached into her pocket, fished out her wallet and presented her library card.

"And what can I do for you, Miss Wolfe?" he really wanted the answer to be "nothing".

"My parents. My dad, he asked me to uh, get a thing from his office." she tried to act naturally, only to realize she didn't know what natural behaviour was like in this situation.

"Well, alright then, go on." he was relieved he wouldn't have to move his ass from the chair for at least another hour.

"Okay, well, I won't be long." relief washed over her as well. The act had fooled the experienced guardian.

"Alright." he just wanted to get back to his novel.

"Okay, bye then."

"*Bye!*"

With her first obstacle cleared, Naomi stepped onward into the elevator, and prepared herself for the second one: finding the office. She had never actually been here before, nor were there any signs or labels to guide her around, an offensive design choice, in her opinion. After about two seconds of thinking, she realized her parents would never settle for anything but a floor high enough to look down on the rest of the people, and pressed button number twelve. The elevator music kicked in for the short ride, blasting "Motorhead" by Motorhead at full volume. There was no end to the offensive choices.

After coming to a full stop, the elevator doors finally deemed to open. They led into a small room, barely big enough for two people, and a solid golden locked door reeking of vanity and narcissism stood before her. She turned the key, pushed the door open, and for a while didn't exactly know what to make of it all. It led to a single opulent room, decorated to mimic some sort of imperial palace from a bygone era. Two golden thrones sat in the middle, with a large sculpture standing behind them, depicting in great detail a bird on fire. It seemed to have a confused look about it. Between the thrones sat a large wooden chest with a small hole at the top, and a label carved into the front: "Offerings to the Fire Bird". "What the shit..." Naomi whispered to herself. In the back of her mind she knew what she was seeing, but she lacked the resolve to outright admit it to herself. She needed to know more.

Back home, she laid awake through the night in her bed, counting down the seconds to her parents leaving for "work". Once gone, she marched in a sleepy haze to her father's home office and found the door unlocked. She had never bothered to actually spend any time in this room before, but now she suspiciously observed it mostly consisted of locked dressers, locked cabinets, and a massive locked table, supporting a computer which was, no doubt, locked as well. Feelings of rebelliousness began to boil deep down inside her soul, and if a life spent devoid of negative consequences has taught her anything, it's that she was completely within her right to grab the crowbar from the garage and pry all the drawers open.

The dressers were, by far and large, filled with suitcases stuffed to the brim with valuable trinkets, gold watches, jewellery, and anything which could be sold for a good handful of bucks. One of the dressers was comically packed with dollar bills of all values, and for a moment Naomi was struck by an intense fear as she entertained the thought of all this being the real family fortune. However, the true treasure of her discovery came from the desk, housing more folders and documents than the national archives, or so she guessed. Naomi examined the pages before her, one by one, and was finally coming around to the idea of putting all the pieces together. Each page contained a name, a pledge to give all to the originally-named "Fire Bird", and the person's signature.

Naomi waited in the upturned treasure trove until her parents came back home in the evening, and once they swung the door open she had a little trouble containing herself:

"You're cultists!" this was the first time she yelled directly at her parents.

"Darling..." Father began, standing as upright as a man with hemorrhoids "We were just waiting for a good time to tell you. It's a complicated business."

"And Naomi?" Mother interjected, truly meaning well "Please don't refer to us as cultists. It's insulting. We're servants of the… well, we don't like to say his name, but… the Fire Bird." there was no hint of deceit in her voice, it was all true.

"Fire Bird? You mean a phoenix?" Naomi allowed herself to be sidetracked. A rookie mistake.

"No, it's the Fire Bird. It's completely different!" there was a slight hint of outrage in her Father's voice, something Naomi never thought she'd live to see.

"Just tell me... where does our money come from?" with great effort Naomi found her way back on track again.

"Now, darling, I need you to understand, this isn't a simple matter, and you have a lot to learn about our ways. It all began when my great-grandfather-" Father's story wasn't meant to be.

"Tell me." Naomi's insistence was almost robotic.

"Naomi, dear, years before you were born we saw the light and started our church. We had almost nothing back then, only a few million dollars to our names we got through inheritance. Things were dire, we just panicked... anyone would do the same in our situation. And so we decided to fully give ourselves to the this… new and… exhilarating lifestyle! Then, I had a dream. The… *our Lord* came down from the heavens and told me it was our lot in life to gather more worshippers. What's more, *He* told me to collect their treasures from them, so that we could pass them on once we reach the afterlife, which by the way, is also full of fire. It also said we could spend as we saw fit." Naomi's mother raised her chin and smiled, firm in the belief she had single-handedly dispelled the entirety of her daughter's existential problems and worries.

"Also, *He* visited me in a dream, too." Father always had something to add. "But I don't remember anything else." maybe not this time.

"...SO... you're telling me, ALL of the money we have, it's..." Naomi couldn't bear to complete the thought.

"That's right, darling. All the money we have will go to *Him* when we die." Father was proud to see his daughter beginning to understand.

"What? No. I meant, all our money is stolen from idiots?"

"Of course not!" Mother was offended. "We've invested a lot of it in the right places. Morally-speaking, Naomi, that makes the money ours." her profound sense of morality was completely undeniable.

A few nights later a mysterious fire ravaged the Wolfe residence, and Naomi's parents saw their fortunes truly given away to their deity. They were less than ecstatic, once again left with virtually nothing and forced to start over from scratch, with only a few million dollars tucked away in their off-shore accounts. They never did forgive their daughter for starting the fire she never admitted to, and without telling her flew halfway across the world to Hungary in an attempt to start the church anew. They kept sending her an allowance of five thousand dollars every month, intending it as a form of lifelong punishment. She had no intention to live off her parents' pity, consistently giving it away to charities. Last she bothered to check up, the few newspapers in the country reporting on Hungary were saying something about a war between the mafia and an emerging cult of pyromaniacs. She even managed to see them in a photograph, at a distance, toting assault rifles before a small but fierce congregation. Despite their corroded history, Naomi was glad to see her parents were doing well. Everyone needs a place in the world.

Roger and Jeremiah helped her find a normal place to live not far from the centre of town, and even helped her find her first job as a housekeeper in an old folks' home. Most importantly, they taught her how to navigate the incomprehensible reality of not having millions in disposable income. It took her years of practice, but she begrudgingly got used to the idea of having to pay bills, rent, and cook her own food, just like the peasants. She even managed to open up her own business, giving painting lessons to anyone with the money for it. Though Naomi had only ever completed a couple of art courses back in college, in a town perpetually-starved for creativity she appeared like the reincarnation of Michelangelo. After the buzz around it settled down, it became a place parents could send their kids to when looking for a moment of peace and quiet. Thirty-three years and eight months into her life, this is where she was spending her day once again, teaching the hopelessly bored about the marvels of using one's brain.

"Let's see what you're doing there Oscar." An hour into her creative drawing class, she decided to have a look at her most promising student's work.

"It's, uhm..." Oscar wasn't sure what to call it.

"It's just a red line. It took you an hour to do this?" hope for a better tomorrow was slipping away from her yet again.

"Yea, uhm. Yea I had to like, get it just right, you know?" the defence began to plead his case.

"No, I really don't know." Naomi wasn't lying. She really didn't.

"It's like, an expression of art, you know? It's an expression... of *me!*" in the cloudy depths of Oscar's mind, the rusty gears began to produce the rare shape of an idea.

"What..." she sighed, "What are you expressing... of yourself?" her only wish was for the class to finally end at this point. No luck, another hour to go.

"Like, I'm expressing, the duality of man, like, inside of me. Inside of like, everyone, you know?" he really believed this would explain everything.

"...Oscar. Your parents pay me a hundred dollars an hour for this. Cut the shit and start drawing." she grabbed his canvas and threw it in the corner, visualizing how nicely it would burn later tonight. It was her trick to decompress.

She gave him a new canvas, and glanced at the other students, who all got the message and were furiously drawing away shapes and colours to be forgotten in just a few days, if not hours. Exasperated, she decided to give them another half hour before doing the rounds. She laid her head down on her desk and set an alarm to ring. When it finally did, she started quietly prowling around her own studio, thoughtfully nodding at works she internally appraised as creative garbage. Just when she thought she might finally nod herself into the slowest whiplash in recorded medical history, one of the paintings caught her eye, and in a non-sarcastic fashion for once.

The background of the canvas was painted black, and on it was the rudimentary shape of a grey-skinned old man, with abyssal holes for eyes and a mouth. From them spilled a river of colour, still in the process of being drawn. He also seemed to be holding his fist near the left bottom corner, his middle finger extended. It wasn't expertly-drawn. She couldn't peel her eyes away from the gruesome tableau, and only after a minute or so did she realize there was nobody at this particular seat.

"Hey!" Naomi loudly and suddenly snapped out of it. "Who drew this?" she scanned the room to find the culprit. Total silence. "Seriously? Who did this? It's amazing." it's not every year she would find a painting good enough to compliment.

"Hey! Naomi!" as if by divine providence, Roger Silver burst into the studio like a bat out of hell. He didn't even give her a moment to reply. "Hey, who the hell drew that?!" he could scarcely believe just how good of an instinct he was endowed with.

"I know! It's actually decent, right?" over the years she had gotten used to his sudden interruptions, as did some of the students who stuck around.

"Right! But, also not right, in a way, if you know what I mean." he waited for a reaction which never came. Naomi had been asked if "she knew" enough for one day. "It's good you're safe. Real good. Jerry should be too, but we have to make sure." the urgency in his voice became increasingly worrying.

"Roger... are you on your... *medication* again?" she paused to gauge his mental state. "Got any left?" her students got used to these types of moments, too.

"No, for the first time in my life, I'm sober." Roger was momentarily proud of this newfound revelation. "But Naomi, something... *SOMETHING*... is about to happen... and whoever made this painting, is involved. I KNOW it." he turned to the students. "Listen up asswipes! I'm locking the door and nobody gets out until we find out who made this painting. I'm ready to die in this room. Are you?" his intimidation tactics rivalled those of the CIA.

After a long and deep sigh, Naomi rectified "What Roger means by this, is, he will go wait outside while I check today's seating arrangement." this turned out to be unnecessary. A loud snore came from beyond the bathroom door. "OH... right. I know who drew this..." Naomi didn't seem too pleased with the information, went ahead and banged a few times on the door.

A few moments later, the door finally swung open, and out marched the titan in teenager form affectionately known as Billy the Third, son to Billy the Second, and grandson to Billy the First. Nobody knew beyond that; for the Billy lineage, the world might as well have never existed before then. He was fairly short and wide, with the common consensus being he had reached his apex in physical development. His plentiful and sagging cheeks as well as his three chins whipped in the direction of his canvas. He saw Roger and the other students congregating around his chef-d'oeuvre, and awkwardly tumbled in their general direction, with a loud wheezing menace: "Hey don't touch that!" he stopped for a breath, "I really put effort into this one!" his bloodshot eyes and general reek betrayed his measly effort to appear innocent.

"Well, well... well..." Roger was stalling trying to think of something clever to say. "Billy the Fourth-"
"The third." Billy was used to making this sort of correction.
"Don't try changing the subject. HOW do YOU know about THIS thing?" Roger's arm dramatically whipped to point at the painting.
"I invented it." a silent, incredulous pause. "What?! I really did." once again, Billy the Third demonstrated how little he knew about the art of lying.
"Billy, you've been in my studio for three years, and the only things you've invented are new ways of smoking drugs in the bathroom. Just cut the crap, will you?" Naomi was inexplicably proficient at communicating with people she herself qualified as a waste of space.
"Okay, okay, fine." Billy waived his white flag. "This guy at the gym-"
"Don't fuck with me, Billy the turd, you wouldn't be caught dead in a gym." Roger finally found his clever thing to say. It wasn't as poignant as he had hoped.
"... Nothing sure gets past you, huh Mr. Silver?" knowing it would annoy Roger, he didn't give him time to reply, and carried on "Fine, I was at the Silent Shark and I passed out after twelve beers. I had a dream some weird dude was going around selling pictures." in Billy's mind, this was enough.
"AND...?" Roger and Naomi exclaimed in unison.
"Oh, and uh, one of the pictures was the thing I painted. I think. I didn't buy the picture or anything." he stopped again, hoping he wouldn't be late to meet his dealer.
"SO? Who is this guy? What did he look like? Where did he come from? Where did he go? What did his hair smell like? I want details, boy, and I want them on a platter." Roger caught the metaphorical scent of blood.
"Uh, he was kind of old, and white I think? Uh, long hair? Kind of looked like a bum, actually." Billy pensively tilted his head to the ceiling at an angle "OH! Yea, one weird thing. He actually smelled really nice, like, roses and shampoo. Also, did I mention it was a dream? Can I go now?" no one ever thought Billy the Third could have helped anyone with anything, but there they were.
"I've got my eye on you... but yea, you can go and... go huff some gas, or whatever you

kids do these days." Roger always liked to have the last word.

"...I'll get right on it. Bye Miss Wolfe. Oh, wait. Can I take my painting?" he was genuinely proud of the effort he put into it.

"Well, Billy, everything you draw in my studio, contractually-speaking, belongs to me. So, no, you can't keep the painting. You can ask your dad about it." for a brief moment, Naomi saw a glimpse of her parents in herself.

"Whatever." Billy didn't have the guts to carry on with this fight.

"Yeah, damn right, whatever." Roger always needed to have the last word.

Naomi turned around to her students, some waiting with bathed breath to see where all of this would lead, but most distracted by the infinitely more interesting digital realms of their newfangled smartphones. They appeared only months ago, and now all hands seemed bound to them. The most effective parasites we've ever created, quiet invaders atrophying our brains. She sighed a sigh of resignation, and let everyone hear the magic words: "Class is over everyone, see you all next time." With the signal given, the conga line of zombified teenagers piled on out of the studio and into the great wild. Roger shook his head in disappointment at this depressing sight: "God save these idiots." Naomi gravely nodded in agreement.

"So... are you ever going to tell me what's going on?... Are the raccoons back?" Naomi would never forget that adventure, carrying its tale into the afterlife.

"God... they'll have to write that on your grave, won't they?" Roger was feeling unusually confrontational today. "Well, anyways, I'll tell you everything on the way to Jerry's. Also grab that dumb kid's painting, we'll need it."

Chapter 4

Today seemed just like any other day to Jeremiah (or Jerry as he was known to everyone, being much less of a mouthful), and it's because until about thirty minutes from now, nothing of note had taken place in his life, just as usual. He slept off the meaningless yet officially-essential work from the previous night, and with the afternoon dawning on the town, he woke up feeling sluggish as usual. "Dreams... dreams..." he muttered half-asleep to himself while turning on his novelty espresso machine shaped in the likeness Mike Tyson, a birthday gift from his mother a while back. He did indeed dream vividly almost every night, but usually come morning only the memory of a memory remained, as if cursed with the inability to leave the planet for a few ethereal hours like every other soul on Earth. Something about the dream he had last night didn't give him peace, but he would have had a better chance at performing brain surgery than remembering anything in his drowsy morning mist.

He looked around his apartment, and for the third or fourth time this week, once again took notice of how little colour his sanctuary carried. The few decorations he had were accumulated as gifts over the years, largely from people with the most basic grasp of interior design, which admittedly, was more than he ever had. The rug was probably his favourite piece, sporting an unusual plaid pattern and laying in the middle of the living room; Jerry genuinely thought it made the place homelier. The Mike Tyson espresso machine yelled out in a warm and fuzzy voice: *"I want to eat his children!"*. The coffee was ready. It had a dozen more quotes in store.

Jerry stepped out on his third-floor balcony, eyes still watering, armed with his coffee and bathrobe, and lit his first cigarette of the day. It had a terrible taste, as if born from a chemical oil spill; just how he liked it. He always did have a sense of enjoyment for these first moments of wakefulness, when he could watch over the entire town, salute the Big Cow in the distance, and imagine for a second there was actually a place for him worth living in. Though this ever-developing sense of nihilism inside of him was once upon a time worrying, these days it became as normal a part of life as the act of breathing. Ultimately, he didn't know it, but through his lackadaisical attitude towards the world and life in general, Jeremiah had made himself into an expendable yet resilient human being who knew better than most of his neighbours what stoicism meant.

Without a second of warning, a bright flash from nowhere and everywhere blinded him for a moment, sending his mind into the realm of forgotten dreams; "So, this is where they all go..." if anything, he was happy to have one less mystery to solve about the nature of life. Images flew by his face one after the other, and though his mind understood what it was seeing, he was totally incapable of describing any of it in particular. Suddenly, one image came to a stop, a forgotten dream without start nor finish, floating in the timeless void of his mental expanse. It wasn't clear to him (few things were in this domain), but the image resembled a world covered in floating colours, an old man with blackened skin at the centre of it all. As quickly and suddenly as he entered the surreal realm, Jerry was thrown right back out of it from the searing agony of burning flesh: he dropped his cigarette on his foot. Whereas most people would have screamed or cursed, Jerry briefly cried on the inside, and carried on with his life.

Back inside his apartment he took a glance at the clock; four more hours before work. He poured himself a cheap beer and sat down on the sofa, looking forward to seeing if maybe this time the world had something amazing to show him. He turned on the television, already set on the Hollow Crest Central News channel, virtually the only one to see the light of day in Jerry's apartment. Things seemed to be rolling along like they always did: a local mother was concerned about the level of traffic near the school, someone from the mayor's party was boasting about how fantastically good they were, and a contorted body with nondescript burn marks was found in the woods right on the outskirts. "Hold on...".

A collective silence washed over the entire town. It wasn't as if they were immortals and had never seen death before, but factually-speaking, the last murder in Hollow Crest took place over thirty years ago, and everyone agreed it was an accident, including the victim. In truth, the town had never seen a cold-blooded and premeditated murder driven by genuine hatred for the entirety of its existence... the people were just lucky. Cold sweat began to run down Jerry's neck as the short segment slipped on past him, and the anchor was back to talking about the mayor's excellent decision to add another bus line. "Is *this* a dream?" the reality wasn't settling in his head, and he wasn't alone.

He stepped back out on the balcony for a moment, lit a new cigarette and stared into the celestial void, bound to never be the same for anyone, he assumed. A selfish thought which didn't account for the world extending beyond Hollow Crest. Slowly but surely, he worked his way through every rung on his cigarette, and having failed to come up with any deep thoughts or rationalizations about what was now bound to become the talk of the town, he was ready to head back in. From the corner of his eye, he caught the unmistakable glint of Roger's 1979 Honda Civic, the paint chipped away in parts, but still gleaming a bright and lively red in others. It was speeding in the general direction of his building, carrying the menace of disrupting Jerry's routine. He walked back into his apartment and took a glance at the clock. Three more hours before work. If he was lucky and Roger didn't need much, he estimated he'd be only thirty minutes late. Worst case, he might have to call in sick for a day or two.

The intercom rang. Three times. Jerry picked up the phone and pushed the button to allow Roger in without saying a word; this routine had almost become instinctual over the years. He stood next to his front door, and pressed his ear against it, trying to catch some sort of signal from the outside, a sign of life, a sign the world wasn't only changing for him. Instead, all he heard were Roger's heavy and hurried steps, entirely masking Naomi's lighter and much gentler gait. He waited for Roger to knock before opening the door, and then a few seconds more; despite having little going on his life, he still wanted to give the impression his schedule wasn't entirely vacuous. It worked like a charm.

He opened the door, and words didn't need to be exchanged for them to let each other know something was wrong. When you know someone long enough, their eyes can become just as expressive as their mouth, if not more. With silence still hanging in the air between the three friends, Roger took off his shoes and sat himself down in the living room, Billy the Third's painting in hand, the front of it hidden under the vast girth of his stomach. Naomi gave Jerry a smile, and feeling equally at home let herself in the kitchen and pillaged a beer from the fridge.

"Jerry..." Roger thought it fell upon him to be the bearer of bad news. "I don't know exactly how to explain this but... something is happening... or something has happened? But some things will definitely happen. Yeah. There's definitely more to come." the stakes Roger was dealing with made it difficult for him to focus, a condition he was generally accustomed to.

"Uhm..." Jerry tried to interject, but to no avail.

"Listen, something, or someone, some being, is out there in the world, and it's coming for us. Well, maybe not exactly *us*, but for our town, or even our area in general. Look, look at this painting. You ever seen something like this before?" he shoved Billy the Third's magnum opus way too close to Jerry's face, to the point where he could smell the recently laid paint on it. He always hated the smell of paint, and claimed he had never painted anything in his life because of it. As he would later confess on his deathbed, he was just, in fact, a terrible artist.

"Hmm...." Jerry took his sweet time examining the painting after removing himself to an appropriate distance. "I'll be damned... Who the hell is this?" Jerry's brain went into a periodic state of shock as it experienced something it had long forgotten: his heart rate rose from a twinge of excitement.

"Wait, so, you've actually seen this guy before?" Naomi's sense of curiosity was also beginning to grow.

"Its uh, it's hard to say. I feel like I did see him... sometime... somewhere. Maybe as a kid? Or in a dream... a television show? A movie? I feel like, I've never seen him, but I've also definitely seen him, somewhere, on the periphery, without knowing..." Jerry trailed off, mustering the entirety of his will to find any real memories of the man in the painting. Alas, the harder he tried, the foggier his recollections became. "So, uh, are you going to tell me where you got this painting from? Who this man is? What anything has to do with anything else?" Jerry wasn't frustrated in the least, he was quite used to the roundabout nature of dealing with Roger.

"Allow me to start at the very beginning-" the flair for the dramatic suddenly erupted from him as he took centre stage.

"We'd be here for years if you did that. We really don't have time... just tell him what matters." thankfully Naomi brought him back down inside the Earth's atmosphere.

"Yeah, okay, fine. Not long ago I had a vision, probably given to me by the beings beyond the cosmos. I'll tell you about them another day, since we'd apparently "be here for years" if I did that." he looked at Naomi with a slight hint of vindictiveness while exaggerating the air quotes. "The vision was that of, well, this man right here. And it really gave me the chills." his audience was partially-hooked. Good enough for him.

"So you went ahead and made a painting of him? Since when can you draw, let alone paint?" Jerry was being genuinely curious, and not facetious. Roger never did develop drawing skills above those of a first-grader.

"Don't be an idiot." Naomi chimed in again, with a much-needed grounding tone. "That was a kid from my class, Billy the Third. He's genuinely a worse painter than Roger, but yea he did do that, somehow." Naomi's voice trailed off as she started to consider how exactly Billy did accomplish this painting, and how she could use it to advertise her own abilities as an art teacher. A catchphrase stirred in her head. "Died uncultured, reborn an artist." she said it out-loud. It was terrible.

"What?" Roger and Jerry chimed in unison.

"Nothing. I need a better slogan. Maybe I can make some more Billies from this town's stock of bored kids." the most painful reaction of all: silence. "Anyways. Back on topic. We don't think it's a coincidence for this man to be popping up the way he does, and we've gotta wonder why we're seeing him."

"Look, what we're saying is, all three of us, and probably Billy, need to stay *real careful* in the near future. Something bad is going to happen. I can feel it. I just know it." Roger returned to the familiar comfort of his doom-saying mood.

"Uhm, I think it already happened." Jerry gauged how soon he'd be able to get to work. Not today, he concluded. "There's been a murder in town." he paused for a moment to let it sink in.

"A what? A murder? Here? No way in hell." Naomi was getting ready to laugh, truly thinking it was all a big joke. The signal to release the humorous floodgates never came.

"Well, it's not official, but I don't think the trees around our town can burn people to death." Jerry was telling the truth. He did not, in fact, think that.

"I wouldn't be so sure anymore, Jerry. Not about that, or anything else." it was nothing new for Roger to be the only enlightened one to truly understand the situation. He briefly mulled over a plan of action in his head. "Alright. So, first thing's first, we need to finally whip out our PI licenses... our, long-ago expired, PI licenses, and get close to this murder thing. Make friends with the cops, the mafia, the cartel, the victim's family... anyone and everyone."

"Sounds like about a day's work." both Jerry and Naomi felt they were in for the longest haul of their lives. "But my question is," added Jerry, "what are *you* going to do?" he wasn't trying to make sure the workload was split honestly, but rather he wanted a forewarning as to the kind of trouble Roger was inevitably about to get himself into.

Roger stopped for a moment, raised his finger in the air, and exclaimed "Meanwhile, I, will investigate the trees… and so on and so forth."

Chapter 5

The lone log cabin sat at the edge of the woods about as far away from the town as it could legally be, its walls bent slightly inwards from carrying the weight of its roof far longer than it was designed to. Most residents of Hollow Crest didn't even know the cabin existed, and the few hikers who did thought of it as nothing more than a fantastic place for pictures. Nevertheless, unbeknownst to everyone, a light did go on every night as the solitary hunter skinned the day's game.

Old Charles Pembroke had lived in this cabin for thirty-five years now, still on the run after the accidental murder of the venerated grocery store's Head Cashier, Clint Krestin, whose skeleton lay buried under the floorboards beneath layers and layers of grieving dirt. Once upon a time, the two best friends decided to film a movie together and prove to everyone they were indeed headed to Hollywood as promised. Old Charles, formerly Young Charles back in those days, found his family's old double-barrelled shotgun and Clint grabbed some blank cartridges from his late uncle's attic for the climax of it all, the scene that would begin their new lives. The gun was fired, Clint hit the deck, and Young Charles realized those weren't blank cartridges after all. And so, Charles began his new life as an outlaw, while Clint began his new life as a corpse. These things happen.

In all his years of solitude his sole limited one-way interaction with society occurred about a year after the accident, when three little brats somehow found his sacred refuge by obviously having far too much time on their hands. Rather than confront or scare them away, revealing himself in the process, he decided to hide out in the attic, splaying himself out over the trap door and peeking through the floorboards, a refugee hiding from his underage executioners. The two boys and the girl with them were about as destructive as Charles had assumed they would be, pushing and pulling the furniture, swinging the drawers open, and generally refusing to behave in any way he'd call civilized. He interpreted it as an additional justification for leaving society behind. Then, he had a spine-chilling realization: he left the bag with Clint's last possessions as a memento down there, a pointlessly dangerous reminder of his own consuming guilt. If those kids brought it back to their parents, he'd have to find another cabin to live in. He wasn't ready for that.

Charles realized he lost sight of them, and started to slither like a silent worm along the floor, peeking through the cracks. His worst fear had come to fruition. They not only found the bag, but were each examining some item from it. The girl was holding a small red Buddha figurine with the face missing, the large kid was holding a set of black cuff links (Clint had the worst taste in fashion), and his friend was carefully studying some cracked wire-frame glasses. Charles then had the genius idea of unleashing a few soft and annoyed moans, playing the part of the ghost haunting the attic of the abandoned house in the woods. He might have been able to make a career as an actor out of such a performance, which sent the three kids barrelling out with high-pitched shrieks, never to return again. As a matter of fact, nobody ever returned there again.

Pushing near his sixties now, he was reminiscing about his early days of survival, and how far he had come from burgling stores for mundane tools and food at night to catching his very own meals, the life still flowing red hot within. He felt the mug it took him three weeks to perfectly whittle to the shape of his lips, and enjoyed a sip of tea. He was still burgling stores at night, but only sometimes. He thought about going back into the world, but decided he would never forgive himself if he got caught after all this time; the mere prospect of failure was far too much for him to face. Little did he know, anyone who could have cared or remembered the name of Clint was long gone, either from the country or the world of the living. As a matter of fact, the investigation into his disappearance was dropped after only two months of half-hearted glances in random patches of the woods. His parents didn't protest. He was always bound to run off on his own, the ungrateful dolt he was. Good riddance, they thought as they moved to Belize the following year. He felt his mug again, brought it to his lips, and took a sip of coffee.

Something wasn't right. The old memories could wait. Old Charles sat there in his chair, perfectly stolen from a patio with criminally-low walls (they were practically begging for it), and tried to figure out what dared interrupt his moment of profoundly-personal meditation. He felt his mug again. Coffee... When was the last time he had coffee? The morning he accidentally made Clint reborn as a corpse. "I hate coffee..." he muttered in confirmation to himself. He grabbed the little tin box sitting across from him, and was assaulted by the smell of foul coffee grains the second he opened it. "I would have noticed..." what little of a heart remained in his chest began pounding faster and faster. The grains were simultaneously rotting and cooking themselves at an unbearable heat, prompting him to chuck the tin to the other side of the room.

In a practiced and controlled motion, surprisingly nimble for his age, he stood upright and quickly reached for the shotgun on the wall opposite to him, an everlasting reminder of Charles' original sin. No luck. The gun was fused to the wall and burned to the touch. "Do... guns do that?" Charles' internal question to himself was genuine. He never was the sharpest tool in the shed. He tried to break free from the cabin's evil grasp through the true and trusted front door, but it too seemed to have fused shut. "God... no way... there's no way..." it looked like the jig was up. They had finally come for him. "I surrender! I did it! I surrender!" he kept on screaming and screaming, hoping the dozens of police troopers which had surely circled the house by now wouldn't tear him up to shreds. No response. After a moment of silence to collect his thoughts, he continued: "Yes! I did it! But I'm not to blame! It was my uncle! You must shoot him instead, if he is still alive! He left the ammo there! I thought they were blanks! Anyone would have done the same! I want a lawyer!" his plea went on this way for a couple more minutes. In his defence, he had no human contact for decades, and had no way of knowing almost literally nobody would have done the same. The greatest speech he had given in his life was only met with even more silence.

Old Charles looked down at his feet, and there he was, or rather, what was left of him. Clint's skeleton was sprawled on the ground, in the same position he had been buried in decades ago, relaxing, enjoying its life of death. The air was becoming heavy, hostile, and weighted harshly in his old and tired lungs. The lines between worlds began to blur. Despite his tremendous ability to accept anything illogical as an explicable occurrence, even Old Charles was struggling with this one. "I, ahh, I didn't hear you come in." He figured staying polite and casual were the keys to success here; at the very least, they cost nothing. "So, how are things with you? Seen, uh, any good movies lately?" Once again, total silence was his only consistent conversation partner. His eyes were swelling up and tears kept on flowing out.

He waited for a few seconds, and then the relatively unthinkable happened: Clint's jawbone opened up by itself, and the skull twisted over to its side. From the mouth some kind of faintly-chromatic liquid began to pour. "Eugh!" It complained with a raspy voice.

"Is it... you?" Old Charles needed to know.
"You..." was the only response.
"No… you're not Clint…"

The liquid was a few centimetres away from Old Charles, now frozen by terror and curiosity in equal measures. The gun. Charles looked at the wall, and sure enough the two were still fused together. He was starting to feel a massive burn from head to toe, and the light of life began to slowly leave his eyes. In a final desperate attempt to escape his fate, he tried to make it outside by using his remaining energy to burst through the door. Charles made it a few feet before giving his last breath under a starry sky. "Ohhhhh" exclaimed not-Clint's disappointed skeleton, before being swallowed up by the restless earth beneath. In a matter of minutes, the rest of the wooden cabin began to visibly darken, and in a distorted agony its planks rotted until the whole construct fell to the ground and decomposed into nothingness. It was the last thing Old Charles ever saw. The air around him lightened and carried his spirit all the way into the afterlife, which might not really exist. Things could have been worse.

Chapter 6

Roger arrived at the scene hours after the news had spread its blackened tendrils over the town, and while the bulk of the mob had left, there were a few morbidly fascinated citizens who weren't anywhere close to having their curiosity satisfied. "Who was he?", "What happened to him?", "Where did he come from?", "Do you think the government did it?", "Where's his head at?", "What was his last meal?" ...the questions only kept amplifying in the face of the ever-stoic Officer Tim, his oversized mirrored aviator shades concealing a lifetime of pain and annoyance with the locals. "Stand back. No comments." He kept repeating in his impersonation of the world's longest standing broken record. The people didn't understand; they needed answers to make for interesting supper conversations. Roger knew there were none to be given, a difficult concept to make peace with for the average person. He decided to use his keen instincts to observe the scene before making his inevitable intervention. After all, they were all his suspects now. He grabbed his trusty spiral notebook and began to write:

Suspect #1: Timothy…? Officer Tim. Occupation: Police Sergeant. Roughly forty years of age. Only motivated by the badge. Zero chance of enough motivation for murder... but too stoic to ignore. Observe further.
Suspect #2: Doyle. Yellow journalist. Waste of a human life, not enough ambition or imagination for anything besides survival, careerism personified. Good prime suspect; I dislike him.
Suspect #3-#8: Unknown quantities. Too much work to sort through…

So went his notes. Roger scanned around some more, and when he was certain there was nobody else left to observe and add to his ever-growing list of suspects, he punctuated the entry with "Signed and notarized, today, Roger Silver". Putting his little notebook away, he assumed his most confident stride and walked straight at Officer Tim, who immediately regretted the general direction his life had taken until this point. Before Roger could even say anything, Tim cut him off:

"Stand Back. No comments. Especially not you." Tim's demeanour was consistent as ever.
"But I am, as you can see, standing back, and not forward. Also, I don't need your comments. No, wait, Tim. I don't *want* your comments. I can't remember the last time your comments actually helped the situation." Roger was banking all his chips on a cheap trick of reverse psychology. He decided he might as well really go all in. "As a matter of fact, I don't think you've ever had an original thought in your whole life. Anything you could tell me about this situation, I already know. Don't even try to add anything, Tim, you'd ruin the mood." he thought it was perfect.
"In that case, Roger, stand back. And no comments." the heavens themselves would give anything to have a protector steadfast and unshakable as Tim.
"Well, then. I'm going to talk to the other people. You know, these people here clamouring for their rightful answers, as guaranteed by *The Law*." Roger's feelings were starting to hurt. He wasn't used to be denied attention. Tim remained motionless in response, hiding out in the safety of his mental refuge.

Roger turned around, and looked at the people who had now gathered around him, waiting to see if maybe he would have some new information about the case. He thought for a moment, his chin in his hand, and addressed the crowd of news-starved onlookers: "Ladies, gentlemen, kids, and all other beings, I am here to do the work... the work the police are refusing to do with any efficiency. You all shouldn't really be here, but you are here. This means you're all suspects under my vigil." he turned to Tim for confirmation, but he had now put on his headphones and was staring into the sky. He was happy, for once. Roger continued. "And so, I'm going to interrogate you all, one by one. The one who did it is among us, I assure you, and I will find him, her, or it. And if they're not here, I assure you, I will also find them, somehow."

"Who are you again?" an old lady was the first to speak up.

"I ride the waves of the universe, and I am whoever it needs me to be. Today, it needs me to be an investigator. If you don't believe me, here's my license." he whipped out his dusty expired PI license purchased on a whim years ago, and flipped it back into his pocket before anyone could have a good look at it. "My good lady, any *good* person should want this crime resolved, right? Right. So, stop being difficult and help me out here, would you?" Roger wasn't fond of people he didn't know, and even less fond of people who didn't know him.

"Here's our address and phone number." she handed Roger a small piece of paper, and winked at him from beneath her sunglasses. She realized it was useless. "My brother and I were just leaving anyway. For our Pilates class." nobody could tell how honest she was being.

"I can hold the side plank for a whole two minutes now." this was the first anyone had heard her brother's voice, unnaturally squeamish for a man of his height and age.

"That's... congratulations. Expect me soon." Roger took a moment to think of something memorable to say in farewell. "Try not to soil yourselves." he wasn't the best at this. Once they left he took a look at the paper: it was blank.

Following suit, the rest of the crowd began to disperse from the scene, and a minute later the only ones remaining were steadfast Tim, unlicensed PI Roger Silver, and Doyle, the professional waste of space. If anyone was going to break the awkward silence, it was going to be him.

"Fancy seeing you here, Roger. I take it your communion with the cosmos carried you?" Doyle sneered. He was prepared for this.

"As a matter of fact, it did." Roger had in earnest forgotten at this point how he learned about it first. "But I'm not about to reveal the finer points of my investigative techniques to you. Tell me, Doyle, what are *you* doing here? Officer Tim over there would like to know as well." he pointed to Tim, still immobile, shielded by his headphones, adrift in his own world with eyes shut tight under his shades.

"It might surprise you to learn this, Roger, but this is literally the only thing anyone in town is talking about anymore. I learned this from my 'communion' with the news station. Didn't your cosmos tell you all this already?" Doyle never passed up the chance to take a jab at Roger's pseudo-science.

"You know what, Doyle? How about you make yourself useful for the first time in your existence, and let me have a look at that notebook you're cradling like a doughnut. If you aren't guilty of anything, you shouldn't have any objections... right?" Roger could feel he was about to expose the weasel out into the sunlight.

"Wouldn't want to make the effort of doing your own work yourself... right? Right." with a satisfied smirk, he handed him the notebook.

After attentively eyeing it for a few minutes and listing through all the pages, Roger looked up at the still-smirking Doyle, and exclaimed: "Is this Spanish? I can't read Spanish, Doyle."

"Better ask your cosmos for a translator." Doyle gently grabbed his notebook back with his ever-present smile.

"I've got my eye on you, Doyle. You're free to go... for now. And write me up an English translation, nobody here can read Spanish." Roger was profoundly offended by his encounter with a language which he not only couldn't understand, but even worse, Doyle could.

"Aye-aye, captain." with an ironic salute, he disappeared in the direction of the town. Tim and Roger were the only ones left.

"Ahem. Officer Tim. I'd like to examine the body before the animals eat it up." Roger did his best to return to the calm, cool and collected air he thought he knew so well. The officer turned to him, sighed, and took off his headphones. Roger repeated his request.

"Come on, Roger. You know I can't do that. We have to-"

"Wait for the crime scene investigation unit, yes I know this, Tim." the frustration was palpable in Roger's voice.

"Then why-" as was the annoyance in Tim's speech at being interrupted.

"Because we both know they're not only hung over from yesterday, but sleeping off the morning drink from today. Come on Tim, we all know how they are, and I'm not blaming them. They essentially haven't had to work for decades. But by the time they get here, you and the body both will have turned into skeletons." for once, Roger's case was pretty solid.

"You know what, Roger? You're actually right. I can't believe it. Let me collect myself from the shock, then I'll lead you to the body. No pictures, no records." Tim was solely fixated on his chance to finally drive Roger away.

"I guess it will have to do. Lead the way!" exclaimed Roger while fiddling with the spy camera he clumsily installed in his chest pocket. A work of modern genius.

Walking right in sergeant Tim's footsteps – and taking crime scene integrity as a rather serious matter – Roger walked for a couple of minutes, up and over a small hill and down some winding paths marked by a series of little red flags, finally leading into a grove few even knew the existence of. Roger couldn't believe his eyes, and neither could Tim for that matter, though he had already witnessed it: rainbow roses sprouting from the ground all over, surrounding the dead body, seemingly wilting before their very eyes.

"Say, Roger, rainbow roses aren't natural, are they?" the sergeant could feel the piercing discomfort of the unnatural.

"Nope." Roger, on the other hand, was excited by the prospect. "I'm going to take one of these. Only one. For analysis... and such..." he saw Tim wasn't really paying attention to him anymore, and took it as his unspoken permission.

"Not a chance, these are staying here, they're government property." he was paying more attention than Roger imagined. "There... there it is. Have your look, Roger. Don't get too close." the once-stoic man seemed caught in a trance of emotions he would never share with anyone.

Roger carefully took a few steps forward and tried to take in every single detail he could. The body seemed burnt, almost charred, and imprinted with lines forming long swirls, spirals and lines. The limbs were contorted. The head was missing. The smell of the flowers was overpowering, only growing stronger by the second. He couldn't stay here for too long. Carefully, he angled his spy-pocket in what he assumed was the correct position, made sure the sergeant was still caught in his reverie, and began snapping one picture after the next. When he was finished getting every single angle he possibly could, he walked back to sergeant Tim to find him half-asleep on his feet.

  "Tim? We better get out of here. I don't like these flowers one bit. Oh yea, the decapitated body is also pretty bad. Tim?" the officer fell like a bag of hammers face-first into the flowerbed. Most people didn't know it, but Roger was actually quite capable of empathy when it was truly necessary. Despite his nagging leg pain and general dislike for the institution of the Law, he dragged the sergeant all the way back to his post. But not before snapping all the pictures his little gadget could handle. After sitting for a bit alongside Tim's fast-asleep body, having a smoke and contemplating the difference in fat content between different types of cheeses, he decided to have a look at the pictures he cunningly smuggled under the nose of the law. All without exception were covered with countless little white spots. Having assessed his own colossal failure in spy craft, he decided to drive the sergeant to a hospital himself. No self-respecting person ought to be sleeping on the job for so long. He took a good look at the woods around him, closed his eyes, and listened to the world. The crime scene investigation unit wasn't coming.

Chapter 7

With Roger out of sight and out of mind, Jerry and Naomi stopped at a run-down cafe to try and figure out what it was they were getting into in the first place, away from prying eyes. The owner behind the counter was fast-asleep, immaculately dressed as always with slick black pants and a red vest. A bit of drool ran down his chin. The customers were used to the arrangement: the coffee was self-served in paper cups, and all the owner ever did was brew a new batch of it. He'd usually brew enough for the day in one go, the enterprising fellow he was. The coffee machine itself was fitted with a coin slot. One dollar per serving. They took a moment to listen to the world around them; silence and stillness take on an unnatural quality when too pervasive. Jerry was the first to make some noise:

"So... what's up?" he asked, hoping Naomi would have an answer.

"Feels like the whole town is about to go mad. Or something else. I have no idea" she didn't.

"Alright, well, let's start at the beginning. This painting, the one Billy made, it's an old man I saw in a, uh, dream? We'll call it that." Jerry was laying the shaky foundations for a grand theory.

"Jesus, you too now?" Naomi wasn't having it.

"Believe me, I wouldn't be caught dead taking a class at Roger's, but something's happening, and until we connect the initial dots we'll be as clueless as he is about... most things. So, as I was saying, I saw this man in a "vision"," Jerry emphasized the air quotes "Billy painted his picture, and Roger was alarmed, I assume because he also saw him in one form or another. Maybe he saw his reflection in a puddle. Your guess is as good as mine, but we'll ask him when he returns. And now, Naomi, we have a murder in town." Jerry allowed a long pause to let the information sink in.

"...So, what's the connection?" the pause was getting too long for her.

"Well, doesn't it feel to you like the two events are related? Besides, if all three of us have witnessed this man's existence in some shape or form, who's to say other people in town haven't as well? Maybe those who haven't seen him only make up a minority?"

"Why, do you think, I haven't seen him yet? Am I not bright enough for him?" Naomi's sarcastic tone hid a tiny bit of pain at having been rejected from the old-man witness gang.

"Well, Billy did paint it in your studio, under your tutelage and instruction. You were also among the first to see the painting. I wouldn't exclude you from our group just yet. Let's make it four." the rusty gears in Jerry's head were starting to grind and turn with the lubrication of excitement.

"All right, Jerry, I'm hooked. So, we have sightings of a strange old man, and a strange old corpse in the woods. Maybe it's the victim himself, somehow? Or they're related?" Naomi's gears were in much better shape overall.

"I... didn't think of that. I just assumed he was a, uhm, criminal of some sort, to be honest." Jerry, unlike most, wasn't hurt by the concept of other people being better thinkers than him.

"Eager to play the hero?" Naomi was right. No response was necessary. "Anyhow, we do have the painting, courtesy of our talented Billy, so we could treat it like a search for a missing person. I think we can take some pictures, print some posters, and hang them up around town. Also put them up on the internet and all that, you'd know better than me."

"Yea, we really do need the exercise, don't we?" Jerry's love handles agreed.

"You're already a paragon of fitness. Oh yea, don't you have work tonight?"

"Not if I call in sick, let's get to it." he thought strolling around town would be a lot more pleasant than work. Most things were.

With their stale cardboard-flavoured coffees behind them, the pair set out to the print shop twenty minutes away, and printed out about a hundred pictures of Billy's painting. Let no one, least of all Roger, say they half-assed the self-assigned job. The occasional pair of eyes would wander over to their station, and an old man, not the one from the painting, even came over to comment on "The beauty of this piece of modern art" and how it "was a reminder of the self-annihilating greed of Man". In his prime, the old interloper used to be a renowned art critic who made and broke the careers of many. After decades of buffoonery, his empty opinions were finally harmless. Too little too late.

From there on out, the two decided to split the main streets up between each other, and both left with fifty posters of the painting, complete with Roger's cell phone number to reach in case anyone recognized the man. The excitement of leaving a comfort zone is hard to resist when one has spent so long in it they remember nothing else. Once Jerry got to the first street of his agreed route, he realized most of his walking would have to be done uphill. Naomi did this on purpose; he really did need to move around some more. With a heavy sigh, he marched onward and began plastering the posters all over. It was already early evening, and most people had returned home just in time to witness Jerry's unusual efforts. From the windows of their cars and homes sheltering them from the harshness of the world, the people casually looked on as Jerry brought warning of an impending doom, one none of them would be safe from. If only they had known any of it, perhaps things could have been different. Perhaps they would have burnt the town down. Or perhaps not; there's no real way of knowing. Having finished putting up about half the posters he held in his arms, a question struck him: "What's the point?". He looked at the few indecipherable faces he could never relate to, still peeking at him from behind their windows, sighed, grew angry at himself, threw away the rest of his posters, and marched back home.

The sun seemed to be setting faster than usual, and the streets grew dark and empty as they do every evening. Jerry forced himself to trot along at a leisurely pace, shooting glances into the homes of the people he had never known despite living beside them his entire life. They were busy with all of life's comforting regularities: cooking, cleaning, watching TV, doing homework, painting a giant canvas of a naked woman based on the archaic photo of a forgotten statue. Business as usual. Life and warmth brimmed from their dwellings, and for a moment Jerry wondered if it wasn't, in fact, he who hasn't made himself worth caring about. A seed of self-loathing faintly burned inside of him; why wasn't he worthy of being one with life's regularities? Maybe it was a blessing, rather than a curse. The night was growing ever-darker.

The street lights weren't what they used to be in Jerry's neighbourhood, but tonight they were acting up more than usual, flickering in and out of existence like the quantum particles composing them. The closer Jerry got to his home, the faster they blinked. The electric eyes watched over him, and in the psychedelic derision of their strobe lights Jerry finally managed to find his building. His head was throbbing from a forgotten corner deep within; he could scarcely remember the last time he had been to a concert this intense. He still had to find his way to his apartment. The lights inside the building began flickering too. Jerry assumed in a few minutes they would blink furiously enough to kill a man, if such a thing were possible in the first place. The headache got stronger. A primal fear began to swell up in his chest, one beckoning him to leave the planet and everything in it; surely, the void would be more tolerable than staying here. He spun around in a three-sixty-degree motion, and realized he could no longer recall his apartment number. Was this even the right building? It seemed to him as familiar as it was foreign. The walls began to melt and drip, the ceiling started spinning, and then, the darkness.

In his panic, Jerry raced around in the black on his lonesome, grasping for any sign of life, light or hope. There was nothing to grasp but thin air. Nevertheless, he continued running like a man possessed, feeling no tiredness until the point he suddenly collapsed and lay there with his eyes open. Breathing was becoming progressively more difficult, and with a herculean effort he raised his head to see a figure towering above him, faint multicoloured lights flowing through it, its eyes seemingly mocking Jerry in his powerlessness. "Mom?" was the only question he could muster before his head fall back on the floor. A single thought raced in his mind, as if implanted there by an outside force: "The slaughterhouse." This helped him none; there was no slaughterhouse in nor around the town. "Get lost!" he yelled into the void, and felt himself pulled back into the waking realm.

The lights turned back on, and Jerry opened his eyes to witness a floor which seemed to stretch into eternity. With a lot of effort, he picked himself up and saw an old woman in a pink bathrobe holding her shih tzu, peeking from behind her chained door. She watched him with great interest, evidently finding more entertainment here than in the rehearsed soap operas the entire block could hear blaring from her room.

"Oh, for God's sake I am sick and tired of you thugs and hooligans wandering in here hopped up on all your drugs! I'm calling the police if you don't leave right now!" God himself wouldn't doubt the wrath in her voice.

"Lady... please... where am I?" Jerry tried to sound as soft and subdued as possible.

"OHHH NOOO!" other neighbours were starting to gather at their front doors to glare through their peepholes. The show was getting good. "You won't fool me, mister! I know bad people when I see them! And you, you're as evil as they come! Get out before I call the police!" the old lady was still young and acutely irritating in spirit.

"Listen here..." something uncharacteristic boiled in the bowels of Jerry's entire being. He suddenly lunged at the door, and before the old woman could close it, he kicked it open and snapped the little safety chain like a twig. "I'm having the worst headache of my life, lady, and you're not helping! I'm just trying to get home! Stop screaming already!" he collected himself briefly and realized, he had entered her living room without a second thought.

"HELP! HELP! I'm being kidnapped! Tortured! Murdered! HELP! HELP!" the old lady's voice rivalled the best alarm systems money could buy.

Realizing it was a bit too late to de-escalate the situation, Jerry ran back into the hall and saw three burly men about twice his size each barrelling down the corridor in his direction. There wasn't much room to manoeuvre... as a matter of fact, he no longer had anywhere to go in the corridor, neither forwards nor backwards; a cement wall on one side, a human wall on the other. "You have the hots for old ladies, pal?!" one of them asked, half-furious, half-curious. It occurred to Jerry he was actually being half-taunted, and was about to enter a fight he couldn't win. Quick as a cornered rat, he ran back into the old lady's apartment – now on the phone with the police as promised – and looked for the nearest window to jump from, which happened to be a few steps to his left. He took a graceless leap in its direction, tipping over a priceless antique stool in the process, and looked through the glass. The fifth floor. "How..." unfortunately, Jerry didn't have time to ponder on his remarkable transcendence of space. He could hear the burly trio in the corridor, and for a second considered the possibility they would make hamburger meat out of him. "Fifty-fifty." he concluded.

Jerry ran further into the apartment, praying to whatever God was out there to find a fire escape in the depths of the nightmare he was now trapped in. There it was. In the kitchen, a second door with a big window leading to the outside world, to his salvation. He twisted the knob and pulled on it. Locked. Of course. He turned the lock, and pulled again. Still not budging. "What the hell?" things were never going to be simple.

"Hah! I super-glued the door shut so scum like you wouldn't get in! You're done for, mister!" the old lady shouted proudly while peeking in from the other room; she had finally lived to see the most important moment of her life. It could only go downhill from there

"Uh-huh." Jerry was way past the decency of normal measures, and grabbed the meat tenderizer conveniently hanging from a nail the wall. He pointed it at the old lady, who once again screamed like a banshee and ran back out into the living room. He heard her crash into something. He meekly hoped she wasn't too badly hurt. With the clock ticking down, he started to smash away at the window in the kitchen. Thankfully, no amount of glue could save it from blunt force trauma. The footsteps of the man were now echoing in the apartment. He could feel the floor shaking with their arrival. Clearing as much of the glass away as he could in one sweep, Jerry began the process of climbing through the gap, one foot on the windowsill, the other over it, and rest of the body following suit. A strong muscular arm reached out around his neck and started pulling him back in.

"You hurt... Miss Dolores... you hurt... all of us..." the large man was already short of breath and found it as difficult to talk as Jerry did listening to him.

Still grasping the meat tenderizer, he struck at the hand reeling him inside. It was enough of a lesson to make it retreat. Jerry took a few steps forward, turned around, and from a safe distance began his apology:

"You tell Dolores I'm real sorry, I've thought about it, and I'll never do it again." he then threw the meat tenderizer back in through the shattered window. "I'm no thief." on these proud parting words he remembered the police was bound to show up any minute, and hurried down the fire escape.

He thought about the antique stool he tipped over, hoped it was going to be all right. Once he reached the ground level and found his way out of the alley and onto the street, he looked up at the building, still caught in the haze of his trip to the void, the adrenaline of his great escape, and realized: "Shit. This really is my building." there was no going back there, at least not tonight. He began wandering in the opposite direction he had come from, thinking about what to occupy rest of his evening with. He could come into work, but the appeal of calling in sick was too big of an opportunity to resist. Besides, he hadn't taken a sick day in two years; legally-speaking, he was essentially entitled to one. Jerry started to feel around in his pockets, and realized he left his cell phone at home. He kicked a small tree branch in annoyance. Time to look for the rare payphone, yet another species dying at the sharp and digital hands of the progressive twenty-first century. There was always one at the convenience store a few blocks away. "The slaughterhouse... I don't get it." Jerry muttered to himself, dragging one foot after the next.

Chapter 8

Naomi carried on with her chosen route, casually putting up the posters without much of a hurry; she had a hard time seeing how this would help them, but deep down, she was genuinely even more curious as to where it all would lead. More importantly, she didn't have anything more important nor exciting to do. Also, this was her proposition, and she would be damned if she was forced to change stances on the matter. She was still lugging the painting around in her portfolio case, making a mental note to return it to the studio come morning. With every poster she put up, a small knot of pain in her shoulder grew. She tried paying no attention, reasoning "I can't possibly be this out of shape." The pain kept growing stronger and stronger, forcing her to lean over to her right. The case with the painting dropped with an uncharacteristically heavy thud and lay motionless, bound to the concrete. The pain began to recede, but wasn't intent on leaving her for good. She looked at the case, more wary than perplexed about the shenanigans it was about to put her through. Grabbing the handles, she tried pulling the case off the ground. It refused to budge by even an inch. "Oh, fuck off..." she cried into the evening in frustration and despair. Nobody was there to listen. She gave it a few more tries and decided it was time to give up before blowing her spine out. One's health should always take precedence. Gathering her thoughts for a moment, she came to the reasonable conclusion she would probably need some help dealing with this nigh-paranormal occurrence. She took her phone out of her pocket and pondered on who to call first: Jerry or Roger? Jerry probably wasn't too far away and seemed largely level-headed, but on the other hand, Roger had the ace up his sleeve of having the glimpse of a shadow of a clue as to what might potentially be happening. The agony of choice.

She decided to take the route of reason and give Jerry a call. "We're sorry, the number you have reached is not available..." Naomi was earnestly beginning to wonder what the hell was going on. She tried dialing it again. "We're not sorry, the number you have reached is not available..." The frail strings of her sanity were being snipped one by one. She felt like setting something on fire. With a deep breath, she reluctantly buried the forbidden desire. She took a look around, and saw the night had somehow already shrouded the town in its embrace. There weren't many street lights where she was, and a couple of them were flickering in needlessly ominous fashion; "Fine, I get it." she reluctantly let out into the world. She dialed Roger's number, hoping to see some light in what was starting to look like a waking nightmare. The phone rang. Once. Twice.

"Naomi?" Roger's voice was faint on the other end, but carried a familiar comfort and relief to her.

"Roger, thank God. You wouldn't believe the shit I'm dealing with." speaking with another human being restored her composure.

"The shit you're dealing with? I'm just done carrying our dear officer Tim to the emergency room. I'm also pretty sure I inhaled some toxic... rainbow-coloured... flowers." Roger paused for a breath, and added "Oh yea, and the doctors here told me I probably need to get checked for eczema... never mind. So, what's this shit *you're* dealing with?" the sarcasm rolled off his tongue naturally after a lifetime of diligent practice.

"...My painting is stuck to the ground, and my shoulder hurts." she complained with great importance after a few seconds of solemn silence during which she processed all he had to told her.

"Wait a moment, *the* Painting, with a capital P, is stuck on the ground?" Roger sounded more alarmed for the painting than himself. Uncharacteristic of him.

"Yea it just, became really heavy and now it's kind of laying here on the sidewalk. Oh yea, Jerry's phone is doing some weird things, give him a call when you get a chance." for a moment she wasn't certain which of the two situations she was more concerned with.

"Listen, we can't just leave that thing in the street, who knows what it might do." the panic in Roger's voice was beginning to bleed over into Naomi's ears. She wasn't too fond of it.

"Yea... who knows what a painting might do to all the people who aren't going to be walking here at this hour in the evening. You know what, here's what we'll do. You get tested for your eczema and let me know when you can get here. The corner of Haddington and Mania. Meanwhile, I'll make a run to the pharmacy near here. My shoulder still hurts." the pain really was beginning to bother her, and the last couple of words were squeezed out through clenched teeth.

"Are you crazy? You can't just leave the painting like that, nobody knows-" few people wanted to take the risk of interrupting Roger, but Naomi was a brave one.

"It might as well be a block of cement at this point. It's not going anywhere. My shoulder hurts. See you soon." and with those words of encouragement, she hung the phone up on him with a rudeness which felt alarmingly natural to her. Now, to find the pharmacy; it was only a few blocks back, she hadn't passed it long ago.

Before leaving the scene of the painting, she took one of the few remaining posters she had, flipped it over on the blank side, wrote on it with her marker she always carried in her trusty pocket. She then folded it, and placed it in the case so half was inside, and the other half sticking out, facing any inquisitive souls which might pass by. It read: "Warning! Cursed painting! Guaranteed bad luck and infertility! Don't touch!" she assumed it was sufficient to deter anyone from touching it. She hoped. Ascertaining this was just about all she could do in this situation, she clutched her pained shoulder and marched forth into the night. Knowing when to retreat is a rare talent; many wars have been won with it.

As always, the streets were calm and quiet, with the people of Hollow Crest having little need for a nightlife to speak of. The majority were more than happy to draw pleasure from the simple things in life; after all, the more complex one's comforts become, the more their standards become unnecessarily demanding. Naomi wondered what kind of stagnation the lack of meaningful changes had brought to these people who had grown so accustomed to the simple life, repeating itself over and over across generations. Was there anything to regret about it? Her shoulder pulsed with pain, radiating through her neck and into the base of her skull. The last time she felt kind of pain, she was a dumb teenager who tried to jump from a tree onto the roof of the two-story house her boyfriend was living in with his parents. In the process of falling she had taken a few tiles and a piece of the gutter down with her. A true heroine's end. If anything could have convinced the boy's parents he was making the wrong life decisions, that was it. She never did see him again.

Her flashbacks obliviously carried her all the way down to the pharmacy, and she only realized she reached it when she had crossed its threshold. Clutching her shoulder, she walked down the aisles, searching for some balms and ibuprofen pills to wash her torment away, just as she had done back then. From behind one of the shelves a young boy in uniform popped out, eagerly holding a box of tissues he had obviously been cradling for a little too long. In a broken voice he yelped out "Please try our new all-absorbent Tearwipers, we're running a special of one for the price of two!". Naomi did her best to ignore him and moved on her way; she wasn't the kind to shed tears often anyhow. She waited patiently in line along with the few lost souls of the questionable evening crowd, and from the corner of her eye she could see the young peddler looking for more victims. A boy slightly older than the first scanned her purchase. In a voice far more slurred than his appearance would have led to believe, he asked: "Hey miss, do you like, cry a lot? We have a Tearwipers special day, just today. Wanna buy some?". The pain, idiocy, the unduly poor speech of the young man, all were weighing on Naomi's shoulder. Is every generation really worse than the last, or is it just a recent phenomenon? The throbbing made her close her eyes and brought out the gravest and most menacing voice her body and will were capable of mustering: "Say Tearwipers one more time and your mother won't have enough of them at your funeral." A shocked, concerned and hostile quiet reigned over the scene. Naomi grabbed her things and left. By her standards, this was very much a historical outburst. The throbbing in her shoulder began to subside a bit. The satisfaction of it was euphoric.

Having popped a couple of pills and rubbed on some of the balm, she felt ready to return to the scene of the painting, and the trip back felt a whole lot shorter with the massive amount of pain taken out of the equation. In the distance she already saw Roger standing at the street corner, looking around, concerned as he always was. As was the case most of the time, she was glad to see him and briefly entertained the prospect of their troubles coming to a good and comfortable ending soon enough; she internally laughed at her own stupidity. She approached him, and he spoke first.

"So, where's the painting, did you manage to take it with you after all? Where is it?" his eyes darted back and forth in search of it.

"It was, uhm, right about here, when I left?" her voice trailed off with uncertainty near the end.

"Well, it's not "right about here" now," Roger emphasized the air quotes "and God-knows who has it or where it is." he was astonished Naomi didn't share his level of concern.

"I see your powers of observation have attained their peak after all these years." her dry tone concealed a slight disappointment with herself.

"Naomi?" he looked her in the eyes.

"Yes?"

"We really blew it this time..." he gazed into the distance, trying to feel with the power of his mind where the painting might be now. He obviously couldn't. Naomi didn't press the issue, knowing how much Roger loved to be seen as mystical and mysterious.

A few blocks down the street, an old car was slowly rolling along with the painting in its back seat, all covered up in a black tarp. A slight heat radiated from it, but the driver wasn't ever going to notice; he wasn't of the sharpest kind. "Think you can just do me dirty like that?" he directed his question at the hula hoop dancer on his dashboard. "I'll show em', I'll show em' all, yeah, they'll see I'm the best. Yeah, I'm not a failure!" the mutterings kept on in this vein during the entire ride home. On the following morning an exciting wave of news was destined to sweep over the entire town, marking a point of no return.

Chapter 9

The light had already faded out from the world of the living, and Jerry was stumbling his way towards the local convenience store. It was an unremarkable little establishment on an unremarkable little street corner, the kind nobody had ever even robbed because of its unassuming nature. Jerry had the impression if someone wasn't looking for this place, they would have a nearly impossible time finding it. And yet it called to him time and time again, day after day, year after year. He enjoyed the peace and quiet he found in this little sanctuary hidden in the midst of the urban jungle, and had the impression it was built solely for his sake. He could be selfish on occasion. From time to time, he wondered how the owner made enough money to pay the rent, but these questions were neither here nor there for him. It could have been a money laundering operation for the cartel for all he cared, so long as it retained its invisible nature. He decided to take a trip inside and buy some cigarettes before heading to the phone out back. The owner greeted him with a knowing smile, and in a broken English accent wished him a great day. Inside was empty as usual, and the shelves half-filled with the kinds of things nobody even knew existed in convenience stores. Jerry briefly wondered if he could ever find himself in a situation desperate enough to buy the ever-so tempting can of "Uncle Vlad's Mystery Meat". Having bought what he came for, he went back out through the door as the polite cashier gave some farewell advice: "Goodbye sir. Chin up, there is no cow on the ice!" he said with a smile and a wave. He clearly wasn't a local, and had no idea expressions don't always translate across languages.

Jerry walked around to the side of the store and witnessed obsolescence in its purest form. The payphone had been subjected to the artistic ideals of what he imagined could have only been a group of super-vandals. Their art was signed: Vince the Prince, 1999. Almost ten years ago now. Vince had successfully conquered and outlived the payphone. "Here's one to him." Jerry muttered to the wind. With a disappointed sigh, he kept on walking around the side of the store to see if the second payphone in the back survived the tides of change. It was old, dirty, and hanging on to life by a single thread, but there was enough of a heartbeat in it to get Jerry's message across. It stood almost under the convenience store's back light, flickering from time to time, constantly threatening to go out without ever carrying through. Directly beneath it was a set of stairs leading down into the store's basement. No light could reach the door at this hour. Jerry began rummaging through his pockets and fished out a handful of nickels and dimes. Just enough for one call. One by one, he lethargically began inserting them until a noise made him jump and drop a few into the darkness down the stairs.

"Hey mister! You seen da colours yet?!" it was the world's stealthiest vagrant, obscured by shadows and yet betrayed by the nauseating stench of beer coming from his shopping cart. It contained all the man owned.

"The colours?" Jerry asked after allowing a dramatic pause to settle in.

"Aye! They was gone for a long time! Don't know how long, never seen em' myself! But now, they're back! Yeah baby, I can feel em!" the elation in the vagrant's rough voice was less and less innocent.

"Well uh, that's good news then, isn't it? I will, uh, definitely let you know if I see them." Jerry said while fiddling with his hands in his pockets, searching for something to defend himself with. Just in case.

"You'll know em when you see em, mister! Oh! They're calling, gotta go!" sporting a never-ending smile, he disappeared down into the darkness of the alley, pushing his cart ahead. Jerry noticed the brief gleam of a comically long knife among the vagrant's possessions. He was better-armed than Jerry all along, as he logically ought to have been, considering his life trajectory.

With the curious little adventure hopefully behind him, Jerry turned his attention back to the payphone. Thirty-five cents had been inserted, fifteen more remained. He realized he'd have to actually look for the change he dropped. It would have probably been more effortless to have simply gone in to work like a regular person. But who was he kidding? He never was a regular person to begin with. Using his dim lighter, he began walking down the stairs and carefully scanning the ground for any signs of his lost change. To his great surprise, he realized the stairs didn't actually lead to a door, but only a door frame, missing the most important part. He couldn't see inside, or at least, there was nothing close enough to reflect the fire from his lighter. Though the rational part of his brain dictated he ought to have been afraid of the unknown, a calming sense of familiarity emanated from the blackness. He couldn't identify it, but if he was forced to with a gun to his head, he would have said there, in the darkness, resided a part of him lost and obscured to the world. For no more than a second, a bright red and purple light flashed at the end of the room. Jeremiah Baxter crossed the blackened threshold, and the world stood dead silent. He wasn't the first, nor would he be the last.
The fire from his lighter went out, and though right behind him, the outside world seemed like an old memory and a dream too distant for him to reach. The red and purple light flashed for another split-second. With an outstretched hand and small careful steps, Jerry marched forward towards the flash, trying not to run into anything sharp and contract some long-forgotten disease of the convenience store basement variety. There were random bits of furniture laying about, an old broken mirror in the corner, a few beer cans and old rags stained by every element known to Man. A few steps in, the light flashed again, and beckoned him onward. A few more steps, and the light reappeared, illuminating the lost fifteen cents he needed to complete his phone call. The light itself seemed to be coming from an errant light bulb, almost feeling to him like a greeting from beyond the frontier Man ought to never cross. In his mind's eye, Baxter felt an icy breath on his ear, a presence he couldn't nor want to chase away. It whispered to him in a low and hushed tone, the voice of destruction itself, the sound of atoms ripping apart... the high and low-pitched, multi-toned symphony of obliteration. In one motion Jerry turned his whole body and swung his arm as hard as he could, hoping to knock out whoever had sneaked up on him. Alas, no one was there, and now he was fairly certain he sprained his neck. He picked up the fifteen cents, cursed at the light, and walked towards the exit. A moment later, Jeremiah Baxter had emerged back out of the darkness, clutching his neck and grinding his teeth. He had a phone call to complete.

Trying to ignore the pain radiating in his upper body, Jerry put the last coins into the payphone and dialed his workplace number. "Hey, Ralph? I can't come in tonight, I'm sick and just hurt my neck. You'll have to hold down the fort. Or find someone else to do it, which really is your style, Ralph." Jerry never really liked Ralph, but he did do his best not to let it show too much. He still had work to do on this front.
"Come on, Jerry, you're not being professional here. I've just finished my shift and now I'm supposed to work the whole night replacing you?" whether over the telephone or in person, Ralph's voice had a droning quality which likely annoyed even his parents. "I have the schedule right here, and it says-" Ralph didn't have the chance to finish; Jerry knew where this was going.

"Shove it up your ass." he said in a surprisingly polite and amicable tone considering the message, after which he immediately hung up the payphone and wondered what the chances were he still had a job. Around fifty-fifty, he estimated.

With the whole evening ahead of him, he also took a moment to ponder on whether or not it would be safe for him to go back home tonight, or ever again. He imagined he would have to risk it at one point or another, despite being certain he would get ambushed by a squad of policemen waiting perfectly still with their guns drawn for him to return. He also took a moment to look back on the events of the last few days, and began to feel slightly worried he had embarked on a path neither he nor his friends were ready for or were even close to understanding… on the other hand, these things happen. He could already feel himself changing, different than when it had started. The longer they get sucked into the spiral, the less recognizable they risk becoming in front of the mirror... and yet, there was no going back now. He had seen and heard the colours, and they entered his life. What to do now? Jerry chose a direction and began walking down the street, hoping some unseen force in the universe would guide his feet to the promised land.

After about a half-hour of walking, gazing into the night sky, and mulling over his thoughts – occasionally sidetracking himself with ideas of how great and worry-free life might be on the moon – Jerry came to a full stop and remembered: the body in the forest. It must be in the morgue by now. With a bit of luck, he might be able to pose as a potential relative and accomplish the unimaginable: get an actual close look at the thing and learn something worth a damn. Besides, he wasn't keen on admitting it, but an unshakeable morbid fascination was gripping him, and in a matter of moments he had subconsciously convinced himself of the vital importance of his mission. He needed to see it because it was important, and it was important because he needed to see it. Besides, few things are as invigorating as the prospect of being useful. Jerry turned around and immediately started backtracking all the way to the other side of town. The unseen force he relied on earlier had been guiding his feet in the wrong direction.

The town wasn't particularly big, but getting around from one neighbourhood to the next could be a nightmare sometimes. Winding roads going up and down hills, dead ends with no warnings, impractical circumventions, and a true lack of public transport worth using, with the drivers themselves getting lost as often as tourists in Mexico. It took him a good hour to find his way through the Hollow Crest labyrinth and he had finally arrived at the town morgue, a relatively inconspicuous building which hadn't seen more than the minimum mathematically-permissible traffic in the last few decades. Its existence was more akin to a relic from days past, kept around and maintained only to remind everyone of how much better things have gotten. Now, it was ironically coming back to life again.

Jerry entered past the automated doors and saw the clerk already asleep at his post. It was barely midnight. The system in place was exceedingly simple: the clerk ran ID checks and led people to the bodies if need be. There wasn't much use for precautions beyond this one, as decades of stable and flawless operation had aptly demonstrated. Jerry looked around at the grim yet tranquil room he found himself in, lit dimly enough not to disturb the great slumber. The droning of the lights was barely audible. Next to the clerk's desk was a mirror, and Jerry found himself caught by his own gaze. It's been a long while since he had a good look at himself, and though he was still theoretically young, the ravages of age were beginning to leave their imprints on him. His dark brown hair now had noticeable traces of silver, his dark-brown eyes started to sag and lost their vibrancy, and the wrinkles were starting to spread. Time was moving faster than he was aware, faster than he had ever wanted to see it move. He was merely caught and swept by the current of his life and those of others, like virtually every person at some point, really. It's unavoidable.

Tearing his glare away from the mirror, he looked over the sleeping clerk, quasi-immobile if not for the small and gentle breaths which moved his rib cage. An older man, likely in his sixties, not too far away from retirement. Or perhaps this was his way of enjoying retirement; for some, facing the prospect of having no designated function is too tough a pill to swallow. After all, feeling useless and inconsequential can be akin to a death sentence. He was wearing his white scrubs and his arms were crossed over chest. Jerry cleared his throat. Then again. And a third time, much louder. The clerk remained motionless. Whatever dream he was in had him gripped tightly in its clutches, and probably wasn't about to let go. Jerry considered slapping the man, but stopped himself short after realizing the opportunity it presented him with. He might fail to convince this man he was allowed in. The keys were right there on the table in front of him. With the certainty of a brain surgeon using a lead pipe instead of a scalpel he awkwardly reached for the keys and brought them back to his side of the counter as they jingled loud enough to reach the high heavens. The clerk was still unmoved, having demonstrably become one with his workplace. Part of Jerry was legitimately impressed with the display.

The morgue door was down the brightly-lit corridor past the clerk's kiosk; contrary to the city streets, it was more difficult to lose one's way inside the morgue. The only other doors were the coroner's office and the bathroom. Fumbling with the keys for a bit, he finally managed to find the correct one and entered the mortuary itself, with the examination suite built-in right next to it. A sheet on the examination table covered what was obviously a dead body... the only dead body which interested anyone in this town.

Shutting the door behind him, he took slow and steady steps towards the ominous sheet on the table. He had already faced death before in his life, like most people, but this time was different. It almost felt infectious, as if waiting to pounce on him the moment he made contact with it. Death is an insidious fellow, capable of worming its way through any crack, fissure or pore should it choose to. Jerry thought for a moment and noticed the report laying on the table beside him. He opened it and began reading in his mind's voice: "Let's see... a John Doe... unknown cause of death... wounds of an unknown nature... missing head... potentially chemical burns and radioactivity... awaiting analysis..." he put the report down. Footsteps were coming from the corridor. Jerry did his best to take on a look of solemn importance and grief. The door behind him opened, and slowly he turned around to see a slightly pudgy, brown-haired middle-aged woman in a doctor's coat, accompanied by what he guessed was a young nurse in training, one with a disconcertingly intense stare. All three of them adopted an air of genuine surprise, and the middle-aged woman was the first to establish a line of communication.

"Good... evening? Are you lost sir? Who let you in here?" her voice was calm and firm, as if she owned everything in the place, Jerry included.

"Good evening, madam." he spoke slowly and paused to buy himself more time. After a moment of uncomfortable silence and nodding, "My name is Jer...ronimous Smith. I asked the clerk to let me in, and, well, he just gave me the keys." he hoped the lie wasn't too apparent.

"I'm Kathleen Morrow, and I work here. So, what *are* you doing here?" her suspicion rising, she motioned her assistant back and whispered something in her ear. Jerry imagined she told her assistant to avenge her, should the need arise.

"Well, you see," another dramatic pause "our uncle William has gone missing some days ago, and I heard you had a body down here you couldn't identify. So, here I am, trying to identify your body for you." after yet another pause, "You're welcome." Jerry was starting to get good at being a snob.

"You don't seem to be very concerned with the idea of your uncle being under this sheet." Kathleen's suspicions were only growing, despite his best efforts.

"Yes, well, you see, we sort of hated him. I'm actually very much hoping it *is* him under that sheet." saying something like this with deadpan impunity felt wrong, but on some level, Jerry was starting to enjoy it all.

After grafting the memory of Jerry's face in her brain, "All right then, before we proceed, we have no idea what kinds of wounds this man suffered, and whether he could be toxic or contagious. You'll have to change yourself into scrubs and put on a visor, mask, goggles and gloves. The changing room is right outside." her practiced manner of speech showed she had given similar instructions a few times before. Unlikely to be a local.

Jerry stepped into the changing room and was handed all he needed to give him the illusion of protection. His own clothes were placed in a bag and stored in a temporary locker. Feeling about as safe from germs as he ever did, he took a moment to reflect on how surprisingly far he had gotten with his lies. He wasn't a practiced deviant of any sort, but it all came a little too naturally to him. He stepped out of the room and back into the examination suite. Only Kathleen remained, with her young blonde and impressionable-eyed assistant nowhere in sight.

"Say, doctor, why didn't you just show me a picture of the man?" with his foot now in the door, Jerry felt safe to ask the obvious question.

"That's part of what makes us take our current precautions. Photographs of the man's face have so far been impossible to develop. They simply become covered in countless white dots. My guess is it has to do with the radioactivity I'm certain he's emitting, but we'll have to wait for further results." Kathleen said as if she had seen it a million times before. She never had.

"And you feel safe being next to it?! And letting me next to it?!" the shock was genuine in his voice.

"I don't, but someone has to do this. And you've clearly gone above and beyond the regular effort to be in here... not to mention, you're the only one here." her sense of observation was already proving greater than what Jerry had anticipated. Another one for his long list of failures.

"All right, on with the show, then." Jerry tried to hide his nervousness with bravado. He was getting better at this, too.

The pair walked up to the table and Kathleen motioned him to back away a little further. With a precision Jerry had begun to see as characteristic of her, she pulled the sheet back and revealed the monstrosity beneath it. A faint smell of sulphur rose to the air and settled into the entire room. For a moment, both of them stood speechless in the face of a canvas used by something neither of them could explain. It seemed as if all the air and water had been sucked out of the man, his skin turned a shade of dark, quasi-black brown reminiscent of tree bark and was marked by spiral-like imprints, not to mention the gaping void where his head used to be. It was more than a mere body laying in front of them on the table; it was a direct line into the mouth of the abyss.

Kathleen cleared her throat and asked "Recognize him?", adding a touch of irony to it.

"Uhm, uncle William, he looked, well, a bit more human, I'd say." Jerry's attention was being sucked into the stump cut off at the neck. A gaping hole of absolute blackness. "He also..." he remembered to stay in character with his dramatic pauses "he used to have an actual head, you see."

"Hah!" Kathleen enjoyed morbid humour, a prerequisite of her profession. Somehow, she seemed immune to it all. "I think you've seen enough sir. Good luck with the nightmares." she motioned with her arm to the door. Jerry didn't hear her. He was absorbed by what he had just been peering into, locked in a staring contest with the stump. She tried again, but louder "SIR! I think it's time for you to leave!" and give him a powerful nudge on the shoulder. She was a deceptively strong woman.

"Yeah... uh... yeah no shit." Jerry seemed dazed, as if something had penetrated all the superfluous layers of protection hanging from him. With the good doctor's help, he walked back to the changing room, and after a few minutes of rest slipped back into his nice and familiar clothes. Everything was in its place. Despite his protests, the coroner insisted on calling him a taxi to drive him home.

After she sent him away, Kathleen walked back into the building and knocked on the bathroom door. "You can come out now Sarah, he's gone." her young blonde assistant stepped out. "Did you get it done?" her voice carried a hint of excitement.

"Yup, nothin' to it." with a cheery motion she handed her a sheet with Jerry's photocopied Medicare card.

"Jeremiah Baxter... Why do you think he lied? Just to come down here and look at the body?" she sounded like she was quizzing her assistant rather than asking her opinion. Such was her manner.

"I... don't think he meant any harm? Jerronimous was a terrible made-up name, he obviously did it on the spot." they both laughed for a second.

"I do think he knows something about this whole thing. He made the effort to be here specifically for this John Doe." she gave a pensive glance to the examination suite room. "I think we ought to have another talk with the man, this time on even terms." she gave a worrying glance at Sarah, knowing full well what she was about to say next.

"Shouldn't we report this to the police?" Sarah's honest reasoning was beyond reproach.

"Think for yourself, Sarah. We have a case full of medical mysteries we've never encountered before. This goes so far beyond normalcy there's nothing for the police to do here." Kathleen's gears were grinding hard in search of a better justification. "Besides, we've never observed foul play of this nature, meaning it might still be accidental after all." her speech cadence was progressively increasing.

"You mean you want to get famous by publishing a scholarly article about this and solving the "greatest medical mystery of modern times"?" Sarah's air quotes and exaggeration did, despite everything, offer a good point.

"Well... don't you?" Kathleen too, had a good point, and much more concise.

After a few moments of silent deliberation, Sarah relented. "Fine, we'll talk to him once more, but if things get, ah, more suspicious, we're going to the cops." she thought it was a fair deal.

"We're in agreement, then." so did Kathleen, who shook Sarah's hand not as an assistant, but for the first time, as an equal and an accomplice. She instantly wondered if she would come to regret this decision one day.

Jerry was dropped off at his home and gave the cab driver a generous dollar-big tip. He looked at his watch. Ten past midnight. He took his chances and slithered by the empty hallways and staircases into his apartment. A safe haven at last. Less than a minute after putting his forgotten phone to charge, he was sound asleep.

Chapter 10

The night might have ended rather tamely for Jerry, but Roger and Naomi still had ways to go; they couldn't rest until they found the damned painting.

"Well, Roger," Naomi contemplated, gazing up at the starry sky, "I'm going home. That's enough for one day." her voice carried a hostile monotony, irradiated with frustration.

"Seriously? You're going to make a giant mess like this, and then leave me with it? You're being unethical." Roger was struggling hard to understand her lack of urgency about the matter.

"It's just a painting, Roger. For all we know it got thrown into some random dumpster..." she sighed and gave those words a few seconds to sink in. "What do you even propose we do? I'm going home and getting some sleep. You should too." her tone subtly changed from annoyance to concern.

He gave her a dejected look, "Yeah, sure, all right. Let's just go to sleep while we're crossing the point of no return to the end of life as we know it, shall we?" Roger's sarcasm spared nobody, not even the most important people in his life.

"The end of life as we know it?" if Naomi's eyes could roll further they would have done a full revolution.

"Listen, I don't know what's happening, but we've been seeing and feeling weird things out of nowhere, right?" his voice gained an extra notch purposefulness when he was about to make a realistic point.

"Right..." at this stage the easiest way to get out of the conversation was to engage in it.

"For the first time since Jesus walked on water, we actually have a dead body in Hollow Crest that looks like he was murdered, and it's turning out to be a giant medical mystery from what I've seen so far. Right?" Roger was being surprisingly sensical for once.

"Right." She started to think she could see what he was getting at.

"And now, the painting of a uh, collective dream? Yes, that's what it obviously is, just vanishes. It's all gotta be connected somehow. There's some real strange bullshit happening here, and we're letting it get more and more out of our hands." a slight rush of adrenaline went up Roger's spine; the feeling of knowing he's right, rather than merely believing it, was one of life's greatest pleasures for him, just like most people.

"So, how does this "put an end to life as we know it"? Weird bullshit has been happening since the dawn of time, Roger. And besides, how was it ever in our hands to begin with? *What was in our hands?*" she wasn't too convinced, and once again angered at having stuck herself in a conversation with nary an exit.

"This is different. I know it. We had some control when we started to notice it, and then when we had the painting. Whatever it is, it will spread, Naomi." he was almost pleading and absolutely serious, a sight which, in and of itself, made her positive there was indeed something paranormal at work.

"All right, let's say you're right-"

"I am right." Roger usefully interjected.

"Yes. Okay. You're right. What do you propose we do? My shoulder is aching, my feet are disintegrating, and I'm about to pass out the second I lay down anywhere..." the exaggerations to her tiredness, if there were any, happened to be negligible.

"Fine... fine..." he ended up relenting to her, as custom dictated. "But you still have to admit I'm right and this is our top priority starting tomorrow morning." he still counted the small victories. They all matter, in the end.

"Yes, you are right, Roger. You're always right... except for the countless times you're not." she didn't want to blow up his ego too much.

"Those times are countless and cannot be counted because there are none of them." his ego had already swelled up to the size of the moon eons ago.

"... Good night, or what's left of it. I'll see you tomorrow." after a brief hug she turned around and began the journey back home. Not long after, she too would be sound asleep in the safety of her own little corner of the world.

Roger was left planted in the middle of the street, in the dead of night, under the soothing glare of the warm lights and calm stillness of the moon. Not a car nor bus could be heard on the roads, not a dog barking, not a couple arguing. Time itself seemed to have slowed to a complete standstill for the sole benefit of giving him a little more of itself to think on his next move. His dearest friends might be out of action, but Roger wasn't about to give up on his venture. Even if he couldn't explain it, a part of him knew a true crisis was unfolding, one scarcely anyone could perceive so far. The painting. After reminding himself he did indeed need to find it, despite not having any clue as to how to proceed, he started to wonder why indeed he was so obsessed with this particular endeavour. After a few minutes with his head bowed in profound thought and his chin cupped in his hand, he came to a conclusion which, in retrospect, seemed obvious to him: it holds some sort of power over people in touch with the energies of the cosmos, like himself. The need to find it somehow grew increasingly urgent; who knows what might happen should masses of people be exposed to it? The reaction of one man often carries little weight; the reaction of a mass can be strong enough to swing any pendulum, both destructive and constructive.

Having failed to generate any actually productive ideas in the few minutes he stood motionless in the street like a horror movie cliché, Roger decided to walk as much of the town as he could, checking as many dumpsters as possible along the way. He also had the bright idea a little later to begin looking in cars and through people's windows, just in case. A few hours of garbage sifting and illegal window peeping later, as the morning sun was starting to come up, he was no closer to achieving his goal. He sat outside a cafe and waited for it to open up. Sleep-deprived and coffee-starved, his brain was still twisting and turning in the meat grinder of its own making. The owner showed up; a tall, slender and older-looking oriental gentleman, gave him a stern, disapproving glance and opened the place up. Roger ordered a coffee, a stale piece of cake leftover from yesterday, and sat down at the table to watch the morning news on the tiny, forty-year old television set still kicking on the counter. A young man who seemed fresh out of high-school was on the screen in an ill-fitting brown suit, trying to read the teleprompter without suffering a panic attack. The words came at Roger's pulsating cranium in short and electrifying bursts.

"...We begin our report today... upcoming city council election... termite-infested school uniforms... a food fight at the chess club..." for the next bit, however, Roger was all ears: "There is a surprise exhibition starting right now and lasting a whole month at the O'Harris Private Gallery, showcasing a single new painting by Billy O'Harris the Third. A hundred percent of the proceeds will go to charity. Touted as the family's greatest prodigy, young Billy is bravely, for the first time, sharing his work with the rest of the world..." the reporter trailed on, but the rest didn't matter to Roger one bit. He spilled his tired mass over into the street, put his fingers to his temples, and tried his hardest to remember where he parked his car. It usually only took him ten to fifteen minutes; this time, it took him an hour.

Chapter 11

Jerry didn't remember his dreams very often, and this was largely because they tended to be rather mundane and uneventful to the point where he could have easily confused them with real memories of his own life. Right now, he was standing in the middle of a dark and empty street, where even the lights had gone to sleep. The sole inconsistency with this picture laid in the sky, as a giant red light kept slowly pulsating above the world. It was terribly annoying and giving him a bit of a headache, which only grew more debilitating as a siren began to screech from every direction. His brain was swelling up, and in the back of his neck, at the point where the spine meets the base of the skull, he felt a tiny drill slowly twisting its way inside. He opened his eyes and looked up: the sun was pouring itself entirely into his room. The phone was ringing. It didn't stop.

He turned over on his bed and looked at the time. Seven in the morning. Too early for social calls or solicitations. The phone was ringing. He did his best to sit up in bed and braved the oncoming headache. He was starting to become accustomed to them. After a few seconds of lackadaisical searching around his room, he found his phone, still ringing, and answered without bothering to look at the caller identification.

"Yeah?" Jerry managed to blurt out through a raspy throat.

"Thank Christ Jerry, you've finally risen from the dead." Roger's annoyed sarcasm was unmistakable. "Listen, while you and Naomi were busy being Debbie-downers I actually made real progress and found the painting." the condescending tone of his voice had a grating nature to it.

"That's great. Really, Roger. Good job." Jerry had some firepower of his own in this regard.

"Now's not the time for this, Baxter. Recess is over." Roger rarely called people by their family names. When he did, it was truly serious. "The painting is at the O'Harris gallery and it's going to be on display for a whole month. Do you understand, Jerry? A whole goddamn month!" every word coming out of his mouth seemed louder than the previous one.

"What I understand, Roger, is that my head is being split in half from the inside and you're about to finish me off with your ramblings." Jerry, on the contrary, was cooler than expected for a man in his situation.

"Rub some lemon juice on your nostrils. It helps. Once you've applied my medicine, head to the gallery, I'm at the cafe across the street." the sarcasm in Roger's voice had been replaced by a dead serious tone. "I'll try to reach Naomi now."

"It's at the other side of town Roger, can't you give me a lift if you need me there that badly?" the prospect of having to leave his home felt particularly unpleasant to him today.

"No can do. I have to stay here. I'm on a stakeout. See you soon." with this curt goodbye, Roger hung up and his voice was replaced by the ever-steady and equally-pleasant dial tone.

Jerry considered following Roger's advice about the lemon juice. Despite all his so-called quirks, he didn't only talk sense from time to time, but also found it in the most unexpected places. If anything, he didn't see what he had to lose. About five minutes later he regretted his decision; the world smelled like citrus and the headache was no closer to passing. He couldn't believe he got roped into this. Again. Deciding to swallow a couple of pills, and braving the throbbing in his skull, he left his apartment through the fire escape door, trying to avoid his neighbours. He wondered how long he'd have to tiptoe around them before they forgot, and if it wouldn't be better to simply present his excuses. But then, what would he say? How could he justify any of it? He'd have to think of something or move to an entirely different area. Maybe even a different country. He hadn't decided yet. Finally, he reached the street level, and started making his way to the gallery. Despite being on the other side of town it wasn't too long of a trip; Hollow Crest had a strangely timely and effective public transportation system.

* * *

Roger was quietly sitting at one of three tables outside the O'Harris Cafe, an extension of the family-funded gallery. He was slowly sipping on his third espresso imitation, pen and notepad on the table right next to him. His gaze was fixed on the entrance to the gallery, guarded by four love-starved giants in black suits and sunglasses. Ex-special forces and armed, Roger assumed incorrectly. From time to time one or a few people would walk in, prompting him to snap their picture from a distance like the professional stalker he was turning into, and jot something down in his notepad.

He had already been sitting here for an hour and had all the time in the world to take a good look at the place. The gallery was unusually well-guarded for the many valuable paintings it contained. Most of them were, of course, under lock and key and rotated for rare and expensive exhibits, which drew connoisseurs from all parts of the country. The top-of-the-line security system ensured no guest could ever set foot in a zone they weren't allowed in, and no paintings were ever left unattended for any period of time. It was the perfect sentinel, and the one lunatic who did try to defy it once disappeared from the face of the Earth... a courtesy of the O'Harris foundation, people assumed. To enter, one had to purchase a letter stamped with the O'Harris family seal of approval, a process which cost a small fortune. However, since this was the family's own exhibit (for the first time ever, it should be noted), they decided give the people of Hollow Crest a once-in-a-lifetime gift and opportunity: a completely free tour of the gallery with the one-painting exhibit as the centrepiece. Hundred percent of the proceeds would still be donated to charity. They truly believed themselves good Samaritans for this gesture.

The building itself didn't necessarily look remarkable from the outside, save for its snow-white coat of paint which somehow remained unnaturally clean no matter what mother nature tried to ruin it with. The windows weren't big nor numerous, to the point where the building required the lights to be on even during the bright of day. It stood on a plot about seven hundred square meters large, adorned with all the greenery and the occasional imported trees the family seemed to be so fond of. He couldn't see the back of it, but assumed there had to be an exit there too, especially if it was a secret. He could all too easily imagine the O'Harris moles scurrying away from a police raid through their hidden underground tunnels. Roger let his imagination run wild for a few moments; he really enjoyed it.

After he finished the call to Jerry, he hung up and quickly dialed Naomi's number. Her phone also kept ringing for an inordinate amount of time. Finally, she too was forced to pick it up in the end.

"Naomi? You have any plans for today?" Roger went straight to business.

"Uhm... Yea but I have this feeling you'll tell me to drop them." Naomi's voice rose by about half a note whenever she got suspicious of anyone.

"Because I found the painting. You know, the one you lost? By your own fault?" rubbing salt in the wound was indeed one of his favourite activities, to the point where he thought about listing it on his dating profile.

"Holy shit you're kidding, right? *You* found it all on your own?" just like Jerry and Roger, Naomi had sarcastic artillery of her own. Maybe it was why they all got along so well together; assholes tend to find kinship in each other.

"I'd me more than happy to explain my detective methods to you, but there's no time. You have to meet me at the O'Harris gallery. Jerry's on his way. The painting is here." Roger's voice once again took on a determined tone.

"I'm sorry, Roger, but I can't revolve the entirety of my life around your, uh, cosmic escapades? I have an actual class to teach in about an hour. Don't you have classes to give as well?" she was trying to sound as kind and respectful as possible, but knew it would hurt Roger on some level.

"Classes? Shit." Roger realized he forgot about his actual day job. "Know what? You're giving art classes. Bring your students here, to the gallery. Make that your class for today." when Roger's brain gears were grinding he really was capable of coming up with productive ideas.

"Hmm..." Naomi briefly contemplated the idea of taking a break from seeing her students' largely worthless and uninspired works, if only for a single day. "Good idea." she liked it more than she let on, and hung up the phone.

* * *

About a half-hour later Jerry walked off the bus and went to greet Roger at the cafe, still sipping on espressos and now launching his assault on an oversized croissant. As much as he was absorbed by his buttery carnage, Roger spotted Jerry from the corner of his eye like a trained spy and waved him over.

"Waiter! Two more espressos and croissants!" Roger belched out. He turned to Jerry and asked "And what will you be having?" in a politely disinterested tone.

Jerry sighed. "I'll have a regular coffee. No fancy nonsense, just for one day." he had already seen Roger animated in this fashion; he knew nonsense was already afoot.

The waiter, who was also the owner, the cook and the cashier, shuffled his seventy-three-year-old frame to their table and set his silver tray down. With forlorn eyes he looked up at the O'Harris gallery and spoke in a voice ground to gravel by a lifetime of joys and tragedies: "He fucked my wife, you know." and the obligatory grieving silence followed.

Roger was the first to regain his composure: "Who did?!" he sounded about as upset as anyone could be for the long-forgotten marital affairs of a total stranger.

"One of those Billy son-of-a-bitches, can't remember the one. Maybe they all did. Wouldn't surprise me, you know." his tone remained strangely indifferent to the painful passage of his life he was laying out. "And now every day I sit here, right across their bourgeois gallery and..." he took note of his customers' disinterested faces "Well, young men, life loves punching people who are down. Let that be your lesson for today." a faint trace of a smirk appeared on his lips, and he returned to his safe haven behind the counter, satisfied with his still apparent use to the world.

Jerry leaned over to Roger and asked the real question: "Roger, what the hell are we doing here?" his face was inadequately equipped from birth to convey the feeling of frustration to others. They probably assumed Jerry was nicer than he really was.

"I thought I'd wait for Naomi to show up before explaining everything. It wouldn't be friendly of us to leave her out of the loop." Roger could barely finish his sentence before biting into his third croissant of the day.

"Fine, but you're paying for my coffees." Sometimes Jerry wondered why he gave in to Roger so often and so easily. Was he truly a friend, or just yet another person taking advantage of human beings? Jerry chased the thought away. They had known each other too long for anyone to be anyone else's tool... right? Right.

The two friends waited for some time in relative silence, with the occasional grunts of displeasure emanating from the cafe owner, half-asleep on his throne. Roger kept watch over the gallery's entrance, jotting down numbers, keeping close track of it. When it occurred to Jerry they will likely end up going into the gallery, a sense of dread he couldn't locate nor explain passed through his chest for a brief moment, and gave him a coughing fit. He ordered a second coffee. About an hour or so later, Naomi got off the bus across the gallery, followed by a dozen of her faithful students. She saw her two best friends in life sitting across the street, and briefly instructed her minions: "Everyone, listen up! Go to the gallery's entrance and wait there for me. I won't be long. Take a smoke break if you'd like." As the teenagers meekly complied with the instructions, she crossed the street and accosted her partners-in-crime.

"Jerry. Roger." she gave them a smile, something she was still surprisingly capable of after observing human stupidity in its developmental stages for years on end. "Nice to see you're enjoying yourselves. What *are* we doing here?" the question was addressed much more to Roger than Jerry.

Roger was chugging down the rest of his coffee. It burned, and he pretended to enjoy it. "Good to see you too. I'm glad we're all here. It's not a moment too soon. Quick, follow me and try to keep up." there was surprisingly little sarcasm or self-awareness in his sentence.

"Roger?" Naomi gave him the pitiful look people tend to have when they're about to hurt someone they love. "I love you and all that, but you can't just string us along one step at a time. You have to, uhm, show us the whole stairwell." Naomi paused "You get the picture." she turned to Jerry in search of support.

"What she said." Jerry dryly let out, piercing Roger with a dead serious glare.

He gave them both a good look, then stared at his feet, then the sky, and finally the empty plate in front of him. He missed his croissant. "We're being invaded." he said in the gravest tone possible, after which he backed his chair up, crossed his arms, and let the information really sink into their minds.

Jerry looked all around him. Life was as peaceful and unassuming as it had always been. "Where, Roger? By who? How high have you been lately?" even a saint's patience can run short, and Jerry was no saint.

"Yeah, I gotta say Roger, this isn't your most sensical moment." Naomi was more unimpressed than angry with him.

"Listen, I don't know how!" Roger too, had a limited reserve of patience. "But the painting, the thing it shows, I've seen it during my hyper-advanced meditation classes. Let that sink in for a moment." so they did. "And don't tell me you haven't seen him either. You recognized him in the painting from Naomi's studio. I, a professional, saw it in your eyes, Jerry. Add the once-in-a-million-years inexplicable murder we've just had, and I think it's obvious, it's all connected. Somehow!" sweat and spittle were flying from Roger's general direction in a torrent of excitement.

"I'll admit, there are unusual occurrences..." Naomi reluctantly conceded. "But what makes you say we're being invaded? By who? A painting? A dreamy old man? Get your shit together. You're gonna need some kind of evidence at some point. You can't spew baseless ideas forever." without his friends keeping him grounded, Roger might have made it to intergalactic space by now.

"Okay, fine, that's my instinct talking. I don't know if we're being invaded. But it sure as hell feels like it, and that's enough in my book..." he noticed his friends were rubbing their eyes in perfect synchronicity "...*but*, I understand if it's not enough for yours. This is why I've asked both of you here. Whatever it is, I intend to stop it right here and now. But I can't do it alone. The gallery is well-guarded and..." Roger's ambition was cut off by a unanimous exclamation.

"What the hell are you planning?!" Cried out both Jerry and Naomi in unison.

Roger motioned for them to lean closer to him, his eyes shone bright at the mere thought of the word, which he let out in a short and excited whisper "A heist!" the reaction of shocked silence by his friends was an appropriate one.

"Don't worry, we're not doing anything now. The place is guarded, but only during the day. Right now, we go in, get a lay of the land, and at night we come back and grab the painting. It's a foolproof plan, trust me." Roger had evidently thought much of this out already, his imagination fuelled by espressos and confectioneries.

"You're saying it like it's a done deal, Roger. Why do you even want that goddamn painting? How is grabbing it going to solve anything at all? To be honest, I'm having a lot of trouble getting on-board with your plan. You realize you might actually go to prison for this, and drag us along with you?!" Jerry had seen enough stupidity in his life, and it disappointed him greatly when it originated from his exclusive inner circle.

"Yea gotta agree with Jerry on this, can't say I'm even close to being sold on your plan." Naomi, on the other hand, was more resilient to it.

"The painting might only be his door to us, but yeah it won't solve anything at all, you're right. You know what, how about we all just hang ourselves and save him the trouble?!" the sarcasm spewed forth from within him once again.

"You don't know that! You don't know anything! For fuck's sake will you ever stop pretending you know everything!?" with these words of anger Jerry smashed his fist on the glass table and produced a visible crack. The owner was still half-asleep, an immovable object in an ever-changing world.

"Since when did you get so angry? You've barely raised your voice at anyone since high-school, but now you're smashing tables like they've insulted your mother?" The patronizing tone was another one Roger had mastered a long time ago.

"He's got a bit of a point Jerry. Not gonna lie, I've also been pissed off as shit lately, and no I'm not even on my period." she knew the detail was unnecessary. "Maybe there is something to it. How about we just go in right now and take it from there?" the earnest desire to move things along was apparent in her.

"Yeah... maybe... may... be... All right, let's go then." after a brief moment of reflection during which Jerry quickly and efficiently mulled over the events of the last few days, the trio crossed the road and walked towards the gallery.

Chapter 12

They approached the large open black gate marking the entrance to the O'Harris territory, watched over by four comically-bulky guards and a sleepy German Shepherd who seemed more intent on playing with them than anything else. They were motioned to come on in, and began making their way down the smooth cobblestone path, winding and zig-zagging without any tangible purpose. An artistic choice, no doubt. Naomi's students were sluggishly dragging their feet a few paces behind them, undoubtedly thinking of literally anything but art. The grass around the path had the faintest red tinge to it, nearly-imperceptible so as to make patrons second-guess themselves. Another sound artistic choice. The trees which the path took them through were ostensibly foreign and oppressively-alien, making Roger wonder out-loud about whether or not they were artificially conceived in an aristocratic laboratory, as a joke. The others pretended not to hear him. Something about the scenery was weighing heavily on their minds, slowly clouding their brains in a dissociative mist making the act of thinking increasingly difficult. One of humanity's more consistent challenges. The closer they got to the entrance, the more this wave enveloped their minds and made them prisoners of the unseen. The thought of turning back washed away into the realm of the physically impossible. The automatic door to the main building entrance was reached, and it slid out of the way accompanied by a series of cheery beeps, welcoming them all in.

Viewed from the inside, the gallery was no less impressive than its outer appearance led the imagination to believe. The floor was polished and pitch-black, the walls were covered in large coloured panels alternating between grey, red, and orange. Jerry silently wondered if the combination was meant to evoke anything other than revulsion. There was really only one main room, with a couple of locked doors here and there where maintenance equipment was held. The natural illumination from the skylights was the only one allowed to touch the various works displayed on the walls and the couple of statues standing in their own corners. The installation of artificial lighting was perfectly calculated so as not to spoil the exhibited art. There were six more guards posted inside, immobile and blending into the room as if part of the show. This too, was a conscious artistic choice. The O'Harris family made very few decisions on illogical whims, it seemed. There was no bathroom; it was located in its very own house fifty meters away from the main building. Nobody dared question the genius of an artist.

There were already quite a few people inside, some dragging their feet about from one painting to the next, with a discernible crowd concentrating around something specific, something the three friends couldn't see through the mesmerized horde. Naomi looked at her students: if they were more brain-dead than usual, she couldn't really notice it. With a defeated sigh, she motioned with her arms for them to explore the place of their own free will. She wondered if there were any among them who weren't simply attending her classes because they were forced to by their parents. Probably not. Art and creativity are a dying breed in a world with an ever-shortening attention span and increasingly easy access to mind-numbing, time-wasting and momentary entertainment. Why create? It takes considerable effort. Being entertained takes none. An annoying droning sounded as if coming right at her from a great distance. She turned in its direction and saw Roger just in time to lean back away from his slap.

"What the hell?!" Naomi exclaimed, giving him back a slap of her own. Roger didn't have the reflexes to dodge it.

"Ow! Didn't I tell you that would wake her up?" Roger sounded satisfied with himself and his foolproof plan.

"What's going on?!" the words came out like bullets.

"You were on the moon." explained Jerry, nonchalantly. "Roger brought you back with the threat of his impotent slap." even if he didn't let on with his monotone voice, he was somewhat amused by the whole situation.

"I brought you back from the clutches of an all-seeing evil and world-consuming despair. You can thank me later." Roger wheezed, still slightly winded from the one-way slapping exchange.

"Guess I owe you my life, then." Naomi's coolness slowly returned to her speech. "I was just doing some thinking, Roger. But I see how you'd confuse that with an all-seeing evil. Foreign concepts are terrifying." her words had an unassuming confidence about them, as if she knew Roger would have no rebuttal. Not a real one, anyways.

"Contrary to some people, I only think about the important stuff. You know? The kind of stuff that puts us at the threshold between survival and total annihilation. For example, I'm thinking about what all those people are looking at," he dramatically pointed in a wide movement to the mass of patrons huddling around what appeared to be the main exhibit. "and more importantly, how many more of them there will be tomorrow. Once word gets around, hundreds, if not thousands will have seen it, and then-" he didn't get the chance to finish his profound thought on this occasion.

"Fine, yes, we get it." Naomi was momentarily tired of Roger's dramatic swings and penchant for the theatrical; she started to believe he had incurable hero complex. There was a time and place for everything, and she sorely wished he could understand this concept. She was destined to carry this wish all the way to her coffin. "Let's just go and have a look first, make sure we're actually talking about *our* painting." her desire to move things along proved itself victorious in the end.

The three friends walked in the direction of the big crowd in front of them, occasionally throwing sideways glances at the other offerings the gallery had in store for them. There were paintings of all styles and from seemingly all known eras of artwork, from a piece of rock holding the portrayal of a caveman's ambitions, to the ridiculously incomprehensible works of the modern era, attempting to delve into the unexplored depths of the human mind. Somehow, none of them really stood out; when every element of a decor is different, the unusual becomes an expected standard. As Jerry inched his way closer and closer to the main exhibit, a feeling of purposefulness began to make its way under his skin, flooding his mind with the impression he was about fulfill a lifelong goal and dream so important it pertained to humanity at large. Like crossing a great valley none had seen beyond. He was full of himself, but no amount of objective facts nor logical debates could sweep this seed from his mind. It occurred to him he and his faithful friends had lost control of something a while ago, maybe even when they decided to head to the gallery. Their meeting with the painting might have always been inevitable. Jerry felt like a sucker.

The crowd was compressed and unrelenting, and the three friends had to slither their way through the sweaty necks and greasy shoulders with all the effort they could muster. Slowly but surely, they found their way to the promised land. Roger was obviously right. It was the painting. Next to it was standing Billy the Third, a grin printed across his face, taking in all the ecstasy of his newfound fame, the glory of being at the centre of everyone's attention. Intoxicated by the abstract fumes of recognition, he stood like a statue in its eternal vigil, a little too still and eternal, remarked Roger. His friends couldn't hear him. He could barely hear himself. For the first time he had a good look at the faces of those they had to worm their way through. They were a suspended mass of human consciousness robbed of any remaining free will. Their eyes empty and minds a blank, they were staring directly at their object of obsession, practically unblinking. Somehow, this felt normal, like he shouldn't be questioning it; they were observing the unrecognized wonder of the world. Billy the Third remained motionless along with his increasingly unsettling grin. Roger took a look at his dear friends. They too were on the verge being sucked into the vortex like all those surrounding them. Feeling himself also beginning to slip, he grabbed them both by the hands and, for the first time in a long while, found an actual use for his hefty mass of a belly. A fat bat out of hell, he plowed his way back through the crowd and outside the gallery, to relative freedom. They momentarily felt sickly and confused, but after a few minutes the feeling began to gradually subside.

"Are you guys going to admit I'm right yet or what?" Roger made sure to pronounce every word slowly and clearly, savouring another victory in his life, no matter how small. They add up over the decades.

"For... yea, we admit it Roger, you're right and wise beyond your years." Naomi's words would have rolled their eyes, if they had any.

"Yea, fine, you convinced us. Something weird is going on and it's making us feel queasy. That's about all we know. What do you propose we do now? Call a team of ghost hunters?!" Jerry's newfound anger and impatience were starting to find their way back to the surface from the depths of his being.

"Well..." Roger gave the idea a serious consideration, "That probably won't be necessary. For now. I think the next step is incredibly obvious..." he looked at his friends, waiting for them to finish his sentence for him. They gave him a wide-eyed stare. "...we have to steal the painting." he pursed his lips and let the idea sink in.

"For starters, Roger, how do you plan on stealing it from the gallery? There are so many guards we stand a real chance of drowning in them." Naomi didn't give Roger a chance to answer before promptly moving on. "Second, what do we do with it if we manage to steal it? What is the point of it? And what makes you sure we'll be able to anyways? Last time I carried it the thing practically turned into a giant cinder block on me." as tradition dictated since their early childhoods, Naomi was making all the good points.

"Those questions are all out of order. First, it's clearly drawing on some evil cosmic energies and radiating them on all those who see it…Or something similar. Some things are still unclear to me, and I'm sorry for that." his friends let him know with their unwavering stares he was getting sidetracked. "If we steal it and put it someplace safe, stop whatever its radiating from spreading, it can't harm anyone else, making us indubitable *heroes*." Roger placed a strong emphasis on the last word. He really did have a complex. "Second, yes it's true there are so many guards right now I feel there's one hiding up my ass, but we're not going to do it now. We'll come back at night and see from there. Besides, I might have an idea or two about getting some help." the words "an idea or two", coming from Roger, caused an instinctive alarm in Jerry and Naomi's conditioned brains. "Finally, I'm just going to go ahead and assume the painting has a mind of its own. It might be a dumb and primitive one, but it's definitely there. It practically forced you to drop it and allowed itself to be carried to the gallery, by Billy the Third as my investigative skills lead me to believe." Roger may have been a buffoon at times, but his seriousness when following a surreal train of thought was unmatched by most.

"So, you're saying," Jerry continued in his stead, catching on to his line of thinking, "if we give it a reason to be elsewhere, we shouldn't have trouble carrying it." Baxter hated how he was starting to see even a flicker of sense in all of this; he wanted nothing to more than to return to his quiet and peaceful existence. Speaking of which... "Well, in any case Roger, it won't be tonight, I actually have to go to work. For survival purposes, you see." the syllables came out quickly and rolled off his tongue, as they tended to do when Jerry felt a bit more confident in himself.

"Are you serious?!" Roger exploded in a sudden and overall uncharacteristic tantrum. "Our collective fate hangs above a precipice, and you're thinking about work?! The cosmos has never seen such a pathetic..." his voice began trailing off, and he caught himself slipping. An ability undoubtedly stemming from the sheer willpower imbued in him by the forces, way up there. "I'm... I'm sorry..." these words spoken sincerely felt so unusual to Roger and sounded like they were painfully excavated from the forgotten realms of his inner universe. "You see what this thing does? It will only get worse before the end, Jerry. Just take your goddamn vacation already, I know you have at least a month of it saved up. You too, Naomi. This will require our fullest attention from now."

"How do you know I have a month of it saved up, Roger?" Jerry was cautiously suspicious. In general, good things rarely came from Roger knowing things he shouldn't.

"Well, you see, remember that time I was at your place a couple of months ago? And you left me for half an hour to run some meaningless errand?" Roger's voice felt like it was trying to backpedal on its own importance.

"You mean the meaningless errand of finding out why my water was cut?" a sarcastic overtone coated Jerry's answer disguised as a question.

"Yes! That's the one!" it somehow flew above Roger's head. "Well, I had to entertain myself somehow, so I looked for any, uh, literature you might have laying about. And uh, I ended up reading your pay stub. Don't give me that look! I'm an investigator, what would you have had me do, watch some mindless TV or read a magazine? Could you imagine me doing that?" he was starting to turn red with embarrassment. Even he knew he had crossed the line.

"Yes, Roger, literally anything other than reading my confidential mail would have been fine." somehow, Jerry was more tired, disappointed and defeated than actually angry at the man. He knew his friend. He liked to think Roger meant no harm and would lay his life on the line for both himself and Naomi. Many reproaches could be made in regards to his character, but lack of loyalty could probably never be one of them. "But yeah, you're right. I probably should take that vacation. Even if it means I'll have to spend it saving, uhm, the world, rather than getting some actual rest." his face started to relax a little bit, and the trace of a smile graced his lips.

"Holy shit! My students!" Naomi was swimming in a world of her own.

She ran back inside the gallery, followed closely behind by her two friends, and wasn't excited by the prospect of what she was seeing. The entirety of the patrons in the gallery had now surrounded the painting, including her students, and were standing like zombies in front of the still-grinning Billy the Third. Roger thought there was definitely something wrong with the kid, beyond the usual nonsense he had swirling in his mind.

"Well... the hell am I supposed to do now? I'm actually responsible for these kids! The hell am I gonna tell their parents?!" her mind was racing at a million miles per hour.

"Nothing much to do for now..." Roger claimed, adopting a deceitful pose of imminent action with his hands balled up into fists and resting on his hips, and his feet spread slightly apart. "... but wait. The gallery does close at some point, and I assume the guards will usher everyone out." he was certain of how things would unfold.

"Say, why aren't the guards affected?" this legitimate question had been swimming in Jerry's mind for a little wile now.

"Hmmm..." Roger cupped his chin in his hand, lowered his head, closed his eyes, and entered what could only be a called an impromptu meditative state. Or he was falling asleep. A passerby wouldn't know the difference.

"Maybe they uh, just don't have the emotional and… hmmm… artistic capacity to be influenced?" Naomi was doing her best to be polite, in case any of them could actually hear her.

"Too dumb to be affected? I think we'd have many more immune people running around if that was the case." Jerry was partially-agreeable to the explanation, but felt it wasn't exactly adequate to cover all the bases.

"What makes you so sure they're not affected?" Roger asked them, quickly whipping his forearm upwards and extending his index finger in the air. "If we assume the painting is sentient, which of course, I correctly do, then maybe these apes are affected differently. After all, I can't exactly know how an idiot would be affected by this, would I?" the question was rhetorical. Jerry and Naomi did their best not to acknowledge it. "In any case, I don't think there's much left for us to do here today. Let's all go home and get some rest, we'll need it. Let's meet back here at one AM sharp." he gave a long and pensive glance at the cafe across the street from the gallery. "We're gonna rock this ship tonight."

Chapter 13

Night had claimed ownership over the skies of Hollow Crest, and at the lonely hour of one in the morning, only the few artistic souls, introverted night shift workers, and professional drunks of the town were still awake.   Silence and emptiness filled the air, and the street lights were working overtime for nobody's sake. The O'Harris gallery still stood in the same place, thankfully, and next to its gate three hooded figures dressed in all black emerged from the shadows. It was firmly locked in place.

"Right..." exhaled Roger, trying to catch his breath under the mask. "I say we find a dark spot along the wall... boost Naomi over... have her tie a rope to something... and then we can climb over..." the ends of his words were fading into pure, thin air.
"You mean so you can climb over..." Naomi's ability to perceive the truth pierced him like a needle.
"It's all right, we should have seen this coming. We'll need a makeshift crane to get Roger over this wall." Jerry offered a smile, but nobody saw it under his mask.
"You two are... *hilarious*..." the lack of wind in his lungs translated to a lack of push in his creative sails. "While I'm actually... dying here..." a strong and painful cramp made him clutch his side. "I think I'm having... a pancreatic pseudoaneurysm."
"I... if that's even a real thing, Roger, I highly doubt you'd get it from a little too much exercise." Naomi was already regretting depriving herself the comfort of sleep, just for this.

After the few moments Roger took to establish he was indeed not dying, but suffering from a cramp, the three stooges walked along the perimeter and found a nice little breach where the top of the wall surrounding the gallery had crumbled away just enough to provide a nice nook, with a foothold to boot. Roger asked them to wait, and after a few minutes brought his old metal stallion of a car as close as he could, aiming to use it as their getaway vehicle. Despite their jabs at their cosmically-enlightened friend, they agreed to do it his way, because after all, he had taken upon himself the role of directing what might turn out to be the adventure of a lifetime. They had forgotten a while back how easily adventures could turn into misadventures; the prospect of being important and rightfully going against the fray is intoxicating in its own right. The two men squatted near the wall facing away, and used their hands to launch a running and jumping Naomi as high as they could. They thought she would be heavier. Instead of landing on top of the wall, she was launched all the way over it and produced a dull thud on the other side. Jerry and Roger gave each other the wide-eyed stare people tend to have when confronted with the reality of their own stupidity.

"It's... it's all right... women... they have a small terminal velocity, they can survive any fall." Roger was doing his best to be reassuring.
"You're thinking of rats and squirrels." Sometimes, Jerry tried imagined a world where Roger wasn't an over-confident fool. He always failed.

A quiet moan of pain found its way to them from the other side of the wall. "The rope you idiots!" it gracefully beckoned them. Without so much as second thought, Jerry threw the rope over, and a few moments later it came back over to his side, now attached to a thick tree branch a few paces away. Roger was the first to go, and Jerry had to find the courage in him to commit an act unbefitting a gentleman, but befitting a truest of friends: he helped Roger stabilize and climb over by pushing on his ass. He produced a considerably louder thud when he finally somehow landed on the other side, and to everyone's amazement, he didn't instantly pulverize any of his limbs in the process. The climb was easy enough for Jerry who stayed in relatively acceptable shape, and the criminal masterminds were reunited at last.

"You okay? Not too bad of a fall?" this marked one of the few times Jerry's concern for another person wasn't totally feigned.

"I'm as good as ever. My ankles are kind of sore-" Roger wasn't the best at picking up social cues.

"Not you, her..." Jerry clarified while closing his eyes and rubbing his hands over his temples.

"Still alive, so I guess it'll have to do." Naomi knew this wasn't the time to berate them for her flight. She could do this later. "So... what's the plan now? I assume we have one?" she suddenly realized making such an assumption might have been giving them too much credit. Then again, she didn't have one either.

"Believe it or not, Naomi, I wouldn't go into this without a true plan of action. For now, we make our way around the perimeter to the back of the gallery, near the big windows installed along the wall the painting is hanging from. Then, we wait." Roger's eyes were sparkling at the thought of having a plan of his work in the real world, and not merely in his imagination.

"Wait for what? Christmas?" Jerry needed more. Something inside reminded him not to trust a Roger plan until it was fully unveiled.

"Then, a distraction. Let's do this. We don't have much time." Roger was fairly purposeful in not revealing everything. He wasn't sure how much they would approve of his methods, and how far he could string them along solely in the name of childhood friendship and vague notions of the greater good, something he himself didn't entirely believe in. At the very least, they didn't have to deal with much of a police presence; the town lost any real use for it years ago.

After a few moments of sneaking about in the shadows around an empty garden, the trio arrived at the tall windowed walls adjacent to the painting. With a bit of effort and angling, they could see a tiny portion of it from the side, enough to ascertain its presence. Roger then motioned for them to follow him into a big bush. This was to be their hideout until the promised distraction kicked in. The bush was big and hollow enough to accommodate three people, and perhaps even a fourth one if necessary. It was quite a convenient tool for any would-be criminals.

"Where are all the guards? Don't think I've seen any outside." Jerry began to worry himself with the suspicious nature of his observation.

"I think there might be some inside... I'm not sure. Don't worry about it." as always, Roger failed to reassure anyone about anything.

"You... think?! Don't worry about it?!" Jerry felt the now-familiar cauldron of rage starting to boil within him once again.

"Just relax for a moment, you're being a worrywart. What we need to deal with is the alarm system. And I just happen to have found a way to take care of both that problem, as well as any guards who may or may not be here. You're welcome." Roger's face adopted a confident smile, his head titled back, and he looked on his friends with the half-closed eyes of shameless pride.

"Out of all the possible childhood friends... why did it have to be you two?" Naomi's interjection drew smiles on all their faces, hidden by the crude masks they were wearing. She wondered how she let herself get drawn into all of this. She wondered why she allowed herself to be born in the first place. The little pyromaniac rebel was still alive and well within her, waiting for the opportunity to grow tall again.

Suddenly, a loud bang from the front of the gallery. A pillar of smoke and ashes rose to the sky as a mighty fire began roaring underneath. The gallery's alarm went off to signal the end of the world. The few guards hidden away inside the employee break room for their night shift ran to the front like not only their lives, but most importantly, their salaries were at stake. The fire was growing larger, consuming any pretentious paintings and pointless knick-knacks it could lay its flaming tentacles on. There was no stopping it. The guards were mesmerized for a few moments, after which they decided to run away to a safe distance and call the fire department, the true professionals they were. On their way off the property, they saw the owner of the cafe across the street standing in front of the fire, his arms crossed, his heart spiritually satisfied. This was a long time coming, he told himself. That'll teach the Billies to sleep with other peoples' wives.

"I'm going to go out on a limb here and assume this is the distraction we're waiting for." Jerry was generally good at going out on a limb and making assumptions.
"I didn't think he'd go that far. I'm proud of him. Yes, let's move." adrenaline forced Roger's sentences to be quick and concise, a quality he would have benefited from adopting in other parts of his life.
"Let's rock." added Naomi, trying to work up her enthusiasm since she was already here anyways. The warm brightness of the flames against the darkness of night helped her with that.

The three masked burglars emerged from the darkness of the bush, and without a second thought, Roger picked up a rock and smashed the glass wall to bits and pieces. It offered no resistance. They went inside the gallery, and witnessed the fire slowly working its way through the fire-retardant layers of the walls. It had eaten away at a good part of the entrance, it was growing and spreading, but slowly and indifferently, as if on its own terms, with personal goals to achieve.

"Well, considering how well the distraction is working, why not leave the painting to burn?" Naomi was making a valiant attempt at bringing logic and sense into this whole mess.
"Because they're almost here..." calmly replied Roger, pointing a finger towards some flashing lights approaching fast. "There's no way the fire will get to this painting before the firemen do." he was correct. The fire didn't seem too keen on reaching the back wall with the painting on it anytime soon.

Having visibly saved the bulk of his energy for this very moment, in one fluid motion Roger glided over next to the painting, grabbed it by the edges, and lifted it off the wall with barely any effort. Despite its size, it felt lighter than a feather. They had what they came for. It was time to leave. The fire trucks were already nearing the entrance, and somewhere in town, an O'Harris was writing a list, trying to determine which of his enemies hated art to this degree.
The criminal masterminds circled back around the wall to their trusty rope, and came to

the realization they couldn't use it to climb back over the other way for it was attached to a tree on their side of the wall. They stood solemn and dumbfounded for a moment. Finally shaking herself from the shackles of despair, Naomi climbed up the rope, squatted on the tree branch, and launched herself back across the wall, this time of her own volition, and landed with feline grace on the other side. In a hushed voice she beckoned them throw the painting over. It took a few times before they heard her over the sound of the ever-approaching sirens and ringing alarm bell. Roger chucked it over in one swift motion and sent it spinning through the air, landing about ten meters away from Naomi. At least the general sense of the manoeuvre was accomplished. It was now Jerry's turn, and with a little more strain than his friend before him he climbed the rope, and made his acrobatic jump to the other side. He managed to snag the sole of his foot on the top part of the wall, causing him to awkwardly stumble over and land right on the hood of Roger's car. It sagged in defeat, its alarm went off for a split second, and black smoke began streaming out from the engine. They saluted the fallen trooper, and awkwardly stood still, waiting for Roger to make his way over. After approximately a minute, they heard a loud wooden snap and the unmistakable sound of fat flesh smacking the ground. The firemen were now rushing towards the fire, and police sirens were also slowly materialising into existence. His ankle sprained and ass on the ground, Roger looked on towards the fire, and watched as the flames began to fade away into smoke and ash, having claimed about half the gallery from front to back and floor to ceiling. The police sirens were still approaching, the bastards.

"I can't run! You have to go without me! Don't try to stay! Leave me!" Roger shouted in desperation over to the other side of the wall.
"Okay!" yelled Jerry and Naomi with a bit too much enthusiasm, fading away into the night and leaving Roger as he so wished. "Also, your car is dead!" Jerry informed him before completely leaving his earshot.

For an hour or so, they wandered around in the eerily empty streets of the town, trying to let the adrenaline wear off and deciding on their next move. Without paying much attention to the twists and turns they kept taking at every opportunity, they had wandered far away into some forgotten part of the city, a section most of its inhabitants weren't even certain existed anymore. Shoddy brick apartment buildings and run-down storefronts made up the vast majority of this neighbourhood, with the lights in peoples' windows being far and few in-between. Even the air itself felt stale and oppressive, trying to push them out of this world they didn't belong in one bit. The lack of life outdoors at this time of night didn't make the atmosphere any more bearable, imbuing every sound with a sharp edge. On the contrary, it seemed as if even raccoons, squirrels and crickets were intent on avoiding these streets like the plague. A world within a world, it housed the forgotten and obsolete of Hollow Crest. They could feel another kind of darkness tugging away at them from the darkened alleyways and vile nooks, twisting the neighbourhood into a shape the mind was almost incapable of mapping. The few street lights littered far and few in-between offered little consolation to anyone trapped here at night.

"So... what's the plan? We keep wandering around 'til kingdom come?" Naomi finally broke the silence weighing so heavily on their shoulders.
"I guess we really should have thought this through. Why do we leave Roger to make decisions?" to Jerry it seemed more like a fact of life, rather than a choice on their part.
"Uhm, say... what are we going to do about Roger? Not that I feel particularly bad about

it, but we did leave him behind-”

“At his own heroic request.”

“Still, I can't help but feel some level of responsibility, don't you?”

“I suppose he is our burden... if only because he's nobody else's.” deep down, Jerry was a tiny bit happy he was indeed their burden to carry.

“So how are we planning to get him out of this one?” Naomi's desire to rescue her friend was driven more by a sense of guilt at this stage.

“You're assuming he hasn't already gotten himself out. He might sometimes be a dumbass of cosmic proportions, but he's more resourceful... more than we know, probably.” Jerry only half-believed what he was saying, but it wouldn't hurt, he assumed, to inject a bit of good old-fashioned positive thinking into this whole situation.

“Right... even so, we should do something come morning, like call the police or the hospital, see if he's been arrested… or something.” she didn't want to add the morgue to this list, but the thought did briefly flash in her mind.

“Sounds about right to me. For now though, I think we have the more pressing issue of, well, just what the hell we're meant to do now?” the frustration was building up in Jerry's voice once again. It had an infectious quality about it.

“How the hell should I know?! Roger was the one who orchestrated this whole thing.” she looked at the sky for a moment, “Holy Lord up above, we're brain-dead.” such was her reasonable take on the situation.

“All right... all right... let's just find our way out of here first and go to... well, whoever's place is closest.” Jerry gave another glace all around him at the dead streets, the dead lamps, the dead alleyways and the dead windows. “For now, we gotta leave the heart of darkness.”

“Jerry? You're starting to sound like Roger. We really don't need more than one of him. Especially not now. Hell, I'm not even sure we can handle *one* of him.” the little attempt at humour drew from her friend the faint trace of a reluctant smile.

“Yeah, now that would be a world-ending catastrophe.”

Right about then, the pair walked across a street they finally recognized, Proud Oak Boulevard. She knew it led to somewhere near her place, and so they decided to keep following it towards more familiar territory. Slowly and certainly, as the sun was closer and closer to bringing a new day, they found their way back into their own world, and her place was finally in sight.

* * *

Roger's foot and shin were throbbing with the agony generally reserved for those truly out of shape, as if trying to escape from his imperfect and sullied body. Naturally, it was futile; all of his limbs and organs were tied down to him, regardless of how terrifying the prospect might have been. He knew he didn't have much time before first the firemen, then the policemen, and maybe even the guards would notice his presence. Thankfully, they seemed to be more preoccupied with the cafe owner, still basking in the light of his life's greatest and most vindictive achievement. He wasn't about to give anyone any resistance, but his gleefully calm demeanour was giving the men around him a bit of pause on what the best method of approach might be. Did he know something they didn't? Was he waiting for them to come in so he could set off a grenade? Obviously, the answer to both those questions was an emphatic “no”, but the whole premise caught everyone off-guard and bought Roger a few precious moments to confer with his cosmic deities and roll away into a further and darker corner of the estate. Maybe he could find a bush to spend the night in, or at least until things calmed down enough for him to somehow slip away unnoticed. He wasn't sure how to elaborate on the "somehow" part, but he was confident the opportunity would present itself to him. As he kept carefully rolling on the ground trying not to aggravate his leg injury any further, he suddenly came to a stop against a wooden wall. The artistically-located bathroom; he was saved. Trying not to make any undignified sounds which might attract even the slightest attention to him, he quietly pulled himself up, stood on one foot, opened the door and managed to slither his way in.

It certainly wasn't the typical outhouse with a hole in the floor, but on the contrary, it was a lavish and excessively furnished bathroom containing all the amenities anyone could desire: toilet, shower, bath, towels, magazines, newspapers, and of course, a mini-bar to help fight boredom. There was even a couch for him to get comfortable. If it wasn't for the lack of a kitchen, the place could have been rented out as a bathroom-centred home.

His first course of action was an attempt at prying the mini-bar open after realizing it unlocked with the help of some form of membership card, probably of the alcoholics' association, he mused to himself. The wooden contraption remained unmoved and unimpressed by his lacklustre efforts. He gave it a good smack as a final resort, and only succeeded in hurting his hand in addition to everything else. Suddenly, he heard faint voices coming from the other side of the door. They were closing in on him, and fast. This was the moment of truth, thought Roger, the instant where all his meditative training and cosmic rapports would culminate to help him find the unlikely way out of this, the way none could have foreseen with mere regular vision. He hobbled to the door as quickly as he could and turned the lock. A few seconds later he could tell the voices were right on the other side, one of them somehow much clearer than the other, and in anticipation of them trying to open it, he yelled out "It's busy! Come back another time!" A surprised silence came back at him from the other side. "I'm having an... ungentlemanly episode. You *really* don't want to be in here." He added with a bit more confidence, certain it would be enough to sway anyone from entering a public bathroom. It would have been, under normal circumstances.

"This is the police! Unlock the door, step away from it and put your hands in the air!" the voice from the other side wasn't messing around.

"Or else what? You'll shoot me for taking a shit?" though Roger certainly wasn't a person of the calmest predisposition, even he found himself surprised at his sudden willingness to tangle with the Law.

"No...?" there was a strange air of surprise about the answer. "We'll take you in a suspect and potential accomplice to the O'Harris gallery arson." a short pause hung in the air. "Unless you try to kill me. In that case, yes, I will shoot you while you're on the toilet." there was an earnest, almost innocent quality about the voice.

Roger was frantically trying to think himself out of this situation. Like many times before, his mind was pulling a blank on him. "I, uh, lost the keys to the door. I can't open it for you." this was the best he could come up with.

"...Sir, you don't need a key to open it from the inside. We'll break the door down if we have to." the voice on the other end was starting to become annoyed on a primal level.

"But you need a warrant to do that!" a flash of relief carried across Roger as he believed he had found a loophole to the situation.

"In this particular case, *sir*," the voice was starting to turn hostile with a hint of mockery behind it, "we really don't need anything."

"Can I at least finish my business before I open it?" like a child trying to delay the inevitable, Roger seemed to be banking his chips at this stage on a miracle which would never come.

"Your business is our business now." the voice paused briefly, realizing how strange those words sounded given the context. "Open the door now, or we're breaking it down!"

"Fine, fine! Keep your dicks in your pants, I'm on my way." Reluctantly, Roger admitted a temporary defeat and unlocked the door, took a few steps back and plopped himself down on the conveniently-located couch.

The door slowly swung ajar, and a familiar face took a peek inside, gun in hand and ready to shoot the evil scum off the face of the planet. Roger squinted for a second as he could hardly believe his luck. It was Officer Tim, whom he so aptly berated not long ago, right before saving his life. Upon seeing Roger, Tim lowered his weapon and held his face in his hand, displaying a profound sadness worthy of a Broadway show.

"No way. Not you again. Why... just why can't I have a normal shift..." Tim was talking to himself more than to Roger.

"Tim! Am I glad to see you!" Roger's enthusiasm was his alone. "You wouldn't believe everything that's been happening here, I've-"

"Been caught red-handed at a crime scene? Just admit it, you helped Vinter set fire to this place because a signal from space told you to do so, or something of the sort, am I right?" the officer's sense of alarm had mostly vanished, yet he still retained a grip on his gun, a profound and unseen part of him hoping Roger would present him with the opportunity to use it. "And don't even think about bringing up the flowers episode. You wouldn't have needed to save me if you hadn't made me show you the body in the first place." the anticipation was a correct one.

It took Roger a moment to process just how bad he looked right now. He had a cunning idea. "What I was going to say, Tim, before you rudely interrupted me, is that I'm glad to see you, because I've taken a massive amount of LSD. I thought this was my home." he tried to give his words a vaguely mystical and droopy quality to make them feel more authentic and convincing.

"You sound pretty articulate for someone on a "massive amount of LSD"." the air quotes were strongly emphasized both in gesture and tone.

"That's just how it is when you're experienced as I am. By the way, where's your partner? I heard *many* voices right before you burst in."

Officer Tim sighed, "Ever heard of a walkie-talkie?" this phrase forced Roger's mouth slightly agape and a vacant stare settled in his eyes. "Listen, Roger, it doesn't matter what you're on. You've been found at a crime scene, while a crime was in progress. I'm taking you in for interrogation. But first, since you're obviously on such a massive dose of LSD, I think I'll put you in the drunk tank for a day or two, and have a doctor look at you." Tim's words were lacquered in a hefty veil of schadenfreude.

Roger gave the officer a good long look, a final vain attempt to buy himself some time to conjure up his great escape from the annoying clutches of the Law. He soothed himself with the idea this small setback was, in fact, a blessing in disguise and all part of the universe's plan which would inevitably see him come out on top as the big winner. We baselessly like to think we're special like that. Trying to keep a proud air about himself, he stood from the couch and hobbled through the pain in Tim's direction. Though the latter didn't have any particular fondness for Roger, to say the least, he remained endowed with a general sense of human compassion and sympathy, and helped his injured suspect make it all the way back to the police cruiser.

On his way to the car Roger managed to get a good look at what was left of the gallery, the front part of it now a lumbering pile of smoking ruins containing the most expensive and artistic ashes in the country, if not the entire world. Such was his personal appraisal. A pang of shame and sadness did wash over him momentarily, thinking about the innocent works of art which gave up their canvases, colours and lives for a greater good they'll never be aware of. Just over half the building was burnt to smithereens, and in an exceedingly rare display of self-awareness, Roger conceded to himself the outlandish idea there might have been a better approach to this whole thing. Nevertheless, it was too late to turn back, and the clock only ever keeps advancing forward, whether in a line or a circle. The main objective, he told himself, had been accomplished. Just as he anticipated, the painting came with them of its own free volition, if it could be named as such, and the gallery wouldn't be admitting visitors anytime soon. His leg kept throbbing harder and harder, the pain beginning to crawl toward his knee, slowly creeping up along the calf. Roger didn't want to imagine where the pain might go to next. Maybe he really did need to see a doctor. Finally, he made it to the vehicle, and created a historical moment by being one of the only ever arrested suspects to have been more eager to enter the back of a police car than the officer escorting them. Tim helped him spill in, locked the door, and went on to have a conversation with a few of the firemen. Right next to Roger was the owner of the cafe, whom he now knew was named Vinter. It never did occur to him to ask for a name. He was still wearing the patented smile of inner peace and satisfaction on his wrinkled face.

"I suppose, I have to thank you, fat man." Vinter eerily smiled at Roger. "Think I really did need that extra push, you know?"

"I really don't." Roger was quite sensibly afraid of being recorded at this moment. His companion no longer seemed to have any fear left him.

"Well, no matter, it's *all right* now..." Vinter stretched his words and took a childish delight in their pronunciation. "I should have done this a long time ago. Never had it in me. Not 'til you came along." he gave Roger another appreciative smile as a way of communicating gratitude.

"Never had what in you?" something seemed off to Roger.

Vinter flexed his muscles and stretched his grin from ear to ear, "The rage."

Chapter 14

Jerry and Naomi were walking down the darkened street at a quicker pace than normal, but not quick enough to attract any unwanted attention. The sound of sirens was fading further and further away, giving way to a soothing silence they both welcomed eagerly. Their veins were still full of adrenaline, and their minds largely devoid of guilt for leaving Roger to his fate. As it should be. They were silently trying to regulate their breathing, and keeping an eye out for any cops who might chase after them. They were in the clear; it was the nearly-perfect crime, the fire and their injured friend notwithstanding. When they finally reached Naomi's apartment, Jerry only commented with "Thank God." before they entered and the door was locked behind them. Safety at last.

The apartment itself was located on the fourth floor of a five-story building, just short enough to prevent a mandatory elevator from being installed, per city regulations. There were many of those around, built decades ago when Hollow Crest was in full bloom and apparently filled with potential. The building itself was fairly unremarkable, its light-yellow brick facade barely standing out from the rest of the monoliths surrounding it. In some ways, it matched quite well with the general spirit of the city. The hallways were obviously old and in need of a few touch-ups, but on the whole, they were clean enough to be presentable to outside visitors. The walls weren't paper thin, but they didn't do a fantastic job at trapping the sound either. The occasional argumentative yell or television set could be heard when they were making their way up the stairs. It was perfect for Naomi. Nobody was up in anybody else's business, and despite being largely invisible, the neighbours still gave signs of life to prevent the building from feeling haunted.

The door leading into her abode was made from sturdy hardwood, a remnant from the times when construction companies still weren't entirely corrupt and had the immense courage not to sell out their principles for the tiniest offering. Not many of those left around, if any. The heavy lock was reminiscent of something one might have expected to find in their ancestral home, and despite actually being easier to pick than a regular lock, it did make the tenants feel just a little safer. An old trick of the trade; people readily settle for illusions if they don't get challenged.

The interior of the apartment was of a largely minimalist design, the white walls being adorned with the occasional landscape or animal painting, and the furniture almost exclusively crafted from wood. There was a medium-sized television in the living room facing a green fabric couch, but it didn't see much usage over the course of the last few years. The kitchen was outfitted with all the basic necessities one could expect, with its sole outstanding element being a round wooden table with three chairs, one of them visibly worn-out more than the others. The bathroom was equally-neat and unremarkable. Both those rooms were reached by an empty hallway, which also led to the bedroom at its very end. It was a fairly-small but rather well-decorated room, especially in comparison with the rest of the house. The bed was covered with a clean and smooth navy-blue sheet, and in the corner stood a wooden writing desk with a computer on it. There were also some wall-mounted bookshelves, housing many classics by Camus, Garcia Marquez, Lovecraft... there was certainly no discrimination to be found here. Everything seemed organized to the point of reaching mathematical proportions, and Jerry silently wondered just how much he was actually allowed to touch in this place, and what the consequences would be of moving something by an inch. Disastrous, he assumed.

The first thing Naomi did was drop the painting off right on her living room couch, after which she stormed into the bathroom and took a long shower. Jerry was left to silently sit on the sofa and awkwardly make friends with the painting. He took a good look at it again, partly because he was curious, and partly because an irresistible force was drawing his eyes to it. It was fifty-fifty. The face of the old man seemed at the same time featureless and all-encompassing, the kind of face one could imagine any man growing old with. His light grey skin was almost glowing in contrast with the darkness of the background, which somehow felt blacker than the abyss, as if it was literally swallowing any light touching it. The liquid coming out of his mouth and eyes had a certain frustrating quality about it, combining colours from all over the spectrum, but seemingly favouring the more vivid and noticeable ones. The more he looked at them, the more had the impression the liquid was moving, trying to worm its way out of the painting and onto the couch itself. Jerry could swear the old man was smiling at him when he looked at his face from the corner of his eye. His hand with the outstretched middle finger remained unchanged.

Imperceptibly at first, he began to feel more and more tired, his eyelids growing heavier and heavier, until they closed down on him and sent him into the strange transitive state between wakefulness and sleep, where dreams and reality melt into one and the same. A raspy voice came down from all directions on him, and all Jerry could do was absorb it in frozen terror: "Too late...". Mustering every inch of willpower he had and didn't have, he managed to open his eyes and snap himself out of the trance. Things weren't looking good. Maybe dragging the painting all the way here wasn't the best idea. Maybe it was best to destroy it? Or was it best to study it? Jerry was mulling it all over in his mind, and as he tended to do when in profound thought, he stared at the ceiling with his mouth agape.

Home is where our heart is, and the unwelcome guest crossed the doorstep into theirs.

Chapter 15

"You're hurting me! I'll write a stern letter about this!" Roger cried as he was thrown behind bars in the police station lockup, Vinter following behind him in a calmer and docile manner, appropriate to those who have found their purpose in life.

"Pardon me, your highness, for the poor accommodations." Officer Tim apologized with a satisfied grin, giving Roger one final prod in his lower back with his government-issued baton, and restrained himself from scratching his itch any further. Annoying as Roger might be, he's just a loony, thought Tim, and as a police officer he was sworn to protect even the dumbest elements of society and follow The Law to the letter. The hardest part of his job, no doubt. "We'll come back for you in the morning. Sit tight for now, get to know each other, tell some stories maybe."

Roger was sitting with his arms crossed and face red with indignation, having evidently found something much more interesting to stare at than Officer Tim, right there in the dark corner of the cell. The redness in his face was slowly working its way toward the rest of his body, and he could no longer pretend he was the stoic macho figure he imagined himself to be. He let out a high-pitched yelp and clutched at his ankle, forcing a tiny bit of pity from and a great bit of amusement for the good officer. The man really did need to see a specialist. With a heavy sigh, he went back upstairs and started to make calls to find a doctor at the unlikeliest time of night. The one at the hospital was busy with a minor operation. The one sleeping at home didn't feel like answering his phone. There weren't many other options for Tim, and he decided to call the idlest medical facility in the city: the morgue. One ring. Two rings. A sleepy voice on the other end "Kathleen Morrow speaking...".

About a half-hour later a car pulled up to the police station, and like a woman on a mission Kathleen barged in through the main doors. Without so much as a greeting she asked Officer Tim to show her the patient.

"I guess politeness isn't a prerequisite when you mostly deal with corpses." Tim was feeling very facetious today.

"It's even less of a prerequisite when there's a live one to deal with." she was still waiting for him to show her the way.

"I... think you'll really get along with our patient." he was too spent to engage in any type of sparring with an equal opponent, physical or verbal. Besides, something told him he was out of his depth on this one.

Lazily, he stood up from his desk, and dragging his feet, without too much of a hurry, shuffled to the downstairs lockup. He opened the door leading to the cell and was almost struck by a panic attack of unprecedented proportions. Roger was still letting out high-pitched squeals in the corner with his eyes closed, while good old Vinter was doing his best to hang himself with a poorly-fashioned noose out of his sweater. It was doubtful whether it could hold his weight, but he was determined to try. The madness in the air was almost quantifiable, and certainly would have been had science managed to progress far enough by then.

Officer Tim reacted relatively quickly considering his training didn't prepare him for this sort of situation, opening the cell door and lunging towards Vinter in one impressively smooth motion. In the process he directed Kathleen toward her patient. This might have very well been the highlight of his career thus far. He started handcuffing the unexpectedly resistant and suddenly virile old man who decided to take the opportunity presented to him by Officer Tim when he forgot to lock the doors behind him. He made a break for the exit. Absurdly nimble for his age, he managed to slip out of Tim's grasp and through the door like a warm stick of chaotic butter, with very little separating him from freedom now. This was no longer the highlight of the good officer's career. As a matter of fact, it might have been the end of it. Completely forgetting Roger and Kathleen, he jumped out in the pursuit after one of the sole individuals he ever arrested whom he could call a true criminal. The doctor and patient were left alone to process what had just happened. The doors were still unlocked.

"Where does it hurt?" Kathleen broke the silence.

"I have an open fracture here, at my ankle." Roger tried to sound as manly as he possibly could.

"You don't know what an open fracture is, do you..." her years of experience taught Kathleen this was likely the start of a long and tedious night, and Lord knows she's had enough of those over the years.

"Maybe, maybe not." there were few greater pains for Roger, like for most people, than admitting he was wrong.

"You... you don't even have a closed fracture. You just have a pretty big contusion. Put some ice on it, champ." part of her was indeed relieved there wouldn't be more work to do on this patient, and another part was annoyed at having been summoned here in the middle of her crucial research.

"Don't you uh, have something stronger than ice, doc?" Roger's eyes pleaded, and Kathleen knew for what. It wasn't the first time she had seen this look in the suffering.

"Fine, here, take a couple of oxy's." Kathleen wasn't above compromising her professional integrity, if it meant it would lessen her suffering at the hands of fools.

"You just carry those around with the prescription and everything?" Roger was at first surprised, and then suspicious of how easily the doctor gave in to his request.

"It's my personal stash. Now drink up and shut up." she instructed him, handing him two pills and a bottle of water.

"Doc, you're my hero, forever and ever. Now, we have to get out of here, this town is about to become very unsafe, for you and me both." Roger was trying to speak as casually as possible in an attempt to make the proposition feel normal to Kathleen.

"*I* have to get out of here, you're right. *You* aren't going anywhere. I don't know what you're in here for, but I'm not the one helping you get out. I've broken my code of ethics enough for one night." when she became annoyed, Kathleen's voice started to take on a higher and sharper pitch, a warning sign for all who might fall to her wrath.

"Hey, correct me if I'm wrong Doc, but you're the coroner, right?" a momentary glare of light shined in Roger's eyes.

"Sure am." the question seemed innocent enough for her to give him a true answer.

"So, you're the one who did the autopsy on that body in the forest, right?" Roger didn't realize it, but in the back of his mind he was starting to formulate a way to not only escape, but also enlist Kathleen in his coming battle against evil. It was definitely coming. No doubt about it.

"Yup." she didn't like where this was going, but at this point she was also just a little too intrigued to stop the conversation.

"Then you've seen what I've seen. You've looked into his stump like I did, and by the Gods of the Cosmos you've seen the evil within." Roger tried lowering his voice to sound more like a preacher, or as he preferred to think, a prophet.

"It definitely defies medical explanation, if that's what you're massively struggling to say." she was quite perturbed at the idea of agreeing on anything at all with the strangely pathetic man before her... and yet, here they were.

"Listen, something's coming for us all, and we're all going to end up like mister medical mystery. Don't ask me how I know this, you wouldn't understand... I am simply in tune with these things. I know you know it too. Even if you don't know it. Your mind still knows it, and that's a fact." Roger was convincing himself once again he was indeed the king of logical arguments.

Kathleen remained motionless and entranced in deep thought for a few moments. She processed everything from the moment she saw the body to the last time she put it on ice, the emotions it raised in her, the dread it excavated from the most forgotten recesses of her mind. She had seen dead bodies before, some even mangled worse than this one, and yet it was the only one whose imprint was left burning in her mind. Contrary to what most people think about men and women of science, imagination and intuition are two of their most valued attributes, allowing them to stretch further the frontiers of knowledge. Kathleen's instinct had been honed and sharpened by years of trying to do her part in the expansion of her field, and right now this valuable tool of hers was saying one thing: there was some grain of truth to be found somewhere in Roger's ramblings. She was entering a domain where logic and rationality only took her so far, and if they were to be introduced into this equation, it would be after all is said, done and solved. Taking perhaps the greatest leap of faith she had in her entire career, under the soothing effects of oxycodone, she agreed to help Roger find his way out.

"Maybe... you're onto something. Don't get your head stuck up your own ass though, we'll need it if you're right to any sort of extent." she was afraid, and rightfully so, that someone agreeing with Roger would inflate his ego a thousand-fold. She was very afraid. "So, I'm just going to leave now, with the doors open like they were... like the good officer intended them to be. You do what you must. You know where to find me, if you need me."

"I will never forget this. We are now bound by the forces governing our fate. Godspeed, fellow scientist!" Roger's ego had indeed inflated a thousand-fold. She was right to be afraid.

Already regretting her decision, Kathleen rolled her eyes at Roger, a reaction he was now immune to. "For the love of all that is holy, please stop talking." she then marched back through the doors with the same determination she had entered them with, and soon Roger heard her car starting up again and taking off.

He didn't know how much time he had to make his great escape, but he assumed it wasn't too long, no matter how supernaturally fast, agile and insane old man Vinter seemed to be. The pills were already starting to kick in, and the pain in his ankle began to subside, giving way to a peaceful calm which finally made thinking possible again. What a saint the doctor was, Roger made a mental note to find a way to thank her later on. Maybe a box of her favourite medicine for her troubles. He'd have to give it some thought. Finally able to stand on his own with only a slight limp, he crossed the cell door, and just like this, in the blink of an eye, officially became a fugitive from the law, likely adding a few years on top of whatever potential sentence he might have gotten. It crossed his mind, and he brushed it away. It didn't matter much now, there were more important things to worry about for one as obviously chosen as he was. With a newfound confidence brought on by the opioid coursing through his brain, he climbed the stairs of the basement and entered the main hall of the precinct. Not a soul in sight. Shoulders high and chest proudly protruding, he walked through the essentially empty space to the front doors, and waltzed right out of it like the criminal mastermind he fancied himself as. Slipping away into the night, Roger left the monumentally barren police station behind.

Chapter 16

Naomi had been standing under the running warm water for about ten minutes now, sheltering herself from the flow of time of the outside world. As long as she stood in the shower, she was an isolated element existing in her personal bubble. Comforting. Naturally, she knew it was a lie, but the feeling of total safety and disconnection was too alluring to pass up. The water had been nice, warm, steady and perfect, which naturally meant it wasn't going to last. In the blink of an eye, it transformed into a scalding stream which caused Naomi to scream and jump out of the shower, bringing her back in the loveless embrace of the real world. She felt betrayed; even her private, timeless sanctuary wasn't strong enough to bar the influence of reality from her. She took the time to look at herself in the mirror. Her hair was still long, black and thick, but she had gained a few pounds over the last year or so. Nothing dramatic, but her sense of shame cared a little. Like for all people who often look into the mirror, her face was slowly changing over the years, but imperceptibly, in a way she couldn't notice. It only materialized a nagging feeling in the back of her mind, the awareness of something she wasn't capable of perceiving in the wheel of life. Hoping it wouldn't change to the point where she would have to make a new picture for identification purposes, she sighed and admitted to herself Father Time would ruthlessly and impartially reign over us all, for the foreseeable future at least. It was time to join up back with the rest of civilization.

After getting dressed and exiting the bathroom, she walked into the living room to see Jerry still staring at the ceiling with his mouth agape. Less knowledgeable people would have called an ambulance with the assumption they were witnessing a man on the verge of death. Being of the more experienced type who had known him for a while now, she didn't blink an eye before snapping her fingers in his face on her way to sit on the other side of the couch, the painting ominously filling the space between them. Jerry snapped out of his trance, and a moment of silence descended upon them, during which they both felt like idiots for having gotten this far and become implicated in a criminal matter. At the very least, the local police department lacked not only the kind of competence which could solely be acquired through experience, but also the type of manpower awarded to the districts with the greatest and highest crime rates. It gave them a fairly solid chance at getting away with it. Jerry baselessly estimated it at around sixty percent, assuming Roger would either keep his mouth shut, or talk too much to be taken seriously. All things considered, the situation could have been worse. Like always.

"So, what the hell are we doing now?" pertinently asked Naomi.

"I... honestly don't know." replied Jerry with a hint of amazement, as if he hadn't considered the need to move forward somewhere. "At the very least, we can always just wait and see what happens tomorrow. This option is always open to us."

"What do you think our odds are on not getting arrested tonight?" Naomi's fear began to grow at the sight of Jerry's clueless viewpoint.

"Glad you asked, I estimated them at sixty percent, if Roger doesn't spill everything. I rate that at about fifty percent." Jerry was glad to have been ahead of the question for once.

"Sounds a little generous." she replied, incredulous.

"I know, but what else can we do? I mean, do you have any ideas?" Jerry wasn't chastising her, it was a legitimate question.

"I don't know why, but ever since this painting appeared, our lives have been slowly spiralling into... something *else*." she put a strong accent on the last word. "Let's try and destroy it. After all, what are we risking?" the idea was sound and logical, at least from her rational perspective.

"You know what? Let's." he had barely finished his sentence by the time he laid his hands on the painting.

"Hold on! Don't go setting my place on fire!" she tried to say it in a joking manner, but her concern for the safety of her apartment was all too real. Not to mention, she wanted to be the one to start the fire.

"Come on now, I'm not Roger. I'm only giving it the knife treatment. For starters." he said, dragging it along into the kitchen.

Jerry took the biggest, meanest and sharpest knife from the rack, and started to work on the painting, adding some of his own lines to the tableau... or trying to, at least. Naturally, it wasn't bound to go as planned. The knife kept slipping off the painting's surface without leaving so much as a trace. He looked at the knife, ensured it was German stainless steel, the only kind he trusted, and that it was as sharp as a knife can be. The canvas remained indifferent to his efforts, the molecules holding steady at his attempts to separate them; an unnatural force kept them bound. Though he couldn't have vouched for the truthfulness of what he saw and heard, he had the distinct impression the old man in the painting unleashed a spirited "Hah!" in his general direction. He started slashing, chopping, heaving and thrusting with ever-increasing ferocity, working himself into a sweat while Naomi watched from the side, doing her best to push away the realization which was creeping its way into her mind. After a few minutes of hopeless and pointless knifing, she put her hand on Jerry's tired and pulsating shoulder, conveying the message it was probably time to stop. No canvas of hers could hold up to such razor-sharp fury. However, Jerry was far from ready to admit defeat in the face of an inanimate object. He looked at her and asked: "Got some lighter fluid?".

She did, in fact, have some, and insisted he carry the painting out in the courtyard behind the building before putting it to good use. Though Jerry was right in the fact he was not Roger, what he didn't and couldn't see was that he was in no state to be trusted with dangerous experiments; his mind was swept up by the hurricane of the war he was now waging. The hour was still dark and nobody bore witness to the second attempt at destroying the painting. They soaked it in as much fluid as they could, and Naomi threw the lit match which started the painting-wide fire near-instantaneously. For a little while it burned, and they even debated for a moment as to whether or not they could smell some nauseating paint fumes emanating from the flames. They were sickening. The discussion, however, was short-lived and settled when the fire went out soon after, leaving a perfectly intact painting behind, every detail in the same place it had always been. It was almost insulting how much it didn't care for them. "Hold on, I'll be right back." said Naomi as she quickly marched back into the building, up the stairs and into her apartment.

She descended back a couple of minutes later holding a few chemical solutions, evidently putting her hands on anything even remotely dangerous she could find. The assortment included bleach, some low-grade acid designed for pots and pans, and a gel for high-temperature stove and grill cleaning. Though she bought those a while back with good intentions to use them regularly, the idea drifted away from her mind when she realized the time and effort it would take from her day. The bottles were all virtually full, and would certainly be enough to ruin any painting... any ordinary one, at least.

They poured the solutions all over their target, and it was almost as if it began to fire back at them. The acids and bleach seemed to be having a violent reaction, boiling and spitting in every direction, with a few drops finding their way onto Jerry's cheek and Naomi's forearm. They burned. The two friends spent a few minutes unwinding with swear words, both real and non-existent, during which time they dashed back to the apartment in panic to run cold water over their injuries. Somehow, the destruction of a lifeless object had backfired on them; few are those who could accomplish such a feat. When they went back down into the courtyard, they predictably found the painting laying on the ground, still as intact as the day it was created. The two friends looked at each other, and Naomi expressed the next logical step in their conundrum: "Let's bury it." They had now become equally-invested in making this happen; it made it personal when it spit their own chemicals back at them. What's more, in theory her idea was sound. In theory, a lot of things are sound.

Grabbing an old shovel she found laying around in the back of her closet designated for the forgotten, Naomi led the march outside to the small deserted park across the street. The night was still dark and silent, and behind their windows people were all soundly asleep while caught in the throes of increasingly violent and colourful dreams, save for the few night owls wrapped in the grip of insomnia. The so-called park only had four benches to it, and a small plot of land barely large enough to host fifty people. The earth was soft and ripe for digging. Naomi was about to do it herself, then remembered Jerry was here, and thrust the shovel into his hands with a demanding look. He sighed, and got to work.

A few minutes later he had managed to dig a surprisingly deep hole, and this without damaging any pipes or other infrastructure. A true miracle which might have been their first real stroke of good luck so far. Silently, Jerry motioned for Naomi to throw the painting in, which she did without too much of a hurry, taking a moment to give it one last good look. Was this going to work? Would the growing cloud of unnatural and violent tendencies hanging over them be dissipated? Would it finally get Roger to shut up about it? Who knows. They were at the experimental stage, which in their case entailed throwing everything at the wall to see what stuck. She tossed the painting in the hole, and spit on it for good measure, which drew a momentary picture of surprised disgust on Jerry's face. He got to work on filling the hole back up, and in a few more minutes it was done. The steady silence was undisturbed once again, the street lights humming a quiet electric melody of peace. Jerry clutched at his back; he wasn't used to shovelling, and his improper form inevitably made him pull a muscle.

"Ow!" he cried out with indignation.

"Seriously? This wasn't much work at all." the surprise in her voice was genuine, but to Jerry it sounded condescending through the filter of his back pain.

"Should've done it yourself if it wasn't much." he pushed the sentence through his gritted teeth. "Anyway, it's happened before. Just need to lay down for a bit." he was doing his best not to take out his anger on her.

"Back up we go, I suppose. Think you can make it?" once again, her genuine concern was received with a hint of mockery by Jerry.

"You'll have to carry me." he was only half-joking.

Grabbing Jerry's arm around her shoulder and giving him whatever support her slender frame could muster, she led him back up the stairs into her apartment, one step at a time. The whole adventure with the painting, which seemed so important in the moment, was already beginning to fade from their memories, but not entirely.

"You really think we're done with this whole thing?" he was partially hopeful, partially wary of expecting anything positive anymore.

"I honestly don't know. We might find the painting sitting in my apartment, just waiting for us to come back. Can't even rule *that* out at this stage." she was being quite literal with her expectations.

"Yeah, I guess we'll see. We've really entered the Twilight Zone, huh?" it was more of a reflection than a real question.

Having finally made it into the apartment, Naomi helped her wounded friend drop himself on the sofa like a dead weight. He moaned and grunted slightly as he turned and twisted himself into a comfortable position on his side. Naomi felt sorry for him, but only a little.

"I think I have a cream or lotion for this. Let me have a look." she was already leaving the room.

"Hey, can you turn on the news first?" Jerry practically had to yell after her.

"The... news? It's the middle of the night." her words came out slowly, as they tend to when someone is puzzled.

"Yeah, just any local news channel. Mind putting it on?" he wasn't yet ready to share his distant suspicion with her.

Allowing Jerry to have his moment of private enlightenment, she put on the Hollow Crest Nightly Journal to his satisfaction, and left the room. It was the only local news channel worth listening to at this hour, being the only one of its kind in existence. For the first few minutes, things seemed rather innocuous: a burst pipeline, a previously-missing child being found, a beloved school teacher preparing for retirement. Charming. However, it took little time for the stories to take a turn off wholesome lane. A feud between neighbours left one at the hospital, a bar fight left two victims in critical condition, a seemingly random battery with brass knuckles, and a gang of looters apprehended after smashing and grabbing two different antique clock stores. The newscaster, a sharply-dressed, jovial bundle of a rotund man in his forties, felt at more and more of a loss. This wasn't planned, nor rehearsed; this was all the good stuff coming live from the crime scene Hollow Crest was slowly turning into.

A moment later Naomi returned with a half-empty Tiger Balm jar, likely far past its expiration date. "It was all I could find, but it should still be good." she reassured him before handing him the little glass container. Expending a great deal of effort, he managed to reach the sore spot with a handful of it and a tidal wave of relief washed over him, but it wasn't nearly enough. Jerry informed her of the fact. Menthol and camphor were invading the air in Naomi's apartment, to the point of turning hostile and battering their senses. Both harnessed their deepest resources of stoicism and tried to ignore the overpowering smell, when the newscaster's eyes were blown wide open as he was obviously fed information over his earpiece. He looked straight at the camera, and did his best to compose himself, but seemed to speak to the people behind the televisions, rather than reading a report. He had no interest in the teleprompter. It's a crutch for the weak.

"Attention, to everyone who is watching, or listening. We have a breaking news report. Coming up... right now." he seemed momentarily confused by his own statement. "We've just received report of three murders having taken place in the city tonight, with six more attempted murders where the intended victims proved surprisingly stronger than their attackers." he allowed a moment of silence to let the news sink into the hearts and minds of the people who had known nothing but stagnant peace for too long, contravening the laws of an ever-moving and turbulent nature. "We... I implore you, stay at home, lock your doors, and take care of your loved ones. Hide your women and children. We will bring you more information as the situation develops. And now, in other news, we can expect some excellent weather tomorrow..." the sweat on the man's forehead was visible even on this substandard television set.

Naomi stood wide-eyed. "Shit... was Roger somehow right? Was he actually trying to warn us about this? Unbelievable." a very real sense of fear was beginning to invade the atmosphere in the room, mixed in with a tiny slice of confusion at their friend's prescient powers.
"Yeah... things are looking pretty bad, between my back and the murders." Jerry didn't make it clear which problem he was more concerned with.
"How do you think Roger's getting on? We did kind of ditch him to, um, the whims of fate." Naomi still felt worse about her role in Jerry's back pain than abandoning Roger. At least for the latter, she had an accomplice; guilt feels much lighter when shared.
"Unless he turned into Houdini and pulled a vanishing act, I think it's safe to say the cops have him. We can head over to the station come morning, bail him out, and listen to one of his insane lectures, always punctuated by how he was right all along." though Roger isn't a career criminal by any stretch of the imagination, it wasn't the first time Jerry had to follow this course of action.
"Naomi chuckled at how accurate the description was. "I guess that's one less problem for us to deal with!" she did indeed feel better, and even a bit chipper, at the idea she wasn't *too* wrong in her behaviour. "Since we're solving problems, I might have something better for your back, come to think of it." her imagination knew no bounds when fuelled by the power of positive thinking.
"I'll just wait right here." he knew better than to believe instant miracle remedies for his ailments, and tried to convey it through his sarcastic tone.

A few moments later, he heard her walking back into the room. The Hollow Crest Nightly Journal seemed to be having technical difficulties, likely with their anchor, he mused, so he switched channels until he found one playing any movie he'd classify as watchable. He landed on a channel specializing in art-house movies, now showing *Liquid Sky*. All he could really process was the presence of terrible actors, a nonsensical plot about tiny aliens searching for heroin, and shoddy camerawork. Just how he liked it. He was near the end of it, right at the scene where the scientist, who performs exactly zero scientific feats, is murdered with a knife in the back. At this precise moment he felt something round about two to three millimetres across press hard and deep against the pained spot in his own back, crushing down on his skin into the flesh beneath, slipping between the nerves, paralyzing him with a fusion of life-altering pain and fear of torture as it slowly wiggled around in circular patterns.

"What... ?!" Jerry asked, his mind attempting to detach itself from the anchor of his body.
"Don't worry about it."
"What is it?!" the fear was worse than the pain at this point.
Naomi retorted in the driest tone possible "My heirloom chopsticks." through the

infliction of a greater pain, the smaller pain passed. Not the greatest design by Mother Nature.

Chapter 17

Basked in the soothing glow of oxycodone, Roger had the impression he could keep barrelling down the street all the way around the world. Not even his cosmic yoga classes gave him this sort of physical freedom. He had mostly forgotten about them by now, and the image of old ladies gathered around the closed doors of his studio gave him a pang of guilt, which then washed over into laughter. It was only a transitional period towards his true designation, he told himself, a machine of destiny which morphed him into the being of supreme importance he was today. He didn't think he was full of himself at all. Persuaded in the importance of his vaguely-defined mission, he fancied himself as a modern-day crusader, albeit with much more reasonable and people-friendly goals. In the midst of the nirvana his mind found itself in, he did, somehow, cultivate the presence of mind to wonder about the most important thing: what's the next move?

Thinking it a good idea to take some time to himself and collect his thoughts, he veered off into a shady alley almost completely covered in shadows, if not for the faint moonlight which found its way through the dark. He missed his car. A few meters in, he found an old milk crate, possibly from the times of the Great War. These things are sturdy bastards. Propping himself up against a wall while sitting on the crate, he entered what he taught in his class as being a complex meditative pose only meant for more advanced acolytes. It had him cross his legs, hold one arm up above his head, and the other one as if cradling an imaginary baby. It helped justify the price hike for his lessons, impractical as they may be. Nevertheless, he believed in it; someone had to.

After managing to move his thoughts away from the ecstasy which was still gripping him, Roger realized it would probably be best to make his way back to his friends, whose abandonment of him at the crime scene stung a little, even though it was exactly what he asked of them. He was truly a man of many layers and contradictions. He opened his eyes for a moment, and the world was so still it seemed to him like time had completely stopped. Of course, he knew it didn't, and was proud of it. He felt confident it was still flowing at a rate of one second per second, more or less.

A voice from the dark bellowed at Roger "Whatchu doin' there mister? This ere's my alley, ya gotta pay the toll."

Still too high and unable to muster his sense of fight-or-flight, Roger yelled back into the dark "I'm a friendly visitor, and come in peace. I'm an ambassador of... Earth." he generously considered his odds of having run into an alien at about fifty-fifty.

The voice was starting to approach him from the other side of the alley "Ya still gotta pay the toll, mister peace."

Roger looked in its direction and was starting to make out the vague shape of a seemingly small man with too many coats on for his frame. "What's the toll?" he didn't feel like moving, and decided to play the game.

"Ya gotta listen to my story." there was something insidious about the words, but Roger couldn't quite make out what. The figure was almost close enough to reveal its face, not that it would have been meaningful in this darkness.

"Well, let's hear it then. But I warn you, it better be good. I have high standards... you know?" he always did like a good story.

The man came forward just a little more to reveal his old and wrinkled mug, evidently formed by a lifetime of hardship and abuse. "Most excellent!" he tried to put a mock British accent on those words, to the chagrin of actual Brits around the world. "Ain't many who wanna listen to me nowadays, or even about me, but I'm here since they made me, and I worm my way in, through all tha little gaps and cracks they's left for me. Jus' can't help it, ya see?”

“Um, yes, I do see.” Roger was too far gone to see much, but he was fairly good at pretending.

“Anywhos, I been seein' things these last few days. Yes sir, I seen the things they keep hidden from all'o'you's. I seen the people, losing their minds, turning on each otha. Can't remember how long I been livin' like this, but I never seen nothin' like it! Not since the moment I been born! I'm between fifty and a hundred, I'm sure!” the man's eyes seemed to flash for a split second in the darkness, and Roger had the feeling there was someone else in there. He promptly reminded himself he was on drugs in a prideful moment of self-awareness. “Why, just hours ago, right across the road from here, I seen a man grab a brick and smash anotha one's head in! Boom!” the man made a loud clapping noise with his spindly arms. “The man gone down, dead when them doctors got here, probably. Cops came along and had the good instinct to *interrogate... me*!” the syllables of the last two words were carefully articulated. “Anywhos, I told em' they wasn't gonna believe me, believe what I seen, believe what I am.” he paused in his storytelling for a bit of dramatic suspense.

“Well? What did you see?” after a moment or two, it annoyed Roger a little bit.

“Ain't you in a hurry. What I seen was the man who did the attack, was the pastor of the church some blocks down! How about that for a doozey?! He just went an'gon' completely nuts. But that weren't the end of it, no sir. When the cops was taking down my statement, gunshots! Blam! Blam! Blam!” he clapped even louder than earlier for emphasis. “Building not even a block away, anotha one bites the dust! I could see him hangin' over the railing, and yes sir, I could see the blood.”

“Why here?” interrupted Roger with an out-loud question he had meant to keep for himself.

“Ah, mister peace, you's ahead of me! I had the same idea. So I started lookin', I walked up and down, left and right, back and forth, you name it. And sir, I seen him! God forgive me, I can't remember where, I think he's takin' my memory... but I seen him! There's a man somewhere in the city, but he's also under it...” he pointed to the floor. Roger involuntarily yawned. “He's dealin' out all the pain and the anger. He's makin' us all lose our minds, and I don't think he can stop, cause he says we made him. I fear I'mma lose my mind too. Ya gotta find him, mister peace, ain't nobody else I met care about this... but I know evil when I see it, and evil don't belong in this world.” on these words the figure started to retreat back into the shadows, with Roger never having seen its face.

“Wait! Who are you anyways?” the strangeness of the predicament was just starting to dawn on him. His fault, for being so accustomed to the unusual.

“It don't matter anymore, you paid the toll.” the voice sounded like it was already deep in the darkness of the alley, and would vanish completely at any moment now.

Roger was still sitting there in his sophisticated meditative pose, but his eyes were now wide open as the gears of his brain slowly ground all the information which had just come into his possession. He was convinced to have been the recipient of yet another cosmic vision. How fortunate. Why him, and why now? Could it simply be because it was just him here, and nobody else? Perhaps his meditations did have some tangible results after all? Maybe he was on the path because the path was solely his to walk. Roger really liked this idea, which was extremely compatible with his ever-inflating ego, at this point likely too large to be visualized by human imagination. However, he wasn't a complete and total dummy, no matter how counter-intuitive it might have sounded. He realized there was a certain chance he was being led into a trap. In an uncharted corner of the city something sinister was awaiting him, of this he was certain. What would he even do if he found this dealer of pain, this man who was making everyone else lose their minds, and could allegedly take the memories of those who see him now? The one who worms his way into every crack and fills the air with madness? No, he couldn't simply rush into the lethal supernatural entity's den without a bit of forethought and preparation... not this time, anyways. For this, he admitted, he would probably need the help of his good friends, who hopefully were still alive, doing well, and likely working a plan to rescue him, he mused.

His mind also wandered in the direction of the woman who made his escape possible and enabled... no, facilitated, his journey upon his all-important predestined path. She might also end up being a player of importance in this whole thing, though at this point he couldn't fathom how exactly. He couldn't fathom many things, and was quite used to working with hunches and instincts. Though they often led him astray, he much preferred to forget those times and remember the ones when they didn't. Memory can be calibrated to suit our preferred worldviews; it's extremely unreliable half the time it even works.

Right at this moment, his instinct brought him back to the ever-important question: what's the next step? He would have called Jerry or Naomi on their phones, if he could actually remember their numbers, or if he had the change necessary to use one of the few remaining pay phones in town, relics awaiting to being swept by the tides of time. He could also walk to either one of their places and hope to meet them there, if they were indeed home. However, the effects of his medication could run out by then, a prospect which frightened him considerably. In addition, the cops might be there waiting for him, and he thought of himself as far too noble a thinker to be caught in such a simple net. Besides, both of them were quite far away, and Roger didn't feel like walking much.

The idea his medication might lose effectiveness soon was starting to grow in his mind like a point of singularity, eventually swallowing all the other thoughts and concerns he might have had. Of course! Kathleen! She helped him escape, and she could likely help him find refuge. Besides which, she might also help him with the medication problem, as she already once did. Two birds with one stone. He didn't exactly know why, but for some reason he trusted the cold and sarcastic woman who broke her code of ethics to feed him drugs and enable his flight. Anyone corrupt to this extent, he thought, seeks to avoid the cruel hand of The Law as much as he does.

Slowly and methodically, he exited his meditative position, and upon realizing how much shoulder pain it caused him after holding it for so long, made a mental note to evolve it into something less physically strenuous. Maybe he could market the improvement as yet another reason to hike the prices on his advanced classes. The possibilities were endless, generally-speaking. For now, however, he had to settle on solely fulfilling the possibility of finding safe refuge without getting caught by the cops one more time. The life of a fugitive was much more difficult and complicated than he anticipated, forcing him to have some newly-acquired respect for Harrison Ford in *The Fugitive*. Now there was a real man, he thought, the kind who knew the meaning of life. Motivated by thoughts of his newfound hero figure, Roger plowed on into the night, in the general direction of the morgue, where he hoped Kathleen basically spent the entirety of both her nights and days.

The streets were still as empty as they were during the beginning of time, and Roger was free to wander in complete safety. One of the only on-duty policemen, Officer Tim, was still very likely chasing after old man Vinter, or at least Roger hoped so. The old man seemed so virile and irradiated with the energy of life, it was hard to imagine fate itself catching up to him, let alone a mere mortal. He closed his eyes and had a mental image of Tim chasing the old man around a public fountain. Assuming it was truth rather than his own imagination, he opened his eyes just in time to avoid running into a street lamp. He probably wouldn't have felt it anyways.

An hour or so later, he finally arrived at the morgue, and found the doors to be barred. He thought about how strange it was for the dead to require safekeeping. If anything, we ought to keep the doors open should they deem necessary to rise up again. He did a little lap around the building, and noticed through his drug-induced haze one of the lights was still on. He tried approaching the window silently and quietly as he erroneously imagined he could, and stuck his round face at a lower corner, more or less unconcerned with the idea of being noticed.

Through the window Roger observed the coroner's office, and his heroine, Kathleen, standing over the one dead body worthy of study in Hollow Crest, carefully doing something meticulous he couldn't quite identify. Probably in the name of science. Did this woman ever sleep? Her dedication to her craft was bordering on the supernatural, and Roger admired her for being nearly as devoted to something useful as he was. Lost in narcotic-induced reverie, he knocked at the window. She was a little too entranced in her own world to hear him. He knocked again, this time hard enough to shake the frame. Kathleen jumped a foot in the air, looked at the window, and unleashed a short but high-pitched scream at the sight of Roger's now-red face pressed up against the glass. A sight to rival any eldritch horror. He knocked again.

Kathleen indignantly paced to the window and slid it open with an angry slam. "Out of all the places on Earth, you had to come here?" steam was practically coming out of her ears.

Roger took a cautious waddle back. "It was the only safe place I could think of. Besides, I think I need more... medicine." the last word came out in an inappropriately suggestive manner.

"For God's sake..." she held her face in both her palms. "I should have known you'd be a world of trouble the moment I saw you." her words were filled with the truest kind of regret.

"Say, what are you even still doing here at this hour anyways?" he took half a step forward, seeing her anger turn into annoyance and disappointment, which he had grown rather familiar with over the years.

"I'm gunning for the Nobel prize in medicine. If I can solve this here mystery," she pointed to the body on the table behind her, still the same as when Roger had seen it, preserved in time like a fly in amber, "I'll definitely be a good candidate for that million bucks. And I *could* use a million bucks." her mind was slowly turning back to other the mystery before her.

"Well, maybe *I could* help you with that one." he gave her a wink, and she shuddered in response.

"How on Earth do you intend to do anything remotely resembling that?" she was getting close to shutting the window down on him.

"I've had a, uh, chance alley meeting with someone, just now. He told me some things, and I think I can connect them to what you have here." he paused to gauge her reaction. The window was still open. "I'll tell you everything, but you have to let me in. I just need a place to stay for the night." he thought for a moment. "And more medicine." he had to give it every shot he could.

Kathleen dropped a sigh heavy as a hammer. "You're not going away, are you?"

"Nope. And I don't think we even have any police left to call until morning, if Officer Tim is still on the chase." Roger making a good point for once caught her off-guard.

"Fine. Climb in here, but you're gone by morning. Also, no medicine, no way. You're a big boy and you can tough it out." She stood back from the window and allowed her nightly visitor to climb in and spill himself over inside. And they say romance is dead.

"Thanks doc, I owe you one." he picked himself up and moved over to sit on a stool a few feet away.

She moved in to close the window and curtains behind him. One peeper was enough for tonight. "Well? Start talking before I really start regretting." somehow, Roger believed in the triumphant power of her anger.

"Well, I met this man in an alley..." Roger relayed to her in great detail as much as he could remember of the man's monologue, without failing to mention his newfound adjustment to his special meditative pose. It took Kathleen all of her willpower to restrain herself from slapping the pretentiousness out of him.

"That's all *very* interesting, but I don't see what it has to do with anything, and I'm starting to regret it." she never did have much of a tolerance for human stupidity, having had to contend with it for most of her life, like so many others before her.

"It's all right, I don't expect you to be as... proficient as I am in the art of deduction." the sting of these words made Kathleen roll her eyes, a reaction burned into her on an instinctive level. He continued. "Let's assume for a moment, what my alley visitor told me is true. In that case, there's a man, or something like one, exerting some kind of *influence* on parts of the town. What if he exerts it in the form of some waves he can somehow control? These imprints on the body that look like misshapen spirals? I say they look more like waves, being all wavy, and such." he briefly paused to give his unusually-attentive listener some time to absorb it all. "I think our man here, somewhere, somehow, ran into the very source of these waves, and that's what burned him up like that. Maybe these are some kinds of waves we've never seen, or some property of them we've never observed. Maybe they're emitted by a radioactive nucleus-type…thing. That could explain the whole... weirdness of the body's state." Roger's mind was burning fuel at one hundred and ten percent capacity, and he didn't even notice his medication had begun to fade away.

After a long moment of introspective silence, Kathleen finally gave her appraisal. "You know, I expected something exactly this dumb out of you. It's all shoddy, and hinges on some mysterious drugged up alleyway encounter. It's not really in line with the scientific method." she had, however, gained a tiny bit of respect for Roger's enthusiasm in this matter, and her voice softened a bit.

"Actually," Roger held his index finger in the air, "I think it also explains why my visitor was all covered up, didn't want to show his face, and was losing his memory. He ran into the source as well, but not close or long enough to be dead like, well, our pioneer here." he dramatically pointed in the cadaver's general direction. "Not yet, anyways. He might be by now." a cloud of sadness swooped over him for a man he barely ever knew.

"Not gonna lie, it's not the furthest thing from the explanation I was looking into. Minus the paranormal rage-dealing alleyway-dwelling ghosts. My best guess is a concentrated spontaneous highly-radioactive event. Something like a radiation or microwave gun. Maybe directed-energy weapons, but nobody has those yet... in theory, anyways." more and more, she was starting to treat him like a normal human being, rather than the bane of her entire existence.

"Okay, maybe your explanation is a little more logical than mine, but I think we can agree on one thing, and it's that we're both on the right track, and should join forces." he gave her a nervous glance. "For the moment, at least. About the future, ahh, we'll see." he tried to diminish his excitement for the situation, not to seem overeager.

"If by join forces you mean you'll report to me any more findings and I keep the Nobel prize money for myself, then yeah, sure thing, we'll join forces." he hadn't won Kathleen over as much as he imagined.

"I was thinking more in terms of combining the power of our collective reasoning to reach new heights of knowledge and understanding. Also, it would only be fair if you informed me of your findings as well. The hypothetical money is hypothetically unimportant to me. You can hypothetically keep it. But for the record, it would be nice if you shared it. I wouldn't say no." with his mind recovered and warmed up, Roger was perfectly prepared to fire on all cylinders with the big words again.

"Fine, have it your way." she was too tired to argue further. "There was one lead I was going to follow. A man came into this place not long ago to see this body. He had a made-up name, so I had his ID copied by my assistant." she couldn't hide the little bit of pride at having accomplished something even remotely and vaguely espionage-like.

"Very clever!" interjected Roger, with a smile and yet another misplaced wink. It made her neck tense up.

"Yes, well, I think you should pay this man a visit. His name is Jeremiah Baxter, and he lives-" she was abruptly cut off.

"Jerry?" Roger broke out into a hearty laughter which lasted a few seconds. "Yea, we definitely should talk to him alright. Him and Naomi."

"You... know him?" she was half-surprised, half-ashamed at not having expected this.

"He's my best friend. Naomi too. We've been metaphorically inseparable since childhood." memories from a bygone life flooded his mind for a brief moment; how quickly it all washes away.

"Never imagined you could have friends." the blow was sharp and would have cut deep had Roger not been hardening against it for decades.

"I'm glad you want to visit him, and I think you should help me get in touch with him. Eventually, when the police wake up in the morning, they'll start looking for me, and probably bring in some reinforcements from the big city. It also likely means my friends will be under surveillance, if it hasn't happened already. I'm going to need a proxy. It's of vital importance, for the survival of Hollow Crest, and the... progress of science." he wasn't sure how to end his plea for help. He tried his best.

"I'll give him one call and ask him to come over, nothing more. How you want to keep in touch after this is up to you." she was helpful to Roger to a degree he really wasn't accustomed to anymore, and it stirred something in him.

"Thank you. I love you."

Chapter 18

The morgue was a little special in the sense it had a disproportionately-large waiting room for people who would, theoretically, line up for one last chance at a conversation or an insult with the recently-departed. In the olden days it served as a waiting mortuary, and one of the fanciest of its kind. The ceiling was far taller than it needed to be and bore the weight of an old cupola in dire need of maintenance. It threatened to collapse in a display of divine wrath. The walls were installed in segments between large columns and were adorned with silver and gold motifs depicting nothing in particular. The white marble floor had fused with a thick layer of dust over the years. Without a doubt, it was the most expensive installation in the morgue, and without a doubt, it was the least useful one. In its heyday it saved exactly zero people from a premature burial, and was actually the cause of a death when a piece of the ceiling broke loose and claimed the life of a nameless worker. He wasn't nameless because he had no name, but there was no one left alive to remember it, which is essentially the same thing. Once techniques had been developed to confirm the deceased were indeed deceased, the useless hall was converted to an even more useless waiting room. The only traffic it saw was the janitor, until the day he refused to enter it anymore on the grounds of having witnessed the ghost of the nameless deceased worker. In reality, he wanted to lighten his workload. Nobody cared either way, his wish was granted, and ultimately the place was closed down and forgotten. Until Kathleen and Roger needed to catch a bit of sleep before the morning.

Using the chain cutters she found in the janitor's closet, which had far too many tools with no janitorial application, Kathleen opened the ancient doors and a gust of musty air shot out from total darkness to greet them. She sent Roger back on a walk to fetch a flashlight, and together they beheld the wonders of the forgotten room. The dust and grime had stripped a good deal of wonder away from it, but it was nevertheless a sight magnitudes more marvellous than the rest of the establishment.

“Wow.” Roger whispered.

“Yeah, not bad for a waste of budget.” Kathleen ejected with a snort.

“So, why are we sleeping here again? There are plenty of beds in the morgue.” he shot a quick raised eyebrow at her, which she thankfully didn't see.

“No, we're not sleeping here, you are. You want to hide from the cops? This is the best place. It's almost got some magic power over people, like they don't even realize it's there until they think about.” she believed none of it. She just wanted Roger locked away a good and safe distance from herself.

“Wait, so how can you think about it if you can't know about it without thinking about it?” Roger was exceptionally talented at deciphering nonsense.

“You... can be told about it. Or read about it. I don't know how this works. Bottom line is, you'll be safe here. See? You can even lock it from the inside” she shone the light on the old rusted lock and prayed to whatever powers were watching over her for this to be enough.

“All right, I suppose this will be good enough. Can I have a snack before bed?” his stomach was starting to rumble.

“I have crackers and baby carrots. It's all you're getting until tomorrow.” Kathleen was already on her way out the doors.

“Oh, well, I think you'll do better next time.” the prospect of such a sad meal sucked a good deal of life out of him. He really needed the rest now.

Kathleen gave her fugitive a small paper plate with the promised carrots and crackers on it, and without even a half-hearted wish for a good night left and slammed the door shut before Roger had any time to speak. He waved his flashlight around, saw a comfortable-looking leather sofa, and laid down on it with his prison meal. How could he be certain Kathleen wouldn't take this chance to call the cops on him? She has him perfectly trapped for them to sweep in and scoop him up. Officer Tim will even likely give her a reward, the bastard, and the government a promotion. She had everything to gain on one hand, as well as everything to lose on the other by not reporting him.

Roger felt a spasm of nervous fear crawl over from the base of his skull to his lower back. On the third hand, what choice did he really have? He couldn't run very far nor very fast, and had an easily recognizable figure. Staying outside was out of the question. He couldn't go back to his own place, nor Jerry's or Naomi's. If Officer Tim hadn't mobilized the rest of the force from their sleep by now, he'd certainly do it in a few hours. The move would be too risky. He thought of checking in to the hotel, but abandoned this idea after he realized there was only one hotel in town, and its only guests at this time of year were a few lost tourists who took a wrong turn. Besides, it would have left a paper trail. He would have been too easy to find. Also, his leg was still hurting. He hated to admit it, but being trapped in the dark forgotten room of the morgue, while being at the mercy of someone who stood to gain the world from betraying him, was probably the best-case scenario for him.

With his flashlight positioned on the sofa so as to illuminate the little plate he put on his massive thighs, he began eating with the melancholy of an oppressed gourmand. All the while, his senses were at their highest points of tension, trying to listen for sirens, footsteps, the SWAT team, or Officer Tim's annoying voice. After having finished the meal which seemed to have only succeeded in opening his appetite and making him hungrier, he stood up and decided to take a short walk around the room to see if there were any hidden passages or such. To the best of his knowledge, old and forgotten rooms always had those to facilitate adulterous activity between neighbouring husbands and wives. The best of Roger's knowledge was sometimes the worst of everyone else's. Slowly and methodically, with the air of a critic walking around a modern art exhibit, he examined every inch of wall he could lay his eyes on, and to his great astonishment, the absurdly large number of leather sofas like the one he had chosen for himself. There were six of them in total, all facing a podium. Like many of their time, the designers of this place expected an impending rise in mystical seances. This may yet come to pass one day; there will never be a moratorium on intellectual regression. The designers will never see it, now united in total decomposition.

To his overbearing disappointment, Roger did not find a single secret passage, nor even a trace of there ever having been one. This was severely at odds with his theory about old rooms and hidden adulterous doorways. He reconciled this dissonance by concluding he was too tired for a comprehensive search, and would have better luck in the morning, if he could remember. With his little tour of the room complete, he sat back down on his personal leather couch, and tensed up once again, scanning for the sights and sounds of those monsters who would take him away for the crime he was indeed guilty of. How unjust the world can be. His body was becoming increasingly alarmed, and he began to doubt whether he would get any sleep on this night. Five minutes later he was sound asleep, but in his dream, he was sleep-deprived and had no choice but to stay awake.

On her end, Kathleen had no intention of calling the cops, or anyone else on Roger. There were many things she wouldn't be willing to admit to the world, and two of them were a complete disdain for authority figures and the longing for an exciting adventure, something she hadn't experienced since the age of six when she got lost in a shopping mall and her parents went on home without her, thinking the experience would help build character. It took her fifteen years to set foot in a shopping mall again. Though anyone looking at her would be completely unable to detect it, she was having a good deal of fun with everything happening around her. For once, she actually felt herself becoming an important figure in her profession, rather than being the attendant for the dozen people who pass away of old age in Hollow Crest every year. She liked feeling important, like just about everyone else. As much as she tended to hate the people around her, she couldn't deny being victim to the same wants, needs and impulses as them. This made her sick and in need of a drink. She sat down in her office chair, opened the bottom drawer kept under lock and key, and pulled out her perfectly average bottle of whiskey along with the accompanying glass. She poured herself two fingers, took a sip, and decided to relive the vigorous days of her youth by drinking it all in a gulp. She forgot how disgusting it was. Then, a miracle occurred: a thought of pure empathy crossed her mind, one she was about to carry through with.

Roger heard a loud knock on the locked door to his private sanctuary, and rose from his sleep-deprived slumber, unaware he had slept at all. He opened the door, and Kathleen thrust into his hands a tall glass of whiskey and a pack of roasted peanuts.

"From my other private stash. Don't say I never did anything for you." the drink had improved her mood rather noticeably, even if only artificially.

"I knew you would do better! Does this mean..." Roger didn't know what he meant by that.

"Good night, you moron." she slammed the door shut on her way out.

Roger sat back down, felt the weight of the offerings in his hands, tried to look at them through the darkness to no avail, and thought to himself in total seriousness, "What a saint, this woman!", without the least bit of sarcasm. With a newfound glee and enthusiasm, he started working on the drink while taking some well-advised peanut breaks in-between. He thought the whiskey tasted great and was likely an expensive vintage imported from Europe, something he made a note to remark upon to Kathleen in the morning, well on its way to end their short night of respite. It was time to lay down again, and fuelled by the power of whiskey coursing through his veins, he managed to fall into the realm of dreamless sleep. Much better than what he had to contend with before.

Maybe things were going to work out after all. Or maybe not. He didn't really know, which remains a capital sin in a world where everyone can become an expert in everything through five-minute videos.

Chapter 19

The morning came rather abruptly for the town of Hollow Crest, as it always does, even though they should have expected as much. The most turbulent night the town had seen in a very long while had finally come to an end, and it was time to tally the damage. One burnt-down gallery, a stolen painting, a jailbreak, two fugitives (if not more, counting potential accomplices), and a police force far too small and inexperienced to deal with it all. Without mentioning the rest of the chaos. Officer Tim spent the night running after old man Vinter until he lost him in the dark winding alleyways and decided to give up instead and catch some sleep. After all, he reasoned, it's not like the suspect would leave town, and if he did, it would make for one less thing to worry about. Roger had severely overestimated the power of The Law in this little corner of the universe.

The morning briefing at the police station was given, as usual, by Officer Tim, who unbeknownst to pretty much everyone outside the police force, held the rank of Lieutenant. This gave time for the Chief Inspector to take his customary morning nap, before inevitably working half a day and leaving for his home outside of town while complaining about heartburn and prophesying how they would all suffer like him when they would reach his old age of fifty-six. For all intents and purposes, Officer Tim was the leading figure in the station, which earned him a modicum of respect in exchange for the burden of all responsibility.

After catching up his thirty-seven colleagues on the changes to the town during their peaceful slumber, he concluded by saying he put in a request to have an Inspector come down and take over, since their own had retired months prior and no one had bothered to replace him. In reply, he was informed of his promotion to Inspector, and was wished the best of luck. The whole room filled with incredulous and doubting eyes, but soon the atmosphere settled into one of complete acceptance. What else could they do? These things happen.

He first proceeded by separating his colleagues into eighteen pairs, assigning the last officer to phone duty. Not a moment later, he laid down a list of priorities for them to work on:

1. Find Roger Silver, look into friends and relatives if he wasn't dumb enough to head home.
2. Find Vinter, likely in some random alleyway.
3. Take statements from the gallery owners and surrounding neighbourhood.
4. Find the stolen painting.
5. Generally tighten up the rule of The Law.

After having carefully studied the list for no more than ten seconds, the eighteen pairs of blue suits split the tasks among each other with Officer Tim's counsel and went on ahead to work. While it certainly wasn't ideal to have subordinates who preferred not to follow his orders and figure things out themselves, it was a natural extension of the leadership they were under. Besides, it lightened the load on Tim's shoulders. In an ideal world, he mused, he could just sit back and watch the station run itself. He then realized they weren't far from this ideal world before the dead body turned up and Roger took a massively irritating interest in it. He almost shed a tear for what could have been, but was enough of a man to hold it back. He took pride in his stoicism, and got to work on doing his part to fulfill the list of tasks written in capital letters on the board behind him.

His first course of action was to place a call to Roger's house, which naturally resulted in no answer nor signs of life. He thought for a moment about the only people he had seen capable of withstanding the presence of Roger in their lives, as a friend no less. He put his hands to his temples and began to rub them as if harnessing a psychic power he didn't have. After straining himself for fifteen minutes, he remembered about this newfangled thing called "social networks" on the internet, and quickly found Roger whose online imprint was exponentially larger than his real-life one. After getting distracted by the unnatural amounts of nonsense he saw on the man's numerous profiles, he looked at his list of friends, comprised largely of distant family members who likely wished to remain as such, a few fake celebrity profiles, and only two who fit in neither group. Jeremiah Baxter and Naomi Wolfe. Assuming Roger would act like he himself and turn to the power of male solidarity in his moment of need, the newly-appointed Inspector placed his first phone call of the day.

The phone rang once. Twice. "Hello?" a surprised voice on the other end.
"Uhm, hello!" Officer Tim allowed the confusing pause to extend for a little bit.
"Yes? Who is this?" the voice wavered with indecision.
"Jeremiah? This is Inspector Tim-" he was rudely cut off mid-sentence.
"Tim? That you? This is Cleary, we just got here, but nobody's home." there was an inexplicable hint of relief at the idea of no one else being here.
"Wait, Cleary? How did you get there already?" Officer Tim was having trouble processing the passage of time.
"We looked up Roger online before going to the car, found this Jeremiah guy. He doesn't live far, we decided to pay him a visit." Cleary was starting to sound a cocky and proud of the good work he supposedly managed to accomplish before his superior.
"And you've entered his apartment without a warrant?" when he wanted to, Tim could be stern as a prison warden.
"..." the question froze Cleary, but Tim wasn't about to answer on his behalf. He let the silence extend for some moments. After mulling it over, Cleary said the brightest thing he could possibly think of: "We heard the phone ring, and it… *warranted* our entry. Buh-bye now!" he quickly hung up, and considering the mess undone, he and his partner left the apartment, without even the courtesy of locking the door.

Officer Tim could hardly believe it, and held his face in his palms for a couple of minutes, trying to shield himself from the radiation of toxic stupidity he had just been exposed to. He firmly believed it was a legitimate way of decreasing one's intelligence, which is why he took pride in never watching comedy shows. He took pride in a lot of things about himself, as well as the idea he was the most prideful person in town. He didn't think of it as a sin or a character deficiency in any way; "One can only take pride in themselves if they have things to be proud of, and there is no shame in that." such was his reasoning. He found his way out of his complex thoughts and back into the real world thanks to a text message which informed him Roger's place was empty and they were waiting for a search warrant to proceed further. After taking care of the request, he decided to give Naomi a call, and hopefully warn her of Cleary's impending charge through her front door. The phone rang once. Twice. Thrice.

* * *

Naomi had just woken up from her sleep to find Jerry still snoring on the couch. She had just taken a shower in her cramped but neat and well-organized bathroom, and almost missed a spot of black mould growing on the ceiling. This was new. She stepped into the kitchen and turned on the coffee-maker, causing it to whine in a distinctly metallic fashion, as if complaining about the pain of heat and electricity. This too, was new. She was pouring herself a cup when the phone next to her rang, startling her and causing a spill. After taking a second to compose herself in the face of the most annoying morning she had in a while, she answered the phone with a tone bordering on the fence between the uncharted lands of grace and animosity.

"Hello." despite her efforts, her manners ended up quite curt.

"Good day, am I speaking with Naomi Wolfe?" Officer Tim sounded very official and authoritative, as if preparing to deliver her news about her son being drafted in the army.

"It's your lucky day." she gave up on trying to sound graceful.

"It really is." Tim smiled at her, then realized he was having a phone conversation, and proceeded. "I am calling you to inquire about the whereabouts of your friend Roger Silver. He's a suspect in an ongoing investigation, so if you've had any contact with him, you're obligated by *The Law* to inform me." he was convinced none could withstand such an organized psychological assault.

"Haven't seen him in a while. What's he done now?" she tried to sound as casual and nonchalant as possible, something she had a good deal of practice in over the years.

"Well, ma'am, I'm not at liberty to say. Do you perhaps know where he might be? Additionally, do you know where we might find Jeremiah Baxter? We have reason to believe the two might be together." it was taking Tim one hundred percent of his brainpower to speak in a manner he judged as the absolute peak of eloquence.

"Did you just call me ma'am? Do I sound sixty years old to you?" she didn't really take offence to it, but understood the need to push back just a little against the authoritarian deity she assumed he imagined himself as. As it turned out, she wasn't too far off the mark.

"Apologies, ma-... uhm, my lady." he didn't want to admit it to himself, but he was caught off-guard by his long-dormant sense of modern chivalry.

"Don't... call me that either. As for Jerry, he's here on the couch. And no, he hasn't seen Roger for a while either, neither of us has. Will that be all?" she was purposefully trying to sound increasingly annoyed.

"If you'll allow me to speak with Jeremiah, then yes, it will be all. Oh, one more thing, two officers of mine are headed for your place as we speak. You'll probably need to have this conversation with them all over again. Also, if you could allow them to look around your place, we'd appreciate it. We don't have any warrants, you see." Officer Tim often fancied himself a grand strategist when it came to manipulating people. Officer Tim thought many things.

"No. Jerry will talk with your officers when they get here. I don't have time for this right now and I'm hanging up. And you, learn how to talk with women before making any more phone calls." on this devastating blow to Officer Tim's masculinity she smashed her outdated phone down loud enough to wake Jerry up. She specifically kept the old model for the catharsis it offered; modern phones are inherently inferior for the inability to slam them down to end conversations.

Jerry rose from his profound slumber with a look of shocked surprise on his face, being unexpectedly torn out of a dream where he was actually a successful person in life. The return to reality is always painful for the dreamer type. He wanted to ask Naomi what happened and whether she heard a gunshot, but before he could open his mouth, she explained the situation to him. Thankfully, the cops didn't know about their involvement in the case, but some uniforms were on the way to ascertain Roger's lack of presence here. Jerry counted his lucky stars, and took his turn in the shower. He too paid attention to the brand-new black mould growing on the ceiling. It's funny, how much can pop into existence with no one noticing a thing.

Already a few moments later, a domineering knock was heard at the door, with Cleary yelling something not quite audible from the other end. Naomi opened it and stood face-to-face with someone a little too eager to finally have a chance to demonstrate how good they were at their job. Without missing a beat, Naomi opened her mouth before her unwanted guest even had a chance to formulate a thought.

"We just spoke with your boss, no we don't know where Roger is, and yes Jerry is here, you can talk to him. And no, you may not enter, the place is cramped enough as it is." she was trying to appear as blunt and annoyed as possible, at least to make Cleary uncomfortable, if nothing else. She closed the door, and after a moment Jerry was the one to open it.

"What can I do for you fellas?" his level of enthusiasm for the whole thing was about as high as Naomi's.

"Jeremiah Baxter?" the officer wasn't impressed with the stature of the man before him.

"The one and only. What do you need?" his voice would remain monotone for the rest of the conversation.

"We're searching for a suspect, a certain Roger Silver, and it's come to our attention he's a, uh, an acquaintance of yours." Cleary paused, trying to put his lack of interrogation training to use and suck out any bit of information he could, which naturally wasn't much. At least he tried, bless his heart.

"Yeah." Jerry was doing his best not to shoot out any unnecessary words. The less they knew, the better.

"Do you have any idea as to his whereabouts? Where we might find him? He's definitely not in here?" the officer was trying to take a peek over Jerry's shoulder. There really wasn't much to see.

"No idea, and no, officer, he's not here." Jerry paused for a moment to stare into Cleary's eyes, then added, "Come to think of it though, he did mention something about heading to Nunavut. The cosmic channels are stronger there. Think he might have set out to fulfill his destiny, or some such nonsense." Jerry's ability to maintain a single voice tone for entire conversations was proving to be a gigantic boon here. Cleary couldn't make out truth from lies to any degree.

"...Nunavut?" the officer repeated, incredulous.

"Ice, seals, Eskimos, the whole package." this was just about the extent of Jerry's knowledge on Nunavut.

"I know what it is... got any idea what he was doing last night? Matter of fact, where were you last night?" Cleary did not, in fact, know what it was.

"If I know Roger he was probably busy coming up with a plan to contact fifth-dimensional beings, or working on an experiment to ascertain the existence of the Almighty once and for all. Maybe both." it took Jerry a bit of effort not to laugh at Cleary, who was writing everything with the dedicated air of a court stenographer. His partner was standing a few feet back, dreaming of the day they'd partner him up with someone else.

"As for me," Jerry continued, "Was here the whole evening and night. That's about as much as I know about the world today.”

“And what were you doing here all night long?” Cleary was gone too deep into his investigative mindset not to ask useless questions.

“We were playing basketball.” Jerry answered through his judgmental half-shut eyes.

“What?” the ambitious officer didn't enjoy being made into a fool. Nobody does, but he hated it more than most. “Sir, I have to remind you this is an official investigation, and everything-” thankfully, his partner cut him off and saved him from further embarrassment.

“Christ Cleary...” the partner gave Jerry an apologetic look, which was returned his way. Officer Cleary was a handful for everyone.

“Right...” the would-be investigator was red in the face. “And I assume the lady living here can confirm that?”

“Yes!” a shout came from somewhere inside the apartment.

“Well, I guess that will be all... for now. If you have any news of Roger, contact us immediately. He is a wanted fugitive, possibly armed and dangerous.” Cleary truly did believe this.

Jerry erupted into a fit of laughter. “Roger? Give me a break, what's he actually done?” he was much better at subtly extracting information than Cleary.

“This isn't a joke, sir. We believe he not only orchestrated the arson of the O'Harris Gallery, but also stole a painting we are told is beyond all known value. Somehow, he has managed to escape police custody, revealing himself in the process as a criminal mastermind.” such was the only type of individual capable of outsmarting the Hollow Crest police force, at least according to Cleary. “We believe he's much more dangerous than we anticipated, and as his acquaintances you must be warned of this.”

“Thank you for performing your duty to the letter, mister policeman.” the ever-so-slight hint of sarcasm in Jerry's voice went unnoticed by the leading officer. His partner caught it though, and cracked a faint grin.

“It's only our job. Contact us if you hear anything from him, alright? Don't be afraid.” On these words, the two officers went down the stairs and left the building, almost knowing less than they did when they had arrived.

After shutting the door, Jerry quickly ran over the events he's been informed of in his head. The big takeaway was the fact Roger somehow managed to escape from the pit Jerry and Naomi had left him in. What's more, he probably found himself a place to lay low, and had the wherewithal not to seek shelter with his friends. How kind and considerate of him. In itself, this was good news. On the other hand, he was now probably the most wanted man in town, which in itself didn't mean much, but the police likely weren't going to stop searching for the sole criminal who escaped them. In the long-term, things weren't exactly looking all too great.

How did they all even get to this point? The question suddenly popped into Jerry's head, as if he hadn't had the time to even think about it before. The supposed danger they were fighting against felt so abstract and vaguely-defined, he started to doubt whether any of it was real. What were the odds they were being dragged into Roger's insane delusions via outlandish ideas and old friendship? Was it just a coincidence violence was starting to rise in Hollow Crest? After all, few things, if any, can ever sit completely still until the end of time; change occurs one way or the other, and perhaps they were simply in the midst of a negative one. Yet, it felt too real and defined to be a coincidence. It felt to Jerry like a collective retribution for a transgression; the cost of crossing a forbidden barrier. The doubts were swirling and settling in his head, beckoning him to leave and drop everything behind. He didn't have to stay here, neither did Naomi, for that matter. They could leave everything behind and move somewhere else away from the madness, and hope Roger wouldn't drag them into the affair whenever he inevitably got caught. On the other hand, is any place on Earth with people on it not only deprived of madness, but also willing to accept them? Jerry wasn't ready to live life of a wood runner, not yet anyways.

Chapter 20

Five years ago was the last time Roger felt the oppressive bellowing of a true hangover, and he had to drink twice as much back then to bring it on. A sign of the times changing, and a sign of his body starting to get fed up with him and his antics, he correctly assumed. He looked around the room, disoriented as can be and seeing triple, until he finally remembered where he was, what he was doing, and just how deep of a pit he had fallen into. It was nice of Kathleen to have sheltered him for the night, but alas, he couldn't sleep in here forever, and would one day be forced to make his glorious return to society. What a shame; he was already getting used to it.

A few minutes of eye-rubbing later, Roger finally managed to stand on his two feet without feeling like he might fall over at any second. He slowly stumbled to the door, and put his ear to it. For a moment, all he heard was silence, and a feeling of great relief had washed over him... which sadly, wasn't meant to last for long. Some minutes later he heard loud and quick steps coming from somewhere down the hall, and Kathleen burst through the door with an unmistakable air of urgency, specifically pertinent to those in the process of regretting their mistakes. She locked the door behind her, and with quick, aggressive motions tried to usher Roger through the window.

"What are you still doing here? Hurry! Get the hell out!" she really didn't want to take the time to explain anything to him.

"What the hell's going on?!" naturally, this wasn't going to fly with Roger.

"Other people work here besides me, you know that, right? Well, they're just about here. Shit, I thought you'd be long gone." the disappointment in her voice, like everyone else's, was Roger's familiar companion.

"That is entirely your fault, for giving me that whiskey." it was sometimes hard to determine exactly how much of his own discourse he truly believed in.

"My fault?! You're the fugitive here. Thought you'd be a little smarter and not sleep for almost ten hours in a government building!" even an iron-willed woman like Kathleen could hardly resist being drawn into an argument with the almighty heir to the Silver legacy. He looked like an easy target sometimes.

"Wait, what time is it?" Roger seemed perplexed at the idea time could advance without his consent.

"It's almost noon. Now hurry up and get out of here! If they find you here, I know nothing about it. Your word against mine." Kathleen stormed out of the room without adding anything. Roger was almost heartbroken.

After taking thirty seconds to try and make himself as presentable as he possibly could given the circumstances, he quietly slid the window open and felt the pain in his ankle return. It wasn't as intense as before, but somehow it felt like it had burrowed its way in deeper beneath the surface. With time being on any side but his, as always, Roger made the brave decision of simply dealing with it and enduring the pain, something he immediately congratulated himself for. With imprecise and unbalanced movements, he slid out through the window and found himself in a small courtyard at the back of the building, facing a small metal gate in a metal fence which seemingly no one ever bothered to lock. The path beyond offered two options: a turn towards the road and back to civilization, or the forest. The latter option seemed the only logical one to Roger, especially considering he didn't even really have a plan to work with yet.

A few minutes of walking later he decided to take a rest on a tree stump in a small quiet clearing, and examine his own failures face-to-face. For the most part, all he managed to do was get someone else to burn down a gallery and take the painting out of the public eye. Even this, might have been done too late, he estimated. He began to shake with rage, one he wasn't used to feeling. Sure, the morally-questionable and intellectually-inferior people surrounding him in his daily life did get his blood boiling from time to time. However, he never felt it towards the most sacred subject of all: himself. Up until now he had been a specialist of the highest order in mental gymnastics, the undisputed champion of shifting the blame, a paragon of self-justification. Up until now, he had always managed to avoid facing the idea of being less-than-ideal.

After about an hour or so of wallowing in the miserable depths of his own mind, Roger was finally ripped away from his self-deprecating fantasy by a powerful sting of hunger. Nuts and whiskey, nutritious as they might be, can only keep a man going for a night... and a man the size of Roger needed a little extra sustenance. He didn't know nearly enough about survival in the forest to last here for any meaningful amount of time, nor was he keen on ever making the physical effort required to do so. But where to go? He had a feeling Kathleen, no matter how much of a saint she might be, wasn't going to shelter him incognito until the end of time. As a matter of fact, she might never shelter him again. Jerry and Naomi were still likely out of the question, and Roger figured he had to assume their phones were under surveillance; no expense was too great to catch a fugitive, at least in his mind.

His hopes were only deflated by the hazy sight which came at him from further down the road into the wild. Squinting his eyes in an attempt to block out any unnecessary light, he could make out a number of trucks driving into town, some of them veering off the road, and the others positioned perpendicular to the flow of potential traffic so as to form a blockade. Most of all, he was dreading the terrifying possibility of having walked all the way here for nothing.

In this state of utter loss and desperation, Roger decided to return to his roots, what he knew best above anything else: cosmic yoga. Assuming a position so experimental it was to remain classified until the end of time, he channelled the bulk of his energy into asking the universe, only slightly wiser than him, on what the next step ought to be. For a while, it felt like the universe was completely silent in response, and his mind was floating in an utterly empty vacuum. He had longed many times for such a moment of stillness and emptiness of mind when meditating, but now was a bad time for it.

About thirty minutes later, the first idea sprang into his head: robbing a grocery store. He really was hungry, but dismissed it as the workings of a mind increasingly drawn into a feverish state of starvation. Or at least, what starvation seemed like to someone who had never experienced anything remotely close to real thing. A few more minutes were spent daydreaming about all sorts of fancy meals Roger obviously wouldn't get his hands on anytime soon.

Finally, an actual idea crossed his mind: Betty, Lisa, Amanda and Marge. His four faithful musketeers probably worried sick about his absence as their instructor. He had completely forgotten about the four women who were inexplicably complacent with his strange demands and more than willing to carry out his bidding whenever he asked. At first, he thought nothing of them and considered their existence in his life an inevitable consequence to being as charming of a leader as he was. Now, they were starting to look like his potential salvation, at least as far as a warm meal was concerned. Though he did momentarily wonder about whether or not they were insane, he judged the risk to be worth it.

The only way to find one of them, he concluded, was to make his way across town back to his studio, where he kept far too much information on all of his clients. He wanted to know about them as much as he imagined they knew about him. He vastly overestimated how big a figure of interest he was in other peoples' eyes. While Roger did have a semblance of a plan, he figured it was risky business to move across town on foot this early during the bright of day. The police were no doubt turning over every stone in search of him, and he wasn't even the type who could lose himself in a crowd... not like Hollow Crest had any crowds for him to lose himself in anyhow. He certainly wasn't going to wait a whole day in the woods either: the hunger was too dominating of a force.

Then, he started to feel a very soft and quiet pulse seemingly coming from up from the ground at him. Roger could see it making its way through the earth and into the air with his mind's eye, and worse, something told him it was happening all over. The internal feeling was barely perceptible, to the point where it could have easily been explained away as the workings of a tired and overly stressed mind. However, with all his experience in piercing the secrets of the universe, Roger unmistakably knew something was afoot, something which filled him with the kind of dread he only felt in dreams so far. It was time to move.

Pulling himself up from the tree stump he was uncomfortably resting on, with the urgency of a man facing the primal fear of hunger – even if it was only a few hours old – Roger slowly began the walk back to town, being more or less forced to take the risk of running into the police. To his surprise, the town felt quiet and empty, practically the same as any other day. No patrol cars rolling through the streets, no tracker squads hunting him down with vicious German Shepherds, yelling at people to lock their doors and close their windows. More than relieved, deep down he felt a little insulted. What matters more pressing than him could they have been attending to? Resolving not to push his luck further than he had to, Roger started walking down from one small street and alley to the next one, hiding behind dumpsters and in the dark corners of the town from random passersby who pretending to ignore him. He did at some point see a patrol car from a distance, but it was so far away he wasn't even sure it was one in the first place.

After finding his way through yet another indistinct alley, Roger could hardly believe the chance encounter the cosmos had evidently set up for him, logically making it a non-chance encounter. Old man Vinter, in the flesh, was standing a few feet away from him, his back propped against the wall of a now-defunct ballet studio. From a distance it looked like he might have been asleep, but his eyes were jumping from side to side, back and forth, caught in a transcendental trance beyond any mere mortal. That, or he was following the erratic movements of a fly. From Roger's perspective, it was a fifty-fifty affair; he was no stranger to either of those occurrences. He was happy to see the crazy old man didn't get caught for his antics, and decided to approach him, if only to thank and congratulate him on a well-performed criminal escapade.

Vinter was startled by Roger's ample appearance right next to him, and jumped away with a scream. "No! I said no!" he would have attracted unnecessary attention, if there were any to be found.

"Shut up old man! They'll get us!" his expression of gratitude wasn't exactly going like he had planned.

"He already... got me..." Vinter's breathing was becoming deeper and more erratic, like a breath of profound panic.

"Since you're here and not in jail, I would say no, he didn't get you." Roger adopted a pensive expression by furrowing his eyebrows. "Say, how did you get away from him? Officer Tim was the high-school marathon twenty-seventh place winner, he was a pretty fast one." In

Roger's world, this was enough of an athletic feat to carry lifelong benefits.

"Nah, not the officer... I was nineteenth in the Marathon of my day... the other guy... it's burning again..." having barely ended his sentence the old man began to contort himself, clutching intermittently at his chest, shoulders and stomach. He reminded Roger of someone quitting drugs cold turkey.

"Hey, are you quitting any drugs cold turkey?" if there was ever a time to be straightforward, he judged this was it.

Vinter couldn't answer Roger anymore. As a matter of fact, he couldn't even really hear him in the first place. A nauseating ringing had settled in his head, complementing the body-wide scorching sensation, which he felt like he was already starting to get used to. He could barely even remember who Roger was anymore, or what they had done the night before. A torrent of wrath began to swirl in the depths of the old man's soul. The more he looked at Roger, the offensively massive and arrogant know-it-all standing right before him, the more Vinter hated him, even if only for the simple reason Roger wasn't suffering as much as he was, the inconsiderate bastard.

After a few seconds which felt like an eternity, he couldn't contain himself any longer and lunged at Roger with unexpected zeal, catching the big man off-guard and sending him tumbling to the ground, his ankle giving up under the enormous shock it was made to endure. Slightly disoriented, Roger saw the old man's hands reaching for his throat, and they felt like burning hot coals when they laid on his skin. Old man Vinter wasn't kidding around; Roger began to fear he unleashed a criminal supervillain upon the world, one who was now intent on improving his craft by claiming his first living victim. However, with the old and burning hands squeezing around his throat, he quickly decided to leave the self-chastising for a more appropriate moment.

Roger might have been fairly out of shape, but he still held a respectable bit of mass, and as a result had a fair amount of muscle to work with, though he tended to exaggerate the potency of his strength in his personal fantasies. In any case, he had more than enough to contend with the old man, who despite being crazy, was old, weak, and in all sorts of pain from head to toe. Roger grabbed his wrists and gently pushed them away from his throat, after which he turned him over onto his back with far less resistance than he had anticipated. He actually felt bad for having to get physical with his assailant, who was still trying to kill him by the power of his intensely unwavering stare. It wasn't a fair fight in the slightest sense of the word.

With its would-be victim having the upper hand, Vinter's unnatural body heat went on the counterattack, burning Roger's hands, still clasped around the pair of wrinkly aged wrists. Roger had the impression he was under some sort of telekinetic radioactive attack, angering him at his own lack of ability to respond in kind. It did make him lose his grip, and not a moment later the old man sprang back up to his feet, dashed down the alley and disappeared behind the corner. Roger was left laying on his side, victim of the most pathetic alley attack the city had seen in a long while.

The pain in his ankle rose to a strong enough intensity to drive him into cold sweats, and it had no plans on letting up. He wasn't far from his studio now, about fifteen minutes on a healthy set of ankles. There was no turning back at this point: he had to bear the pain, or he would likely end in a lock-up a little more secure than last time, and without any crazy old men or suspiciously-amenable doctors to help him out. He looked around, and noticed a set of dirty old pipes resting a few feet from him. With a monumental effort he managed to grab one and turned it into a walking stick. His genius, perseverance and quick thinking truly knew no bounds, a thought he encouraged himself with. His hands and neck still felt hot and buzzing, but it was tolerable, at least for the moment.

After vowing to get his revenge on Vinter and carefully checking to make sure no police cars were patrolling up and down the streets, the crippled, self-proclaimed guru on the subjects which truly matter in life continued his journey towards his studio. The further he walked, the more suspicious he grew about the lack of police activity, and the more he feared they were setting an elaborate trap for him. The anxiety made him want to stop in his tracks, but unfortunately for him, his good fortune prevented him from doing so; there was simply no reason with zero observable danger. Even Roger couldn't get himself out of this one, especially with his stomach rumbling like a biological earthquake with greater frequency. It was such a pressing concern for him he was already in the process of forgetting his alleyway assault a few minutes ago.

Finally, half an uneventful kilometre later, he was finally able to see his studio, a ray of enlightenment in a sea of cosmic darkness. To Roger, said darkness manifested itself mainly in the form of the town's sole strip club next door to him. His eternal nemesis he had been fighting against for longer than he wished to admit, for it stood as proof of his impotence in the face of greater debauchery. He wondered whether Vinter would be up for another gig, should he find enough of his sanity to coordinate another arson. He discarded the idea, realizing the old man would probably set fire to the entire neighbourhood if given the chance. Part of him was afraid he'd do it without even being asked to. He really hoped the police could catch him soon, or that he would drive himself past the horizon and become someone else's problem. Both options suited him just fine.

Though his dojo was in sight, he wasn't about to simply barge in like a clown and give the cops an easy target to take down. He fancied himself smarter than most clowns. Finding yet another perfectly-angled dumpster on the other side of the street, Roger positioned himself to watch his own front door and tried to spot any signs of activity. For the moment, everything was at such a standstill time itself didn't feel like moving.

He waited for ten minutes, twenty, thirty. Still nothing. Some of the strip club workers having a smoke break outside noticed him, and he caught them giggling from the corner of his eye. Evil can manifest itself in many ways, and Roger believed it most often manifested itself in the form of attractive women. This was the reason, he told himself, he had never been with an attractive woman, and was naturally proud of it. Not many remained in the universe who shared his purity of thought and soul, of this much he was certain.

With his eyes transfixed on his studio, he failed to notice one of the girls from the club casually approaching him. She was a tall red-haired amazon wearing shorts, knee-high boots, a bomber jacket, a massive head of hair comparable to Medusa's, and most offensively, somehow, she made it all work together. She was about two meters away from Roger when she decided to catch his attention.

"Psst!" her loud whisper immediately drew a reaction from him.

"What? No, I'm not in need of your services!" he was always the uncrowned champion of jumping to conclusions.

"You think me a whore?!" in the blink of an eye she covered the distance between them and slapped his wide face, leaving a stinging red mark on it. "Fine, have it your bitch-ass way!" she began stomping back.

"Wait!" Roger whispered loudly. "I'm sorry! I've had a bad day! And my ankle hurts!"

somehow this was enough to stop the lady in her tracks. For a second, he even stopped himself in his tracks, wondering when he had the time to become so apologetic. This wasn't like him. There was a time when he would have banished this demon of debauchery to the eighth circle of hell, but now, he felt she had something important to say, and he needed to know. After all, they had been door-to-door for such a long time, and only now were they talking. "Please! What were you going to say?" he wasn't used to pleading much, and coming from his unpractised self it had an uncanny characteristic to it. Still, the lady didn't mind. She had seen worse.

She sighed, "I saw the cops goin' into yo place, never saw them come out." she tried to get a good look at Roger, attempting to gauge what kind of person she was dealing with here. She settled on pathetic, which to be fair wasn't too far off the mark.

"They're coming out now!" Roger cried out and pulled the lady with him behind the dumpster. "Can't let them see me, or you talking to me! They'll take you too! Shhhh!" his desperate eyes were enough to convince her he was either truly innocent or a dangerously impotent maniac. Either way, she judged it was best to play ball right now.

Two policemen came out of his studio in a hurry, and only seconds later a squad car with its lights and sirens on full blast drove by, picked them up and carried them off to unknown horizons. A minute or so passed, and Roger felt like he could finally breathe again. More importantly, he felt an immense satisfaction in knowing he was right and there was, in the end, a trap set for him. He also managed to feel a slight concern for whatever might have happened which exceeded in importance the manhunt after him. He looked at the lady he dragged behind the dumpster; she remained quiet and still as a statue. Roger was impressed by her ability to follow his instructions. She was impressed by how bad of an idea it was to warn him of anything.

"All right, they're gone now, we're safe." Roger shot her a smile which wasn't reciprocated.

"Fantastic." her sarcasm was unbearable.

"Hey, what's your name? I'm Silver, Roger Silver, but my friends call me Roger, and also sometimes Silver, and government employees call me Mister Silver." he looked at the sky for a moment, lost in thought as to whether he covered all the names people used for him. Either way, it had to do.

"Lucinda." she answered after a moment of internal deliberation as to whether or not she should give him her real name. Naturally, she decided against it.

"Well, Lucinda, if you ever need a favour, let me know. I'm your man. I never thought the likes of you and I could join forces or see eye to eye, but here we are." he shot her another smile, one he tried to calibrate as normal and friendly. It still wasn't reciprocated.

"The likes of you and I?!" she knew what he meant, and took offence to him, dangerously crazy or not.

"Yes, I meant the likes of me, a guru of cosmic meditation, and the likes of you, a..." he paused, finally noticing the pit he was digging himself into.

"A... what? Say it, what you mean!" she wasn't about to let him off the hook. She could be dangerously crazy too, when necessary.

"A bride of debauchery." Roger gauged this was perhaps the best euphemism he had come up with in his life. Definitely in the top three. He winked at her, without knowing why.

The lady whose name wasn't really Lucinda hid her face in the palm of her hand, and couldn't for the life of her ascertain the sort of person standing in front of her anymore. "I'm goin' back to my girls now. No objections?" she felt just a little safer now, enough to ask his permission to free herself from behind the dumpster.

"Zero objections, Lucinda. You are free to go." he waved her on back out into the street, which she crossed about as fast as she could to her friends. They were going to make fun of her, and she vastly preferred this fate to Roger's company.

With the way now about as clear as it would get, Roger walked on to his studio and finally managed to cross the front door. The familiarly stale air of his sanctuary soothed his nerves for a moment, bringing him back to a simpler time when all he had was the opportunity to enlighten people about the ways of the universe. They'd have to remember his teachings and manage on their own, for the time being. He had faith in them.

He locked the door behind him and pulled down the curtains, then changed his mind and pulled them back up again, in case someone would notice their new position. He changed his mind for a third time and closed them again, preferring the brief privacy they would offer him, something he had been deeply missing for a while. Feeling about as safe as he potentially could in his situation, he took a minute to look over his haven, and once again lost himself in reminiscence of days past. One minute turned into ten when he finally snapped out of it, and noticed something was amiss. A detail which only stood out to him now: above the giant six-foot tall mirror which stretched across the entire wall hung Roger's favourite inspirational poster, but it seemed to be ever-so-slightly off-centre, no more than a millimetre or two. It displayed a pitch-black background with a white text written in Comic Sans: "*I think; therefore, I'm thinking.*" He pulled up a sturdy chair which he had specifically bought for its ability to withstand large weight loads, climbed on it precariously, and slowly began peeling the poster away. It was coming off way too easily, like it hadn't been glued there for years and years on end, and this gave Roger a rush of anxiety. If they had found the inhumanity to tamper with his favourite poster, there was no telling how far these animals would go. After carefully laying it on the small table which he referred to as his office, he grabbed his emergency military surplus flashlight from his doomsday emergency cabinet (any self-respecting guru ought to have one) and began examining the wall behind it.

Inch by inch, no crack or hole could escape his superhuman focus, and finally he found one bigger than the others, and more importantly, it didn't look like a natural product of erosion and lack of maintenance on the building. It was perfectly circular, and he had no doubt someone had drilled it in there, with the cops being his number one suspects, of course. He shone the flashlight inside and brought his eye as close as possible to have a look. As far as he could tell, there was some kind of unidentified black device in there. In other words, he had no idea what he was looking at. However, this never stopped Roger from reaching the conclusion he wanted to, and after a about half a second's worth of reflection, he concluded the place was bugged. While he didn't know nearly enough about police procedures to ascertain the legality of the situation, he was both slightly surprised and tremendously flattered to have been considered a high-enough value target for a wiretap, likely the first in Hollow Crest. He really was moving up in the world.

Following his brief yet fulfilling moment of self-congratulation, Roger realized he was likely being listened to by an agent in a van somewhere, complete with the dark suit and sunglasses. He probably heard him walking around, or at least moving the chair. Without missing a beat, Roger put on his worst Southern accent and loudly exclaimed to anyone spying on him: "Yup! That Roger fella ain't here! We best look at... the other end of town!" After putting the poster back up and swiftly grabbing his emergency supply kit as well as the address book from the hidden drawer of his desk, he stomped loudly to the door, carefully scanned the area to ensure no special agents were waiting outside to arrest him, left his studio, and waved a dramatic goodbye at it, the way children wave at liberated balloons floating to heaven.

Once on the street, he found himself frozen for a moment, as an idea was being birthed in the recesses of his entangled neurons. With as determined a stride as he could manage with his ankle, he approached the ladies of the club next door, still gossiping with each other on their endless smoke break.

"Greetings, ladies of the evening!" Roger proclaimed in an uncharacteristically jolly voice. They simply eyeballed him with confused faces lacking any answers. "I've come to offer you all the chance of a lifetime! If you let me into your club so I can make a few phone calls, I will gift you all one month of free classes at my studio. But probably next month, this one is turning out a little busy. That's right, it's a once-in-a-lifetime opportunity! If you miss it, you kiss it, as they say." he was satisfied with his sales pitch, though he was a bit rusty due to years spent with a regular clientele.

"Nobody says that." answered the unnaturally-skinny blonde.

"What kinda classes we talking about?" asked the one with the leopard-print purse.

"Cantchya see? Fitness classes!" the other blonde yelled out mockingly. They cackled hoarsely in perfect unison.

"Fitness? Don't even bring that up in my presence." Roger wasn't about to be deterred by the opposition. He really needed that phone, and was prepared to descend into what he thought of as hell to get it. "What I'm offering is something much more profound you will never find in your internet videos and whatnot. What I'm offering is the deepest and truest kind of spiritual connection to the universe, a bridge to the forces from the great beyond manipulating us like pawns. Don't you wish to know what's out there? To cross the frontiers of human knowledge? That's what I offer at my studio, at a reasonable price for most people. I offer-" Roger could have gone on for much longer, if he hadn't thankfully been interrupted.

"We'll let you use our phone if you stop talkin' right now, how about that?" not-Lucinda chimed in.

"That works. Where is it?" though it hadn't unfolded the way he planned, the end result was still the same, giving Roger every reason to pat himself on the back.

"Take a left when you go in, then turn right at the second corridor, then walk all the way to the end." explained not-Lucinda, with a pensive finger on her chin and her eyes rolled toward the sky in deep recollection.

"I will never forget your kindness, ladies of the evening. I-" he really wasn't used to being interrupted this much.

"Stop calling us that, for fuck's sake." the leopard-print purse lady made her annoyed presence known again.

"Yes, uhm, if you *ladies*," he made a brief pause, to ensure this was indeed an acceptable way of addressing them, "if you ever need anything, let me know. I offer shelter and knowledge to all, except the people I don't like." and there were indeed many people Roger didn't like... certainly more than he did like.

Following those words, he stepped inside the club and began journeying the labyrinth of depravity towards the sole phone in the entire establishment. First cell phones came along and launched an attack on landline phones, and now word was spreading about the imminent takeover of smartphones, coming along to finish the job. People must have really taken a liking to making themselves available to annoy twenty-four-seven, not to mention easily-tracked by the government. Thus Roger explained it to himself. Finally, he could see the payphone at the end of the hallway so unkempt one might have thought it was built by a previous civilization. By some miracle of engineering, the phone was still functional.

With his mind being focused on a singular task, Roger hadn't yet taken in his new surroundings, also partly because he felt like he had walked into the den of The Beast itself. At this time of day, however, it was still largely empty, and no gratuitous revelry was taking place. This calmed him down a little bit. The music was still blaring loud and hard, with the sound system being dysfunctional to the point where everyone was afraid to touch it. Over time, they began treating it like a sentient machine which already knew best what to play, when, and how. The owner was all too happy with this development, seeing an opportunity to save money on technicians. The girls hated it at first, but then got used to it. Nobody really knows if the music ever stops.

Roger finally found his way to the phone, and in spite of the flashing neon lights capable of driving even the non-epileptic into epilepsy, he began to list through his address book to look for Betty, Lisa, Amanda and Marge. The emergency supply kit was already coming in handy, containing a stash of quarters he could use to place way more calls than the payphone had seen in the last year. He though about who to call first, and decided to simply go in the logical order. He was about to dial Amanda's number, but then remembered her confrontational attitude, as well as the fact she didn't have a phone in the first place. Betty was up next, but she wasn't picking up the phone, and he was astonished, incapable of imagining any reason for her not to be home. With the third name on the list, Lisa, a ray of hope finally shone through for him.

"Hello?" her faint and tired voice on the other end made Roger temporarily forget about being in the den of all evil.

"Lisa! Am I glad to hear you!" Roger had to yell out every word to have any hope of overpowering the obnoxious music.

"What? Please turn down the music dear, I can't hear you." she disliked the sound as much as he did, but didn't have any anger left for anything in her heart.

"It's me! Roger! R-O-G-E-R!" he was yelling at the very top of his lungs.

"Roger? My God, where have you been? We're worried sick, you know? We got your word out in the internet, and then you were gone! You know, we're still showing up to your classes, in case you come back!" the happiness in her voice was truly genuine.

"Really? I..." for the first time in world-knows-how-long, Roger actually felt a bit of true sadness and empathy at someone suffering because of him. The sensation felt relatively new and uncomfortable. "I need your help Lisa! Can I come to your place? I need help! I'm being pursued!" he had to yell this phrase several times over before she finally understood him.

"Of course, dear! Anything for you! You remind me of my grandson, but he's a lot more handsome! Anyhow, my address is-" Roger enjoyed cutting people off.

"I know what your address is, I'll be there soon!" he could hardly contain the excitement at this turn of events.

"What? How? And where are you now, dear?" as confusing as this was for her, she couldn't think ill of him, nor virtually anyone else for that matter.

"I'll explain everything later! Later! Also, I'm in a strip club! See you later! I have to go *now*!" with this rather unsatisfactory explanation, Roger hung up and began the mile-long trek to what he hoped would be a private little sanctuary for him in this town.

Chapter 21

It wasn't too long after the police left when Jerry got a call on his phone. It was one of his colleagues, the steadfast kind who never missed a day of work and has never taken a moment of vacation in his life. The conversation was brief and fairly one-sided, with the colleague urging Jerry to have a look at the news, under the pretense none of them might have a job in the near future. Before Jerry could ask for more details, his colleague hung up on him. Something told Jerry no matter what happened, he would have been left without a job anyhow, with the way things were progressing for him.

He turned on the TV set and called Naomi over to share with her yet another display of madness in a world sliding further and further into the realms of the dangerously ridiculous. The local news network was live at the scene of what was, without a doubt, the most eventful day in the town's history yet. It was happening at The Big Cow, where Jerry still worked, but only theoretically. The police surrounded the area with confused looks, and paramedics could be seen on the sidelines waiting to help. In the distance a crowd of people spectated the whole affair, fascinated by how terrifying and unusual this day was turning out for them. With an air of morbid sadness which he hadn't quite mastered yet, the news anchor turned to the camera and finally explained the situation:

"This is Hal Collins with Hollow Crest News. I'm at the scene of a major panic which, as far as latest reports indicate, has claimed the lives of at least six people, and injured a dozen, if not more. Witnesses report all cows began to behave violently and erratically at virtually the exact same moment, which allowed many of them to break out from their enclosures… during the chaos they themselves engineered. The question stands as to whether or not it was a planned uprising. It is said city inspectors have recommended the upgrade and maintenance of the enclosures during the last two inspections, placing the fault for this event on the owner of the company. Strategic decisions are being made at the moment to ensure the safe extraction of those still inside and held as hostages." following this declaration, Hal looked behind him to see the many officers standing idly by, in any process but strategic decision-making. He cleared his throat and carried on. "The cause for this event is still under investigation, as is the extent of the damage it has caused. The police are advising people to stay in their homes, if possible. Or, if they prefer, they can join the row of spectators a hundred meters or so behind me. I am also being informed an animal rights protest group has begun forming. This is Hal Collins with Hollow Crest News, we'll be back with more details." the screen faded to black and was promptly replaced by a milk commercial.

"I hate milk. Always have." declared Naomi, her memories reeling back to the days when her mother forced the evil upon her.

"Looks like you're getting your wish, and more. The fight for bovine freedom has begun." Jerry couldn't help but chuckle at his own take on things. "Hah."

"Think you'll still have your job by the end of it?" the question was only half-rhetorical.

"Your guess is as good as mine. Depends if the cows surrender or not, I suppose. Not much use for a security guard when there's nothing to guard. Although, maybe government regulations will let me keep my job. It's all complicated." it was indeed complicated, especially for someone who was largely ignorant of the subject.

"The hell you think is happening there anyways?" her tone gave Jerry the impression she was expecting the answers on a silver platter.

"Why would I know?" he had no answers, nor platters.

"Between the two of us, you're the one who works there. So, your guess is technically better than mine." this was the kind of sturdy logic Jerry couldn't argue against.

"Mad cow disease." he guessed, bearing a stoic face.

"Mad cow disease?" she responded in the process of attempting to murder him with her stare.

"It's what I said." he decided it was best to go all-in on the theory he had pulled from the unexcavated depths of his rear.

"Coincidentally, all at the same time? Right after we've gone on our little adventure?" she had a hard time understanding the leaps in logic he appeared to be making.

"What are they acting like? Mad cows. Means it's mad cow disease. Simple, and elegant." Jerry was starting to feel tired of the whole thing, and angry he had to live in this town specifically, rather than any other one on the planet. A whole world of towns to choose from; how could his parents have gotten it so wrong?

"You've been spending far too much time with Roger. You're starting to worry me. More than usual." there weren't many people in this world Naomi could be concerned with; he should have felt honoured.

"Yeah, that'd be enough to drive anyone mad. Maybe that's what happened. Roger went in for a little midnight talk with them, dropped something in their water." his wave of self-pity was thankfully fading away; he had no time for such trivial pursuits.

"A vial of mad cow disease?" she mockingly interrupted his reasoning.

"Might as well be. Maybe something stronger, like cow LSD. Hmm..." he wasn't certain of it yet, but part of what he said as throwaway conversation filler seemed to ring true.

"I think you're...?" Naomi trailed off with surprise after a moment of reflection. "I think something poisoned them." Another moment of silent reflection passed. "Shit!" she exclaimed in loud and piercing fashion. "Quick, we gotta dig the painting back up!" she was already on her way to getting dressed and grabbing the shovel.

"What's the painting got to do with it? Matter of fact, I feel pretty good not having to lug it around anymore." Jerry's objections were duly noted with a stern silence, but not much more. "Fine, fine, wait for me." he never could get the better of any woman. Following her down the stairs he found the opportunity to throw in a couple more last-ditch effort objections her way. "Isn't it a bit too bright and early to be doing this? People might actually see us. Wouldn't want that to happen." this just about covered all the excuses Jerry had left to avoid moving.

"Everyone's either glued to their TVs watching the news or seeing it unfold themselves at the Big Cow. Or they're at work. If anyone sees us, we'll just say we're... treasure hunters." the plan seemed fairly foolproof to her.

"Fair enough." he waved his white flag.

Without missing a beat, they left the building and walked in silence to the spot where they had buried the painting, Naomi wielding the shovel like her trusted family sword, but only for so long. Naturally, it was Jerry who was going to do all the digging. The streets were once again quiet and empty, but a certain feeling of tension hung in the air, almost as if the oxygen itself had gotten ever-so-slightly thicker. Jerry couldn't remember if breathing always felt like this, or if he was pathetically out of shape to the point where he couldn't admit it to himself. Then, he wondered on what the difference was: even if breathing wasn't always like this, he was still out of shape and knew it. If not for being yet another one of many champions in mental gymnastics on this Earth, he would have addressed the issue long ago. Now, he was likely heading to face an unknown evil with it. Tough luck for those who don't make their own, he thought. He then retracted the statement in his mind, thinking of all the people who died before having had a chance at making their own luck. He simply settled on "tough luck".

They had finally arrived to the spot where they buried the painting at the park across the street, and Naomi ceremoniously handed him the shovel. Jerry sighed and began to dig while she stepped expectantly to the side and waited. No more than fifteen seconds had passed when a sweet and charming old lady furtively approached them. Jerry stopped digging and turned to greet their visitor. The old lady gave them a kind, soft smile, and spoke first.

"What the fuck do you think you're doing, you disgusting animals?! This is a public park! A public park! A public park! You think you can just dig wherever you like?! I can tell real city workers from the fake ones! Yes, I can! I can tell them apart, I can! I'm calling the police, and they're going to shoot you, and I'll watch! I'll watch and laugh!" somehow the old lady managed to keep her charming smile throughout the entire tirade. Thankfully for Naomi and Jerry, she walked about as slowly and methodically as she articulated her words, giving them plenty of time to work with.

"We're treasure hunters!" Naomi thought it was worth a shot. Jerry was starting to feel a headache coming on.

"Nazi hunters?" the unforeseen assailant was momentarily confused.

"No, treasure hunters. Treasure hunters." repeated Jerry through an annoyed expression.

"Treasure? Here? I warn you! I'll know if you're lying!" she kept her right index finger pointed at them, as if it was a gun ready to shoot.

"Yeah it's... a treasure from the times of the Great War." Naomi took a bit of pleasure in having to flex her creative muscles. "American family came back here with a treasure they took from... a treasure cabinet." evidently, they needed a little more exercise. "But they also happened to be wanted criminals. For theft. And so, they buried their treasure somewhere around here not long before they died in a... parachuting accident. It was tragic." she stopped her story, seeing the old woman was slowly analyzing the information in her decaying organic processor.

"Well, if you find the treasure, half of it is mine too! If you found it, I found it too, because I'm here now!" visions of riches she didn't even know how to spend flooded the old lady's mind.

"Definitely, we'll give you a call, write you a notarized letter, and deliver the treasure personally when we get it." Jerry's monotone delivery didn't ring any alarm bells in the woman's mind, which in itself was suspicious, since it was practically made of those. "Let's exchange information. We'll give you our names, and you give us your address and phone number."

Following a long moment during which time felt like it was forced to a complete standstill, the old woman finally spoke up. "No! I knew it! You just wanted to get under my dress! I'm calling the police, and don't try to stop me! Don't you even try! I won't be stopped!" with these words of terrifying conviction the woman began the thirty-minute long march back to her place around the corner. Jerry and Naomi had more than enough time, or so they hoped. There likely weren't even any cops left to answer her call at this stage.

After a few minutes of hard work on Jerry's part and leisurely rest on Naomi's, the shovel finally struck against a distinctly familiar surface. He could already feel the unnatural stench of the nauseating fumes escaping from the earth, with a strong and unmistakable aroma of wrath. He was starting to feel angry with himself for having dug it up again. After clearing the earth around it a little more, Jerry jumped back out of the hole to stare at its contents with a racing heart. The painting was still intact, but it seemed to him as if the paint itself was leaking from it and was being absorbed by the earth, flowing ever deeper into the underworld. The flow wasn't stopping, fuelled by a seemingly everlasting supply of colours. Jerry and Naomi both looked at each other, and words weren't necessary to understand what they had to do next. They had to remove it from its niche. They had to stop its violation of Mother Earth. Whatever it unleashed was flowing deep within the soil, and would worm its way into the water, the roots of plants, trees, and any other crevice it might find along the way… if it hadn't done so already.

With a heavy sigh at the impending display of manliness he was about to put on, Jerry jumped back into the hole, grabbed the painting by its edges, and tried to pull it back out. It was barely budging; something was clearly keeping it there. Grabbing the shovel once again, he started to dig further down, trying to clear the soil beneath the painting and sever whatever was keeping it there. After a minute or so of exhausting toil, Jerry recoiled out of pure instinct, doing his best not to puke from revulsion. As far as he could tell, the painting had sprouted roots, and they went far deeper than he cared to imagine. He knew he was witnessing something which should not be in this world, something defying the laws of nature, physics, religion, and everything he had learned up until then. This was his first eye-level glimpse into the naked world beyond his own, the loathsome side of man-made reality no one ought to be privy to.

Caught in the deep throes of a primal panic, he couldn't move a single muscle nor utter a sound, his jaw slacked open and motionless. His consciousness was twisting and turning on itself trying to make some kind of sense of it all, but his subconscious was steps ahead, crying out a warning alarm for the terror it was witnessing. It knew things wouldn't be the same anymore, and what's worse, it was partially their fault, in a sense at least... the subconscious too, loved to blame itself. While the gears of Jerry's mind kept spinning out of control, Naomi nudged him with her foot in an attempt to snap him out of it. It seemed to have worked to an extent, as he slowly turned his head to meet her worried stare, his own eyes carrying the terror of forbidden knowledge. Thankfully for him, it was knowledge he didn't understand. Their stares locked for an uncomfortable moment, and bit by bit his senses found their way back, forcing him to grimace in terror once more at the re-realization of what he was witnessing. Starting to lose hope, Naomi grabbed him by the arm and helped him climb out of the hole. She then had to climb in herself to retrieve the shovel Jerry was unconditionally refusing to return for. Once she was down there, she understood why, and jumped back out faster than she had jumped in.

"So, uhm, what are we dealing with here?" Naomi's question was delivered in a practical tone, as if expecting a prefabricated and reasonable answer to it all.

"Roots?" this was just about the most reasonable answer Jerry was capable of providing.

"All right, how deep do they run, do you think?" she was doing her best to approach the illogical situation in the most logical manner possible, a question of maintaining a sense of much-needed normalcy.

"Deep enough to hold the painting down." the appearance of rational thinking was calming him down a little bit.

"So, at least a few meters deep?" she was trying to visualize how far the roots could realistically penetrate the earth.

"Yeah, assuming they're not growing any bigger, the bastards." he was developing a hatred for these roots, as if without them everything would have fallen neatly into place.

"So, what are they for? Don't roots, you know, usually feed trees and all that? Does the painting need to eat? What does it eat?" the chain of logical reasoning was starting to come under the threat of the supernatural.

"Food, I suppose." Jerry was also doing his best to treat this situation like a normal and explicable occurrence. "Maybe water, too." he didn't want to sound like too much of a sarcastic dick, at least not with Naomi.

"Good guess. Glad you're here." she gave him the cold, dead, unimpressed stare she had mastered over the course of many forgettable encounters. She knew he hated it.

"Fine, I have a confession to make. I feel like we're out of our depth on this." part of him was hoping Naomi would agree to just drop the whole thing and pretend it never happened, allowing him to keep on going through life as a willingly blind bystander.

"Can you think of a single person who would be in their depth on this?" no such luck.

"All right, but some people are probably better qualified than us to tackle this." the responsibility of dealing with all of this was really starting to weigh him down.

"Got anyone specific in mind?" she already knew what the answer would be.

"We need Roger here. He might just be deluded enough and, uhm, "out there", to deal with this." the idea of pawning the responsibility off on his friend seemed rather alluring at the moment, especially since in his mind, Roger would be more than glad to take it upon himself, his ego preventing him from doing otherwise.

"And how do you propose we find him?" once again, she knew what the answer would be.

"I have no idea." he confessed, his head bowed down.

"Short of bumping into him on the street or him getting arrested, I don't think we're going to find him anytime soon. If the police can't do it, I don't think we'll have much better luck. Also, stop trying to pawn the responsibility of this bullshit off on anyone else." she didn't even give Jerry the time to ask the question she knew he wanted to. "Why us? We're the ones who got pulled into this mess, nobody else, probably by virtue of being like nobody else in the first place. If you find yourself in the middle of a catastrophe that isn't yours, there's probably something you can do about it… question is, are you ready to make the effort it requires? Are you ready to do your duty as a human being and not close your eyes on the darkness taking over right next to you? What I'm saying is, don't be a little bitch. We're at the right place and have the awareness of seeing it happen. All down to bad luck, Jerry. And yes, I don't know why, but I sure as shit think we made it all worse by burying the painting, which by the way we still need to deal with. This is our mess to unravel, and the sooner you accept that, the sooner I can shut the fuck up and stop being pissed at you." she was indeed getting just a little tired of his lackadaisical attitude.

"I'm sorry." he genuinely let out after a long moment of silence, which both of them passed staring in opposite directions. "I'll be honest, I'm scared." she shot him a slight look of surprise following his honest confession. It took just a little bit of restraint not to mock him for it, as she would have usually done. "Things are getting worse around us, and we can all feel it. First the body, then the random murders and violence the other night, now the cows, and I can only guess what'll happen in the next season." they both reluctantly smiled. "What's scaring me more than anything is we're still groping around the dark in this mess, we're trying to grasp for explanations and meanings, but we're just being swept along for the ride. We have to figure out what we're dealing with, this has to be our first order of business. If we don't, we're all going to die, and that's a fact." he didn't, in fact, know whether or not it was a fact, but he thought it helped to get his point across. The point being, he was afraid.

Naomi's fiery anger at him gradually subsided into understanding. "I get it. I do. I'm scared too, and I'd bet everyone in the town is, even if they don't know it. You're right, we can't stumble around in the dark anymore. Look where it's gotten us." She motioned with her head at the uncovered painting, still showing signs of life and leaking its colours into the earth. It even looked like it pulsated once or twice. "But I have no idea where to start, it's not like there's a manual on this." her gaze trailed off into the distance. "... Is there?" she wondered in earnest.

"Is there...?" he echoed her question, but with a stronger twinge of hope for a better future. "What it would it even be titled? "My Possessed Painting and I"?" anyone but Naomi would have wrongly interpreted the question as a mockery. She knew better.

"Think the library is worth a shot?" her suggestion spawned from the myriad of mystery shows she had watched as a child. The library was always a place for answers to be found in an unrealistically short time frame.

"We still have a library?" asked Jerry, with an astonishment nearly equal to the inexplicable course of events his life had been following. "Didn't the protesters for the right to illiteracy accidentally blow the place up years... and years ago?" he was doing his best to recollect a strange and idiotic time he was now starting to get nostalgic for.

"They only blew up a part of it. No one was hurt. A couple of years later, an anonymous donor funded the repairs and modernization of it, but it didn't get any publicity. I'd bet pretty much everyone in the town thinks the place is still dead. The only mention it got was a tiny one-paragraph article in the newspaper. I wouldn't know about it either, but my former neighbour was really into conspiracies and an unstoppable blabbermouth. At least, until I referred to her to Roger's... what does he call it these days? The Loose Brain Dojo? Guess she found someone who would listen to her... her missing half." she allowed herself a smile at the thought of Roger finding his other half in that woman.

"Hey..." the flame of an idea ignited in Jerry's eyes. "Maybe that's exactly the type of person we need to have a look at this. If she's that deep into conspiracies and exchanges them with Roger, she might know something we don't..." his train of thought came to an abrupt halt.

"Oh, trust me, Jerry, she knows literally everything we don't. And more." she interjected with a smirk.

"That's great news." lost in the throes of his reasoning, he was unable to detect the all-too-apparent sarcasm. "Who knows, she might even lead us to Roger, in a perfect world. Although, then we'd be walking around with a fugitive. I suppose that's a bridge we'll cross when we finally get there. Listen, how about this, I'll head to the library and, uhm, try and do some research in hopes things work out like they do in the movies. Meanwhile, you go see that former neighbour of yours, tell her about the situation, but keep details to a minimum. If she's as crazy as you make her sound, she won't have much trouble believing anything you tell her." Jerry's spirits were lifted from only moments ago, now having a semblance of an actionable plan to work with.

"Not the worst plan I've heard. What do we do with the painting? I don't think there's much danger of it leaving this spot." she gave it the look of hatred and disgust one reserves for their worst nemesis. "But I guess there is the danger of more people stumbling on it. Something tells me we don't want more panicked chickens running about and crying about the end times." this understanding came to her on an instinctual level she couldn't exactly understand yet.

"Yeah, we have to bury it back up, all we can do for now." he closed his eyes, knowing exactly what would come next.

"Yeah, you gotta bury it back up, best get to it." she handed him the shovel with a content smile, and watched him work some more for a few minutes. "We can have some lunch at my place before we head off for our, uhm, excursions." neither of them had eaten for a while, having more important things to worry about than survival.

Exhausted, more mentally than physically from all the digging and reasoning they had been doing, they shambled back up the stairs to Naomi's apartment, and if any neighbours had been around to see them they would have given them the stink eye. While Naomi was busy fixing up plates of rice and chicken, Jerry turned the TV back on, curious to see how the cow situation was being handled. After a few minutes of weather reports and couple of commercial for a tooth-brushing timer application and a two-hundred-dollar hair straightener, the truly important news of the day finally came back on. He turned the volume all the way up for the whole world to hear.

The news anchor looked a whole lot livelier and more jovial than he did the previous time around, an unnatural and rotten admiration almost bursting out from within him. "This is Hal Collins with Hollow Crest News, reporting live from the bovine crime scene of the century at the Big Cow! Ow!" he closed his eyes and grabbed his forehead for a moment. It passed. "First, I am proud to relieve you all by saying the animal rights protest group mentioned earlier was clubbed into submission and forced to disband by our brave policemen! We don't negotiate with terrorists! But this is old news. We've received reports our policemen went to war with the cows, storming their stronghold and taking no prisoners! There were several wounded on both sides, and reportedly four incidents of friendly fire, at the very least. Though the cows suffered a few casualties of their own, their leader managed to break through the police line and lead them out into the wild. In response, the police decided to help the army in closing down all roads in and out of town! Oh, did we forget to announce it? A military cordon is in effect due to the danger we present to the outside world! We've estimated there are approximately thirty cows roaming our city and/or its surrounding area. Exciting stuff, isn't it folks? I tell ya, these cops really put the "laughter" in slaughter!" Hal burst into an uncontrollable laughter for about two minutes before whoever was in charge of the channel wisely decided to cut back to weather forecasts.

"What the hell..." Jerry thoughtfully muttered to himself.

Chapter 22

At this point in his career as a criminal, Roger had developed quite the proficiency for hiding behind large dumpsters and bus stops while avoiding the gaze of occasional passers-by who had zero interest in him. He thought of himself as becoming a master in the long-lost art of invisibility; after all, if nobody did see him, who would be there to tell him otherwise? The town still seemed almost totally bereft of police presence to him, constantly altering his state between relief and anxiety, a regular system he was now accustomed to. He knew something wasn't quite right, in addition to the many other things which already weren't quite right. Having moved on his feet in one morning more than he had in a month, his energy reserves were already dwindling, and his stomach reminded him of the ample void he had yet to fill. The courageous man he was, Roger did his best not to let it deter him, stopping only every five minutes to whine a little bit. Finally, after the tremendous efforts he dedicated to his journey, he could finally see Lisa's little cottage, standing on its lonesome near the edge of town marked by an impenetrable forest. He momentarily wondered how she always managed to attend every one of his classes on time.

The little house stood in the grey area between being too close and too far from civilization, just the right spot to seem like a bit of a mistake, a product of a bygone era which no longer had its place in the modern world. It was more akin to a cabin, made entirely of pine wood and barely accommodating enough for one person to live in. A short brown picket fence surrounded the property, though it was more decorative than anything else, incapable of even keeping a toddler from breaking through. Surprisingly to him, the grass was of a deep green and healthy hue, obviously subject to meticulous love and care by its owner. Roger couldn't help but stop for a moment and take in the beauty of the world apart he was witnessing. With his back turned to the rest of the city, he felt like he existed in a pocket dimension, one he didn't mind spending the rest of his life in. However, he reconsidered once he realized it meant he wouldn't be able to teach his ever-important classes, and decided to keep his adventure in the current dimension.

Snapping himself out of the trance through sheer power of will, he stealthily barrelled towards the cabin and gave the front door three loud knocks. He heard a laboured shuffling somewhere behind it, and gave it there more knocks, in hopes of accelerating it... to no avail. Just when he was debating whether he should knock at the windows, the door gently creaked open and out peeked the kind grimace of an old lady in her seventies. She held it open just wide enough for her face to show, and she stared at Roger without saying a word. He thought about saying something, and even went as far as slightly opening his mouth, but thought better of it, deciding to play ball with the guardian of the house. A minute went by. Then two. There was something solemn about the quiet, but more importantly, Roger was getting hungrier by the second, and after getting a good measure of the smiling face at the door, he finally broke the silence.

"Greetings, woman." he was hoping to take her back to what he imagined was a nostalgic past when he believed such greetings were in vogue. She gave a slight nod in response. He took it as a sign to continue. "I'm here to see... LISA." he enunciated every letter of her name clearly to make sure he was getting through to her. "LISA. Is she here? I have a meeting with her." the old lady kept smiling in response, unmoved by anything Roger had to say. He looked at her, debating whether or not he could push his way past her without being charged with assault, if not murder. Part of him enjoyed the idea of being thought of as a hardened criminal, finally getting the thrill of the bad boy experience, something he never could get quite right, no matter how hard he tried. Just as he became lost in his fantasies of what a criminal mastermind with his level of intellect might accomplish, the door swung open wider and a more familiar face finally showed up.

"Oh dear, hi Roger!" Lisa cheerfully shouted at the top of her collapsing lungs. "Pam! Out of the way!" she directed the other old woman, still standing at the door and smiling vacuously. "My apologies dear, Pam is my sister, and she hasn't been quite right in over fifty years now. She used to run with the wrong crowd..." a forlorn look came over her face. "She wanted to prove herself to them. Oh dear... she tried to rob a man with nothing but her fists. She really was a tough one, that Pam." a sad smile born of nostalgia came over her. "It's too bad she never learned to throw a punch. It all happened so long ago..." she briefly paused again, taking the time to recollected the whole story in her head.

"And?" Roger was about as patient and polite as he could be in this situation.

"Oh yes dear, and what?" she seemed confused.

"You were telling me about... you were just about to invite me in." he saw his chance to cut the historical exhibit short.

"Oh right! I didn't finish telling you about Pam! Where was I?" the excitement of re-telling her favourite story lit her eyes right back up.

"At... the mugging?" Roger was prepared to endure virtually anything for the sake of finding a safe place to eat.

"Oh, right! Well, first she tried to scare him, and scare him she did. So much he belted her right in the jaw!" she imitated the motion of a right hook, which Roger found adorable to his own surprise. "She ended up in a coma, and unfortunately her gang democratically voted her out. Never was quite right after that. What a shame, I thought she had it all planned out." her smile disappeared once again, giving way to the sadness which arises from eternally-lost potential.

Roger raised his eyebrows as high as he could to the sky. "I guess... times must have been incredibly different, for any of that to make sense." he really was making a valiant effort at being understanding, but only the few who knew him closely would have realized it.

"Want to know what I think, sweetheart?" the question was rhetorical. "I think that drama queen Pam has been *faking it this whole time!*" she yelled those last few words out as loud as she could. "Maybe when she came out of her coma she had a few problems, I'll admit it, but since then she must have healed up! It's been over fifty years now! I think she's just in love with being a lazy government leech and doesn't want to let go of her extra disability allowance! She's faking it! I know it, and I'll prove it!" family life is always a complicated affair.

"Those are some real... twists and turns you've got going in your life. We'll be sure to meditate on Pam's condition in our next class. Even if you're right, she might have been doing it for so long, she has convinced herself of her own disability, even though it's not there. But technically, it is there, because she's creating it by thinking it is there, even if it's not there. So, who's to say it's not really there? You following me, Lisa?" though he was speaking with total honesty, he hoped she wasn't following, so he wouldn't have to deliver on the promise one day.

"One hundred percent!" Lisa was excited to hear more from the true master of the universe.

"Lisa? Can you let me in now? I've paid the toll by listening to the story, and have even offered you my counsel on the matter. I've more than earned the right for a meal or three." he would have spent all day standing outside the door if he hadn't asked to come in.

"Of course, dear! Please come in and make yourself at home. And don't mind Pam, she can be a troublemaker sometimes, but deep down she's a good person and has a good heart. I hate her." with these words of wisdom she stepped aside and allowed Roger entry through the doorway, barely wide enough to accommodate his width. This didn't affect him: he had grown used to turning sideways when entering rooms.

The interior of the cabin looked larger and more welcoming than Roger had anticipated, decorated in a rustic but cozy manner. All the furniture was wooden and from a deep past he was too young to have ever known. Somehow, it was all still standing strong and giving the middle finger to Father Time, despite the apparent lack of care and maintenance. There were two small rooms, a basic kitchen, and a bathroom just large enough to fit an insultingly-small tub inside, fit only for a contortionist. The house was lulling him asleep, almost outright asking him to stay forever and ever, but he knew these sorts of comforts were reserved for people who had spent far longer on this Earth than him. Lisa led him to the kitchen table, put away the dirty old pipe he had been using as a walking stick, and had him take a seat while she prepared a full-course meal with all the meat and vegetables Roger could ever ask for.

After gobbling up more than any normal person ought to in a single sitting, he finally felt whole and ready to face the dangers of the changing world. A Roger on a full stomach was a veritable force to be reckoned with, thought admittedly not for too long; evil beware. He took a good look at Lisa, sitting and admiring the ever-pleasing sight of someone else enjoying her cooking. He thought about whether to bring her up to speed on his important quest, to drag her into it, and what purpose she could possibly serve. He decided to give it a shot. After all, she was old enough to decide what she did or didn't want to be dragged into.

"All right, Lisa?" he took on an air of grave importance.

"Yes, dear?" she seemed a little worried about what he could possibly tell her.

"I have a few things to tell you. First of all, I'm a wanted fugitive by the police. Se-" it took no time for her to interrupt him.

"Yes, I know dear, it's been announced over the radio this morning, and then at noon again." she seemed unperturbed by this news so far.

"Well, uhm, that's excellent." this really took him by surprise. "I guess, second of all, I'm spearheading a battle against an evil which found a home in... somewhere in our town. It's just, sitting there, and slowly turning the whole place into a cesspool of violent degenerates. Something's crashing back on us, like a boulder we needlessly pushed uphill years ago and forgot about, or like a corpse we buried ages ago coming back to life to strangle us… or a retribution for crossing a forbidden line. I can feel it. Yes, that's it. I'm afraid it's all quite vague for the likes of you. I never thought I'd say this, but it's almost as bad as communism. We have a new number one enemy for the time being. People have already died in the last few days, and it won't get any better." he was trying to contain his excitement at letting this information out into the open and enlightening someone new about the truths of the universe.

After a few seconds of mulling it over, Lisa came up with a question. "Who are we fighting for, dear?" it didn't seem very pertinent to Roger, but he obliged with an answer.

"...The greater good. God. The people. The Lost Kingdom of Atlantis. Take your pick, it doesn't really matter. Myself, I choose to believe we are fighting for good and people, Lisa. It's a classic, it's muddy, and doesn't beg to be defined further. It's perfect." he couldn't help but colour the answer with a sarcastic tone.

"You think we're good?" the warmth was all gone from her face; only existential dread remained.

"We... yes, we're the good guys here. No two ways about it. I, for instance, haven't killed anyone, nor do I plan on killing any innocents. The things we're up against are very much okay with killing innocents. As a matter of fact, I believe it's their number one priority." he could hardly believe this was the part of his story Lisa was struggling with.

"How do you know all the people who died weren't bad? Oh, I don't know, it all sounds like one big kerfuffle, dear." she was increasingly doubting her good status with the big guy upstairs, right before she started doubting his existence as well.

"Lisa? You're not helping with your negativity here. As someone more experienced than you in these matters, you'll just have to accept my conclusions and the undisputable facts I presented." he was putting every ounce of effort into sounding as structured and calculated as he could manage, as well as fighting off the ever-growing desire to sleep after a meal of historical proportions. "I'm asking for your help, and Pam's if possible, to do just one thing. I just need you to let me stay here. This is the only safe place I have left, and if I don't have a safe space to retreat to, this whole town will end up doomed to... total damnation." if he could only get a place to stay and eat out of all this, he was ready to consider it a monumental victory.

"Oh, I don't know dear, our house is small, and Pam can be noisy, and what if the police show up?" she was voicing the concerns not because they were real, but because she felt it was her duty as mistress of the household, something she took very seriously.

"I'll sleep in a corner, Pam doesn't bother me, and if the police do get me you can just tell them you had no idea. We'll say I told you my house burnt down. Besides, you're old enough to play the dementia card. Nothing should happen to you." he cupped his chin in his hand, deep in thought. "You know," he leaned down and whispered in her ear "if I stay around, you can have an extra set of eyes on Pam, and if she is faking it, we'll have a better chance at catching her." his bargaining offer was too valuable for Lisa to ignore.

"Oh, all right, Roger!" the warm smile returned to her face, and everything in her little pocket world was right again.

With all matters about as settled as they could be, Lisa bade roger farewell and went to sit on her favourite antique chair a few feet away from him and turned on her radio to some news channel nobody had ever heard of. Roger was amazed at the fact the antique was still holding together and supporting her weight, being likely older than the combined ages of everyone in the house. Quality craftsmanship, even for the simplest purposes, is a bit of a lost art nowadays, naturally due to the corroding questions of cost and profit. Though he was bound to them like any other human on the planet, Roger hated having to constantly weigh them against each other in every facet of his life, and relished the few moments he didn't have to. Most people would have sworn Roger only delighted in harassing others and spreading misinformation, but he still found room to appreciate the mundane. He traced the contours of the antique chair with his eyes for so long it seemed like he wanted to eat it, and was only satisfied once its image was burnt forever into his retina. A reminder of simpler and sturdier times. But were they better, or merely a different incarnation of the historical cycle? How does one exactly even qualify "better", if the only times they truly know are their own? All eras are always remembered fondly by those who prospered by personal standards, and painfully by those who suffered, no matter where in time and space they might have been. Nostalgia for a time and place a person hasn't experienced tends to be a painful mistake, but one which seldom gets exposed and corrected. Ignorance, as it turns out, isn't always bliss.

Just as Roger was about to proceed into the deeper layers of his intellectual excursion past the unmappable regions of his imagination, a small disturbance in the air caught his attention. It was a faint noise he couldn't quite pinpoint, going up and down and pitch, almost like a radio transmission meant for the naked ear. He was looking around the room, but no matter where he concentrated his attention, it started to sound like the noise was coming from every other place. He remembered then about the CIA's brainwashing experiments which they were surely still conducting, and was relieved he had mentally conditioned himself against this eventual scenario. If the government was finally cracking down on him, they were too late.

However, instead of subsiding, like Roger was mentally willing it to, the noise only gained in intensity; he knew he was dealing with something else. He looked over at Lisa and asked her if she could hear it.

"Lisa, are you hearing this crap?" he unnecessarily yelled a few feet away from him.

"Oh, yes dear." she didn't seem nearly as perturbed by the occurrence as him. In fact, she was acting about as natural as ever.

"It doesn't bother you?" he shouted even louder, more out of general frustration over the auditory assault which he couldn't stop.

"Yes dear, but, what can you do? Life goes on." Lisa might have very well been the reincarnation of a Zen master.

"Is this a common occurrence in... these parts?" he waved his arm across the apartment in one jerky and graceless motion.

"No dear. As a matter of fact, I think it's the first time. My memory isn't what it used to be, but at least *I'm not pretending to be crazy!*" those last words were unleashed with the kind of venom nobody really suspected Lisa of having within her. Probably because she saved it exclusively for her kin. She smiled at Roger and he decided to abandon this line of questioning.

A few seconds later, the sound seemed to get stronger as the pitches and frequencies flew to increasingly distant extremes, and soon they weren't the only ones to feel the effects. Electric appliances began flickering on and off, while Lisa's beloved radio transmission was starting to twist and turn into aggressive pulses of static at random intervals. The event didn't last for too long, and a few seconds later the noise receded to its previous levels, with the only difference being Lisa's radio still emitting nothing but static. This too, didn't last for long; an old raspy voice began to talk.

"Uhhh....uhhh...ahhh...Down... Down... Down...uhhh..." and so on and so forth, the hypnotizing voice on the radio kept repeating the mantra, and nobody could understand its meaning, nor stop listening to it. All the radios and televisions in town were blaring the message, and not a single person was capable of shutting it off. As a matter of fact, nary a single person was even capable of moving.

Roger tried to plug his ears with his massive hands, but it didn't make a lick of difference. He could sense thoughts and feelings trying to burrow their way into his psyche, and while he was momentarily happy to have the ability to fend them off, he was subsequently angered by how much others surely lacked his mental fortitude, making them vulnerable targets to this sort of sonic attack. The transmission was even making him want to puke and caused his nose to start bleeding, but thoughts of all the marvellous food he just ate gave him the strength of will to pass yet another trial from the universe. He glanced over at Lisa, who was, both surprisingly and unsurprisingly, sitting still and listening attentively to the broadcast, just as she had been before it started. Now there was a woman who could calmly sit through the end of the universe, which gave Roger a newfound measure of respect for her. A few minutes later, it was all over, and the regular news broadcast from the same station nobody had ever heard of resumed on Lisa's radio.

"Damned commercials, they just keep getting more and more intrusive these days!" though her body language could never betray her under penalty of death, Lisa's words did finally show some chips in her perfectly stoic facade, Pam-related outbursts aside. This was about as much of them as Roger would ever get to see.

"Something tells me this wasn't a commercial... Lisa." he paused for a moment, looking up at the ceiling. "Although... what do you think they were even selling?" with how far and quickly technology had advanced in the past couple of decades, Roger found it hardly possible to be sure of anything anymore.

"The internet." the response was concise and presented like an undeniable fact of life.

"Your theory is something I'll deeply consider." he managed to sound honest and courteous when saying that, partly because he truly meant it. "However, I think my theory is a better one." he paused, trying to come up with said theory.

"Well, what is your theory, dear?" she gave him about two minutes of meditation. Two more minutes than anyone else would have likely given him.

"It's evolving, stepping up its game. The *thing* I told you about. I think recent events have... increased its outreach. Something is feeding it, maybe metaphorically." this was the best he could come up with, which was enough for the moment as the main goal remained to counter Lisa's internet commercial theory.

"I don't know dear, he didn't sound all that evil to me. Matter of fact, he sounded confused like my late uncle Gerald, may he rest in piece, the evil bastard." as it turned out, her complicated family life ran deep.

"Well, Lisa, I hate to break it to you this late into your life, but evil doesn't always look or sound evil. If it came in a bag labelled "evil", I think our problems with it would have been resolved long ago. Actually, it often comes in a bag labelled "good". Are you trying to defend the bastard on the radio?" it suddenly appeared strange to him how hard she was trying to steer him away from his own infallible theories.

"Oh dear, you know you're the only for me, Roger." she gave him a smile and a wink which warmed his heart but also made him throw up in his mouth a little bit. "I'm just trying to help you how I can. After all, I've lived for a long time and have a lot of wisdom stored away in here." she gave her head three knocks with her knuckles, wearing her patented forgiving smile which he still hadn't found a way of wronging. Yet.

"I don't doubt it for a second." he doubted it for much more than a second. "But you have to understand, I'm the conductor of this symphony, because the universe has decreed for me to be who I am. You can come along for the ride, Lisa, but don't be surprised if your deductions fall flat compared to mine. And don't get discouraged either. Most people tend to make the wrong conclusions where I make the right ones." the arrogance and confidence were almost oozing out of him.

"Not a problem, dear." but even those weren't enough to shake Lisa's demeanour, keeping her warm expression through thick and thin, except when it apparently involved her family members.

His head still ringing and the mantra from the radio still being chanted in his head, Roger couldn't do anything but lay down and close his eyes for a little while, only to be stuck in a dream where he was failing to fall asleep. Again.

Chapter 23

Jerry stood in front of the Hollow Crest Library, the building which, strangely enough, contributed to the town's inception. The first settler in the region, whose name only went down in history as Marvin the Woodsman, intended on living a life of complete solitude and isolation from the rest of the universe in the company of his small book collection. The bellowing infernal machines of an industrial age devouring the old world didn't agree with him. He had enough of the trials human society inevitably carries along with it. As is often the case, life had different plans for him, and no sooner had he built his shack, travellers from all over the land began using it as a landmark in their cross-country journeys, some begging him for shelter. Not to be outdone by the forces of destiny, Marvin expanded his shack to include guest rooms, and charged a toll of one book a night per customer. While the approach did dissuade some people, more than enough adventurers were willing to pay the price for a roof and a stomach-churning meal in the midst of a wilderness inhospitable to the uninitiated.

Before he knew it, word had travelled around about Marvin's reasonably priced accommodations, and he was forced to expand his shack into a real house with an actual library. Books from all over the world on all manners of subjects found their way into his humble abode, and for many people, his house became the destination of a journey rather than a point of respite. The more his library grew, the more connoisseurs it attracted to the region, and the more obscure his collection became, spanning dozens of languages and including countless unknown authors for whose works Marvin attempted to take credit, albeit unsuccessfully. In only a few years' time, his shack had grown into the region's most valuable treasure trove of knowledge, and at this point he completely abandoned his struggle to remain alone against the will of fate. Those attracted by forbidden and occult literature had begun settling around in the area, with their life goals being the study of Marvin the Woodsman's ever-expanding library, half of which he hadn't even had time to read by that point. Only a few years later, the emerging nearby town of Hollow Crest swallowed it up, with thriving modern workshops, electricity, and markets to boot.

Marvin's fate remained a bit of a local mystery for as long as those alive remembered him, but even his story was washed away by the merciless tide of time. On a late night, one of Marvin's patrons saw him walking around listing through one of his most recent acquisitions, a book with no author nor title. Entranced by the pages, he walked into his study and locked the door behind him. This was the last anyone saw of him, disappearing without even the trace of a struggle or a chance to berate destiny for his unfulfilled desire for solitude. He had been entirely plucked out from the timeline. Perhaps he did get the last laugh over his destiny; these things happen. The library came under the care of the town's short-sighted mayor, who saw no reason to maintain it for the lack of immediate profits it was bringing.

For a couple of decades, the locals took it upon themselves to care for and add to the library, but as their clocks ticked down and their children spread away into the great wide world beyond, there were simply fewer and fewer left who could want, need or appreciate everything it had to offer. The thirst and love for knowledge slowly gave way to complacency and pointless distractions, and so the library fell into a sorry state of disrepair and general invisibility. Its existence was threatened like never before when the group of anti-literacy protesters accidentally set fire to the place in their glorious attempt at self-recognition in a world all too happy to accept them anyhow. Thankfully, the fire was set not to the library itself, but the ancient living quarters which had once served as yet another one of Marvin's ill-fated attempts at segregating himself from the world. The entire scene was reminiscent of a failed high-school play, and the firefighters took only a few minutes to bring the whole show to a close.

Following the incident, there was the question of whether or not the library was even worth spending the money demolishing, since it would inevitably crumble on its own in a decade or two at most. The alternative of building a waste-high picket fence and a couple of warning posters was being explored when a mysterious benefactor called in, taking it upon himself to restore and fund the library's further maintenance. It seemed an attractive deal, pawning off the management of a building which was becoming a sore point in the town's landscape, and so nobody questioned any of it.

After the restoration, which mostly repaired the damages and modernized the infrastructure, the library actually opened up again, with a real librarian working there. It received few visitors, being largely limited to rare book collectors, who in their own right were also fairly rare. Jerry had the impression the place was restored to look exactly like it had been at the time it was the bustling centrepiece of the landscape. The architecture looked like it was planned on the go, and the walls had far more imperfections than you'd see in modern structures. Nevertheless, it stood tall like a dying beacon incapable of reaching total annihilation.

His moment of reverie behind him, Jerry had some new thoughts swimming in his head. Namely, the fact he didn't know what he was looking for, how to determine what to look for, or even describe to someone else what he was looking for. After a few minutes of fruitless labouring in his mind, he crossed the threshold in hopes the librarian would be a little wiser in these matters than him; after all, as far as everyone was concerned, she spent her days and nights here, locked away with her books for company. Marvin the Woodsman would have died of envy.

From the inside, the library looked exactly like the outside would have led one to believe; rustic and out of place. Virtually everything inside was made out of wood, which made Jerry shake his head at how little people learn from history; the place was asking to be burned down. He was partly glad not to have brought Naomi along. On the other hand, it did give off a rather cozy and friendly atmosphere; the payoff was most certainly worth it. To his left he saw a door labelled as "Living Quarters – Staff Only", and on his right was the wide entrance to the library itself. He felt like he was the only outsider to have set foot in the building in a fairly long time, but every surface was neat and wiped down, the floors washed, the air lightly scented with flowery aromas he couldn't identify. He felt special and had the impression he was being expected all along, even if he knew it was a selfish thought to have. Selfish thoughts too, have their place in this world.

He cleared his throat and ejected a loud "Ahem!" which echoed throughout the place. No response. His curiosity getting the better of him and he decided to have a look around on his own, on the off chance something would jump out at him. The books were classified into multiple sections, and navigating them was going to prove a little more challenging than using a search engine. There wasn't even a computer to consult, and the catalogue, if they ever had one, was likely in the librarian's possession. The many sections he was surrounded by included famous novels, moderately well-known ones, lesser-known novels, completely unknown works, books with authors, without authors, with titles, without titles, in English and other languages, and this was just in his field of vision. He saw the shelves stretch onward and curve behind the corner, where a sign hung with the label "Rare Books". He stood still, and at a complete loss. He wasn't automatically entitled to a research montage as he had hoped; unfortunately, things did not work out like in the movies.

A few paces behind his back, an unenthusiastic and gravelly voice startled Jerry. "Can I help you, sir?"

"Uhm." Jerry turned around, trying to appear manly rather than startled. To his surprise, he was standing face-to-face with a young black-haired woman with pale skin, likely in her early thirties and dressed as if for a funeral, complete with the hat. "Hey, name's Jerry." he gave her a chance to reply, but she didn't take it. "I was wondering if you could help me. I'm looking for something particular... but I don't know what it is." he was already regretting sharing this with anyone.

"I'm afraid you'll have to be a little more specific than that, sir." she seemed far more composed than him, despite having very little communication with others.

"I'm looking for books about, well, evil, I suppose." he hoped it would narrow it down enough.

"This doesn't narrow it down, sir." foiled again.

"Let me think for a moment." she obliged him, standing motionless and barely blinking. "I'm looking for non-fiction books talking about, uhm, inexplicable events of madness and rises in violence... a violence that can take over the minds of people? Does that narrow it down any?" he felt like a fool saying these words in front of anyone; not believing in the apparently-supernatural and inexplicable had been a point of pride for him since the one time in high-school he was made fun of for believing in it.

"Yes, that does narrow it down." her words remained neutral and calculated, almost convincing Jerry he was standing in front of an attractive robot whose voice and appearance had been mismatched as a joke. "You'd be surprised, but we probably have a few books on the subject here. Follow me." she started walking down the lane to the rare books section, motioning for Jerry to come along. "I'm assuming you only want books in English?"

"You're correct, afraid I'm a xenophobe." he was doing his best to alleviate an atmosphere which he felt was tense. She didn't react in the slightest. Professionalism at its peak.

"Mind if I ask what this is for? Personal interest? A research project? Writing a book? It might help me make the best recommendations to suit your needs." the perfection and precision of her wording was tensing him up even further.

"It's for a... documentary I'm making. On supernatural evil in small towns. It's going to be big. I even got Zak Bagans to give an interview. It'll be the next Titanic." he figured the more confident he'd sound in his own lunacy, the easier it would be for her to buy it.

"We'll just say it's research then." nothing in the world could faze this woman. She would recommend books even through an earthquake. "Please, have a seat over here. Give me a few minutes, and I'll try to bring you the texts you're looking for." after seating him at the reading table, she disappeared into the darkness of the aisles.

Jerry assumed she really wasn't enjoying his company, and he wasn't entirely wrong, having hit all the wrong notes in such a small and easy conversation. Sometimes he wondered what was actually wrong with him, and then reminded himself the world is a fairly wrong place as a whole; there wasn't as much shame in being swept up in an irresistible current. He was quite surprised at how helpful the unsettling lady was being to him, as if today was the day his expectations would be constantly defied and subverted. In the few minutes he was waiting, he resolved to try and defuse the tension, which may or may not have actually been there.

As promised, a few minutes later he heard footsteps coming back from down the aisle, and she appeared before him with a few books in her hands. She set them down before him in a practiced, almost ritualistic fashion, deliberately placed her hand on top of the stack, and warned him. "Sir, I am legally obligated to warn you, these are rare works which cannot be taken outside of this establishment for any reason other than to save them from impending destruction. If you are caught trying to steal any of these books, we are completely within our rights to shoot you down on the spot." on these words she flashed him the gun she was carrying in her shoulder holster under her blouse. Jerry was confused, petrified, and slightly captivated by the display.

"Got it. So, uhm, not many other clients around, huh?" his tension defusal skills needed some work.

She gave him a look of sadness and nostalgia for a time she never experienced. "Spoon-feeding the brain is in vogue." she cracked a semblance of a smile at Jerry, realizing he might be one of the few to whom this new norm didn't apply. Despite himself, he did manage to hit a single note correctly. "If you need anything, just shout. The sound carries everywhere, an anomaly of our architecture."

"Will do. What's your name, by the way? I'm Jerry." for the first time the intonations of her voice resembled a human rather than a robot, calming him down a good deal.

"I remember, you introduced yourself five minutes ago." human or robot, her memory was certainly much sharper than his. "It's Laura. I'll leave you to your research now." and so she did, waltzing back to wherever she had appeared from.

Jerry was now left sitting with the four books she had brought over. They were titled as follows: *How I Survived the Afterglow* by Ryan Chezemir; *The Faces Behind our Mirrors* by Barbara Tinsley; *The Well who Killed My Town* by an unknown author; and *The Blackened City* by another unknown writer.

The first book was more akin to a personal journal detailing the author's lifelong struggle to survive against something he first categorized as the "most insidious and invisible of all evils known to mankind". It retained Jerry's interest initially, until about a dozen pages in he realized this evil the author was talking about was sunlight, an unstoppable killer on Earth only stopped by roofs, walls, curtains, and opaque objects in general. About thirty pages in, after ascertaining he was indeed reading a serious book and not a parody of some sort, he set it aside making a mental note never to devolve to this stage of insanity. He was confident he wouldn't anyway, but he still had enough time ahead of him to get it done.

The second book by Barbara Tinsley was essentially a manifesto by the author attempting to make her case for mirrors being windows into alternate dimensions. Her main argument was foolproof from head to toe, resting on the fact mirrors mirror their surroundings and don't accurately display whatever objects they're reflecting. In addition, she also detailed many mystical experiences with all sorts of mirrors, often witnessing the presence of beings and objects which weren't really there. Naturally, none of those experiences ever occurred in circumstances where they could have been recorded or observed by reliable witnesses. Conveniently enough, Tinsley also left out her history of hardcore drug abuse and increasingly frequent stays at the asylum. Jerry was starting to feel just a little desperate, and wondered whether all those who dabbled in the inexplicable were either deranged or just charlatans. This question also applied to himself. With a sigh and a hint of frustration he tossed the book aside like a used napkin, and immediately regretted it when he realized just how old and frail those volumes really were. They weren't of much use to him, but someone clearly saw tremendous value in them.

The third book was already promising right from the get-go, featuring black and white pictures as well as an anonymous author, which at least made it less likely to have been an attempt to garner the type of fame which offends other people. The pictures featured a tiny village somewhere in the woods, with about a dozen or so log cabins inside a depression, spaced a few meters away from each other and placed in a circle. There were only men in the pictures, most of them aged from their early thirties to their late fifties, with a couple of outliers. They were all bearded, dirty, wearing large woollen sweaters, hats, and thick leather suspenders with imposing boots which made their feet look a few sizes too big. There was also a shed with axes, hacksaws, hammers, and plenty of other tools Jerry didn't know the name of. This made up the sum of the pictures in the category the author labelled as "Before the Well". The next category featured a single picture, aptly titled "The Well". Predictably, it depicted a well in the middle of the houses. The author added a note, claiming they were ordered to build it as soon and as deep as possible. After the pictures, came the diary. Unlike the authors of the first two books, this one seemed to only be interested in conveying facts, rather than embellishing everything around them; he would have never made it as a modern journalist. Jerry deduced he must have been a military man for the extremely concise way he delivered information, as if he was gathering a report for his superior. Some segments of it had even been redacted:

"[Redacted] of Hollow Crest. Coordinates: [Coordinates Redacted]/ Date: 05/17/1955/ Time: 10:44PM/ Author: [Redacted]

The purpose of this text is to document an even of unknown nature and origin. The following entries use the day the well was built as day zero. It's convenient.

Day 3: Four of us complained about nightly discomfort, an inability to sleep, and observed momentary rises in our bodily temperatures. I had a nosebleed in my sleep.

Night 3: Personal Bodily Temperature measurements. 10PM: 36.7C / 11PM: 36.5C / 12PM: 37.8C / 1AM: 36.7C / 2AM 36.6C. Further measurements weren't possible due to need for sleep. I hate it.

Day 5: Eight of us are reporting the afore-mentioned discomforts and fluctuations in temperature. A request was sent via radio for a doctor. Denied. Assholes.

Day 7: Richard didn't wake up for roll call. Found him passed out in his cot with a small puddle of deep-red viscous blood near his bed. We successfully awoke him. He claimed to remember nothing besides sleeping, and ascertained himself as being in perfect health. Most of the men voted in favour of not pushing the incident any further for fear of depriving Richard of work he was in desperate need of. They like him more than me. I hate Richard.

Day 8: Woke up with a burning sensation in my chest. A strange wave-like shape began to appear on my forearm, not dissimilar from a burn. Nausea and a profuse nosebleed followed. Missed roll call and was advised to spend the day in bed. I saw fear in the men's eyes. Cowards. The twelve of us potentially sick with something. The well must be the cause. Likely unearthed dormant bacterium. Cannot risk returning to civilization and bringing it back. My mission is successful. Everything else, a failure. A meeting is called for tonight to decide on what to do. I still hate Richard.

Night 8: Our council agreed on total isolation until the condition passes. One way or another.

Day 10: Eric lunged at Mosley with an axe. Killed him in a single blow. He said it was the logical course of action. He then claimed he was "probably right". The men looked at him with pity, but they wondered if he might indeed be right. I had the same thought.

Day 11: Tired of waiting. We all agreed the well was likely to blame. If we've uncovered a disease, we must do our best to cover it back up. The process has begun to fill it with dirt. It's my turn to haul in twenty minutes. May no one set foot on this land ever again.

Night 11: Marek screamed through the night and gave nobody a chance to sleep.

Day 12: Marek was found dead in his cot with unsettling burn marks over his body, Similar to the one on my forearm. The blood still poured from his nose. I clogged it with bottle cork. Effective. Is this my fate, too? Gabe claimed he saw a light coming from the well at night, for no more than a split second. Randy claims Gabe is an idiot. I agree.

Night 12: Cries for help woke everyone up. Gabe was trying to claw his way back into the well through the dirt we sealed it back up with. It took three of us to restrain and tie him up. He kept yelling about going home. None of us are.

Day 13: Gabe was found dead and still tied up in his cot, an axe sticking up from his head. Eric called it mercy and apologized. All was forgiven.

Day 14: Nine of us left. Some better, some worse. I can still walk, at least. Randy'll be the next to go. Good. Never liked him.

Night 14: I killed Randy in his sleep. Eric was right. He's probably in less pain now.

Day 15: I apologized for my actions. All was understood and forgiven. To think this was all it took to achieve an understanding and forgiving social order.

Day 16: The juniors among us, Eric and Billy, decided to set themselves on fire and purge the sickness from within, just in case it would weigh their souls down too much to reach the heavens. Nobody stopped them. Bright boys. They'll get far in life.

Night 16: The burning pain is increasing in intensity. If I allow it to continue, I won't be able to walk soon. There's only one option for a man in my condition: to leave my mark in the history of this world and be the last man standing. I won't let anyone bring me mercy, only to be forgiven. It's not right. I walked to Richard's cot, but he wasn't there. I assumed he had the same idea I did. I went for Jack, the oldest and most pathetic alcoholic among us. He wouldn't be missed anyways. Bad luck. He was already dead. Real bad luck. I crossed Richard on my way back. He was also looking for me. I was faster and far less brain-dead. My hammer came down on his head, and my sleep improved. I STILL hate Richard.

Day 17: Either Dale or Vincent went hunting last night as well. Danny took his own life in his cabin and left a note. No one bothered to read it. The three of us gathered in the middle around the well, and decided to dismantle the structure as best we could. Too little too late. It was symbolic. Once we destroyed it, we decided to act like gentleman and settle our differences in a three-man fight. They stabbed each other at the same time. Victory is mine. Request for a doctor still denied.

Day 18: The air feels different. Alone among men and kindred only with the implacable shepherd. A lot of time to work on my prose now. I should set fire to the cabins... I've set fire to the cabins. Kept one of them for myself. If I die here, I'll die in a comfortable bed.

Night 18: The invader in my body finally showed his old, revolting face to me. I saw him standing in the corner. He was radiant. I insulted his mother.

Day 19: The burning is only getting more intense. I wish there was someone else to share it with. My nose is bleeding without pause.

Day 20: This will be my final entry. My strength is waning and the pain is only worsening. Whoever finds this, stay away. If someone does mourn me, I'd appreciate it, but it's not required. I hate Richard.

-Signed: [Redacted]

The rest of the book contained more pictures of the area, information on its surroundings, related folklore legends, and a whole lot of other things Jerry really didn't feel like going through. But he had to, and he knew it. There was something strange about the book, besides the obvious. The pictures held a certain familiarity in them, and he decided he'd study them more a bit later. After all, he still had one more book to go through. For the first time in a very long while now he actually felt like he had something to work with, however small or redacted it might have been. It gave him a newfound hope for a better tomorrow, the invisible ingredient sorely lacking from his world.

He doubted he would find something more relevant in *The Blackened City*, but he still gave it a chance and immediately regretted even touching the thing. It turned out to be the thorough depiction of a nightmare dreamt up by the most extreme racist Jerry had ever come across in his life. He wondered if the librarian was playing some kind of practical joke on him, and couldn't decide if it was funny. Disenchanted with his new acquaintance, he stood up from the table and decided to leave the books there rather than take the effort of returning them. This ought to teach her a lesson, he figured. However, she was one step ahead of his loitering ambitions and seemed to manifest from thin air the moment he stood up.

"Done already?" she inquired rhetorically.

"Did you think it was funny? That "Blackened City" business." he was inquiring more out of curiosity than annoyance, though it was present as well.

"I thought it was extremely funny." she elaborated without missing a beat. "Were you going to leave without returning the books to me?" there was no ill will in her voice, only amusement.

"As a matter of fact, I was. This is my contribution to the fight against racism. By the way, any chance you could lend me the book about the well? It was riveting. I'm thinking of replacing my sleeping pills with it." he didn't have any sleeping pills. Jerry never had much trouble sleeping throughout his entire life, the lucky bastard.

"No." she held his gaze while he anticipated further clarifications which never came.

"Well, see ya later, Lara." he pointed his finger-guns at her as he began to slip away.

"Laura." she unenthusiastically corrected him.

"I know what I said." the phrase was accompanied with a smile and a wink, which he later came to regret. Her shut-eyed rebuff pierced his neck with a sharp pain.

Chapter 24

Naomi stepped off the empty bus in the quiet residential neighbourhood which over the years came to be known as The Sanatorium. Three-floor buildings held together by weathered bricks, housing roughly two dozen units each, were packed in tight swathes on both sides of the road, though they also somehow found the room to squeeze a grocery store and a clinic among them. Over the years, elderly people had trickled into this area more than any other, a phenomenon which simultaneously had no explanation and too many explanations at once. Everybody had a different theory, ranging from the self-sufficiency and the low rent prices of the neighbourhood, to signals beamed by aliens light years away. However, few of them had thoughts on the subject as profound as Amanda Rayburn's, whose door Naomi was standing in front of, mentally collecting herself to cross its threshold. She knew there would be no turning back from the world she was embarking into, but it had to be done for the simple constraint of having no better things to do. While she was waiting, gunshots rang out in the distance, followed by a guttural scream. She decided it was time to knock. Nary a second had passed before a series of metal clanks heralded Amanda's appearance as she carefully opened the door a crack, still held in place by three little chains. Naomi was about to say something, but Amanda, wearing a wrinkly doubtful grin and one of her many turquoise antiquated dresses, motioned her to stay quiet, and carefully examined what she could see of the outside to make sure this wasn't an ambush by the secret services. Finally, she nodded approvingly at her confused solicitor, already regretting the decision to come here. After removing the three chains from the door, she swung it wide open and beckoned Naomi to jump in as quickly as possible. She obliged, hoping this wouldn't be how her life ended.

"Good day miss Rayburn." she was finally allowed to speak.

"Naomi, right? I got a good memory for these things." by the time her sentence was finished she had already lit a cigarette. "I know why you're here. You've seen the shit happening around town and you finally came around to see the truth." she smiled, basking in an aura of self-satisfaction.

"What... truth?" she was afraid to ask, but there weren't many other options for moving the conversation forward.

"That I was right about this shit all along..." her thought was interrupted by her own brash cough. "...and you all thought me crazy. Kept talking behind my back. Talking and talking. Well, who's talking now? Idiots." it hadn't even been a minute but she already succeeded in making Naomi both hate her and feel sorry for her casual brand of insanity at the same time.

"Do you mind not calling me an idiot? And since you're right about everything, I guess you wouldn't mind explaining it all to me? Assuming I'm not beneath your life-changing revelations." politeness and civility always prevailed.

"Hah, you're all so soft these days! Yeah, I can tell ya everything, but you better keep up, cause I got work to do and I ain't saying shit twice." she went to take a puff from her cigarette and realized it had gone out. She flared her nostrils at it in frustration and lit it up again, knowing it wouldn't be the same now. "This ain't the first time it happened, oh no. My daddy, God rest his soul, he told me many years ago before my time people went ahead and killed each other like this again. More or less. Now, it didn't happen right here in our bit of the town, somewhere further out in the woods, so nobody really knew about it 'til later when they found em' all dead. Course, most of the place was woods back then." she blinked furiously as the smoke streamed in her eye. "One of em' even wrote down a journal, and my daddy got his hands on it for a while, copied it by hand. Oh, I still remember, how he read it to me as a bedtime story over and over again... Oh, how I loved that story..." a tear came to her eye for fond memories of yesteryear, frozen in the amber of her mind. She then remembered she was talking to a person, and not a mirror for once. Quickly, she collected herself. "Anyway, the shit that's happening here now, it happened there too in that journal, and whoever wrote it, he thought it started when they dug up a well." she took a moment to catch her breath. She wasn't used to making such long discourses anymore; her best days as a doomsayer were fortunately behind her.

"A well? And let me guess, a ghost crawled out of that thing? It's a bit too cliché these days, don't you think?" she still wasn't sure what to make of the story as a whole, but mocking it was her way of lightening the mood just a little. She really didn't like the idea of a crazy conspiracy theorist being actually right about something, even considering what they say about broken clocks.

"Don't mock me girl! I've seen more than twice as many ghosts as you have!" though she was old, there was still a very real fire behind her eyes. The will to live ages last.

"Any amount multiplied by zero is still zero." Naomi knew this was one of the more unnecessary responses she could have given, but the opportunity was too great to resist. Right before Amanda was about to burst in flames on the spot, she decided to apologize. "I'm sorry, I don't know what came over me. Please continue."

"As I was saying..." it took her a few greedy breaths to calm down, but her enormous life experience allowed her to succeed. "This has nothing to do with ghosts, and not even the Japanese, believe it or not." she was dead serious. It did not, in fact, have anything to do with the Japanese. "I think they dug up some kind of... government virus when they built the well. I've done my research, I know they experiment with chemical and biological warfare on the regular population. We're all guinea pigs for the government to experiment on. Someone was sent there to dig up a virus on purpose, it's made the people in the journal go crazy and kill each other. Now, they either dug it up again, or they've gone and made an aerosol version. There it is girl, your truth." she put on the prophetic smile of someone privy to life's unattainable secrets.

"Do you have... any proof... for any of this? Where's this journal now?" Naomi could feel she was on the trail of something, but what it was or whether it would help her was hard to gauge.

"You can read the journal yourself, it's at the library, last I heard. And, you didn't let me finish my story." she lit another cigarette barely a minute after finishing the last one. A truly enduring woman. "There's something you won't find in the journal, or the news, or anywhere else in the world. My daddy told me he met the author of the journal. He didn't tell me his name. Didn't want me close to that government filth. But my daddy, he said the man used to be a soldier... or a criminal. Can't remember. They were the same to him. And from what he told my daddy, he was being sent to work and live there as punishment. Back then, the government was trying a new program in secret, cutting down recidivism by forcing former prisoners to live far outside of cities doing lumberjack work. It worked, but only technically..." she seemed momentarily lost at the idea the government could have done something right, even if it was in the most technical and roundabout way possible... all while benefiting from her government-issued pension cheques.

"So, you're saying they ran an experiment on people because they were criminals?" Naomi was at a tremendous loss about what to believe, if anything at all. She had no way of knowing what percentage of the story was truth, and how much of it was Amanda's conspiracy-driven fantasies.

"That's right." she gave her a strong affirmative nod, pleased to see at least someone was smart enough to follow along with her. "Not many were gonna miss em', and if anyone did, they could just tell em' they died in a prison fight. It was the perfect plan." she got up uncomfortably close to Naomi's face to deliver the last line.

"What were they even testing?" she asked, backpedalling as politely as possible from Amanda's smoker breath.

"Weren't you listening girl? Biological, chemical warfare. Viruses. Chemicals. Biology. There were other words, but I can't remember em' now. Probably testing some shit they could poison their enemies with to make em' kill themselves. And the government has only one real enemy: The People." in Amanda's head, all the pieces of the puzzle had fallen into place.

"I see. That's definitely something to think about. By the way, do you know where Roger might be? I actually came here to see if you had any idea." she felt it was high time to steer the conversation back towards something less susceptible to conspiracy. The idea that a grain of truth might be found in there, however, refused to leave.

"Hah, showing your true colours I see. You didn't care for the truth in the first place, did ya?" her accusatory tone was starting to sound just a little dangerous to Naomi.

"You got me there, Amanda, I'm just here for the food." she was hoping a little more humour would stop the old woman from suddenly jumping at her with a knife she was certainly hiding somewhere underneath her dress.

"You can see he ain't here, not sure why you're sticking around." she pursed her lips and squinted her eyes menacingly in Naomi's direction. "What's he done for you to come looking for him here? Aren't you best friends? Is the government after him? What's happening to him?" the concern she was showing for the sake of her guru, and likely the only other person willing to listen to her ramblings, was a tad touching to Naomi, nearly making her forget the head of bouncing marbles she had to deal with in front of her.

"He's... on the run. I don't know where he is, or what's happening to him. We lost touch with him not long ago. I figured he might have been hiding out here with you, since, I'm guessing, you got along so well." she did her best to put on an air of deflated sadness, disappointment and powerlessness.

After savouring a moment of watching her standing there all dejected, Amanda's heart softened a bit and she took pity on her visitor, young enough to be her daughter, not that she ever wanted one. "Here, have a cookie from my private stash, it's free this time." she pointed to the glass jar on the counter behind her.

"That's... that won't be necessary, I don't think. I can't eat baked goods. It's against my religion, you see." she was mortally terrified of those cookies being poisoned, and wondered how many lives Amanda had taken over the course of her existence. Any guess was as good as any other one. She then quickly marched towards the front door and started undoing the seven locks which kept it stuck firmly in place, in addition to the three chains allowing it to open a crack. "It was very nice seeing you again, Amanda. Thanks for all the help. Stay away from that... biological chemical warfare, now." finally, the last lock surrendered under her stressed and trembling hands.

"Wait..." Amanda almost sounded like she was pleading. "He might not be here, but there are others like me."

"Other conspiracy theorists?" Naomi was truly surprised by this piece of information.

"No." the dryness of her tone properly conveyed the offence taken. "Other old crones who go to his dojo. Matter of fact... they're boot lickers and ass kissers of the highest order. I think they're in love with him. If anyone would let Roger hide out with them, they'd fit the bill. Marge, Lisa and Betty. I'll write you down their addresses." with a renewed sense of purpose she hadn't experienced in a while, Amanda went to fetch her ornate pen and extra-thick writing paper.

"Couldn't you give me their phone numbers instead? Or just call them right now to save us a bunch of time?" she wasn't thrilled at the idea of having to possibly visit three more addresses today. Getting around the town seemed to become increasingly dangerous in the modern climate of societal dissatisfaction.

"Hah, don't use phones, got no need for em'. Nobody calls me, and I call nobody. When they'll start beaming signals into our brains, the phones are where they'll start. We're always holding em' to our heads, and they use radio signals." as she was educating Naomi on the finer points of telephone-based mind control, she finished writing down the addresses and names of the three old ladies she thought of as her friends, despite holding a fistful of disdain for them in the far reaches of her segmented psyche.

"Thanks, Amanda. I actually mean it this time. You're a little crazy, but you're alright." Naomi was finally starting to understand what wavelength she had to adjust to.

"Hah! Honesty at last. I don't think *you're* alright, but beggars can't be choosers. Drop by when the world ends. Or don't. I don't care. Now scram!" if there was one thing Amanda respected above all else, it was honesty in all of its insulting glory.

Naomi walked out from perhaps the most frightening situation she had found herself in recently, and was somewhat amazed at her own survival instincts, or more precisely the lack thereof, having allowed herself to walk in there in the first place. Though their interaction ended about as well as it could have, she hoped never to see the woman again. However, taking into consideration how life tends to work, her desire not to see Amanda again essentially guaranteed she would very much see her again one day. Probably.

She looked at the piece of fancy paper she left the apartment with, and was simultaneously struck by the perfection of the handwriting, and disgusted by its proximity to the reviled Comic Sans font. It seemed reasonable to start with the first name on the list, especially since it was only a fifteen-minute stroll away; just enough time for something to go wrong. As she put the note away in her purse and started walking, she realized she'd be going in the same direction as the gunshots she heard before entering the apartment. The streets weren't very busy, with the occasional pensioners slowly creeping down the lane in their cars and elderly passers-by shambling around in search of proof confirming bygone days were indeed better. For a brief moment, the world felt normal and nothing was amiss. Only for a brief moment. As she turned the corner down the street she saw where the gunshots had come from earlier. Two teenage boys were standing not far from the street corner, crouched over a man who had evidently been shot in the chest. He had the look of a rough worker in his late forties, his face and fingers bloated by years of friendship with the bottle. Taking a few moments to catch her breath and collect herself, she hurried over to the kids, wondering in passing why no sirens were to be heard. Both boys swivelled their heads at her in unsettling unison, without any semblance of concern for the gravity of the situation. They were both wearing baseball caps, one red and other yellow, and seemed no older than fourteen or fifteen.

"Whatchu' want, lady? We're busy!" blurted out the red cap with the hostility of a honey badger defending its territory.

"Busy with what? What's going on here?" Naomi couldn't hide the stress the situation was putting on her shoulders, her hands quivering at her sides.

"We shot him. We didn't mean to. Are we going to be in trouble?" the yellow cap meekly barged in, evidently afraid of spending the rest of his life in prison.

"You... shot him? Is he still alive? Did you call an ambulance?" she seized control of her nerves and muscles, and reached down for the phone in her pocket.

"No way lady!" the red cap couldn't stay silent for long. "We told you, it was an accident. We didn't like him anyway. It's too late for the doctor anyways. Stop bothering us!"

"You knew him? Where's the gun?" without making any sudden movements, she was slowly unlocking her phone and dialing the emergency number. All she got was a busy tone, and the sense of creeping dread sent an obvious chill down her spine. She physically shuddered against her will.

"He's our uncle." the yellow cap elaborated. "He bought us guns for last Christmas. He told us yesterday to take them everywhere with us. He was going to teach us to shoot today." he understood the gravity of their sin, but the potential consequences didn't have time to be processed yet.

"So you figured he'd make for a good target?!" something boiled inside Naomi at the sight of corruption having discrimination for neither age, gender, nationality, nor anything else.

"Shut up! You'll get us in trouble!" the red cap gave his partner-in-crime a smack across the face in vain attempt to preserve their innocence in the eyes of the law.

"You're already in more trouble than you can imagine. You can run away from the country right now and they'll know it was you. Fingerprints, DNA, eyewitnesses... life in prison, kid. Life in prison." she took a sweet delight in saying those last three words. "So keep talking, maybe they'll let you out by the time you're forty."

"Well... well..." the yellow cap was trying to push something out through his tears. "He told us to make sure the guns worked, so we pulled our triggers to check, and they worked..." the realization of what they had done was too much to bear for him.

"Where are your guns now?!" she was having just about enough of this. After all, she couldn't be expected to shoulder every single burden in her path, especially if its an inevitably by-product of the spirit of the age.

"In the car! Just leave us alone already!" the red cap pointed down the street about ten meters away, where an old beige jalopy rested with its door open and a streak of blood sporadically leading to the crime scene.

Naomi backed away, and tried dialing the emergency services once again, only to be greeted by the familiarly frustrating beeps. She sighed, and went ahead to the bloodied car a few paces in front of her. She thought it was preferable for her to have the guns rather than running the risk of having those kids come back for them. The police obviously weren't interested, and she couldn't stay there to babysit them the whole day. After all, she too, had a fugitive to find. She approached the car with a sense of hesitation, and began to notice a strange odour seeping from within it, something she couldn't quite place and had never experienced before. It made her want to throw up her insides, but she made the expert move of holding her breath while looking for the guns. The car seemed older than her by a wide margin, likely running on arcane energy and virgin sacrifices at this stage of its existence. Apart from the splashes of blood, the inside was surprisingly immaculate and made it easy to grab the two pistols from the floor, both of them Glocks, something Naomi knew because of all the times she had seen them in terrible movies with names she always forgot. Quickly stashing them in her purse, she backed away from the car and took a glance at the kids, who were still crouched over their dead uncle, either in morbid fascination or entranced in a spiritual exercise. After hesitating for a minute, she decided against keeping the guns. They breed nothing but destruction, born from Man's intimate relationship with violence and his puzzling, self-destructive desire to snuff out the lives of his own kind. It has ruled us since the dawn of time. She chucked them over a nearby fence in an alleyway, and watched them fly out of her sight into a pile of trash. She looked back at the kids, told herself they probably wouldn't budge from there for a while, and she would try to ring the police a few more times. If not, their parents would surely find them one way or another and ground them for a week without food. It's what she wished she could have done.

Leaving the whole scene behind her, she kept on walking to Betty's house, or at least she hoped it was, still harbouring a slight fear Amanda might have sent her on a fool's errand for the sake of her own amusement... which to be fair, wasn't completely unfounded. She tried calling the police a couple more times, and while the first attempt gave her a busy tone, the second one got her closer to her goal. An automated message began blaring through her phone: *"Thank you for putting your faith in the Hollow Crest emergency services department, where we're always ready to serve you at our convenience. Unfortunately, we would ask you put your faith elsewhere at the moment due to an ongoing crisis, partially of conscience. If you have any questions, please feel free to find the answers to them on your own with the help of the internet. Once again, thank you for putting your faith in us, and have a nice day."* when the message ended, it was once again replaced by the busy dial tone which Naomi started to find comforting for the repetitive familiarity it created for her. Finally, after a fifteen-minute walk which proved far too adventurous for her taste, she finally made it to Betty's supposed home, the left side of a duplex built following a perfect mirror arrangement, back when architects were allowed to draw a bit of inspiration for their deeds. She rang the doorbell a couple of times, and heard some shuffling on the other side. After a few moments, she rang some more and even gave a few knocks for good measure, only to be answered by a more aggressive and purposeful shuffling sound. Finally, she yelled out "Betty! Is that you?! Open the door it's important!", which by miracle got her point across, and the door opened wide before her.

"Oh, I'm so sorry, people tend to forget about me and I'm just not used for them to remember my name. Please come in dear, I've just made some tartar steak, you can watch me eat it." her offer was quite sincere and she didn't even give Naomi a chance to respond before pulling her inside a cozy, tidy and surprisingly well-decorated abode. The aesthetic was rather minimalist, but somehow worked well with the glass table and black kitchen counters; a paradox in and of itself.

"I'm Naomi," she explained, following Betty to the dining table, where she had indeed prepared a tartar steak for herself. "and Amanda gave me your address. I'm looking for Roger, he's in a bit of trouble and I thought he might have decided to stay here." she had a hard time concealing her disgust with a steak prepared against all natural and human conventions.

"Oh no! No! No! No! Not Roger! He's the only one who remembers my name! Amanda is such a sweet girl to have sent you here, but he's not here. I wish he was. Actually, now that I remember, I did have a missed call from him earlier, but he didn't leave a message. I was going to call him back, but then Ghost Hunters came on, and I forgot all about it." she seemed rather disappointed with herself at not having been able to provide Roger with the help he surely needed.

"Well, that's good news at least. If he called you, he might have called the others. That only leaves Lisa and Marge. Please tell me you have their phone numbers." she really wasn't excited at the prospect of having to make more potentially-wasteful treks through town.

"Why, of course dear, I'm a technologically-informed woman, as the young people say nowadays." she had strange ideas of the things young people said nowadays. "Just give me a few moments to finish my steak, and I'll get them for you."

"That..." she once again tried to swallow her hatred for the raw heresy on the plate in front of her. "would be much appreciated. I've done enough walking to skip the gym for a week, I think." a sense of relief washed over her and the tension in her neck and shoulders began to vanish into thin air.

"Say, while we have time and I'm still eating, mind telling me why you're here?" her eyes were blank as if laying their gaze on Naomi for the first time ever.

"Uhm..." this sudden turn of events caught her off-guard, and she went ahead and tried to re-explain in a nutshell everything which had happened since she walked into the house.

"Oh yes, Roger! What kind of trouble is he in?" somehow, her admiration for him had lowered considerably since the last time she mentioned his name.

"He's running from..." after giving it a moment of thought, she considered it wouldn't be too dangerous to tell this woman things like they were. What were the chances she would remember them? "He's running from the police. He orchestrated the arson at the O'Harris gallery, and he's been on the run ever since. Also, he took up the gauntlet against an invisible and vaguely-defined enemy which is swallowing to the town. In other words, he's the closest to a hero Hollow Crest has ever had." the mere thought made her stop in her tracks.

"The O'Harris gallery burned down?! Say it ain't so! I always loved their modern art displays! I never understood them, it was amazing!" she was lost in a dream for a second, going through images in her mind's eye of paintings and sculptures she could scarcely describe for her inability to understand what they were meant to represent.

"It had to be done, according to Roger at least. There was a painting being displayed there... and... well... it had to be removed. The fire wasn't really planned, but it's just how things turned out." she was trying to sound apologetic, realizing she played a hand in destroying something this lovely old lady had integrated into her past, and what few memories she had left of it.

"The painting... oh, you mean that new painting by Billy the Third?" Betty's enunciation began to change just a little bit, seeming just a tad sharper and more purposeful to Naomi, whose shoulder started betraying her once again, pulsing with signals of pain.

"Yeah, the same one. You didn't go to see it, did you?" the cozy apartment began to turn claustrophobic.

"Of course I went to see it! Didn't I tell you? I loved that gallery!" Betty was now staring at her guest with eyes open wide and unnaturally awake. "Oh dear, I don't... feel so good. Looks like…" she wiped the red streak flowing from her nose in an absorbed fashion. "I'm bleeding? Oh, my head! It hurts! I'm guessing you could never get such a headache, with that empty head of yours!" the lovely old lady's demeanour was seemingly no longer her own, having taken yet another sharp turn.

"What the hell is this? What's going on? Talk to me, Betty." a switch flipped inside Naomi, and forced her into a composure so solid and unbreakable she herself didn't even know was possible.

“I'm just an old lady, I can't help you... Nothing will help.” a hint of foam began to appear on the corners of Betty's mouth.

“Betty? I think you're having one of your episodes. I'd call an ambulance for you, but they're all busy last I checked. How about nice little trip to the hospital? How does that sound?” she was gently feeling for something she could use as a weapon in her purse. She regretted never buying any mace.

“Hah! I'm not about to make it easy for you. Oh no, I'm staying right here, with my episode, thank you very much.” Betty's body didn't seem to be handling the situation all too well, turning into a strange shade between red and purple. She could hardly keep her head steady, swivelling it this way and that at random. The nosebleed kept diligently flowing.

“If you have any conspiracies to share with me, now's the time. Otherwise, I think I'll just be off. You probably really do need to visit the hospital though, for what it's worth.” she was doing her best to draw anything out of this situation, but unfortunately, she lacked both experience and education in negotiating with such clever and unconventional adversaries. Also, the radiating pain in her shoulder was increasingly difficult to endure, but she was putting on a good poker face.

“My oh my, you really are useless!” the sentence was punctuated by a roaring laughter, after which she stood up and with a laboured heftiness began reaching for the big kitchen knife on the counter. A smile coloured her face.

“You really need to take your medication.” Naomi raised her chin in the air and scoffed before running for the door without looking back even once. Betty couldn't hope to catch up.

Chapter 25

Roger woke up from his slumber feeling about as unfulfilled as he had entered it, and would have felt at a total loss if not for the tremendous meal which still kept him full. He looked around and couldn't see nor hear Lisa and Pam, though they weren't really the noisy types to begin with. As a matter of fact, he figured, they were trying to stay as silent as possible for his holy sake. He made a mental note to thank them for it a later, more appropriate time. Trying to sort the thoughts in his head as to the events which led him here, Roger made a terrifying realization: he was out of oxycodone. He wondered about whether Kathleen would help him again, but decided to leave it as a last resort because of all the trekking yet another trip across town would involve. Using phones was out of the question for him: too risky for the country's most wanted criminal. Taking a deep breath and gathering his resolve, he tried to stand tall and predictably enough, his ankle snapped him down with torturous agony. If this was indeed only a sprain, it was evolving into something a whole lot more terrifying for him. He let out a short girly scream and hoped there was indeed nobody to notice it. Lisa and Pam remained silent. For the first time since his ill-advised jump over the fence to the O'Harris Gallery, Roger felt a stab of uncertainty as to what awaited him. He always knew the answer to everything, which paths to take, which to avoid, and how to overcome any manner of enemy, whether physical or spiritual. Now, however, he couldn't ascertain whether or not he really knew how to proceed. As a matter of fact, his overactive imagination carried him to the beginning of a long downwards spiral, one which started with ankle pain and ended with total paralysis and at the mercy of an angry mob, surely already assembling and clamouring for his head. He was afraid, but only a little bit. So far, he had put off really examining his battle wound, especially after a licensed doctor took care of the problem in his stead; in truth, more than anything, he was an avid believer in the power of denial. If he could successfully convince himself to deny the existence of a problem despite factual proof to the contrary, the evidence would eventually rearrange itself to suit his needs and desires. As he was painfully learning, this theory wasn't entirely true.

Telling himself the time had come to face the music, he pulled his pant leg up and wished he could coil back further in terror and detach himself from his leg completely, if it was indeed still his. The place where the pain congregated on his ankle was swelling with bright and aggressive colours, as if an entire chemical spill had occurred on a surface of three square inches. Aesthetically-pleasing, the colours were changing, vivifying, muting, transmuting, glowing, and seemingly attempting to spread to the rest of him. After thinking about how hard he was going to sue Kathleen for the low-quality illegal medical care she provided him with, he focused his attention to the problem at hand. Turning on his power of logical thinking, he began by ascertaining the speed at which the swelling was spreading to the rest of his body. After a few minutes of observation, he concluded the situation wasn't as grievous as he first thought, still having a couple of days or so before it really became a problem. Perhaps even more, if he put his mind to it; maybe the case for the power of ignorance wasn't completely lost yet.

An idea struck him. As old as Lisa and Pam were, they were surely ordained by the government to be on heavy doses of various drugs, victims of the countrywide conspiracy to save money on pension cheques. Or at least a cane, perhaps even a wheelchair. He understood he was more of a beggar than a chooser right now, but he certainly didn't have to like it. The only thing he could do from his pathetic position was try and summon some help, and so he began to yell with authority: "Lisa! Lisa! Lisa!" It took about ten mentions of her name before he started to hear slow shuffling footsteps from another part of the house, seemingly miles away. Finally, a head popped into the room, and to Roger's dismay it wasn't Lisa.

"Pam? You're not the right one." he declared with angered annoyance with the help of which he was hoping to improve his authority in a home he was only a guest in.

"Hmm. Hmm Hmm." Pam gazed on at him with a strangely disenchanting smile and kept humming the little dissonant tune to herself. She had mastered the coveted art of both acknowledging and ignoring people at the same time.

"Pam, where's Lisa? We have a situation here, and I'm going to need some drugs to get through it. Say, you must have a bunch of drugs, right Pam?" he wasn't certain what he was hoping for, but he figured it was better to bounce his thoughts off of her, no matter how ineffectively, rather than being left alone with them right now. After all, distraction can also be an excellent remedy for nagging pain, albeit temporary.

"Haa... haa..." she sounded like an alien trying to emulate a human laugh. It was far less disconcerting when she was simply humming at him.

"Did no one teach you not to laugh at the unfortunate?!" Roger was offended by the idea a woman so old could have so little class. Then, he backtracked and understood the implication. "You must be on the best drugs money can buy, right Pam? That's your secret, isn't it? Lisa is right, you are faking it, but you can't not fake it because of that good stuff you're taking. Am I right?" the satisfaction of unravelling the truth behind a conspiracy decades in the making was almost making him forget about his far more immediate problem. "If you give me something of whatever you're taking, I'll give you some free classes at my studio. Hell, I'm feeling so good about this, I won't even rat you out to Lisa. How does that sound?" in the depths of his heart, Roger earnestly believed this was the kind of offer one couldn't refuse.

"Ptooh!" Pam spat on the floor, slowly rotating until she was facing away from the room, and resuming her journey about the house. One day Roger would come to terms with his lack of omniscience, but it wasn't today.

After waiting for about ten minutes to make sure she wasn't off to fetch him her experimentally-powerful government-sponsored painkillers, he sighed and decided he'd have to rely on himself for a change. He wasn't comfortable with the idea, but as his father loved to say, there's a first time for everything, especially being a dimwit and running out of people to leech off. Roger always held the inaccurate memory of his father in high esteem. Looking around the room for something to prop himself up with, he finally settled on a wooden baseball bat sitting in the corner. He could imagine neither Lisa nor Pam making any use of it, but it looked to be pristinely maintained following a history of heavy usage. He then mused at the possibility of Lisa having lied to him about Pam's past... in theory, she could have made up the part about her sister being a mugger. It was a compelling story, but Roger was starting to see some holes in it. Slow as a snail but sure as the rising sun, a sense of unease was beginning to crawl up his spine; the safe sanctuary he found for himself didn't seem like much of a haven anymore. He was about to stand up and try to walk out of the house, until he remembered he was still indeed a wanted fugitive and probably wouldn't be very mobile while using a baseball bat as a cane for an ankle which seemed to be disintegrating with every step it took. Slowly putting his weight on the bat while trying to figure out how to best use it for a purpose it wasn't meant for, he hobbled on to the living room where the sixty-inch television was glued to the wall like the central object of worship. Still no sign of Lisa, and perhaps thankfully enough, no sign of Pam either. He wondered whether or not she ever left the house as he briefly searched for the remote and turned on the news channel, only to be greeted by the worried, pimple-ridden face of what could only be described as a high-school student posing as a news anchor. His voice shook as he took his time to carefully pronounce each word the teleprompter was feeding him.

"...of violence have climbed by over one hundred percent in the last days, and experts are projecting an exponential increase. Police Chief Halversson has reportedly made requests for reinforcements to be brought over from neighbouring towns. She claims the situation is under control, even if it may not look like it at times. She said, and I quote, "Even if you have a thousand murders a day in this town, compared to the national population, it's still an invisible dent nobody will notice. What I'm saying is, don't get your panties in a bunch, people." end of quote. There is the additional issue of potentially running out of space in the morgue, and a lack of hospital staff to treat the victims. Coroner Kathleen Morrow had this to say, and again, I quote, "We're gonna be puttin' bodies in the fridges and beer coolers if this keeps up." end quote. I guess we'll need a bigger mortuary, right folks?" a strangely abominable silence filled the air for a few seconds. Creative liberty has as many downsides as benefits. "Ahem, end of my quote. Anyhow, we've gotten reports decisions were made on the federal level on how long to maintain an impenetrable cordon around town. The need for martial law is also being investigated." a few more seconds of silence as the anchor allowed suspense to fill the air, as if he was announcing the winner of a lottery. "Aaaannd... We are indeed being cut off by the military at every conceivable exit from the town for the, I quote, "foreseeable future", end quote. I repeat, the town is encircled, martial law is in effect, and no hope of escape remains. A bit extreme, if you ask me, but nobody ever asks me. The victim count of what can only be described as a sweeping madness, so far tallies one hundred and twenty-seven dead, and three hundred and thirty-four wounded. The good news is it brings us much closer to the national average after all the years of peace we've had."

The rest of the words which came out of the anchor's mouth sounded blurry, vague, and indecipherable to Roger, who was standing frozen in shock and fear, barely able to process the numbers he was hearing. How did it all go so bad so quickly? He began to wrestle with the idea of defeat; he was too slow and meandering, having barely gotten any closer to the nature of the malaise gripping the town. Now, he was going to pay for it, and so was everyone else. His imagination began to race as it tends to. He listed through all the possible outcomes this situation could have in his limited mind, from an unexpected reversal of fortune to total annihilation at the hands of the army, preoccupied with stopping the spread of whatever was tearing Hollow Crest at the seams. It didn't help. He cursed himself for his laziness, and heard a shrieking laughter behind his back. It was Pam. However, this laughter was different, more aware and menacing than before.

"Hilarious, isn't it? I'd laugh too, if I wasn't the chosen one to stop this." his pride was hurting, and he was incapable of hiding it.
"You were right." Pam's pronunciation was crisp and clear, though her voice had a certain rusty quality to it; her vocal cords didn't see much action over the past decades. Also, Roger just noticed, she was holding an antique knife with a few rusted spots on it. She began to approach the crippled chosen one about as quickly as she was capable, shuffling one foot after the next. This made her only a step or two slower than Roger himself.
"I don't have time for this!" he declared with indignation, and swung the baseball bat at

Pam's hand, knocking the knife out and likely shattering her bones in the process, although she didn't give any indication of minding it. "Let this be a lesson to you! No conspiracy flies above my head!" Roger boasted at the top of his lungs while pointing the bat like a sword at Pam's chest. Two seconds later, he brought it back down again to be used as a cane, his ankle coming back at him with a real vengeance. "I'll be on my way now, so don't try and stop me, or... you've seen what I can do!" his voice roared through the house and made the foundation shake; it was a flimsy construction. Slowly, he backed up until he had reached the door, keeping his gaze on Pam the whole time to ensure she wouldn't slowly sneak up on him with some other knife she had hidden elsewhere. "Tell Lisa I said hi, thank you, and goodbye. Thanks for everything. Bye-bye now." Even in the most precarious of situations, it wasn't a bad idea to remain a gentleman, or try and pretend to be one, at the very least.

Stepping outside into the streets elicited images in his mind of some of the tamer apocalyptic stories he had read, with deserted towns seeped in oppressive atmosphere, where seemingly no danger was in sight, yet laid in ambush behind every corner. If Roger could take at least one positive note from the recent developments, it was the possibility the police weren't concerned with his fugitive status for the moment. Maybe Officer Tim had even forgotten all about him, having moved on to the bigger and better duty of stopping the town from falling apart to a plague of wrath and hatred. He still hadn't settled on a concrete definition, but he liked the sound of this one. The idea almost felt correct to Roger, but it was missing something, including a scientifically-verifiable factual basis, but he wasn't about to get picky with his evidence, or lack thereof. One of the many inner voices buzzing constantly in his head suggested he was on the right path, and another called him a coward for having spent most of his time evading a pursuit which may or may not have been happening. He would have to get these voices checked out some day. Inhaling a deep and unsatisfying breath, he admitted to himself he probably wasn't going to be able to solve this crisis on his own, regardless of how chosen he might fancy himself. Maybe, he mused, it was possible for there to be more than a single cosmically-chosen one, in case the first one failed. Screams in the distance diverted his attention from his profound moment of introspection, and with a highly developed instinct he hobbled to a nearby trash can and crouched behind it on one knee.

The screams sounded like they were coming closer and closer, but Roger couldn't see their source yet, which caused him a great deal of worry since he felt unprepared to deal with invisible entities, despite having supposedly mastered the art of being one himself. An interminable minute later, he finally saw a group of people rounding the corner about fifty meters away from him. There were about a hundred of them or so, and it was perhaps one of the most progressive and culturally-diverse angry mobs Roger had ever seen. It was composed from people of all ages, shapes, sizes, genders, colours, creeds, religions, political beliefs, scientific convictions and dietary restrictions. All these different people had smelted themselves together into a mass of emotions with a singular and primitive mind, and as far as Roger could ascertain, with a single, annoying purpose: to grow and scream until his eardrums burst. He couldn't tell if the scream was one of joy, anger or sadness, but it was certainly loud enough for him to consider reporting it for noise pollution. As the mass barrelled down the street its extremities were lashing out violently and childishly at any nearby cars, shop windows and house doors they happened to pass by. He even witnessed an elderly yet determined store owner come out to try and defend his life's work, only to be sucked into the mass, adding yet another one to its count. When it came upon the intersection, four police cars pulled up and eight men and women in uniform, woefully under-equipped and abysmally-trained, were standing face-to-face with the greatest threat they had never imagined. Without missing a blink, they opened fire into the crowd which wasn't about to stop its movement anytime soon.

Generally-speaking, the threat of death is quite an effective one when it comes to dispersing large congregations, especially ones which aren't fighting for their freedom or right to a normal life. However, as was becoming apparent, this wasn't a regular crowd, and its fallen members only allowed it go faster, removing weight from the total bulk. Soon enough, the officers were all swallowed by the indefatigable torrent of lost souls; all that remained on the street were their upturned cars and the bodies which the mass had shed away upon their deaths. "Wrath unites people." Roger expressed with an air of wisdom. Even if he himself was the only person in front of whom he could appear intelligent, Roger wasn't about to miss the opportunity.

Thankfully, his unrivalled ability to hide behind garbage bins served him well once again, and he thought about integrating this element to his classes, at extra cost naturally, when they would eventually resume. The crowd had passed him by without paying any mind to him, and it never occurred to Roger he simply wasn't an attractive addition to the grand mass, despite its overwhelming variety in members. It was likely better this way; maintaining high morale is important. With the immediate danger behind him and the headache-inducing screaming fading away into the depths of the streets, Roger knew what he had to do, though he had been putting it off fearing for his life, something he would never admit to anyone for the rest of his days. Not even to himself in front of a mirror. He knew the answer lay somewhere in the central underbelly of the town, behind, or beneath a non-existent slaughterhouse, and he knew it might turn out to be a one-way trip for him, wherever it was. The fear of his own mortality wasn't something he was used to struggling with, like most people, and the experience of overcoming cowardice in the face of true necessity is the kind of barbed gate everyone must go through for the first time. Not everyone comes out triumphant. A sense of shame washed over Roger as he began to redden, followed by confusion at the fact he was experiencing shame. A whole new world of uncomfortable sensations was opening up to him, and he hated every second of it. With his stolen baseball bat (and potential crime weapon) at the ready to double as his cane, Roger began the trek back in the general direction of the town centre.

Because of his unimpressive traversal pace, he decided it would be a good idea to use this time to make the kinds of reflections which might actually accomplish something besides massaging his tremendous ego. The first order of business was figuring out where the nearest slaughterhouse was, and to this end he decided to buy up some maps from local convenience stores. Fortunately for him, Hollow Crest wasn't the biggest town and there were only seven stores which might have qualified as the convenience type. Unfortunately for him, there were a whole seven store owners who were rarely happy to see him. His ankle was already whining at the thought of the coming journey. He asked it to be quiet. The first one was only a five-minute walk from Lisa's place, ten to fifteen minutes at Roger's pace. When he arrived in front of it, an idea came to him to help shorten the investigation, and he gave himself a literal pat on the back. The store was standing out in the open surrounded by a parking lot, which itself was surrounded by rows of houses packed so tightly they pressured alleyways out of existence. He walked inside the convenience store and was greeted with a double-barrelled shotgun pointed at his face.

"State yer business, jackass." the sixty-year-old store owner behind the counter was doing his best impression of a terrible Texan accent, complete with a plaid shirt, bell-bottom jeans and cowboy boots. He wasn't the kind of man to be messed around with.

"I come in peace, you shit-eater." Roger figured it was wisest to engage the man on his own level of intellect. Thankfully, he didn't wonder how it came so easily to him and attributed it to his unequalled talent of adaptability, proving himself worthy once again of his place in the hall of fame of mental gymnastics.

"I don't think them baseball bats be a sign o'peace." he pulled back on the imaginary pump of his double-barrelled shotgun and made a clicking sound with his mouth. It took Roger a few seconds to process it as a threat.

"It's not a baseball bat, it's my cane. I use it to walk. My ankle has been through more than I can describe to you. I'm just here to buy a map of the city. Surely, I don't have to explain to you the importance of my mission." Roger gave the man a slow and understanding nod after delivering his demands.

"Ye dun' look like a... uh... mapologist. Use yer computer like all dem stupid teenagers. I got enough prawblems here as it is. State yer real business, or get tha hell out!" his fake accent was starting to grate on Roger's nerves, who instantly pegged it as fake despite never having heard a true Texan accent in his lifetime.

"Do I look like one of your stupid teenagers? How about you tell me what problem you're dealing with here, I'll help you solve it, and then you won't shoot me and hand me a map. It's a matter of life and death. I'm asking you kindly, for now." it was increasingly difficult for him to hide his annoyance in the face of someone so intellectually-inferior to him.

"I ain't tellin' you mah prawblems, you chickenshit bootlicker!" with the gun still pointed at Roger, he quickly used one hand to grab an old folded up map beneath his desk and tossed it in his direction, hitting him in the left cheek in the process. "Now git! Git!" as a final warning sign he fired his gun into the ceiling, sending a cloud of dust scattering across the whole room. They both coughed for a few seconds.

"Thank you, mister Texas." unleashing a sound similar to a cat puking, Roger bent down and picked the map up, opening it on the spot to make sure he wasn't being duped. "This map is from 1967! I'm going to need something a little more recent. Also, I'm not paying for it, because I feel like I'm being duped now. Me, an honest, law-abiding, tax-paying citizen. You should be ashamed." Roger once read it was always beneficial to flip the tables in any kind of argument, and he did his best to follow this creed when he wasn't getting his way.

"The only one I got. I ain't tellin' you twice, now git!" the fake cowboy's eyes were lighting up with a kind of rage he probably once saw in a Western movie.

"This was the second time you told me. Technically, the third time, since the first time you said it twice. But..." mister Texas was about to say something, but Roger kept on going and interrupted him with tremendous success. "I think I've made my point clear here. Never try to dupe an honest citizen, we always get the upper hand." Roger turned around and, from the corner of his eye, saw a man's foot sticking out from behind one of the more distant shelves. Having had a gander at the type of problem the store owner was dealing with, he accelerated as much as he could and by his crippled standards, flew out of the store with his antiquated map in hand. He made a mental note to declare he wasn't willing to pay for items more often in the future; it seemed to work.

He opened the map from the bygone age in hopes it still remained current in the present day. According to the map, the convenience store in front of him was a church, and all the houses around him were nothing but barren soil. It was definitely not current. The more he looked at it, the more he saw things which hadn't been around for a long time anymore, as well as emptiness destined to be filled up in the decades to come. It was a window into a quasi-alien world, one he was certainly glad to have never been a part of. Life without the comfort and laziness afforded by modern technology? Inconceivable. He was just about ready to throw the map away right outside the convenience store, but something caught the eye of his subconscious, and he couldn't stop looking at the whole thing. While it may not have been current, perhaps it still held some truth in it, something which the eye of the present wouldn't even know to look for. At a first glance the design of Hollow Crest felt unremarkable, perhaps even a little random and impractical in certain sections. Many streets led to dead ends, and while some neighbourhoods had grid arrangement, others were more akin to unravelling spools of spaghetti. And yet, there was an undeniable overall cohesion to it, with all the different sectors interlinked, supporting each other's existence and development into what the town was destined to become in the modern age.

After about ten minutes of staring at the map and mentally complaining into the void about his ankle pain, Roger finally made his first crucial observation. All the smaller streets were connected to the bigger ones, and they, in turn, all connected to the slaughterhouse, which rested at the centre of town. Eventually, it was destined to turn into the Big Cow, whose owners became far more preoccupied with shedding milk rather than blood.

Chapter 26

Jerry had just barely set one of his feet outside the library, when a disturbing sight caused him to jump right back in, yelling for Laura with the piercing distress of a lost puppy. A few seconds later she appeared in front of him as if from thin air, calm, collected and robotic as the first time he had met her, which he could remember as if it happened yesterday. He once again felt a silly shame for his deplorable behaviour in a house of learning, but soon reminded himself that, unlike Roger, he actually had a reason for acting insane this one time.

"How can I help you now?" her facade of monotonous indifference began to give way to monotonous annoyance.

"We have to get out of here, no time to explain! Is there a back exit to this place? A secret bookcase maybe?" he could barely get his breathing under control.

"You will take the time to explain. Or I'll take the time to call the cops." her patience was obviously running thin, and understandably so. The library wasn't seeing many visitors these days, but it was still preferable to such an agitator.

"Damn it lady, this place is about to burst in flames, and you're worried about explanations?" he momentarily clutched at the base of his neck and bent over in pain. A few seconds later, it passed. "Come with me if you wan to live." He always dreamed of delivering that line in total honesty one day.

"No." Jerry's surface-level pop-culture reference wasn't enough of an argument, but then again, it was coming to a point where it wasn't necessary. A noise was approaching closer and closer from the outside, and for a moment Laura was excited at the prospect of other, more considerate customers to help out.

At a brisk pace she left Jerry planted in the middle of the room like yet another fixture among the empty reading tables and wooden chairs, unable to decide on whether he really wanted to go through the trouble of helping someone who would likely prove herself to be a contrarian at every possible turn. Unable to find in himself the apathy to simply leave her behind, he followed her to the front door, a few steps behind. She opened it, and her eyes widened in terror, finally showing a bit of emotion and assuaging Jerry's worries about her being a cyborg. The angry hive-minded mass was barrelling down the street, and was headed straight for the library. They were now close enough for their wrathful chant to be heard, and its illiterate lack of sense and cohesion broke Laura's heart. She jumped back, slammed the door shut and turned the key, which would do literally nothing to stop the advancing tide of regression. Turning to Jerry with a stare so savage and yet purposeful it reminded him of a documentary he once watched on Scientology, Laura stormed off somewhere in the twists, turns and book-lined rows of the library. She returned a few seconds later with a shiny revolver which looked like it had never been used. In her small hands the thing looked comically oversized, almost like a toy designed to intimidate would-be robbers and general scumbags. With the brave determination of a warrior meeting her destiny, she unlocked the door, marched out onto the porch and waited for the incoming doom to advance closer. This was her territory and she was going to fight for it, even if technically-speaking none of it actually belonged to her. In a more real sense, her territory wasn't marked by walls, ceilings nor ownership documents. Discovery, exploration, knowledge, education; this was her territory, and it had been declared war upon by the blind fury of mankind once again. Rational thought always stood in the way of exhilarating, raging madness, but which of the two was bound to triumph? At this moment, it was certainly appearing like the latter was taking the upper hand. Jerry joined her at the entrance, with the crowd now being close enough to make them feel uncomfortable.

"So, uh, got enough bullets for everyone?" he was trying to put his manliness on display and hide how worried he was to be a potential witness for multiple homicides.

"I definitely have enough for you." her burst of attitude made Jerry turn sideways and brought about an uncomfortable silence, only bloated by the raging crowd's demoralizing cacophony. She regretted it a little bit, but promised herself she would resist the urge to apologize for anything. "I apologize for this. But I always knew this day would come."

"*This* specific day? I knew about it too, it's always been on the calendar." he was intent on showing her he had some venom of his own to dispense. The crowd was inching ever closer, and even swallowed a few new members along the way since Roger had first seen it.

"..." she pursed her lips in frustration and gazed at him with more animosity than she did towards the real problem at hand. "I knew this day was coming because... I can't tell you why. Let's just say someone told me, and leave it at that." she knew there was no way Jerry was going to leave it at that, but he simply had no time to protest in the moment. If they didn't make a move soon, the crowd was going to swallow them up as well. "I can't let this place fall." she declared heroically as she fired a shot into the crowd, hitting a middle-aged woman in her clavicle and slowing her pace down. All in all, a rather ineffective attack. "Shit, I hoped they'd scatter." it only made them walk a little bit faster. "That was about that, I suppose. Follow me, there's a back exit." she seemed to take the entire situation rather well for somebody who supposedly couldn't afford failure. If anything, firing a shot at the crowd had livened up her senses. Frighteningly so.

"Finally going to show me your secret bookcase?" Jerry did his best to put on his seductive tone.

"Oh, please shut up." she appreciated it even less than she let on.

Jerry began running behind Laura after she locked the door again and took the lead, but after a second, he made her stop and wait for him as he went around to look for the first book he ever wanted to rent from the library. She wanted to tell him something, but he hushed her and ran off into the aisles. A few moments later he returned empty-handed, only to see her standing there with the book in her hands. Naturally, he didn't think to ask the librarian for it. With a curt nod of acknowledgement and gratitude, he motioned her to continue the great escape from the house of knowledge, the crowd now banging on its front doors; they were fancy and visually-evoking, but certainly not solid enough to withstand anything beyond a bit of wind and rain.

A few more seconds of running later, they found themselves at a dead end, and Jerry felt like no inconvenience nor incompetence should surprise him anymore. Before he could open his mouth and berate her, she pulled on a dusty tome and the secret bookcase exit started to open up with a slow creek. The mechanism was old, rusty and lazy, taking its sweet time to swing the shelf open, taunting them with the allure of freedom. Jerry tried to fill the silence and asked her if she had seen any good movies lately. He succeeded in only making the silence even more prominently aggressive. He wished she could at least curse at him and tell him how much of an idiot he was. Anything was preferable to this. Thankfully, the unstoppable force from the outside broke through the door; the sound of wood and glass being smashed gave him something to comment on, something she couldn't simply ignore.

"I hear them smashing the wood and glass. Come on, you can't simply ignore this." to Laura's chagrin, the door was only a quarter open now, and she could not, indeed, ignore what was happening there.

"I know. What do you expect me to do? Call a handyman?" this was, without a doubt, the most aggravating day in her life, and she was already thinking about all the bestselling stories she would write about it. A thought flashed through her mind out of the blue. "I wish I was stranded alone on a deserted island." she declared to Jerry, as if waiting for his response to conduct some test of character.

"Yeah, sounds good right about now." though he didn't have the greatest sense for conversing with women, even Jerry understood how unwelcome she felt his company was at this particular moment. The door was about halfway open, and they could now hear footsteps behind them as the crowd was spilling into the library.

"To hell with this." Laura started trying to squeeze herself through the gap before them which was still opening far too slowly. She wondered if whoever built it was a sadist and intended on giving people false hope. "I'm stuck." she unceremoniously informed Jerry a second later.

"Just wait a couple of seconds, it'll open further, no need to worry." despite knowing there was a tremendous need to worry, he nevertheless recognized the eternal importance for a man to be macho in all possible circumstances.

"Either kick me through or fight them off!" a hint of panic was detected in her voice. As it turned out, she was claustrophobic.

"Sure thing." Jerry gave her a good kick in the shoulder, and it finally pushed her past the door. He looked behind him, and could already see the mass spilling into the aisle. There was no time left; he had to squeeze through as well.

Sucking his stomach in and making himself as slender as can be, Jerry was about to try and fit through, but abandoned the idea before even starting it. Even at its fully opened position, which it was bound to reach within a year or so, it barely created enough of an entrance for Jerry to fit through. In this great hour of need, the pain in his neck made its grand entrance once again, firing him up like never before. Unleashing a primal, blood-curling scream which hurt his throat, he grabbed at the bookcase door, and used the element of pain to fuel the fire of manliness within him. He didn't tear it right out of the wall like he had hoped, but he did make it open just a bit faster and managed to squeeze through, nearly compressing himself into a pancake. Thankfully, the aisle he was standing in was narrow, and the angry mass, which he could hear wrecking the library already, was only able to pour towards him one person a time, sometimes coming to a halt as a second person tried to squeeze past the first. He did have to deliver a couple of kicks while pulling the door closed to keep them off, but on the whole, he and Laura made it through the ordeal rather successfully, if one didn't count the fall of the library as a failure, which Laura certainly did. Jerry hoped to see her on the other side of the door waiting for him, but alas, he found himself walking down stairs into a pitch-black darkness, and was forced to make a testosterone-fuelled effort not to whimper. He imagined a labyrinthine expanse stretching before him, complete with deadly traps and a roaming Minotaur for good measure. He called out into the darkness, but only heard his own echo in response. He tried to grasp at the walls, and ascertained he was surrounded by concrete which, at the very least, gave him more certainty he wouldn't end up as a cave-in victim. He called into the darkness for Laura once again.

"Laura! Answer me, damn it!" unwittingly, he was starting to sound like an overbearing husband trying to connect with his distant wife.

"I'm here!" from the darkness a voice reached him, but it was too distorted by the walls for Jerry to recognize it with certainty.

"Where is *here*? It's all dark, for Christ's sake!" he was starting to feel a little better about his own shortcomings.

"Follow the wall!" the voice from the darkness cried out again.

"Lord..." he whispered to himself. "There are two walls! Which one?!" he was just about ready to walk back into the library out of sheer exasperation, even if it was probably in the process of collapsing.

"I don't remember!" this was the last time the voice from the darkness would guide Jerry.

"Great! Thank you! Thank you very much!" Jerry thrust his face in the palm of his hand and was just about to sit down for a breather when he heard a scream in the blackness ahead, a scream he couldn't quite place, a scream which chilled him to the bone and made him stop in hesitation, regardless of how manly he was.

The only way to proceed was forward, and though he wasn't particularly afraid of the dark, he was certainly terrified by this specific darkness. Choosing the right wall to lean against, via the logic of being right-handed, he began to slowly advance onward, shuffling his feet like a zombie, afraid of tripping over anything or falling down a bottomless pit. The passage felt like it was inclined downwards ever so slightly, with the air becoming hotter, heavier and more nauseating with every step he took. He wondered whether this tunnel connected to the sewer system, hoping it wouldn't. Though the path was winding left and right, it remained straightforward the whole way through, and surprisingly enough, didn't seem to hold any traps in store for Jerry. The only problem was its progressive slope toward the bowels of the earth, leading him further and further away from the surface. His power of logical rationalization was put on full display during this descent, as he kept imagining the types of underground facilities which would have this sort of complex tunnel system, repeating himself he was getting closer and closer to a luxurious elevator which would take him out to the sweet air of freedom. He tried to will his idea into existence, but Roger's teachings failed him. He couldn't hear Laura any longer, neither her voice nor her footsteps in the dark. He assumed she was waiting for him at the exit, having walked faster by the power of being more courageous than he was.

After a few more minutes of meekly stumbling in pitch blackness and inhaling an increasingly oppressive atmosphere, a wave of uncomfortably unnatural heat began to pulse at him from the distance. He stopped for a moment, grasped around to get his bearings, and realized he had come at a four-way crossroad. He felt something wet dripping from his nose, and it smelled like iron. In an attempt to ascertain where exactly the source of the heat lay, he licked his finger and lifted it to the air. According to his scientific method of thermal detection, the source lay to the right of him, so naturally, he went in the opposite direction, and to his great relief the air felt like it was decompressing, becoming a little easier to breathe once again. The sharp pain in his neck which he had already forgotten about came right back out of nowhere just to remind him of its existence. It forced Jerry to stop for a moment while clutching his neck in agony, which had absolutely no alleviating effect. Just like the times before, a few seconds later it subsided, leaving his ears ringing with fear and disorientation rather than pain. He thought he heard a faint laughter followed by an offended cough somewhere behind him, but he had spent so long in the dark he had a difficult time trusting his senses. Time felt like it had come to a complete halt, the sense of touch slowly left his hands from being raked over concrete for so long, and he no longer had any idea of how much he had been walking. He figured this is what it must be like, to become nonexistent to the world above, to be free from all its rage, murder, envy, jealousy, greed, annoying colleagues, taxes, diseases, loud bikers, terrible books, death... and life. There were many things he was tired of, but for the sake of being totally fair to himself, he tried to look on the good side as well. He already missed the kindness, humour, friendship, love, annoying colleagues, taxes, loud bikers and terrible books. He felt conflicted by the idea life wasn't exclusively terrible nor flawless, but was starting to accept the notion. Subsequently, he also remembered he was, as a human being, doted with a survival instinct, and soon it would prod him to move along back into the land of existence, surrounded by the living. After all, he doubted there was either food or a toilet to be found down here, and he thought it would have been rather ungentlemanly to die without either.

He got up, placed his right hand on the wall, and proceeded to move further in the direction where the air was getting lighter and lighter. The hint of a metallic taste appeared in his mouth, and he hoped really hard the spontaneous bleeding would get itself back under control. He had no time for such concerns. Though his hand was almost completely robbed of sensation at this point, he could tell the texture of the walls had changed ever so slightly, some tiny patches being smoother than others. His heart then raced with excitement as his feet stepped on a floor inclined upwards at a forty-five-degree angle. It felt slippery and unstable, but with both hands pressed on the walls to his sides, Jerry brought the inner athlete out of himself and started the laborious crawl upwards. His thighs and calves were on fire, and he regretted not having spent more time working out; he should have known he'd end up in a situation like this. However, all the pain in the world was washed away the second he saw a hint of light, something his eyes had mostly forgotten in the unknown amount of time they spent in its absence. Thankfully, the increase of light was rather gradual, and he didn't have to deal with pain in his eyes as they adjusted to it. One more victory for the little guy. After a minute or so of climbing, he finally reached an old rusted grate, and gave it a good, frustrated push and flung it open. Exhausted, covered in sweat, grime, and a strange blood-like slime, he emerged from the bowels of Hollow Crest and took a moment to just splay himself on the ground and catch his breath. Wherever he had ended up, it was large, empty, and he noticed the only source of illumination was coming from a few hanging light bulbs which seemed at odds with the rest of the room.

After dreaming for a few minutes and musing on how proud he was of himself for having made it through the ordeal, he remembered about Laura, and sat up to look around, but unfortunately, she was nowhere to be seen. She might have gotten lost down there, but he knew there wouldn't be any rescue party without an actual light source. Besides, he told himself, she was the kind of lady to shoot into crowds of people and apparently knew this day was coming; she'd be just fine on her own. Looking around the room a little more attentively, Jerry realized he was actually sitting on what appeared to be a large dish or platform, curved downwards ever so slightly towards the grate he had crawled out from. There were some large metal machines which he couldn't clearly identify. As a matter of fact, the entire place seemed to be made out of old and rusted metal, with its ability to stand up against the ravages of father time being nothing short of supernatural. Jerry briefly pondered on whether or not this could be chalked up as proof for the existence of the divine, and then realized he had more pressing matters to worry about. With the ache in his muscles having subsided a little bit, he stood upright and decided to look for the exit to the room. The light bulbs weren't showing him much, but he did spot a ladder which seemed like it led to yet another grate. There was more light coming from this one, and he could even spot a well-lit ceiling which seemed to him vaguely familiar for some reason. He put his fingers through the grate to get a good grip, and gave it a push upwards as hard as he could. It budged only by a centimetre, giving Jerry the impression it was locked from the other side. He got a good grip again, and before he could give it another push a shoe came stomping down on his fingers, causing him to scream in both pain and terror, giving his voice a strange frequency he himself had heard. He didn't however, let go of the grate, and within a moment a flashlight was shining down at him through it.

“Don't move! This is the Hollow Crest Police Department! Come out with your hands off the bars and in the air!” a familiar voice bellowed from the other side of the grate.

“I would, if I could open it.” Jerry managed to hide his pain through gritted teeth.

“Stand aside, perpetrator!” the owner of the voice from the other side slid something, and pulled the grate open. “What the hell is this?” Officer Tim seemed perplexed and in dire need of a few hours of sleep.

“Jeremiah Baxter, plumber extraordinaire, at your service.” he explained as he nonchalantly climbed out and propped himself up against a nearby wall with a gun still pointed at him.

“Well, well, well. What a coincidence, just the man I've been looking for.” Officer Tim holstered his weapon, feeling evidently no threat from the suspect who had essentially appeared out of thin air. “But let me guess. You're not *actually* a plumber, are you?”

“Got me there, officer.” he gravely nodded.

“So, what *are* you doing here?” he pointed an accusatory finger toward the hole in the floor, as if it was responsible for spitting the man out into the world.

“I work here. This is my regular commute.” Jerry had finally recognized the walls and ceilings. He was in a sector of the Big Cow he virtually never saw, one dealing with certain packaging and manufacturing processes which had been explained to absolutely nobody outside of those working with them. It made the whole thing look a lot more suspicious than it needed to be.

“Hmm... we'll verify that...” Officer Tim nodded thoughtfully as he was scribbling on his notepad the words “sewer commute” followed by three question marks. “And in what capacity do you work here, Mister Baxter?”

“Security guard. Helluva job, right?” he cracked a friendly smile which was reciprocated with a serious frown.

“Right. So technically-speaking, everything which has happened here was your fault, correct? You're the security guard, and the security of the place has been compromised. We haven't even caught all the cows yet.” Officer Tim was laying a clever trap and was about to perhaps bag the most important culprit he had ever come across in his life.

“Yeah, I'm a regular patriot for bovine freedom.” he couldn't help but sigh at the absurdity of the question.

“Hmm... yes, we'll verify this, too.” Officer Tim's notepad was seeing a lot of action today. “Well, that's the small talk over with. Now, for the real question. Do you know Roger Silver? I know you do, don't deny it.” he was now pointing his pen directly at Jerry's forehead.

“I do know him, I'm not denying it.” his sole concern was avoiding contact with the tip of the pen.

“That's right, don't deny it, I have your confession now.” his eyes lit up as if he was on the verge of uncovering a deep-seated conspiracy at the core of human existence. “Do you know where he is? Are you harbouring a fugitive down there with you? Is he down there, through the grate? Don't lie to me, I'll know, I've taken lie detection courses and am a certified lie detector." he was dead-serious about it.

"Oh, you mean the course consisting of five videos of five minutes each? Yeah, I also took it a while back." though Jerry knew what course he was talking about, he had never taken it, for he at least wasn't susceptible enough to be conned out of a hundred dollars.

"Ah, a fellow... connoisseur, I see." for a moment, Officer Tim let his guard down and was charmed by Jerry for being the first and only person who recognized what he was talking about. "Ahem. Yes, well, don't try and change the subject on me. You haven't answered my questions about Roger." he thought he did a good job of catching himself slipping and putting his professional air back on before anyone noticed.

"Yeah, he was down there with me, but he was too tired to make the climb up, so I told him to rest a bit. He should be about halfway recharged. He might not be down there anymore though, if he heard you talking." Jerry had an amazing idea.

"Well then, I suppose you'll have to climb down and fetch him for me." Officer Tim turned it into a terrible idea.

"I can't, I'm afraid of heights, and the dark." the tables were turned right back once again.

"But you literally just came out of there, and you claim this is your normal commute. How do you explain that?" the good officer's instincts told him something wasn't right here.

"I'm not going in there, I came out of there. And I came out of there, because I'm afraid of the dark, so I couldn't stay in the dark. I'm also afraid of heights, so I couldn't stay on the ladder, and had to climb out. You see, I was already in there, and since I'm afraid of being in there, I had to leave, and I can't go back in." he hoped the chain of logic was sound.

"How did you end up there in the first place, then?" Officer Tim was now massaging his temples, trying to take it all in.

"It's my regular daily commute." Jerry explained after a brief moment of silence. He gave the officer a puzzled look, trying to suggest he was the crazy one for not following his logic.

"I'm... going down there. You stay right here, I only have one set of handcuffs and I'd rather use them on Roger. I mean it, you don't move from here." it had never occurred to Tim people could give honest promises without ever keeping them.

"I promise, honestly." he really did make it sound believable and good-natured.

"Thank you for your cooperation, I'll be sure to make note of it." he declared, while making zero note of it in his little pad. He opened the grate, and commenced the climb down in search of Roger. Jerry waited a few moments until the officer was on the lower rungs of the ladder, and left the room in search of a more familiar area of the factory, one he could get to an exit from.

Upon finding an unassuming and barely visible door in the corner, he took his chances and crossed through, finding himself in a brightly-lit hallway, which in turn brought him to the janitor's closet. On the other side of the closet opposite to him was another door, and a familiar sight of relief finally appeared before his eyes when he entered it: the men's bathroom so many hours had been spent in hiding from the cameras. The perks of being paid by the hour. Finally, he was back on his own territory again, but even so, things didn't feel entirely right; the air was thick and unwelcoming, lodging itself with contempt inside his lungs and almost refusing to leave when exhaled. Unfortunately though, he still had nowhere to go but forward, and it was only a matter of hours before Officer Tim would realize Roger wasn't, in fact, down where he went looking for him. Taking as deep and unsatisfying a breath as he possibly could, Jerry pushed the door out of the bathroom open and was greeted by a sight equal parts mystifying, beautiful, and terrifying. He found himself in the main production area, only it appeared more like a slaughterhouse, the bodies trampled by hoof marks strewn about here and there; the unlucky ones who didn't have time to escape before the great uprising. Jerry couldn't decide what was more worrying between this and the fact a couple of cows remained there, planted still, in perfect peace and harmony where the workers usually stood. He couldn't even be certain they were alive, but assumed they were since he couldn't afford to take any chances. For the moment they paid him no attention, but he knew his good fortune could change in an instant. If Officer Tim had the wits to get past them, so did he... assuming the good officer hadn't been chased into the room where Jerry met him.

 With the grace of a cat in severe need of a diet, he pressed his back along the wall and began to slither down towards the door to the locker rooms, which would eventually lead him to the reception area, and hopefully to the outside world once again. How he already missed it in all of its infinite stupidity and human error; it was part of him, and he was part of it, whether he liked it or not, and he certainly didn't like it. He wondered how his good friends had been getting along, how his mother was doing in her beauty salon in the Bahamas, and whether or not Laura had died down there in the tunnels. He felt like a bit of a wimp for not braving the dark and ultimately falling victim to the same fate as her, and made a mental note to do something courageous sometime soon. Maybe he'd repair the library in her honour. Or perhaps plant a tree. Whichever was cheaper. He didn't know her *that* well, unfortunately. She was also the kind of woman to shoot into a crowd without hesitation. He mused about making it a smaller tree, and settled on buying a cactus and naming it in Laura in her honour. The profoundly introspective meditation he was having managed to divert his attention from the surreal danger he was surrounded by, and before he knew it he was only a few steps away from the locker room door. Upon reaching it, he realized it was the women's locker room, and with the fear of being branded a pervert outweighing everything else, he took the few extra steps to the men's locker room instead. He waved goodbye to the cows, who had nothing to say to him in return.

 To contrast with everything he had just seen, the locker room was a welcome sight of cleanliness and organization, as if it had just been thoroughly scrubbed a few minutes before he got there. The janitor certainly wasn't the kind of man to shirk his duties. He went to his locker to see if it had anything he might want to take with him. For starters, there was a small backpack, with an old wooden police baton and a flashlight. Those were his tools to fight the crime which never showed up at the factory. After carefully shoving inside the bag the book he had been holding under his shirt since the library, he crossed over into the reception area, only to be greeted by a squad of policemen, all pointing their guns at him. He never knew the town had so many of them to begin with. The searchlights all turned directly at his retinas started to give him a headache, and he had a difficult time hearing all the conflicting instructions the cops were shouting at him. One of them threw an unprompted flash grenade at him to the chagrin of his colleagues, and for a few moments everyone was writhing around in total pain and disorientation. Jerry's neck took the opportunity to give him a few more seconds of suffering. Finally, one of the men bravely stepped forward, his gun held in a shaky hand and pointing at Jerry, only to grab him and shove him in the back of a car. He was happy to finally be relaxing on a warm and comfortable seat, especially since they had apparently forgotten to cuff him, and couldn't help but lay on his side and fall asleep. He momentarily dreamt of himself starring in a beef jerky commercial, until he was fortunately woken up by another officer pulling him out of the car and calmly leading him next to a pillar, a bit further away from all the commotion.

"I am detective Holmes. Sherlock Holmes." the man informed Jerry while presenting a gaping smile missing a few teeth, worthy of the Victorian England stereotype every step of the way.

"I'm General Bonaparte. Napoleon Bonaparte." Jerry put one hand behind his back and the other on his chest while thoughtfully gazing out into the distance.

"A clever ruse, if I've ever seen one, my dear chap." detective Holmes was clearly a local, but was doing his best to put on a vaguely British accent. His best was far from being good enough, or even remotely good, for that matter. "But I know you are not Napoleon... for you are too tall!" he cracked a smile and hoped his heavy-handed sense of humour, self-appraised as the most refined in town, wasn't too refined for the lowly likes of Jerry.

"It's the only logical response to meeting the renowned Sherlock Holmes in person. You're missing your deerstalker hat though. That's a few points off your total." he was still uncertain if he was dealing with someone whose parents thought it a good idea to name their son after a fictional character, or a simple, run-of-the-mill extravagant detective whose investigative abilities were only surpassed by his incompetence.

"Come now, as I'm certain you know, I am far too young and real to be Sherlock Holmes. I legally changed my name whence I made detective, and am exploring the logistics of opening up my own private practice. Say, would you be interested in legally changing your name to Doctor John Watson?" the question was an entirely serious one, and demanded a serious answer.

"I'll think about it. For the moment though, Jeremiah Baxter suits me fine." he never did think about it further.

"Ah-hah! You have revealed your name to me without me even needing to ask it." he closed his eyes and played an imaginary applause in his head. "And how can you explain your presence here, mister "Baxter"? Do make it a convincing one, I shall know if you're lying." his eyes did have a certain truth-seeking character to them. There was a chance a competent detective was hiding somewhere behind the façade of a buffoon.

"I work here." he opened the bag he was still carrying, and took out his ID from a hidden inside pocket, certifying to detective Holmes he was indeed an employee. After about a minute of holding his identification in his outstretched arm for the detective to study, he got tired and put it back in his bag. "Heard there was a commotion here. I'm the security guard, as you probably know by now. Thought I could do something to help the situation. I couldn't. So, I grabbed my things and left. Then I got assaulted by ten policemen for no reason. That's my story, detective, and I'm only saying it once." he was afraid he'd get details mixed up if he was made to repeat it again and again, one of the most effective interrogation techniques known to man.

"Would you like to know how I know you're telling the truth right now?" the chance to educate someone on his methods always gave the detective a thrill unlike anything else.

"Not really, I don't. I just want to go home, get some sleep, and start looking for a new job, just in case I end up with the shit of end the stick here. I'm leaving now." without receiving permission he already turned to leave.

"I haven't given you permission to leave." He whipped out his badge and identification, which Jerry should have probably asked him for at the start of the conversation. "We're not done here yet."

"Lord have mercy." Jerry eyes made contact with the detective's, holding his stare for a second, and then rolled towards the ceiling.

"Save your wits for the gallows, friend, you'll need it." the dramatic declaration had no visible effect on Jerry's appraisal of the situation. "Well, I'm sure you'll hang, one day, in some fashion or another. But for now, tell me, did you see another constable in there?" his needless usage of British and sometimes archaic terms shrilled into Jerry's ears.

"A con... why yes, sire, I did see another constable in there, by the name of Timothy. He went down a grate and I never heard from him again." the detective was too enamoured with himself to realize he was in the process of being mocked.

"And why did he go down the grate?" he squinted his eyes and brought his face within inches of Jerry's.

"Because he was looking for either a fugitive, or an adventure, I can't rightfully remember which. As a matter of fact, I can't remember much of anything and think I have a concussion from the flash grenade one of your men threw at me." he realized it was time to cut this conversation short; this was one detective capable of talking his ears off until the end of time.

"That was me. I threw the grenade." his confession was coloured by pride rather than guilt.

"Ow! I'm feeling extremely nauseous and dizzy, with a hint of vomiting coming up. If you'll excuse me, mister Holmes, I must find my way to the hospital now." once again, without waiting for his permission, he turned around and started to leave.

"I haven't given you permission to leave yet." the detective didn't like others dictating terms. He waited a minute while pretending to be thinking something over in his head, though he had made all of his brilliant decisions and deductions long ago. "I am now giving you permission to leave." he brought his hand up to his temple and gave him an army salute. Briskly, he turned one hundred and eighty degrees, marched towards his colleagues, and relayed to them what Jerry had told him about Officer Tim. Two of the policemen began to suit up in some heavy-duty gear and check their equipment.

With the episode now behind him, Jerry turned around and finally got a good look at the town for the first time in a while. The Big Cow stood on a slight hill at the centre, and considering there were no large buildings or skyscrapers, the industrial facility ironically offered the best possible view of the area, and tourists were even led up to its roof, the few times they did end up stranded in Hollow Crest. At first sight, the city looked the same as it always did, largely devoid of activity, with the buildings, stores and houses standing tall like Jerry always remembered them. Together, they mixed and matched to make up a sprawling landscape which almost made the city look bigger than it was in reality. However, he couldn't shake the feeling that something was different, and soon he managed to figure out what it was: the thick plumes of smoke rising from various points in the distance. They weren't always there. It seemed obvious in retrospect. At first, he thought they were the result of barbecue fires, until he realized they only looked so small because they were far away. He was exhausted; it was a lot of physical activity he went through in such a short amount of time.

He noticed a bench to the side, under an inviting patch of shade, and he finally sat down for a good bit of uninterrupted rest. He felt depressed and discouraged at the sight of his town being torn apart from within by its very own inhabitants, and he began to wonder how much of a push they really needed to allow their inner violent nature to fly. Nearly every human being has potential within them for both extreme good and evil, but for some reason, most of us like to think we're only capable of one or the other. We breed suffering like an endless commodity and dish it out across the entire world, through the whole range of species, races, living and nonliving beings. It's quite fortunate we haven't mastered intergalactic travel to any significant level. If we did, we'd manufacture and deliver our purest and highest quality suffering to the ends of the universe. We've been soaking the Earth in blood, guts and misery since we've had the wherewithal to bludgeon and stab our peers. Suffering breeds wrath, which in turn, only breeds more suffering. We're primed to dish out hatred for things we are told should not be. But how long until we do away with ourselves as the things which should not be? A self-inflicted extinction isn't all too far away, it might not even require tanks, war planes, aircraft carriers, nor soldiers; only the ravaging potential of human emotion and ignorance. Jerry wondered if humanity deserved as much, and under the crushing weight of his cumbersome thoughts he fell into a peaceful and gentle slumber, right there on the bench, under the shadow of the tree.

Chapter 27

Naomi felt sickened as she tried to swallow one large gulp of air after the next, the thick atmosphere of the town shearing her throat like a thousand razor blades. The oxygen itself was taking on a poisonous aspect, and it seemed every square inch of air around her was pressing down violently on her body in an honest attempt to disintegrate her. This annoyed her greatly. She was still standing outside Betty's door, though she wondered whether it was still accurate to think of her as such. The old lady seemed have turned into something rather offensive and off-putting, giving hints of latent murderous ambitions in the process. Was her real personality finally shining through, or was she too, a victim of the fate befalling the rest of the town? Few, if any, had predicted the emergence of such a maelstrom, and even now that it was here, all around her and them, they still failed to notice it, all too complacent and happy to be sucked into its vortex. Most people don't even need a reason to show their violent nature; they only need to be spurred to it as part of a greater movement. Speaking of the greater movement, Naomi turned her head to look down the street and saw the giant mass of hateful, contorted and cheering faces spilling in her direction. It had grown a fair size since her friends had successfully avoided it, now numbering hundreds and hundreds of members. The hive mind kept on rolling and consuming, fulfilling its senseless purpose as an agent of violent assimilation. Naomi looked at the congregation and felt like a deer stuck in headlights for a moment, unable to move an inch. Suddenly, she heard a knock behind her, and turned around to see Betty banging on the little glass window at the top of the door. She smiled pleasantly and pointed at the oncoming crowd. Naomi flipped the middle finger at her, and started to run down in the street in the opposite direction. Her shoulder wasn't doing her any favours, though it did seem somewhat less bothersome to her ever since she stepped outside the house. Thankfully, her mind was, at the moment, distracted by more important matters and didn't pay any heed to pain nor discomfort. She wasn't a particularly gifted athlete, but she could run fast when she had to do, and soon enough she had lost herself in the winding streets and uninspired alleyways of Hollow Crest.

She stopped for a moment to catch her breath, and clutched at her side in a vain attempt to improve her recovery from a cramp, a lifelong nemesis of hers. She wondered if the outside world had any inclination as to what was happening here, or perhaps more worryingly, whether the outside world was going through the same thing. There was also the possibility people on the outside did know, but couldn't bring themselves to care about such a small and insignificant town. Cities with dozens of millions of people exist all around the world; what is one whose population is measured in thousands worth in the grand scheme of things? If it doesn't hit close to home, why bother reacting? Yes, most likely, she told herself, this was how it was all unfolding. She guessed the military cordoned the place off completely because they were dealing with some kind of chemical warfare, but she suspected the cause of it all was much more insidious. It was almost as if it had all been conjured, in one way or another, by the sullied path of destruction and cannibalism our recent ancestors, and those before them had been following; something, or someone, pushed the rotten fruits of this path to the surface. Maybe they could only stay hidden and buried for so long. Whatever the precise case was, the big picture was starting to become increasingly clear in her mind, while at the same time slowly robbing her of hope a remedy could be found. She wasn't about to lay down her arms and wave the white flag, but she wanted to do something more than go down with the ship and become absorbed into the mindless horde, which seemed increasingly inevitable in the end. "Well, at least I'll always have this option." she mused sarcastically. The streets were now mostly empty, but it felt different from before. Whereas the silent nature of the town was formerly born from the inner peace of its denizens, now a grounding fear was reigning supreme. The sounds of hammers and nails along with occasional faint screams and sobs came from behind the walls of the houses turned into shelters, and not tombs, she hoped. Some were preparing to keep the zeitgeist out and ignore it, others were all too keen to join it.

With her head spinning she hadn't taken the time to ascertain her surroundings, and upon doing so she realized she made it to the old ostracized quarter of Hollow Crest, one of the founding neighbourhoods of the actively crumbling city. Once a trading hub and shopping district, now it was home to low-income housing and served as an enclosure for all the city's undesirables, the elements which didn't fit in, the gears with no matching mechanism. Every town has these types of people, but what can anyone do? They too, have the right to live. The buildings themselves were all five floors-tall with no elevators, their crimson brick walls in dire need of maintenance and repairs. Naomi rarely dared to venture here, and could hardly remember the last time she had visited the place. For most people, it was an invisible part of town whose existence they forgot about the second they learned of its slightly higher crime rate, even if the crimes weren't too serious in their nature. It didn't serve as a prison for undesirables, but rather, as a refuge for the lost who were likely to stay that way.

Despite knowing where she was, Naomi felt a soothing relief beginning to wash over her, and the air itself seemed to have gotten lighter; it was no longer burning and slashing her throat with every breath. For the first time in a little while, she actually felt safe, and her muscles which had been tensed up for far too long relaxed themselves. She fell unconscious like an ungainly sack of potatoes. She had a dream about Roger, who came to her dressed exactly how a child would describe a pirate. She laughed at him, and he stood dejected for a moment. This was the extent of it. Naomi never had any meaningful dreams in her life.

She sensed people gathering up around her, and heard voices from the beyond deciding on her fate. She just wanted some sleep, and mustered the final remnants of her strength to kindly ask the otherworldly figures to shut the hell up. In a matter of seconds, her body went from feeling granite-heavy to feather-light, and in hear dream Naomi was floating through an endless void which smelled of gasoline, and occasionally, dumpster bins. She quite enjoyed this new arrangement for her life, and after pondering whether or not she ought to remain a vegetable for the rest of her days, wisely decided against it. In what seemed like only a split second later she opened her eyes and found herself in a cramped, dank room on a surprisingly clean wooden bed. The dim light of the evening crept through the windows and illuminated a night stand with a glass of water on it, along with a plate of dried mystery meat and bagels. Not the oddest meal she ever had, and with her ravenous hunger giving her little choice in the matter, she almost instinctively began to stuff it all down her throat. After washing it down with the water marked by a suspicious twinge of chlorine, she got up out of bed and stumbled stealthily toward the door, behind which she heard unfamiliar voices. Without a second thought, she burst through the doorway, her eyes still-half closed, only to be faced with a family of a husband, his wife, a grandmother, an uncle, four children, three cats, a Shih Tzu and a parakeet. They watched her in astonished silence, and she returned the favour. The dog was the first to break the silence, barking at her in an uncertain and menacing tone, conflicted about her presence, and sensing his owners' apprehension as well. She then noticed something strange and perhaps a tiny but unsettling: there didn't seem to be any electricity in the house. All the lights were off, no television nor radio was heard, no computers turned on, nor were there any electric clocks to be seen. Candles were already laid out in strategic places, and with the setting sun the grandmother was poised to light them all, following a carefully-elaborated routine which evidently held some meaning to her. The house seemed quite small, and Naomi couldn't fathom how it accommodated so many people without sending them at each other's throats. On the contrary, they seemed about as happy and at peace as anyone she had seen in the past few days. Yet another miracle of the human race. The children, having already gotten over the shock of her presence, resumed playing the games they were so entranced with. Naomi figured it was time to speak up.

"Hables Espagnol?" she gave it her best guess.

"What? We're locals." the uncle retorted, stepping into a ray of light, flashing his coarse and weathered face at her.

"Oh, my apologies then." she looked at him with embarrassed eyes, and he gave her the international nod of forgiveness. "Could you tell me where I am? What happened to me? Who you are? Why do you have no electricity? I'm sure I can come up with more questions, if you give me some time."

"For starters," the father spoke up with a heavy and commanding voice "you're in our house. You passed out on the street and the people brought you here. You slept for three whole hours! How lazy can people get?!" his indignation delivered through furrowed eyebrows gave her an unexpected slap on the psyche. "First you eat our food, now you complain about electricity? If I had my electric drill right now, I'd-" thankfully he didn't manage to finish the sentence before being interrupted by grandmother.

"I didn't raise you to be a crybaby! You'll have to excuse him," she turned her massively overweight frame to Naomi, "but he's a bit of a crybaby. It's all my fault, I should have never signed him up for badminton as a child. He was never the same since." she shook her head with the heavy burden of someone marked for life by a terrible mistake. "There's no electricity, sweetheart, because we've been completely cut off from the outside world. In every way possible." her calm enunciation helped to soften the blow of the news.

A cold sweat instantly passed over Naomi's brow. "What do you mean, cut off in every way possible?"

"Just before the power went out, we were constantly watching the news. The town has degenerated, so many people have gone mad, so much violence..." she shook her head once again, this time with zealous disapproval. "If there are any normal people left, they've barricaded indoors and are hoping to wait this whole thing out. But they'll run out of food. The situation went out of hand so quickly, the military was called in, and they've blocked all the exits. The journalist even said they were thinking of putting a glass dome over us, just to make sure. Then, just before the power went out, he said the decision was made to put our town completely off the grid. No electricity, no food, no water, no nothing. We're a small town, and we only have so much in stock. We might as well be on a deserted island." she nodded at Naomi with her lips pursed, thus driving home the gravity of the situation.

"Do they know what's happening? Is there some kind of bio-warfare going on? A new disease? Lack of proper education? Psychic gangs? What is it?" she really didn't like where all of this was going. With the arrival of the military, it felt like an imperceptible timer had started.

"My dear, the journalist knew nothing. I can't even be sure he wasn't making all of it up. But that's probably what they'll say no matter what it is. A new disease or some... psycho bio warfare agent by the CIA. Whatever it was, it swallowed us up and took us back to the dark ages. Sometimes they flicker back on, but only for a second, then everything shuts off again." she began to light the candles around the room.

Naomi looked out the window. "This part of town doesn't look too bad. Actually, it doesn't look affected at all, ignoring the whole electricity thing." her brain was immediately firing on all cylinders trying to figure out why.

"You got that right, it's the only safe place... shit!" she somehow managed to burn herself with a match. "You're welcome to stay here with us, I see you're of a tough kind, maybe you could teach my son to toughen up a bit!" she enunciated the last part loud enough for his benefit.

"Mother!" the prodigal son objected, but in vain. All ears were deaf to his protests.

"I don't know if I can, I have some friends out there... and, well, you won't believe me, and I don't care, so I'll tell you. My friends and I, we might have provoked the start of this. Or we failed at preventing the start of this. Or we simply witnessed it. We're still uncertain. About a lot of things. Most things, in fact. I don't think there's a manual for this scenario. But we did seem to get a bit of a forewarning," she grasped her shoulder, which suddenly starting pulsating with a few doses of overdue suffering. "they're still out there, and I can't leave them behind. It isn't right. My parents were cultists, I have to be better, otherwise my life would be a waste. Do you understand?" Naomi's frenzied eyes gazed deep into the grandmother's soul.

"I do, my child, I do understand." the grandmother understood only that she started to have second thoughts about letting her stay.

"When I find them, can I bring them here?" her voice suddenly took on a pleading character.

The grandmother wisely looked out the window, and pretended to mull it over in her head. She knew her answer in advance considering her unwavering adherence to principles of kindness, but wanted to put on the air of a careful and thoughtful person. "If they're alright and promise not to eat much. But you'll have to take turns using the bed in the guest room, or sleep on the floor." part of her was taught to always offer her hospitality to people in need, but another was really hoping she wouldn't have to.

"It's a deal." Naomi quickly blurted as she grabbed and shook her wrinkly hand. "Could I please have a flashlight? It's getting dark out there." grandmother obliged. Determined the find the only two people who, for better or for worse, she actually cared about, she marched on out through the door and back out into the streets.

So long as she stayed in the neighbourhood of the forgotten, as she had started referring to it personally in her head, she felt quite safe and even cozy in a certain sense, the kind of coziness one can feel when surrounded by genuine kindness. She thought about where she could find Jerry and Roger. The electricity in the town was out, and night was starting to settle in. The grandmother was right. The street lights did periodically flash, but for no more than a second. Darkness was wrapping its way over the town, and soon, she mused, people would come out with good old-fashioned fire torches and bring the whole show to a close. She remembered Jerry was supposed to have gone to the library, and though it was a long shot at this stage, she still believed it was her best chance to find him. Like most of the places in town, it wasn't too far away from where she was... and like just about every place in this town, it was out there, where things weren't safe. Where a swelling mass of incomprehensibly angry townsfolk was roaming about, moulding and congealing together into one grotesque organism capable of only absorption and annihilation. This sighting alone must have been enough to get the military closely-involved, she figured correctly. Besides, who knows what other devils might be roaming the evening, many times more terrifying than any Jehovah's Witness? And yet, she was driven onward by a simple fact: all and everyone she had to live for were in this town, and she'd end up profoundly bored and empty should it all disappear. This fate terrified her to the core, more than death itself.

Taking care to conserve her batteries, Naomi could still make her way using the dim light of the evening for the moment, and she had trouble believing just how much the town had changed in the last few hours. Streets were nigh-unrecognizable, littered with the dead and wounded, with nobody around to tend to them. Windows were either smashed or barricaded with shoddy planks barely capable of stopping a toddler. Down the street, a group of people seemed intent on burning down a watch shop for the express purpose of flushing out its owner. He had long caused them headaches with his eternally-delayed promises of repairs, and they had the bright idea of making him pay for it all. Naomi carried on. What could she do? One can't stop all the mad people in the world. One must stop the madness, if they are to stop anything at all. Random pieces of trash and rubble, with occasional pieces of clothing and dirty bandages were strewn about and seemed to crowd every square inch of space where Naomi had a mind to place her foot. To her relief, she did see a couple of other people like herself, furtively moving along the streets and trying to avoid certain death. She directed them to the neighbourhood of the forgotten, and had to remind them such a place did indeed exist in this town. They pretended to trust her.

She was just about five minutes away from the library when she was passing a store with its windows shattered. A hand shot out from the darkness and grabbed her by the hair. The arm felt strong and sinewy, and Naomi was dead certain it was covered in ashes and grease, though she had no specific reason to believe this. She noticed the edges of the shop's window frames still housed long and sharp glass shards. In a moment of unusual clarity, she threw her whole bodyweight forward, bearing the pain in her scalp and pulled the arm along with her, right into the jagged protrusions. She didn't turn to see the damage she had caused, but it was obviously sufficient as it made the arm retreat with a piercing howl back into darkness. Feeling empowered and with nobody to express herself to, Naomi yelled into the black void inside the shop: "Anyone else want some?!" clenching her fists in nervous anticipation. Satisfied and relieved at the lack of answer, she continued on her way, paying much closer attention now to any windows on her path. It was getting darker still, and it was time to bring the flashlight into play.

When she finally arrived at the library, her heart sank and dropped momentarily. Its doors had been shredded into nothing but chips and splinters, and she could already see from a distance the mess which had been made inside. Not a single book nor shelf was spared the collective rage of the rabble which passed through the building, and finding anything at all in there felt like asking for a miracle. Nevertheless, Naomi pressed onward, and began to climb over the overturned piles of furniture, loose pages and covers; the concept of total chaos materialized. After a few preliminary hello's shouted at random, she felt confident the place was indeed empty and started scanning it with a more thorough approach. There was a sense of relief at not seeing any signs of death or wounding, but the destruction felt like it harboured a different sort of aggression, something primal and profoundly anchored in human nature, something capable of holding hatred against the sacred concepts of learning and knowledge. Few things can claim to be as vile.

With her head lost in her own philosophical musings about the evil men can do, she barely reacted to the loud knock which seemed to come from somewhere deep within the library. For the second knock she stood at complete attention, her back stiff and coiled, ready to run away at the speed of an Olympic champion. Her hand shaking slightly, she gathered the resolve to proceed, and was enticed further by another, stronger knock. After wandering for a minute, Naomi thought she identified the source of the sound: a bookshelf which seemed strangely intact compared to the others. The knock sounded again, coming from the other side. The bookshelf moved slightly, and a woman's pleading groan was heard on the other side. Another knock. And another. Each time, the shelf moved further and further, and Naomi realized she was looking at a shockingly-stereotypical secret door. She tried grabbing onto the edge with her fingertips and pulling it back, but her help ended up being more symbolic than anything else. Finally, after giving what felt like every ounce of her body and soul to the effort, Naomi stumbled back as the door swung wide open and a young woman emerged, falling to the ground with staggering momentum. She murmured to herself "They'll never have my library...".

Chapter 28

Jerry awoke a couple of hours later, still on the bench, from a gentle prodding in his knee cap. The air had gotten cooler, and he noticed a large and imposing figure towering above him, leaning awkwardly on a baseball bat and shifting from left to right in a stance of discomfort. It took him no more than a few seconds to recognize Roger, who instantly plopped down next to him, letting out a big sigh of relief in the process and grabbing his ankle to prop it up on his knee. He looked at the strange swelling on his skin, then at Jerry, then back at his ankle with righteous indignation.

"Can you believe this shit?!" Roger decided if there ever was a time to skip the pleasantries, it was now.

"I can, Roger. I see it." Jerry was still half-asleep and was considering turning this bench into his new temporary home. He felt his pockets for a smoke. No luck. Thankfully, Roger came prepared, and as a sign of true friendship shared one. After a minute of tense relaxation, the conversation continued. "How did you even know where to find me? The cosmos?" contrary to most people, Jerry didn't mock him when he brought up the cosmic forces. He was past getting any fun out of it.

"In a sense. I got this map from a convenience store, from an older time before ours. I made the astute observation all roads led to here. It used to be the abattoir. Well, most of the roads anyways. The important ones. Here I am now, to fulfill our destiny. Where's Naomi? And how did you know to be here?" Roger was satisfied with the explanation he had provided. He was, after all, following methods incomprehensible to most, if not all of mankind.

"Me and Naomi split up after we tried to dig the painting back up again-" Roger was already out of his mind at the news.

"You what?! Again?! Tried to?! What have you both done in my absence?!" he was getting paler by the second. Even the pain in his ankle receded to an uncharted depth of his mind.

"Relax, will you? Not like we're making anything worse. We tried to destroy the painting, but nothing worked, so we thought it would be best to bury it. We did it outside of Naomi's apartment. We came back to it later, and tried to remove it, but the thing had sprouted... roots of some kind... and it was leaking. So, we left it alone again. We're wise like that." Jerry could only feel he had done something not quite right, but had no idea why.

"You've mixed the symbol of hatred with the element of earth. It then seeped into the element of water." Roger nodded with grave wisdom while clearing up absolutely nothing for his friend. "I too, had some time to think while I hobbled my way over here. While you slept, I thought. I mean, I always think, but this time, I thought even more. I did twice the amount of thinking in half the time." he rubbed his afflicted ankle and pursed his lips in anguish. "For starters, we didn't really notice any of what was happening around us until it was so obvious we couldn't ignore it, right?"

"Right. Nothing more than a feeling." for once, Jerry was genuinely curious about what Roger had to say.

"Second, we were barely affected, yet nearly everyone else seems to have gone mad with... we'll call it bloodlust, because I really like that word. It's like we're not even part of the reality we're observing. Correct?"

"Correct, probably. I'm not the best person to ask."

"Of course it's correct. Those two factors can be explained away with one simple truth:

we are disconnected outliers of society, and the scourge taking hold of everything is of a unique nature. It is rooted in the tainted actions of humanity at large, a humanity we're mostly disconnected from, likely by virtue of our inherent superiority, if I had to take a guess. It was somehow created... *by Man.*" the last two words were emphasized with a heavy dramatic tone. "You saw that giant mass of people running around and wreaking havoc on everything? None of them are outliers. They're active members of the social mass, and are connected to each other by ephemeral means. Over-connected even, maybe."

"I agree, whatever all of that means." Jerry only interjected to offer himself a bit more time to process everything Roger was unloading on his half-functional brain.

"This Man-made scourge, it brings out the worst in people, the worst Man is capable of... because that's what gave birth to it in the first place. *The worst thing Man is capable of.* We can only guess as to what *that* is." Roger ploughed onward, no longer paying attention to whether or not Jerry was listening to him. "Bottomless wrath, hatred and senseless violence are the worst we're capable of, I would assume. They work like pendulums; the potential for it is always there, but they need a push, and once they get it, they swing harder and wider as they draw more people in and gain momentum. The doomsday machine is already built into our nature, and even if I can't permanently shut it down, I want to know that I'm right. We have to find the source of the scourge. We have to stop the pendulum. Otherwise..." he looked up at the darkened sky with an air of pride, "Otherwise, only the outliers will remain. And there aren't enough of us." he cracked a knowing smile, still looking upward, now convinced of the altruistic purpose of his existence.

"Can't say I have any arguments against anything you're saying. Your guess is as good as mine." this was Jerry's way of agreeing.

"My guess is much better than yours. Anyways, that's all I got for now, and I'll need a couple more years to meditate on this topic. Also, you didn't answer my important question. How *did* you know to get here? And where *is* Naomi? It's important, trust me." he casually put his hand on Jerry's shoulder, and let it rest there in what he considered a sign of trust.

"Like I said, we split up. She went looking for you at a former neighbour of hers she referred to your... Loose Brain Dojo." though it was the only of its kind, Jerry struggled to remember its name in times of need, of which this was the first. "Haven't seen nor spoken to her since. As for me, I followed the oldest movie trope known to mankind and went to the library to see if I could find anything." he took a break in his story for a wide and lengthy yawn.

"And?" Roger didn't appreciate this storytelling technique.

"... I forgot what I was saying."

"Did you find anything in the library?" Roger looked at him, slightly incredulous. He wasn't used to being the one asking normal questions.

"Right, yeah I found an old book." Jerry recounted in vague details the journal he found in there. "Long story short, something somewhat like this happened before, on a smaller scale, and somewhere around here. It also had to do with a well, at least according to the author."

"I'm guessing it doesn't seem like much to someone with your lack of training in the ways of the cosmos, but Jerry, you've uncovered an important clue, and you don't even know it. Blessed be the Cosmos. Repeat after me." the life had returned to Roger's cheeks.

"No."

"Right, what am I thinking? I have to explain it out-loud for you to appreciate it. You've confirmed my hypothesis-"

"The one you developed right now on the spot?" Jerry asked mockingly.

"Yes, that very same one." there wasn't even a hint of shame in his voice. "My hypothesis according to which there is a much stronger potential for hatred and the like specifically in our town... and it has been this way for a while. What year was the journal from?" Roger had fully assumed his role as a detective.

"1955 or so, if I remember right." in spite of all it had been through, Jerry's mind still found the space to store small facts which seemed insignificant at first.

"Interesting... interesting indeed. Whatever happened, it must have happened even before that. Anyways, what happened next?"

"Then the mass of angry people burst into the library and seemed intent on tearing it apart. The librarian opened a secret passage for us to escape. Classic trick. It led us into some dark tunnels, and then we got separated. Things were confusing down there. I'm not exactly sure how, but the tunnel led me to a room deep inside the Big Cow, and there I met Officer Tim." he suddenly remembered Roger was still a wanted man, but only technically. His crime didn't seem at all important anymore.

"Officer Tim? How's the man doing?" his concern for the officer was entirely genuine, and definitely unusual.

"Still trying to do his job. I couldn't stop him from going into the tunnel, but I'll be honest: I don't remember if I even tried." a short involuntary laugh escaped Jerry's mouth. "Then I made my way out to the front door and a bunch of cops greeted me." he pointed to the entrance, and realized there was nobody there, save a strange man visibly hiding behind a grey column, evidently intent on eavesdropping their conversation from an impossible distance. He decided to let him be for the moment; Sherlock was no imminent danger to anyone. He turned back to Roger "Do you know where the cops went, by any chance?"

"As a matter of fact, I do. I got here about half an hour ago and had to hide in the bushes for a moment. They were arguing about whether they'd actually get paid overtime for standing around at the entrance. Then, they decided their shifts were over and they had the God-given right to return home. And so, they all did."

"Just like that?"

"How else?" answering a question with a question was one of life's little pleasures for Roger. "I hate to say it, Jerry, but I think we'll have to go back into those tunnels you tried so hard to get out of. I myself likely won't be able to join you on account of my deteriorating ankle," he shoved it closer to Jerry to make a point about the terrible pain he was having to deal with. "as a matter of fact, I'm thinking of amputating it. It's not the most important organ in the body-"

"It's a limb, not an organ." Jerry interrupted in a rather casual manner. "Besides, I really don't feel like going down there myself. It's dark, cramped and confusing. A bit of fresh air is what I really need now. To hell with it all. If people want to eat each other alive it's their prerogative." he was feeling tired of it all, tired of being pushed to do things he didn't entirely want to.

"I'll save the philosophical argument for later, but Jerry, somehow I doubt the government will allow anyone to leave this town anytime soon. As a matter of fact, I wouldn't be surprised if they're preparing to nuke us out of existence, just to make sure whatever happened here doesn't spread around to the rest of the country and remains a secret. They have really small and quiet nukes these days, don't doubt it. Second, if too few people are left, we lose to means to maintain all of our modern luxuries, and I think even you aren't willing to give that up." Roger knew how to be persuasive when he had to be.

"I wouldn't mind living in a ghost town." Jerry, however, was his toughest customer so far.

"Even one without internet? Electricity? Gasoline? Cars? Televisions? Radio? Shops? Refrigerators? Air Conditioners?" Roger wasn't about to give up. He had an important mission to accomplish, and come Hell or high water, he'd get Jerry to accomplish it for him.

"Yea I could do without those things. Maybe I'll reconnect with nature and start a one-man hippie commune." there was no palpable sarcasm to his words.

"Even without... functional plumbing? Toilet paper? Working bidets? Are you really prepared to venture back into the stone age? Because you're what? Tired?" this was Roger's final gambit before whipping out the philosophical arguments.

"..." Jerry paused in his mental tracks for a second. Life without toilets did feel unfathomable to him. "Fine, that would be an issue, I'll admit it... but still... what am I supposed to look for down there? My torch is barely functional and I haven't used it in weeks, it's pitch-black darkness down there-" the man who hid poorly behind the column made his entrance onto the scene.

"Yet mine is perfectly functional!" he waived his flashlight in the air as he jovially strode towards them wearing a now-familiar smile lacking quite a few teeth. "Holmes, Sherlock Holmes, at your service!"

"Who?!" Roger seemed offended and held his baseball bat menacingly, trying to warn the approaching detective not to get any closer.

"It's... Sherlock Holmes, he just told you. He's been spying on us the entire time we've been here. Don't worry, he's fairly harmless unless you're allergic to terrible accents and impressionable personalities." he waved the detective to come closer.

"I dare say, gentlemen, I believe you've cracked the case, and this even before I, the great, renowned-"

"The case could still be yours, if you're willing to brave some dark tunnels." Jerry wasn't sure how many more times he could hear the name of the legendary character associated with the buffoon in front of him before losing control.

"You and I shall go together, whilst your injured compatriot stands guard for us. You will have the honour of being *my Watson*!" he really did make it sound like an honour with the deepest implications.

"Can't lie Jerry, it's a fantastic idea he's got there. I'm all for it, which means your vote doesn't even count anymore. Thank you, Mr. Holmes, for your assistance." he extended his hand to the detective, who shook it cautiously without breaking eye contact. "Being an officer of the law, he'll lead the way, so if anything happens, Jerry, I think you'll have ample time to run back and tell me all about it. It's a deal then." he nodded at Jerry with the air of a man making a difficult sacrifice for the greater good. "Besides, Officer Tim is still down there, and the librarian might be as well."

"Fine, fine, I'm going, Roger, no need to get your philosophical arguments in play." he smiled at his long-time friend and admired his desire to do good through other people's hands. "What are we looking for, commander? We need an objective, we can't wander around aimlessly."

"For starters..." Roger put his finger to his chin and craned his head sideways in a pose he erroneously assumed was elegant. The other men looked at him with begging curiosity. "For starters, find Officer Tim and the librarian. Then, look for literally anything that doesn't belong in a secret underground tunnel complex. Anything that stands out, especially man-made." these were the most coherent orders Roger could manage.

“About as concrete of a direction as we can get out of him.” Jerry explained to the detective. Roger heard him. “You seen any rope laying around? So I can find my way back when the Minotaur tries to eat us.” the detective bravely concealed his outrage at such a poor attempt at humour.

“You're the one who works here, Jerry, not me. I only see the rope of destiny.”

“All right, we'll go looking for some and head on down. You do stay up here, and if Naomi comes around, for the love of all that is holy Roger, don't send her down there with us.” Jerry's concern for the one decent person in their little group was greater than for his own life.

“I promise.”

“I mean it, Roger.”

“Fine, I really promise. No backstabbing.” he had never quite mastered the art of making believable promises, and wasn't about to start today.

“Good luck. Off we go, mister Holmes.”

“Onward, my dear Watson!” excitement took hold of every fibre in the detective's body.

“Call me that again and I'm leaving you down in the tunnels and sealing the grate.”

Jerry and his companion spent a couple dozen minutes looking around through the expansive body of the Big Cow and finally found a stock of long and thick ropes a few dozen meters each. They attached them together, and figured they had enough for however much exploration they were preparing to conduct down below. Meanwhile, Roger stood outside with an air of importance and tried not to worry too much about his ankle. It was only a limb, after all, and he still had so much more thinking to do.

The three men made their way through the factory back to the grate where Jerry had emerged from hours earlier, and almost instantaneously an uneasy feeling rumbled in their stomachs. The gaping darkness was pulling them in, and their survival instincts were sounding every red alert they could possibly manage. In spite of it all, Jerry and Sherlock readied up, and bidding farewell to Roger, perhaps for the last time, began their descent down the forty-five-degree slope Jerry had only barely managed to conquer.

With detective Sherlock's military-issue light shining the way, the tunnel took on a different air, its lifeless concrete walls, floor and ceiling inspiring anything but safety and confidence. The turns seemed more numerous than he had remembered them, but then again, his memory relied entirely on his sense of touch and lack of proper orientation. He took the time to notice there were no signs of rodents, spiders, insects, nor life in general to be found. A slight hint of nausea settled in the pit of his stomach. They kept on walking without much direction, laying the rope behind them, turning left and right at the detective's whims. His companion was far more entranced with his perceived progress than the lack of it.

“How far do you think these tunnels stretch?” Jerry had an inkling there wouldn't be enough rope to cover their exploration.

“A tad too far for my taste.” the detective replied with concern. “We ought to direct our exploration towards zones of greater discomfort. I take it you and I are suffering from the same onset of nausea at the moment?” for increased dramatic effect, he shone the flashlight on his own face while speaking.

“You got that right... Don't know about you, mister... detective, but seems to me we're already doing that. It's getting worse.” a prickling in Jerry's throat gave him a short coughing fit. “Who even built this place? And when? And how long can we stay down here before we puke our guts out completely?" he was suddenly having second thoughts about once again following Roger's poorly formulated plan. It was a terrible habit of his, and he made a mental note to get rid of it as soon as he had the chance.

"So many questions, young man! Let's go over what we know. People built this. Sometime before today. And we can at least stay down here for as long as we've already been down here." the gears were turning at the speed of light in the detective's head.

"..." Jerry wasn't sure what to say. "Are you certain you're a police officer? Let alone a detective?"

"Do not waste time questioning my authority, young man." he was above such petty criticism. "Evidently the meaning of my message was completely lost on you. We have not much to go on, and the only way forward is, well, to move forward. And so, I propose, my fellow comrade, that we proceed onward as planned and seldom dawdle as we did just now." without giving Jerry a moment to get an answer in, he turned around and walked further into the belly of the beast, his reluctant companion in tow.

The sense of nausea was rising ever so subtly, and soon it was accompanied by a faint and warm breeze emanating in pulses, bearer of a revolting and unnatural sensation. The further they were edging into the tunnels, the stronger the breeze blew at them, and the hotter the air got. Holmes puked a little bit. Jerry put his hand on his shoulder and motioned him back. The detective shrugged it off and insisted on going further. His savage eyes carried the mark of a man far too close to forbidden knowledge to back off. Jerry understood the lethal determination which carried the detective on his two feet, and knew protesting was useless. Inching further and further back, he kept increasing the distance between himself and the detective, to the point where they ended up a few meters apart. Suddenly, Jerry thought he saw a flicker of light as he walked past yet another intersection of the tunnels. He tugged on the rope and ordered the detective to stop. Naturally, he didn't listen and kept on going. The light appeared once again in the same place he had seen it, but this time it was pointed straight at him, and inching closer in his direction. At first it moved slowly, then faster and faster, and before he could turn and run Naomi's voice called out to him from behind the light.

"Have you been down here this *whole* time?!" Naomi was understandably worried at the dishevelled state of her friend.

"I did go out for some fresh air. Also, I found Roger. Well, technically, he was the one who found me. I know where at least one of the exits to this place is, leads to the Big Cow. My efforts haven't been completely useless. Oh yeah, Roger thinks he has most of this thing figured out." as briefly as he could, he relayed what he could remember of Roger's explanation for the events around them. "Not that I'm a huge believer in his cosmic nonsense, but unless you have a better theory I think it's all we got for now." he was happy to see someone who wasn't half-insane, and it made him a bit more talkative than usual.

"Well, you've been a little busier than I imagined. I myself avoided death multiple times, but I'll tell you all about it later. I also found your librarian, she's alive and well-" a face peeked out from behind Naomi's back.

"You abandoned me! You're the king of all cowards!" Laura was spitting rancor at him in a twist of rage with cruel intentions.

"It wasn't my fault! You didn't tell me which wall to follow, and then you disappeared! You're the one who abandoned me! You're the coward!" Jerry wasn't about to take any of this laying down; he despised being called a coward, largely because he thought it was at least partially true.

"Can you two fight later please?! I'm about to puke my guts out." the nausea was creeping further and further into her guts, and Jerry remembered how he had hoped only minutes ago to keep Naomi from being down here.

"Right, we have to find Sherlock first." they both looked at him completely unamused.

"He's a detective who changed his name legally. Came down here with me. He decided to take point and then ran off-"

"Can't stop abandoning people, can you?!" Laura was prepared to take every possible jab at her defector.

"Ahem," he gave her a long and stern look, "he ran off, and we should go and get him. And before you ask, yes, we had the bright idea of laying a rope to find our way back." he looked at Naomi for some positive reinforcement. She obliged by nodding at him. "Most importantly, I think he's losing his mind."

"From playing a character, or being down here?" Naomi inquired with a hint of sarcasm.

"Both, probably. Let's go, the longer we talk, the deeper he'll go, and the likelier it is-" he looked at Laura, anticipating her reaction. "the likelier it is we'll have to abandon him."

"How are you friends with this man?!" Laura turned to her own newfound friend, and menacingly squinted her eyes when silence was the only answer.

The three then picked up the rope which the detective had helpfully laid down on his descent into madness, and with Naomi's flashlight they crept along the corridor with Jerry taking point. They turned a corner, and saw the tunnel going down, deeper into a hideous darkness heralding the rot of mankind. The air felt thick as molasses, synthetic and hostile, attacking all of their senses at once, and they wondered how the detective managed to get this far. The descent ultimately ended in a room with a short ceiling and a floor made of dirt rather than cement. In the middle of the room stood a stone well, and in it streams of multi-coloured liquid slowly crawled up the walls, flowed and poured over the edges. A faint light emanated from within, and despite every human and inhuman instinct telling Jerry to run away, he couldn't help himself. He had to look and see what was inside. He needed to gaze into the abyss. He glanced around the room, and noticed the detective was nowhere in sight. There was only one place he could have gone. Cautiously inching forward and trying to fight off the indomitable nausea smashing his solar plexus like a battering ram, he peeked over the surface of the well. It ran deep. He inched closer and closer, looking down on the walls up which the vibrant liquid flowed. It must have been at least two dozen meters deep, but at the very bottom, in the darkest void he had ever gazed into, Jerry saw the unmistakable glint of a rage-scorched human stare along with the faint smile of a knowing retribution. The figure also seemed to be holding its middle finger up at Jerry, but he couldn't be certain. The sight made him coil back in terror, and pushing his way past the women, he started to run back to the exit following the rope, yelling for them to join him as quickly as they could. He wasn't proud of losing his cool to this extent, largely because he knew Laura would take a stab at him again, and he wasn't certain how much further demoralization he'd be capable of withstanding.

Jerry wasn't the fastest runner, and the two women almost caught up to him not far from the upwards slope leading to the grate which stood between them and freedom. Out of the darkness, a hand came down on Jerry's shoulder, hot, heavy and desperate.

"It really is your regular daily commute, isn't it?" the tired voice of Officer Tim was a soothing sound for sore ears.

"Your...?" Naomi looked at Jerry, but decided not to intervene, having obviously missed some important elements of the conversation between the two men.

"My daily commute. And I've brought you two along to give you a tour of the factory. And I'm not even afraid of the dark anymore, because they brought a flashlight, as did I, even though it barely works." Somehow, Jerry had a good memory for the lies he told specifically to Officer Tim.

"Who do you think I am?! A brainless imbecile who can be jerked around by the nose?!" his sudden outburst put Jerry and his companions on edge. "Visiting hours for guests end in the early afternoon, and it's already past 9PM! On top of everything that's happening with the cows, you'd violate your inner workplace visitation laws as well?! I thought for a while you needed to be sent to a good old-fashioned prison, but now I see... you deserve to be in the asylum!" the officer was working himself up into a real frenzy.

"Well, I do have something of interest for you, venerable lawman." the sarcasm flew miles above the officer's head. "I did find Roger, the same one you've been looking for this whole time. I can even lead you to him, but we'll have to make a deal." Jerry knew his friend couldn't keep running from this one determined policeman forever, especially if life ever returned to its normal disposition. He did his best at coming up with a plan to nip this in the bud once and for all.

"Of course, there we have it, the words of a true crook. Let me guess, it will be a deal I cannot refuse?" the man's spite quickly gave way to mockery.

"You can definitely refuse it. As a matter of fact, you can do literally anything you want and can do. Technically, there's always a choice."

"Spit it out then, and be careful. Anything you say right now will be remembered by me to use against you in a court of law." the time spent down in the tunnels had robbed the officer of what little patience he had left after the worst days of his career had started.

"I'll lead you to Roger, and even convince him to be cooperative with you." he knew there was no way he'd convince Roger to be cooperative with anyone. "He'll tell you the entire truth about anything you want to know, no bullshit involved." an explanation from Roger without bullshit was like rain without water. "I just need one thing in exchange from you. If he does have to answer for anything before the law, let him roam free until his trial. Give him the full presumption of innocence he... deserves." both Naomi and Laura were impressed at how diplomatic Jerry managed to be, especially since the matter revolved around Roger's fate.

"As if I have a choice!" Officer Tim pressed both palms to his eyes and suddenly realized how tired he was from all the chasing and suspect hunting he had been going through. "Fine! I'll think about it! Now lead me to him!"

"That's... I kind of need you to agree here Tim, and not just think about it. Otherwise, I can't tell you where he is. If anyone can understand it, I know it's you, Timmy." his attempt at being friendly sounded more like ridicule than anything else.

"You don't get to dictate terms here. I remind you that not telling me the truth is a crime: obstruction of justice. Right now, you're obstructing my investigation, so really, I should be arresting you now." he looked at Naomi and Laura. "And you two as well for being his accomplices. Clearly, I have more power here than you could have ever imagined, Jerry. Tell me where Roger is, right now, or as God is my witness, I'll arrest you all and call in the FBI." whether Officer Tim could actually enact his threats or not, he truly believed he could.

"Hey! You guys alive down there!?" Roger's voice boomed down through the grate and into the tunnel. Officer Tim smiled and began to climb up the slope to the grate where his most wanted nemesis awaited him.

<h1 style="text-align:center">Chapter 29</h1>

The grate opened and Officer Tim burst through like a bat out of hell, flying at Roger with his fists ready to strike. Out of fear and survival reflexes, Roger swung the baseball bat he was propped on in an upwards motion, striking the officer in the armpit and sending him careening to the side until he hit a wall.

"Assaulting a police officer. Now *that's* a felony. I really got you now, Roger. No way out. You're done for." the ambitious officer declared while clutching his armpit and nursing what he secretly believed to be a fracture of some sort.

"You're the one who assaulted me! In the name of the law, you must identify yourself before making any sort of intervention. For all I knew, you were a deranged mutant of our sewer network. The resemblance is uncanny." Roger had been accused of worse over the years; he knew how to play his own legal defence in an informal setting.

"We'll see what the judge has to say about that. But first thing's first. The fire at the O'Harris Gallery. I have it on good authority you're the one who masterminded it. Come quietly, or the pain will be unbearable." he was starting to whimper, and the others felt a bit of pity for his unimpressive pain tolerance.

"And who is this, "good authority" you speak of?" the emphasis on the quotation marks was so extreme Roger thought he'd break his fingers.

"That's none of your concern. I won't divulge my witnesses; you might go ahead and kill them. What do you have to say for yourself?" the trap was set, and the officer knew his prey was about to blindly walk into it. "A pure confession from the depths of your heart is the only way out of this."

"I didn't do it."

"What?!" the officer was absolutely stunned. He had done everything like they taught him to, softening up his target in all the right ways, making him ripe for the killing blow. He began to doubt the power of online courses on interrogation techniques, and a few more things along the way.

"If you're going to make any additional accusations, I demand you provide me with a lawyer, and preferably one who knows what he's doing. Until then, Officer Tim, you can talk to the hand." with a tremendous display of sass Roger put his hand up in the officer's face and turned his head sideways, but still looking at him from the corner of his eye.

"I'll be damned..." he whispered. "You'll have your lawyer all right. This isn't over, just so you know."

Roger was about to answer with something, but then he noticed the three others climbing back out of the tunnels behind him, and could hardly contain his joy at being reunited with his friends once again, even if they brought a stranger along. He gave Naomi a wide smile and instantly began to recount to her everything Jerry had already told her. He didn't let anyone get a word in edgewise, and so they patiently listened to his explanation a second time. Unlike Laura, who was standing and pouting in light of the repetitive nature of the situation, Jerry and Naomi understood the need to allow Roger to indulge himself in his self-professed superior understanding of the world around him; after all, who doesn't feel better when they believe to hold secret knowledge the majority aren't privy to? He was the type of person whose success and ability to function effectively depended entirely on his sense of self-worth. A soothing silence followed during which the three friends looked at each other with relief and a hint of admiration, while Laura and Officer Tim felt like fixtures unfortunately misplaced in the tableau.

"So, have you found anything down there? Also, where's Detective Holmes?" he looked at Officer Tim for a second. "Are we dealing with a shape-shifter?" he privately asked Jerry in a hushed tone. Jerry closed his eyes and rubbed his temples in response.
"No... Roger...how the hell do you manage to have coherent thoughts in-between all the… other ones?" there was no hint of malice nor hatred in Jerry's voice, only friendly curiosity.
"One thought at a time." the answer was vague and sounded just profound enough for Roger's taste.
"Yeah, anyways, we did find something down there. A well, with bright liquid pouring out of it. I looked in and I'm certain I saw someone at the bottom. I'm pretty sure he gave me the finger. I think that's where it's all coming from. This might actually be it, for some reason. I assumed you'd be able to fill in the blanks by now." he kept his surprise hidden at Roger having been correct in sending them back down there.
"That's a good start, my friend, but I'm afraid this was only the first of many expeditions down below." the news didn't seem to surprise Roger one bit. "We still have to figure out the best way to deal with it, and soon. I'm starting to feel a little hungry. All this waiting around while you do the hard work is starting to wear on me." he rested his hand on Jerry's shoulder.
"I'm only going back down there if you lead the way. I'm not a mole, Roger." the sweaty hand on his shoulder was starting to feel uncomfortable. He courageously let it be.
"You guys are pathetic." Laura suddenly chimed in. "One abandons everyone he sees and the other can't be bothered to do anything but order everyone else around!" they looked at her without answering, implicitly agreeing with her accusations. She tossed a folder and what looked like a bronze plaque at their feet. "I found it in the well room. While Jerry here was busy running away like a little girl." she gave him an evil eye he wouldn't soon forget. "Also, I do have a gun. We could just try and shoot down the well."
"You do that, let us know how it works out." Naomi stood up for her friends in her own way, despite knowing Laura's accusations weren't incorrect.
"Will do." failing to catch the sarcasm and anxious to solve things on her own terms, she grabbed the old flashlight from Jerry's hand and went on ahead to conduct her experiment. The others waved her goodbye.
"You know..." she turned to Roger after Laura vanished from their sight. "I did end up in a neighbourhood that seemed unaffected earlier. They even offered me safe refuge, but had zero interest in doing anything that would involve any amount of effort. They also seemed a little crazy, but of the harmless kind."
"Interesting... very interesting. What neighbourhood was it?"
"I... I can't remember? It's slipping my mind somehow. The place was... unremarkable. I'm sure I could find it, if I saw it again. Point is, if I had to peg them as anyone, it would be outcasts. They might even have measures of... self-sufficiency, to some extent. And food." Naomi saw the lights flashing in Roger's eyes. He was probably holding back additional complaints about his hunger. "Anyhow, what are these all about?" she pointed to the floor.

Wasting little time forgetting about the existence of their gun-toting comrade, they all turned their attention to the folder as well as the plaque she had left behind at their feet. Considering where they were allegedly found, the group quickly concluded there was a great importance to them. Even Officer Tim joined in, for once agreeing on something with Roger, who, through a twist of fate, had become his greatest nemesis. He didn't have a very high standard for making enemies, and deep down he wanted one who would prove to be his equal and push him to greatness, a Hector to his Achilles. Unbeknownst to himself, Officer Tim never did have the makings of greatness in the first place, and the search would prove futile until the end of his days. He took initiative and was the first to grab the plaque and read its inscription. Putting on his best lecturer's impression and lowering his voice an octave, he read: "*This foundation for a new and ground-breaking step forward for the human civilization, propelling it into the Age of Atom, was laid in the year of our Lord 1954, in honour of General Hallard Krestin, for his courageous deeds, personal contribution and sacrifice for the coming brave new world.*" he paused before proclaiming the end of the reading.

"Hallard Krestin? Is this some kind of terrible joke?!" Officer Tim blurted, offended at having read what he thought was the old-time equivalent of an archaeological prank.

"Be quiet, Timmy, we still have this folder to go through." Roger held it up for everyone to see.

It was bound in leather and closed with the help of a zipper, which started to fall apart when Roger began to pull on it. Shrugging his shoulders at the damage he was causing to the relic in his hands, he kept going until he pulled out an old journal with its pages stained in yellow and with old rusted blades protruding from it. Carefully so as not to cut his hand, he opened the little book and noticed the cover was partially burnt. He listed through it, and decided to read the last entry, with the reasoning it was most likely the important one. He read the General's account of his surprisingly tame mission which involved getting smuggled north of the Canadian border and observing other people doing their duty. Then, he read it again, this time out-loud, for the benefit of the group. He listed back a few pages to look at the previous entries, and when he was convinced there was nothing of note to be found anymore, he carefully laid the journal back down on the dirty floor. A faint bang was heard from deep within the tunnels. Then another, and another. "Idiot." muttered Roger under his breath. The collective nodded in agreement.

"So, what do we have out of this? Hollow Crest was built or named in honour of this general, who was secretly smuggled here to... watch something explode? Years before they even started building. This is getting us nowhere." Jerry was about to learn just how wrong he was on this account.

"You are wrong on this account, Jerry." Roger put on the smug and all-knowing air everyone around him had already become accustomed to. We are pliable to the extent dictated by necessity. "He didn't just watch something explode. *Propelling it into the Age of Atom*". I have good reason to believe he witnessed the explosion of a small nuclear device, maybe even planted underground to some extent." the theory was taking on a more concrete shape than it ever had in his mind. "Did you notice the date mentioned by the general? July 17th, 1945."

"So?" Jerry and Naomi asked in unison, relatively unimpressed by their friend's lecture so far. Officer Tim started rubbing his armpit again.

"So?! On July 16th, 1945, the first nuclear explosion in the history of the world took place! The mission the general went on was a continuation or a derivation of the project... a long-term study of the bomb's effects on both nature and people. It's what I would have done if I was the government. They blew it up, and sometime later the people from the book you found…" he vigorously pointed to Jerry as if they were in a courtroom. "…the ones building the well, they came around and all died. That was meant to be the foundation for Hollow Crest, and it explains why the plaque and preserved journal were next to it. I do believe they realized they've made a mistake when the well builders tragically passed, and decided to cover the whole thing up, literally. They covered it in dirt and land, and built a rudimentary complex for their… observation and research purposes." he had to take a moment to catch his breath. He wasn't used to speaking for so long without taking any breaks.

"Following your theory, I have a feeling these researchers met the same fate as the builders." Naomi was buying him a few more seconds before speaking.

"Almost the same. They weren't at the same proximity to the well as the builders, so the effects took longer to make themselves known. Then, they covered it up again, literally. They buried the mistakes of their past, and on this new foundation of nuclear pollution and deathly decay our dear beloved city was built." He dramatically waved his arm around the room, in his imagination pointing to the entire city beyond it. "At first, the slaughterhouse was right here, as I discovered from the archaic map that one… rude and ignorant convenience store owner gave me. Bless his heart. The blood trickled down into these passages, soaked the earth, and eventually found its way down to ground zero." he shuddered at the mental imagery he had just forced himself to process. The others didn't find it so disconcerting. "Whatever they created down there, it was kept at bay for a few decades for how deeply it ended up buried. It turned into more than the sum of its parts… a giant, backfiring mechanism by… Mother Nature. Against us. It's now set in motion, and I don't think we'll ever know peace again, even if we die one day. How are we going to destroy something propagating through means even *I* can't hope to understand? It's absurd." Roger was once again winded and bowed his head to try and hide his poor lung capacity, but everyone saw through it.

"They should just nuke the place." Officer Tim offered a brilliant suggestion.

Jerry gave him a stern look of disappointment. "You know, with people like you around I think we're headed for total annihilation one way or the other, no outside influence needed."

"I-" the officer was about to dig his own grave even further when he got interrupted.

"You've done more than enough, Officer Tim." Naomi chimed in. "We're all tired, hungry and thirsty. How about you put your police privileges to use and raid a burger joint for us. Our lives depend on it, and we can all agree on how important our lives are."

"If it's the name of keeping me… us alive, I cannot refuse your request." he smiled and winked at Naomi. She realized he might have taken a liking to her, and the idea caused her enough concern to distract herself from the more important problems at hand. Off he went into the night, to raid a burger joint.

"What's the plan now?" she was eager to keep trudging forward, unperturbed by their lack of resources. The three friends were alone together for the first time in what felt like an eternity.

"First, I must eat." Roger, however, was a good deal more perturbed by their lack of food and water.

"We can still come up with a plan while we wait for those to come in." Jerry astutely noticed. Just as he said that, the grate opened and Laura came back out with an unmistakable air of disappointment. She didn't seem to have her gun anymore.

"I took a few shots into the well. Then dropped my gun in it. I don't have it anymore. If only someone with strong hands would have volunteered to do it for me." as was becoming a habit for her, she looked at Jerry with scorching venom in her eyes. She really had it in for him, to the point where the others didn't know whether to laugh or prepare themselves for an impending assassination attempt.

"You made your own choice, not much we could have done." he was starting to become increasingly adept at rolling with her punches. She pouted in response and pretended to become absorbed in deep thought. He turned back to his friends. "You know... not being able to destroy the thing in the well isn't much of a problem." his friends craned their heads at him in surprise, and even Laura was curious for what he had to say, though she'd never admit it in a million years. "Maybe we don't need to kill it. What if we just bury it up better than it has ever been buried before? I'm thinking cement down the well, fill the tunnels up all to the way to the grate here and the library. It will at least buy us time. Then we go on from there. Move everyone out of here, mark it a dead zone. It was born from the destructive nature of humanity, and while we exist in it, so it will too... if I even remotely understood anything Roger said... assuming his theory is even partially correct. Best we can do is shield ourselves from it, and stay away from its influence as much as possible." he was looking at his friends' feet, a habit he had when elaborating out-loud while thinking as hard as he could.

"What a magnificent set of thoughts-turned-words, Jerry!" Roger had adopted yet another one of his strange meditative poses while his friends weren't looking. "Give it a couple of decades and you can hope to become as perceptive as I am. I couldn't have said it better myself." most people would have taken this as an insult, but it was truly the most heartfelt compliment one could ask out of this man.

"Not the worst thoughts I've heard, but we are facing a problem when you're done patting yourselves on the back." Naomi was about to rain on their parade. She had no choice. The storm wasn't waiting on them. "Where exactly are we going to find the cement and the workers to fill the whole place up? And don't even try telling me we'll do it ourselves because none of us have any experience with this sort of matter to any extent. And no, Roger, having a great-grandfather who once worked in construction doesn't count." her anticipation of Roger's non-argument was a question of reflex at this stage.

"We'll cross that bridge when we get to it. For now, I think there are a couple of things even *you* forgot about, my friend." Roger couldn't maintain his meditative pose any longer and propped himself up against his baseball bat again. "There are two other sources we'll have to bring back to the well before we seal it all off, otherwise it will all be for nothing. The painting and the body. I'm positive they're poisoned with the image of the scourge and serve as... independent sources, or proxies, or something of the sort. It's complicated, and if I had the time for it, I promise you, I could definitely explain it."

"At least we know where to find them. How are we going to split this up?" Jerry thought the endeavour was futile, but it seemed preferable to at least occupy himself with something other than twiddling his thumbs. After all, potential death, no matter how probable, is still vastly preferable to guaranteed death.

"Well, you could say I have a bit of a thing going with Kathleen, our local coroner, so I should be the one making the visit to her." he briefly glanced at his ankle; the pain seemed to have subsided slightly compared to earlier, and at least the unnatural swelling wasn't getting any larger, nor spreading. "Since you two buried the painting together, at least one of you should go for it."

"Naomi and I will get the painting." Laura suddenly gave them a sign of life. "There's no way you're leaving me alone in all of this, and there's even less of a chance I'd rely on either of you two for anything." she used both hands to point at Roger and Jerry simultaneously, incidentally appearing as if she was trying to shoot them with her finger-guns. She holstered them. "I'm sticking with Naomi, at least she seems capable of rational thought. Also, since I don't anticipate enjoying the sight of a dead body, we'll be going for that... painting." her case was sound and logical from start to finish.

"I guess that settles it." Jerry no longer took offence to Laura's incessant outbursts of anger. As a matter of fact, he was beginning to warm up to her, and chalked it all up as a quirk of her personality. It occurred to him he'd likely be fairly bad at identifying potential maniacs. "I'll go with Roger to meet his one and true love." Jerry declared unironically. Naomi snickered. Nobody in the room believed Roger had anything going with Kathleen, but they indulged him. It's what good friends are for.

"But first, the food." Roger pointed to the window through which he could see Officer Tim making his way back, two huge grocery bags in each hand. His morale perked right up at such a wondrous sight.

Officer Tim walked on to them, with the proud grin of a hunter carrying back his biggest catch yet to feed the family. He placed the bags on the floor, and with joy began listing the products he had acquired in his raid on a deserted supermarket: "Potatoes, regular and red onions, garlic, parsley, dill, vinegar, olive oil, bananas, apples, pineapples, beans, rice, dried peas, soy beans, a frozen chicken, one kilogram of ground beef, corn cobs, spinach leaves, a frozen pizza and two boxes of cereal." he held his arms out while his companions looked at him with the kind of incredulous confusion he had yet to experience in neither his current lifetime, nor any preceding one. Only Naomi brought him out of his trance of pride and happiness when she asked him "how do we cook it?".

They all feasted in silence on the fruits and dry cereal while shooting glances of scorn at the officer, who was in the process of failing to jury-rig a cooking station. It crumbled a couple of minutes into the project. It looked much better and sturdier in his mind's eye, but for some unknown reason, reality refused to bend to his imagination, and he took offence to it. Finally, he relented and joined the others in one of the least satisfying meals he ever had the displeasure of eating. Once they were all finished, they went over the plan once again, and it was brought to everyone's attention Officer Tim had no duty assigned to him. Seeing it as his great opportunity to prove himself worthy of his title, he declared he'd take it upon himself to secure the workers and resources to seal the place up completely. With sighs of disbelief and eyes rolling like billiard balls, they all parted ways without knowing if they would ever see each other again. They would.

Chapter 30

Slowly but surely, with Roger leaning on both Jerry's shoulder and his baseball bat, the two men walked down the street as they used to in better, happier days when they were still young enough to be intoxicated with both alcohol and the naive idea of a future with limitless potential. Eventually they both learned, like everyone else, the future's potential becomes exponentially limited the further one gets into it, not to mention it was never even close limitless in the first place. So many things are decided for us at birth, from our genetic makeup to the path life forces us to follow, it's a wonder anyone still believes in the concept of true freedom and complete free will… not to mention the all-encompassing and unbending laws of nature. Even knowing what they knew today, with all the lessons taught by life, they still yearned for the bygone days when the illusion held up and allowed a truly carefree attitude to reign. Even the air they breathed and the sun on their skin used to feel different. Regardless of how hard they tried to dream, the reality they were currently walking through was bringing them back down to Earth with virtually every step. They could hardly believe the society which seemed perfectly peaceful and functional only days ago had collapsed so quickly... and perhaps more frightening, so willingly and right under their noses. The unspoken words were understood: the potential for this exists everywhere humans reside.

The streets were dark and largely silent, with the remaining few who hadn't lost their minds trying to keep the attention away from themselves, perhaps hoping to wait it all out. There was no way of telling how many remained, but for all intents and purposes, Hollow Crest seemed to have become a ghost town. Windows were smashed, cars were upturned, the roads littered with skewered trash bags and debris giving off a heavy reek which made the air feel dense and poisonous. There was no getting away from it. From time to time, Roger nearly tripped over unexpected pieces of rubble and cursed the government for letting it get so out of hand, and maybe even being responsible for this in the first place. When Jerry asked him to clarify which government he was talking about, Roger responded with *"THE* government." while pointing his index finger to the sky. Jerry gave the topic up immediately. Thankfully, all the time Roger had spent running around town gave him the knowledge of a tour guide, and he already knew exactly which streets would bring them to the coroner quickest. They hoped the body was still there and they wouldn't have to hunt around town for it. Despite their good intentions, neither of them had the energy for extended escapades anymore. Being the good guys requires a tremendous amount of effort.

They both praised the forces that be when they arrived to the main door of Kathleen's office without any superfluous adventures. This felt like a totally new experience. The lights in the building were off and they could see through the small glass panes on the door it was barred with some sort of metal pole from the interior. They deemed it a good sign, hoping the place might have been spared the fate which seemed to have befallen the rest of the town. They also deemed it a bad sign, since now they would have to find another way in. "No good deed goes unpunished." Roger wisely remarked, while Jerry rubbed his eyes, and held himself back from asking him what he even meant given the context. They started creeping around the building, and were momentarily mortified by all the bodies strewn across the yard, white sheets tied to them and flapping about. The toll was starting to feel heavy, soaking the air with outlandish rot. Trying to find a way in or a sign of life, they noticed what they were looking for at the window to the autopsy room. There, by candlelight, a figure stood hunched over the body, likely Kathleen still working away towards her Nobel prize in medicine, as Roger figured.

"What a woman!" Roger exclaimed with a loud whisper.

"She's the one you have a thing going with?" Jerry decided not to be sarcastic, despite how appropriate it might have been.

"She's the one, Jerry. *The One*." without even realizing it he pressed his face up against the window with his cheek flattened against it. A bad habit of his. The figure turned around, screamed, and pointed something in Roger's direction.

"Get down!" Jerry tackled his friend to the ground just in time to avoid the gunshot which shattered the window.

"What a woman!" he was even more enamoured with her. She could do no wrong.

"Yeah, she's definitely the one for you." he brushed a few glass shards off himself.

"Do you really mean it?" there was an uncharacteristically honest hope in Roger's eyes.

"If not her, then who?" the logic was sound, solid and unshakable.

A revolver-toting hand crept through the broken glass window, and soon a face popped out behind it. "You have five seconds to get out of here. Five..." the voice was familiar, but it wasn't Kathleen's.

"Kathleen?! Even your voice is more beautiful than I remember it. I think the recent events might have given you some of your youth back." he was blushing at what he thought was an over-the-top compliment.

"I'm Sarah, her assistant. Kathleen is sleeping, we've been hard at work. Hey... aren't you..." she took a closer look at Jerry, who helped her out by shining the flashlight at his own face, blinding himself in the process. "Jeremiah... Bexter? Baxter?"

"Yeah... wait, how'd you know?" he was a little worried at the turn the events were taking.

"Kathleen had her copy your ID because she thought you were suspicious." Roger obliged with the explanation.

"I see they even got you in on it. Let me guess, what a woman, huh?" he began the laborious process of standing up and helping his friend up with him. "So, have you found anything Nobel-prize worthy yet?" he turned to face Sarah.

"No, not really, nothing of much note. Other than the fact the body can't seem to stop emitting radiation and we can barely make a scratch on it with our tools, nothing special." she had a smug air of self-satisfaction, and then remembered this represented the entire sum of their learning. An intense jolt of pain made her grasp the side of her skull for a few seconds. It subsided. "If we had the tools to match our ambitions, we would have learned more by now."

"Aren't you a little under-protected for something that constantly emits radiation?" Jerry looked at the body on the table with apprehension. It didn't really matter who it was, but looking at it tugged at something profoundly buried within him, calling back to the sort of all-consuming fear children fall victim to.

"It doesn't emit enough to be dangerous. I don't think. Most of the time, anyways. Like my mentor says, there is always a price to be paid for scientific progress. This time, it's a bit of exposure to radiation." she seemed entirely convinced the risk was well worth the reward. The pain dwelling in her skull agreed. "What are you two doing here anyways?"

"We came here to take-" Roger felt his friend's elbow nudge him in the ribs. It hurt more than either of them expected, and he doubled over from the shock.

"We came here to take part in the research you're doing on the body. Also, Roger wants to see your mentor, declare his undying love for her, and all that." he quickly glanced at his friend, still slightly bent over in pain.

"I guess I can let you in, we could use some help. At least someone to go out and find more whiskey." she glanced at Roger, automatically pegging him as the least useful one of the two in her mind.

"We'll take the front door, Roger here has a recently hurt ankle and theoretically hasn't been able to climb through windows since he was twenty. I think I did watch him climb a fence once, if that counts for anything." he grinned to himself at the cheap quality of his pot shot.

"See you in front." she disappeared from the window with grace and swiftness.

"Why didn't you let me tell her the truth?" Roger asked as they were making their way back around to the front.

"Use your head for once. They're obsessed with researching it for their damn prize, and she had a gun pointed at us. You really think they'll be agreeable with our idea to throw it away and seal it off forever? I think she would have killed us on the spot if we shared the idea with her."

"Hmm... there's a chance you might be right on this one." admitting other people could also be right didn't come naturally to him, making the moment all the more important in his biography.

"We'll have to find a way to steal it from them, and then carry it all the way back to the factory. Even if you weren't injured, I don't think we'd be able to make the entire trip on our own. Got to think of transportation." he didn't like the challenge ahead of them one bit; Murphy's Law loomed over it.

"We'll just wheel him out of there. They must have gurneys here, somewhere. I could also distract them with my many charms, intellectual or physical." Roger winked at him.

Jerry shuddered in disgust at the suggestion. "We'll... see what the situation calls for. Don't go around getting physical on them for no reason. Let's see what things look like inside."

When the two friends had walked back around to the front of the building, Sarah was already standing there, visibly annoyed at having been made to wait for so long. She removed the metal bar, ushered them in, and locked the door up behind them. The place, for the most part, looked relatively clean and untouched by the chaos of the city. There were strategic candles placed here and there which helped them find their way to the autopsy room while guided by Sarah's ambitious gait, still clutching the revolver as if she knew to expect the worst from them. Considering her goals and theirs, she was mostly correct.

"Kathleen is sleeping in her office." she pointed down the corridor.

"I know where it is." Roger proudly declared. "I should go ahead and pay her a visit."

"She's resting, I just told you." the irritation in her voice was palpable. She was also quite clearly on edge and the facade of calmness she was putting on started to fade, piece by piece.

"I know, I'll just sit in the corner and watch her sleep. When she wakes up, she'll be overjoyed to see me. I guarantee it." he gave Jerry a quick and barely-perceptible nod, indicating he had some sort of a plan up his sleeve.

"You should trust him on this matter. He definitely knows how to cheer people up. It's his greatest talent in life." against his better judgment, Jerry was going along with the improvisation.

"Fine... do what you want just... don't wake her up. I mean it. You might become the next corpse we study. Hah." though young, Sarah was already developing her coroner's sense of humour, raw as it was.

"You can always count on me. Not like I'm going to, *knock her out*, or anything." Roger tried to send a coded message to Jerry as he left for Kathleen's office.

Jerry rubbed his temples in agony at how poorly encrypted it was. By divine intervention, it somehow wasn't intercepted. "How about you show me this miracle of science then?" he feigned curiosity towards Sarah.

"This way!" at the mention of her obsession, life seemed to seep back into her tired eyes.

As they walked down the hall, Jerry was fairly surprised to see how well everything had withstood the localized apocalypse, showing no signs of damage besides the lack of electricity. "Couldn't you guys afford a backup generator?" he had the strange urge to find any flaw he could to complain about.

"Why? The dead don't need electricity." she glanced at him with her eyes half-shut. It was a valid point.

"Hasn't anyone tried to break into this place?"

The question made Sarah stop in her tracks. "Yeah... but they… changed their minds." her regretful gaze at the floor told Jerry she wasn't telling the whole truth, and probably never would. He had no leverage over her.

"Are we going to stand here all night?" he was becoming increasingly irritable the further they walked down the hall. He felt it was unbefitting of himself. "I'm really sorry, it was unbefitting of myself." They resumed walking. Sarah didn't seem to be paying much attention to him anymore, transfixed on something in her very own private world. "Did you find out who the dead guy was? When was he from? Where was he born? What kind of music did he like?"

"Jazz." only questions about the matter at hand were capable of snapping her out of the introspective trance she kept falling into.

"That's all you got?" he tried to sound unimpressed with the results of her work.

"Well..." she looked at Jerry as if appraising the discretion of a child. "The police tell Kathleen things, and I overhear some things. The rest, she tells me herself." she felt the exclusive knowledge of things hidden from the public elevated her status in life. "They can't confirm it, but they think the man was Charles Pembroke. Disappeared a while back in these parts." she realized she was divulging this exclusive knowledge, making her status in life that much less special. "I've said too much. There is more, but I've been sworn to secrecy."

"What a shame, I can only imagine all the useless bits of knowledge you're keeping from me." he was starting to grow exasperated by her attitude towards the world around her. She didn't seem to care about it much either way, a philosophy he could definitely relate to. Seeing it from the side, however, was far more frustrating than he could have imagined.

"They would definitely be useless to a smooth brain." she had more bite than he anticipated. They finally arrived to the autopsy room. "There it is, have a look, take some pictures, chip some flakes off if you can. If you can find something we haven't I'll..." she fell into deep thought once again. "I'll admit you're better at this than I am. I'm still taking the credit for it though." this was the greatest offer she could legitimately think of.

"Sounds good." he wasn't sure how to proceed at this stage. On one hand, she definitely wouldn't leave him alone, and on the other, even if she did, they were still lacking the means to transport the body. He knew he had to be clever, to improvise the greatest story he could to wheel this body out of here. Every ounce of creativity he had flowed through his arteries and into the centre of his consciousness. He casually walked around the table, until he was within arm's length of where Sarah was standing. Suddenly, he whipped his head right towards the window, and exclaimed: "What the hell?!".

"Wha-" Sarah turned to look, and the world went dark.

Jerry had smashed his fist into her jaw while her attention was diverted. She was out cold. This turned out to be the pinnacle of Jerry's creativity when under pressure, and he considered the mission accomplished. After the flow of adrenaline slowed through his body and his senses went back to normal, he looked over Sarah to make sure she wasn't injured. On the contrary, she seemed fast asleep in a pleasant dream, and it occurred to Jerry she likely wasn't going to wake up soon, having evidently worked for days without rest. For that matter, neither was her boss. With one down, he made his way back up the hall and went into the direction Roger took off in earlier. The place was dark and unfamiliar, but it wasn't so big as to allow him to get lost easily. In only a few minutes, he saw another room with candles burning in it, and through the narrow glass pane on the door saw Roger on the other side, sitting on a leather ottoman, nursing something in his hand. Quietly, he turned the handle and pulled on the door, making it open with a very loud creak to which Roger reacted by nearly spilling his drink and frantically putting his finger to his lips. He pointed to the other end of the room, where Kathleen was laying still. Roger couldn't take his eyes off her, but couldn't bring himself to walk closer either. Deep inside, however, they both knew; they were bound to be hit close to home sooner or later. The darkness helped to keep the illusion alive, but it was time to dispel it. Jerry shined the torch on her, and the light bounced off the small hole in her forehead. Roger crushed the glass in his hand, cut himself, and began to cry. He could hardly even explain it to himself, having always believed to possess the powers of rational thinking and stoicism which come with his level of enlightenment. He had barely known Kathleen for any amount of time, but she stuck out his neck for him, and the utterly insane, uniquely strange man he was, Roger believed he had fallen in love with her. He didn't remember the last time a woman under the age of seventy treated him well. It only took him a few seconds before he started blaming himself, although he had no idea as to what he could or should have done to avoid this.

"You really liked her, huh?" Jerry finally dared break the silence.
"Maybe." Roger confessed in a broken voice.
"You think the assistant did it?" he tried to move the topic on a more logical plane of existence.
"There's nobody else." a few tears were still streaming down his face. "Where is she now?!" the all-consuming fire of vengeance suddenly ignited his blazing eyes.
"I knocked her out. She's in the autopsy room, and I think she'll be sleeping for a while. Roger, you'll find the time to grieve, but now we have to-" he watched Roger as he stormed with an unsteady gait, still propped on his bat, out of the office and down the hall toward the autopsy room. Jerry understood exactly what there was to fear, and immediately chased after him. His first instinct was to grab him by the arm, but Roger just shrugged him off like a pesky mosquito. His size wasn't just for show. Nevertheless, he kept following him, until he stood over the sleeping beauty. "Don't do it, it's not worth it."
"It's not right for her to keep on living while having taken Kathleen's life. I'll bet my life she'll be pardoned for it too. The old insanity defense. Where's the justice in this? *I* will bring justice to this land." though he spoke of action, he didn't seem too keen on actually going through with it. Not yet, anyways.
"But it's not for you to judge, Roger. Besides, we're not even sure she's the one-" he regretted bringing up the argument as soon as it left his mouth, realizing it would rile his friend

up further by forcing him to justify her guilt.

"Not even sure? The inside of the place is all clean, she has a gun, she has a motive with that meaningless Nobel prize of hers. There is literally nobody else." the picture seemed clear as day to him.

"Can you still be one hundred percent certain of that, even with everything that's happening around us? Come on, Roger, I know you'd like to punish her for this, but if ever the presumption of innocence should be a thing, it's in times like these." Jerry thought he felt the tides turning in his favour.

"Yes, Jerry, I can still be one hundred percent certain of that, even with everything that's happening around us." his gaze didn't leave Sarah's face, peaceful as ever. In her dream, the president was awarding her a medal at the local gas station. She smiled.

"They've worked in proximity to this body for a while now, they might have been driven to insanity. We don't even know if she can be held liable for her actions... if it's her." he was a firm believer of vengeance not being a solution and was prepared to hold his own until the end.

"She was perfectly liable when she greeted us, and I'm sure, when you knocked her out. And it is her, Jerry. You know it. I know it. She knows it. The Cosmos knows it." Roger was trying to convince himself as much as his friend. He had never considered how difficult it could be to end a human life until this moment, and even knowing all he thought he did, a deep barrier in himself he didn't know existed was preventing him from acting. Facing down against the reaper wasn't nearly as simple as he had imagined, no matter how much self-education he had in the philosophies of stoicism and idiocy.

"You're not a murderer, Roger. She is. If you kill her, you'll become one. The world will have the exact same amount of killers it did before. And Kathleen... she'll never be back, no matter what." he put his hand on Roger's shoulder.

"So you're saying... I should kill her, and then kill myself?" Roger severely misunderstood the message.

"What?! No. You should not kill her, let it be, and not soil your life for something that can't be changed. There are others waiting for us, living people, Roger. Think of your Loose Brain Dojo, those old ladies of yours need your guidance. What would they do without you?" Jerry shot a quick internal prayer in hopes this was enough to stop his friend from having blood on his hands.

"You're right." the sense of duty was one which was always successful in temporarily bringing the crippled guru down to the realm of rational thought. "We'll do what we have to for now. After this is over though, as the autopsy room stands witness, I'll dedicate every moment of my life to bringing her down and then making her life a living hell."

"Sounds good to me." he thought it was a bit of an extreme approach to the situation, but it would have to do for the moment. After all, maybe things would end up taking care of themselves, should everything end in total oblivion. "Did you find any stretchers on wheels? I don't want to ruin my jacket carrying him by hand."

"I think I saw one in the hallway. I'll find it. Tie her up so she doesn't escape" Roger's face was still red, but the tears of grief had already started to dry up with the prospect of a new and better tomorrow. He seldom enjoyed dwelling on the incomprehensible phenomenon of his own emotions.

With Roger having left the room momentarily, Jerry pretended to obey his command and placed a piece of loose rope around her wrists. From a distance and to the untrained eye, it looked like a perfectly-acceptable knot, but she'd be able to slip out of it when she'd eventually wake up. It also occurred to him he might have broken her jaw, and she'd be in a lot of pain. He shrugged his shoulders at the thought, and soon Roger returned with a big and luxurious stretcher, the kind they probably reserved for the Pope. With a lot more effort than they had anticipated, they shifted the body over from the table onto its modern carriage. Strapping it in for a comfortable ride and attaching the flashlight to the front, they carefully began the process of wheeling it back to the Big Cow. He tried not to show it anymore through the amount of concentration he was dedicating to the task at hand, but Roger's internal world was torn apart and he knew things would never be the same; a new stage in the evolutionary process of his mental cocoon had been set in motion. Jerry could feel it and respected his friend for how he was handling it.

On their way back, the city felt like it had rotten one step further, and even the precautions taken by those who shuttered themselves in were proving largely futile. The yells of wrath, insults and curse words were starting to take over the calm silence which had permeated earlier, and there were even some people who had taken to the streets in vague protest of the government's inability to keep people reigned in and bars open. Gunshots began to resonate from multiple directions in the distance, accompanied by giant spotlight beams undressing the night sky. Things were discouraging. Those who had left their homes seemed to instinctively clump together into like-minded groups, the thoughts and motivations of their individual members eventually becoming indistinguishable from each other. Roger even put his bat to good use and smashed the foot of a raging lunatic who kept walking besides them and insulting their mothers. They all needed to let out some steam. Children were even starting to join in with their parents, following in their methods and footsteps even from young and formerly-innocent ages. They too, became one with the mass, even faster and easier than their seniors. Despite their collective anger, they all felt a sense of fulfillment, of belonging, of the sort of happiness which comes along with societal validation.

The conditions in the streets weren't exactly conducive to wheeling a stretcher through them, but nevertheless, after many grunts of pain and effort, the two men had finally managed to bring their morbid bounty to where they were all supposed to meet back. They were the only ones, and decided to do the one thing they possibly could: wait.

Chapter 31

Naomi and Laura were walking down the pavement at a rapid and steady pace, uncertain about what they should be talking about, if anything at all. They were starting to get used to the conditions of their beloved city; the state of ruin was something they were becoming strangely comfortable with, and even surprisingly adept at navigating. This was especially true for Naomi, who as if by instinct knew exactly where every piece of rubble was, where they ought to hide to avoid people, where they should walk in the shadows and how to avoid any nasty surprises in blind spots. She figured if she had to, she could probably live under these conditions for the rest of her life, and perhaps even make a worthy documentary subject out of it. There was even a certain charm to seeing the world in the way it was being presented to them; there is a beauty in chaos, even if its principal feature is allowing us to appreciate order. Besides, she knew most people would go through their entire lives without witnessing anything even half as unusual, which made it a bit easier to cope with the idea they might not make it. She did her best not to think about that scenario.

On her end, Laura kept ruing the day she allowed Jerry to enter her library, focusing the brunt of her hatred on his person for, as she saw it, his contribution to the destruction of her castle. She created an alternate reality in her mind where the place was still standing thanks entirely to Jerry's absence from it, and slowly it took on the form of fact in her head, rather than fiction. The hatred also stemmed from a shame she experienced towards her own self at having failed to protect the sole bastion of knowledge for miles and miles around, despite having been warned about this day, as she saw it, by her mentor before her. She remembered perfectly the parting words of wisdom he had for her on his luxurious retirement party: "There will come a day when you'll have to stand up for what you believe in and keep this library alive, against all odds." Little did she know, he was afraid of loan sharks setting fire to the place after he failed to repay his debts to them. He worried for nothing. They preferred to burn down his house instead.

"Why are you friends with those clowns?" Laura shattered the sweet sound of nothing. She simply had to know. Naomi wasn't caught off-guard.

"Why do you hate literally everything you see, hear and touch?" she had already prepared this reply well in advance.

"How can you not hate self-serving, selfish assholes who only think about themselves? I'm not just talking about your friends. They're everywhere, stinking the place up, revelling in their lack of education, their lack of general knowledge about anything, taking pride in ignorance..." she had to stop for a moment to take a deep breath before proceeding with her tirade. "...they take pride in being idiots and cowards. They make knowledge lose its value, and they pass those values on to their children... we're a single hair away from regressing back into the stone age." she had been holding on to these thoughts for a while now, waiting for an unsuspecting victim to unleash them upon.

"Are you accusing Jerry and Roger in literally all of that? They're guilty of some ignorance, at most." she tried to keep her tone even, in spite of how much her companion was driving her up the wall.

"*SOME?!*" she seemed prepared to end Naomi's life right then and there.

"Fine, massive ignorance, for one more than the other. But they're not... wicked people. They're doing what they can to save what little is left of the town, more than you at least. You should be grateful to them."

“They'll save it by burning it, you can count on that. It's the way of the intellectually-deficient.” this seemed to be going nowhere. She decided to change the topic. “Anyways... where are we going now?”

“Somewhere you'll have a chance to demonstrate your intellectual superiority once and for all.” Naomi accentuated her sentence with a sharp exhale through her nose.

“I already did that when I became *The* librarian of this town. Are you planning on answering my question?” a small vein of indignation began pulsating next to her temple.

“We believe the thing in the well is not only spreading from the source, but two other things in town. One of them is a corpse. The guys went to get it.” and took themselves the easy job, she thought to herself. “The other thing is a painting made by a student... or former student of mine at this point, I guess. Billy the Third. Long story short, we tried to destroy it, didn't work, then we tried to bury it in a park and it sprouted roots.” she stopped, realizing her story was sounding increasingly dubious with every sentence. Then again, the limits of normalcy had become irrelevant a long time ago. “We weren't able to get it out of there, and it was leaking some nasty liquid, so we decided to leave it be.”

“What a brave decision you all made. Keep it up, and I'll start believing you're cut from the same cloth as those two. Did you actually try to do anything to get it out of there?” the condescending tone came as naturally to her as breathing.

“We...” Naomi reddened a bit in the face. “We pulled on it. Real hard.”

“That's... it?”

“What's it?”

“Lord high above... is that the only thing you had the wits to try?” Laura was almost prepared to cry faced with this level of incompetence and lack of critical thinking skills.

“It wasn't exactly a priority back then... oh shit!” they had arrived at the end of the street from the park where they buried the painting, and in the distance she could see a small crowd gathered around the hole, now completely uncovered. There seemed to be a trickle of people coming and going, like cars at a busy gas station. “What does your superior intellect say about this?” she hushed her voice down to a whisper, even though they were well out of earshot.

“Hmmm. They're definitely drawn to it, I can infer this much.” they both slowed their walks down and tried to be more careful with their flashlight.

“You and Roger would be perfect for each other.” strangely enough, the suggestion wasn't sarcastic.

“Are you-?! That *self-centred swine*?” it ought to have been.

“I was being sarcastic.” she lied her way convincingly out of the situation. “Any other words of wisdom to go along with your observations?”

“It looks like... they're either being... brainwashed? Or recharging there? They're not too transfixed to never leave. There's a constant flow of them. This is surreal... I'm sure there's something at the library to help us...” she craned her head up to the sky to simulate a state of deep thought.

“Forget about your library! We don't have the time to be searching through twenty dusty tomes for a vague clue that would likely take months to unravel! We have to act, and now. I have... a cunning plan... unless you have one...?” her voice trailed off as she too fell into deep thought. They both stood motionless like that for about a minute or so.

“I have nothing. Fine. What's your plan?”

“What?” Naomi was surprised at how unlike her it was to admit defeat, and so easily. “Did your superior intellect actually fail you? Oh dear, now we're done for.” her condescending tone was no less annoying than her unenthusiastic companion's.

"I have nothing, as in, I have nothing for now, and you said you had a plan, so let's hear it. Otherwise I'm turning around and going home." she crossed her arms and stood there like a petulant child.

"Mmhhmm. Anyways, my plan is simple. How good of a runner are you?" she already knew the answer, but she had to give it a shot, for equal opportunity's sake.

"I'm wearing high heels, and running away from or at anyone or anything is beneath me." spoken with the confidence of true bourgeois delusion.

"I assumed as much. I'll distract our little crowd and hopefully get them to chase me. I'll make a few trips around the block, while you figure out how to get that painting out of that hole." the plan seemed about as solid as it could be in every respect to her.

"I already know how I'll get it out of there." she reached inside her sleeve and unsheathed a large hunting knife. The beam from the flashlight made it gleam. Naomi recoiled more in surprise than terror. This Laura had a truly unhealthy obsession with weapons, but thankfully she ended up on a life path where they came in good use. Things could have easily been different.

"Well, I'm glad you of all people came prepared for this." she closed her eyes and took a deep breath. "Let's rock."

"Ugh, I hate that expression." Laura had the uncanny yet strangely common talent of finding even the most obscure and unexpected ways of souring the mood.

With Laura taking a few steps back so as not to draw attention to herself, the two women slowly kept creeping up the street which gave off an increasingly chemical smell the closer they got to their objective. They started breathing a little heavier, their feet were dragging a little slower, and their minds were clouding a little faster. A strange fatigue began to take hold of them, the kind which accompanies headaches and irritating social situations we can't get out of. Nevertheless, they pushed onward: they both knew there was nothing better to do tonight anyways. Though Laura would never admit another person superior to her in any respect (anything anyone was better in happened to be beneath her), but she was starting to develop a certain amount of respect for Naomi, even playing around with the idea of taking her in as an unpaid intern at her library. She thought it was better to bring it up later, once it was certain her beloved workplace wouldn't totally go up in flames and be buried as a pile of ash. On the other hand, Naomi was placing little confidence in Laura's ability to get the painting out of there, and was afraid she'd end up running from a crazed mob with nothing to show for it. She was always a fast and enduring runner, but she was far from being in the best shape of her life, and this without taking into account everything happening around her, including the lack of sleep and proper nutrition. The adrenaline was doing its holy work, but its effects can only last for so long, and she was afraid of simply passing out without warning. She tried to motivate herself with memories of her family, and upon remembering the kind of cult-leading family she had, saw her morale sink even lower.

Finally, they were within range to attract the crowd's attention, and Naomi froze in place. She looked back with her flashlight and saw Laura standing in a dark corner, motioning to her with angry gestures to move the light beam away from her. Naomi obliged and turned her attention to the crowd gathered in front of her. Something about them seemed off, and it wasn't them behaving like battery-fuelled zombies. She had expected a crowd of angry people foaming at the mouths, willing to chase her down the moment they saw her and knew she wasn't one of them. Yet, they all seemed fairly calm and even bored by what they were witnessing down in the hole. They were well-dressed and well-groomed, surprisingly hygienic for a local apocalypse. There was no hint of wrath nor malice in their gaze, and in the whites of their eyes Naomi could see a world of pain and sorrow. They still didn't notice her presence. Finally, she decided to set her plan in motion. She jumped out from the shadows and began flickering her flashlight at them while yelling out "Hey!" over and over again.

In one swift and dazzling motion, a tall black gentleman turned in her direction and looked at her with great puzzlement, then put a finger to his lips and shushed her. Once she obliged, he turned around and started looking at the painting again, as if he had forgotten her. Naomi turned to her companion in the shadows, shrugged her shoulders and motioned for her to stay there and wait. It was unnecessary. Laura wasn't about to divulge her presence in the face of so many people if she could avoid it. As a matter of fact, she hated big gatherings in general, and even if these were normal circumstances she'd avoid all those people like the plague.

Naomi came in closer and started pushing her way through the small gathering, which she estimated at about forty people from up close. With slight grunts of displeasure, the people moved out of her way until she made it to the edge of the pit. It was much wider than the hole they had dug up last time, almost looking like a crater with the painting as the epicentre of an explosion. There was a light emanating from within, the roots seemed to have sprouted more numerous and deeper than before, and the liquid was pouring out of the painting and into the soil. The people around seemed both mesmerized and completely unfazed by the display before them. Naomi tried to make her way back through the crowd and found the tall black man who shushed her, the one person there seemingly still having some form of awareness to him. She tugged on his sleeve to get his attention, and he abruptly slapped her hand and looked down upon her.

"What do you want, miss? Can't you see we're busy here?" he pointed to the unnatural pit.

"I can see you're all... extremely busy. What with, if you don't mind me asking, good sir?" she was going a little overboard in her guess as to the gentleman's age.

"Where the hell did you learn to speak like that? You think I'm old as a mummy for you to talk to me like that? I'm barely older than you!" he evidently took offence to it.

"I just assumed..." she clamped down and a burst of frustration found its way through her voice box. "Just tell me what the hell you're doing here, all right? How complicated..." she realized she was turning into Laura, and at an alarming rate.

"Hmph." he studied her expression for a few seconds before proceeding. "We're thinking on how to get the thing out of there. Everybody's too scared to go down there, but we're also too scared to leave it be. Who knows what it could do when we're not looking? So, we stand here and watch it. I, myself, think it's a neat solution. Very forward-thinking." he gently tapped his temple with his finger and gave her a knowing smile.

"Yes. Very. Forward-thinking." it occurred to Naomi those apart from the social mass still existed in it. Introverts aren't all relegated to a single neighbourhood. The realization made her feel a little safer. "I might have a solution to your problem. My... friend... and I, we came to get this painting out of here and get rid of it."

"Your... friend? Who? Where?" he began actively scanning the area around him, but could only see the darkness.

"She's hiding not far, we thought you were bloodthirsty maniacs and I was trying to get you to chase me. It's when I was yelling at you." she clarified without any superfluous emotions.

"Well, I'm honoured, miss, that we failed to meet your expectations." he gave her another smile, this time with a forgiving motivation behind it. He was too wise to take offence at anything but a grossly inaccurate appraisal of his age.

"She's all about logic and reason, so I think she'll volunteer to go down there to try and cut the roots off." she lowered her voice, inviting the man into a strange complicity he had no interest in. "Laura! It's safe! They're not maniacs you can come out!" she yelled into the blackness behind her.

"Tell the idiots to leave! I hate crowds!" a slashing response shot out from the darkness.

"Well, that's her, in case you couldn't have guessed. It's-" she was cut off by the man's hearty laughter.

"Yeah. That's Laura all right. Come on out, Laura, nothing for you to fear out here."

Cautious footsteps began approaching them from the shadows. "George? Is that... you?" for some reason Laura's voice didn't sound as happy as it should have to encounter a familiar face. She came out of the shadows and could now see him clearly. "Oh, for fuck's sake, even *here* and *now* there's no goddamn escape from you. Naomi, meet my deadbeat of a former... third husband. George. And now, forget you met him." a scornful fire set her eyes ablaze, the kind she hadn't showed to anyone in a while. A woman with many hidden layers of hatred.

"Nice to meet you." she decided to play along as best she could. The last thing she needed was getting drawn into some sort of spat between divorcees. These types of pleasures could wait a little while longer.

"Likewise." Georgie sounded more and more like a gentleman. "Our light was short, bright, fierce, and full of hotel room damages." nobody asked to hear this, but there was no stopping the man now. As much as Laura claimed to hate him, she flashed him a split-second-long smile. "And it would have lasted to this very day... if it wasn't for my second lover's fault." he glanced regretfully into the distance.

"It was...your lover's fault... that your marriage was ruined?" Naomi was having some trouble following the logic here.

"Naturally! She went ahead and told Laura everything about the eleven times I cheated on her. Can you believe it?" offended, he turned to Laura with a pleading voice.

"George...?" her voice started to break, as if she was about to start choking on tears any second now. "Fuck off, will you?" she regained her composure as fast as she had lost it.

"A real iron lady, huh?" he remarked to Naomi who awkwardly stood there, hoping this interaction would one day come to an end. "It was so long ago... can't you find it in your heart to forgive me? I'm not as old as I look, and I swear on all I hold dear I've learned how to do laundry myself. You were right. It is fairly easy." he unleashed another hearty laugh, evidently satisfied with his own attempt at humour.

"Long ago? It was a year ago, you hopeless buffoon!" her yelling was starting to draw the attention of the other people gathered around the pit, some of whom started shushing her.

"How about we get down to business?" Naomi finally found it in her to move the conversation along to something more important. "Can you help Laura get down into the pit?" she asked George, almost rhetorically.

"What the hell for?" his happy demeanour had quickly shifted to one of suspicion.

"Remember this?" Laura brought her hunting knife up to eye level. "I'll admit one thing, this was a great gift."

"It's a testament to my love for you, forever carved into eternal, non-biodegradable steel." George was still trying to win back his youthful and frankly attractive (ignoring her personality) ex-wife.

"I'm about to carve this blade into your face. Out of my way." She pushed past him and the people, who still maintained their air of indifference at a woman armed with a knife slithering her way through them.

Having finally made it to the edge she stood for a second, her survival instincts keeping her frozen in place at the sight unfolding before her eyes. Even though she had been given an overview of what to expect here, seeing it in person hammered layers of her subconscious she couldn't even guess existed. In a short moment, she understood exactly why all the people standing around couldn't go in nor walk away. The terrifying has always elicited a curious attraction in people since ancient times; no matter the ominous tales about the other side of the mountain, eventually people did find the courage and curiosity to cross over it. She closed her eyes, jumped feet first into the pit, and finally drew some sort of reaction from the crowd, whose members began to mumble and whisper to whoever they were standing closest to. However, none of them interfered, all watching with great interest what was about to unfold. Some of them were even on the verge of yelling out wise advice urging her to be careful. It was the most entertainment they'd had in a while.

Laura landed with a splash into the liquid which was seeping into the soil, and in certain places it arrived all the way up to her ankles. She felt her feet burning and knew she needed to act as fast as possible. She began hacking away at the roots of all evil. One by one, they were severed by her knife, and even though the blows weren't particularly strong, they were relentless and purposeful. As a matter of fact, they were quite weak, and only Laura had the contrary impression for how much effort she was putting into them. In the midst of this frantic hacking she had failed to hear George's warning of "Cannonball!" as he too jumped down into the pit, splashing the liquid onto everyone's clothes, and even into some peoples' faces. This too, was an attempt at winning Laura back. He stood there for a moment as she hacked away, and then extended the palm of his hand to her, beckoning for the knife so he could continue her work. With her feet burning up and lungs sucking for every bit of air they could find, she gave it to him without hesitation and began to climb out of the pit with a bit of help from those on the edges. They were now transfixed by George's hacks and slashes as he tried in vain to imitate techniques he saw in old martial arts movies. Thankfully for his ineffective methods, Laura had already done most of the hard work before him.

Standing a bit to the side, the iron lady took off her shoes and examined her feet. They were partially burnt, with the skin peeling off and boiling in some places. She clutched her fist and contained her need to cry from a sight equal parts agonizing and terrifying. Naomi sat down and put her arm around her shoulder, in a weak attempt to offer some superficial comfort. "You've done enough, stay with George for now. I'll carry the painting." Naomi proposed, and Laura quickly agreed with regretful head nods. The idea of self-sacrifice for some sort of uncertain greater good has always been a difficult one to process.

Only a couple of minutes later, George had finally finished hacking the roots off, and with a satisfied glee carelessly threw the painting in Naomi's general direction. It landed on the ground a few feet away from her, narrowly avoiding members of the crowd who had just enough time and reflexes to move out of the way. The strange vibrant liquid still spurted from it, but in a broken rhythm and uneven distribution. Meanwhile, inside the pit the severed roots seemed to have sprung to life and began hissing while violently flailing around, objecting to being separated from their source. Without an ounce of fear and every ounce of self-assured stupidity,

George began slashing away at them with the knife, avoiding their unpredictable blows with the grace of an overweight ballerina, putting on the show of a lifetime to win his ex-wife back. His audience was as impressed by his display as they were stupefied by his lack of common sense, urgently beckoning him to come back where it was safer. George heard none of it. Large swathes of his body had been covered by the burning liquid and all he could see was an all-consuming bloodlust manifested in a frantic duel of Man versus the unnatural. He never did stand much of a chance. After a few minutes, despite the excellent shape he was in, strength began to leave his body as pain and weakness nested instead, betraying the entirety of his plan to put on a heroic display of his immense worth as a human being. Taking a few steps back, he collapsed against the edge of the pit, and proudly announced he was going to take a nap, asking everyone to wake him up in thirty minutes for the second round of the duel. He promised it would be no less exhilarating than the first. Once they heard him snoring, the people pulled him out and laid him down on a nearby bench. He was breathing quickly. Too quickly. His pulse was going through the roof. A self-proclaimed doctor emerged from the crowd, and upon inspection, announced there was nothing he could do, for he wasn't really a doctor.

“I'd love to stay with you, but I really have to get going now.” Naomi declared as she grabbed the painting from the floor, carefully holding it by the edge with one hand.
“I changed my mind, I'm coming with you. This place is starting to grate on my nerves.” Laura already started walking back. “Are you coming, or what?” she seemed to have fully recovered and was back to her old antagonistic self.
“Didn't you want to stay with George? Looks like he might actually need you back there.” she was trying to gauge what kind of game her companion was playing.
“I only wanted to stay to watch him suffer for a while. Now that he's passed out, there's nothing left for me there. Except for my knife. I'll be right back.” a couple of minutes later, after prying it out of George's spastic hand, she was all set and in a bit too good of a mood to return back to the Big Cow. “I'm back. Let's go. Now.” an unsteady note in her voice betrayed her air of confidence, exposing before Naomi her profound fear and agony masked by layers of vulgarity and stone-cold endurance.
“Let me guess, I'm the one who's going to carry it all the way?” she already knew the answer.
“Yes. It's your painting. Pretty talentless too. Besides, I did the hard part...”
“So did George.” she was getting better at finding opportunities to strike back.
“I did over half of it, which is more than you've done so far. You're also the one who buried it. I shouldn't even be helping you, so just thank me and move on.” she was ready to end the conversation.
“Thank you, my liege.” so was Naomi.

With the vibrant and luminescent liquid spilling behind them and leaving a trail bright and obvious enough for a blind man to follow, they marched on in silence through the dilapidated town which had already started to feel familiar to them. “How quickly we get accustomed to things”, Naomi remarked for her companion to completely ignore her. Laura made it seem like having these sorts of discussions about universal truths and realities of the human condition were also beneath her, like most things in her life. After all, in her mind, discussing it implied either incomplete knowledge or a lack of confidence in what is already known. She always assumed she had both in spades, and therefore had nothing to discuss on this front: it was all simple and obvious to her anyways. She never would understand why people didn't share her point of view on the matter and why they bothered to engage in trivial conversations leading to the same tired conclusions and well-explored dead ends. Wasted time and resources.

A noise began to brew behind them, and looking back, they once again saw the ever-swelling mass of pointlessly angry people flowing through the street, bigger than ever before. Naomi wondered whether they ever had time to eat or go to the bathroom; it seemed like a commitment with few opportunities for rest and relaxation. However, even this circumstance no longer fazed the two ladies as they calmly and naturally sought cover in a nearby deserted building. Soon, all the buildings threatened to follow suit. It was more of an annoyance than an actual threat at this stage, but their powerlessness in the face of it all kept nagging at the backs of their minds. It was a slow but certain demise, and this is precisely what made it such an irritating burden to carry. Their only solution was not thinking about it and trudging onward in the hope they could make some kind of difference. Even if they couldn't undo the harm which had already been inflicted, maybe fortune would find a new champion thanks to their efforts. After a relatively long time, the mass had passed on and they resumed on their silent journey through the night. Following what felt like an eternity of bitter silence, the Big Cow was finally in sight.

Chapter 32

Officer Tim was a man of initiative, the kind who thought it best to charge ahead first and ask questions later, but simultaneously giving people the benefit of the doubt until they themselves provided a reason to think otherwise. A man of hidden and contradictory depths. He was disappointed in himself for having failed to catch old man Vinter, even though he chased after the sprinter far longer than any of his colleagues would have. He was certain there was something foul and unnatural at play, but he couldn't quite put his finger on what, and kept a mental note to confer with his Ouija board when he'd get the chance. He was a firm believer in there being powers beyond the realm of current human understanding, and he thought a wide swing was the best approach to the matter. His home was chock-full of talismans, medallions, charms, and wards from religions most people didn't even know existed. One of them was bound to be the correct one. He assumed his wisdom was beyond his years, and the ends would always justify the means for him. However, for the first time as far as he could remember, he couldn't see the ends, and even less the means to reach them. His immense sense of wisdom failed him, and none of the protective trinkets nor prayers he learned could help him out here.

He was wandering through the streets, trying to come up with a plan on how to seal those damned tunnels up for good. Roger and Jerry knew more than they let on to him, he was certain, and he even began to have doubts about whether or not they were his friends, hurting his feelings a little bit. There was a lot happening around him he couldn't understand, but he assumed it was just a matter of time to let it all stew in the subconscious, where the true and clear picture might be formed. His assumption never did prove correct. He tried to examine every detail of every wall, door, facade, park, and store he came across, hoping to find some sort of clue from the greater powers governing his life on what he ought to do now. After all, he gave quite a big promise before leaving, and he'd be damned if he returned without fulfilling it. For this reason, he was considering not returning at all and waiting it out in the deepest basement he could find. He reasoned he could go out and raid grocery stores for a little while and keep himself sustained, if need be. The thoughts felt shameful and unworthy of an officer of the law, but what could he do? Unbelievable as it might be, Officer Tim was human too.

About a half-hour later, as he was about turn the corner into a smaller street without any rhyme nor reason, he heard rhythmic footsteps booming from up ahead. Under the cover of shadows, he subtly slid up to the corner of the building and peeked his head around it to see seven figures marching down the street in perfect synchronicity, all holding something black and shiny in their hands. One of the figures was slightly in front of the others, leading the pack. They seemed far too reasonable to be locals, Tim figured. Assuming a stature of strength by puffing his chest and stretching out his shoulders, he rounded the corner with an air of absolute authority, the sheriff of a town fallen to banditry and disorderliness.

"In the name of the law, identify yourselves!" he pointed a dramatic accusatory finger at the figures before him, who responded by pointing what they had in their hands at him. He recognized those as assault rifles, and his throat was instantly dry. However, he knew better than to back down now. "If you don't identify yourselves, I'll be forced to arrest you all for obstruction of justice!" the threat drew a chuckle from one of them, and he stepped forward.

"Brigadier-General Salazar Darling Grundy. Hold fire, men. You, identify yourself." his voice was even, confident, steady, and had a certain commanding nature despite having a noticeable softness to it. He was wearing a helmet showing no hair, a respirator mask, a leather satchel, and a set of green army fatigues without insignia. The men behind him were similarly dressed and donning their own menacing gas masks.

"Police officer Timothy Krestin. I too, will hold my fire." he put his accusatory finger back in his pocket. "I'm glad you've run into me, Brigadier-General. You're just the man I was looking for." in the grey mist of his mind a plan began to brew.

"It is you who ran into me." Grundy politely corrected him.

"It is my town, so I'm right on this one. But, that's not important right now." Tim did not accept any corrections. "Brigadier-General-"

"Call me Sir Grundy."

"...Sir Grundy, I-"

"I changed my mind. Brigadier-General sounds better." annoying people was both an interrogation tactic and a favourite past-time of his.

"...Brigadier-General, I've come to report to you-"

"So, you admit it is you, who ran into me!"

Officer Tim closed his eyes to contain the frustration, and pressed on. "I've come to report to you I know how to solve the crisis at hand. Me and a... rag-tag troupe of mine. All we need are perhaps fifty trucks' worth of cement, maybe a hundred, I haven't done the math. We also need them as fast as possible, I'm sure you understand." the light of hope was shining brighter and brighter in his eyes.

"All I understand is you're breaking martial law being out at this hour. I have every right to gun you down where you stand."

"Then do it!" he clumsily unbuttoned his shirt and presented his bare chest, supposedly for them to shoot.

"I said I have the right to do it. Not that I'm going to do it. You need to work on your comprehension skills, officer. Besides, I have orders, from high up." he pointed a finger to the sky.

"What orders?" Officer Tim calmed down, but his shirt was irreparably ruined, which was bound to put a damper on the coming days, if they were indeed fated to him.

"Top secret orders. From the highest levels." the brigadier-general teased.

"And what do they say?" he wasn't about to drop the subject.

"I suppose... nothing can change your fates now. My orders are to erase this town from the face of the Earth. We have some real heavy artillery waiting just outside of town. All records pertaining to or mentioning Hollow Crest are in the process of being destroyed as we speak. It will even be struck from historical records and satellite images." the announcement came with the pride and love reserved for a government one truly believes in.

"But..." Officer Tim knew there was some flaw in the logic, something he could exploit to his advantage, something obvious, and then it finally hit him during the most important eureka moment of his life. "You'll still know about Hollow Crest."

"What?" Grundy was blinded by his admiration for the upper echelons of command, as well as their incessant praising of his abilities and trustworthiness... most of which came right before his current mission. He squinted his eyes at the officer as if trying to hypnotize him, and slowly he was starting to understand.

"They'll kill you after you've finished your mission. And your men along with you. If they can erase a town from existence, they can probably erase a person." he could feel Grundy leaning further and further to his side rather than his masters'. "You've been given a criminal order, and as an officer of the law in the town you're in, I order you to disregard it." he felt confident enough to start giving orders again.

"There is a chance you might be right, officer. However, this solves nothing. If I won't do it, I'll get court martialed, someone else will come along and take a right where I took a left." the roles had now shifted, and the brigadier-general was looking at the police officer for counsel on the situation.

"Maybe... You can convince your commanders. Convince them the place can be saved with a hundred cement trucks."

"I must see for myself what you need all those trucks for. But... if I have the evidence, I could stand a chance at convincing them human lives must be saved... even if only for experimentation. I don't know if they would ever let any of you leave. Including me. I'm not privy to much, but they all seem extremely concerned not with the town's existence... but information about its existence." he put the index and middle fingers of both his hands up to his temples and pulled them back a bit, plunging into deep thought, a sign his men had already come to recognize.

"There's no time to waste, you can massage your face on the way there. I'll even do it for you, if you'd like." the offer was as genuine as anything could be.

"Men! Form up! We're following the officer! Jogging speed, engaged!" in the blink of an eye they were all primed and at the ready, looking at the officer, waiting for his signal. Once the glory of the spotlight had passed through Tim's mind, he began his leisurely jog back toward the Big Cow.

Chapter 33

When Naomi and Laura arrived at the Big Cow, they saw Roger and Jerry sitting and waiting there, with the body laying on the stretcher, patient as ever. They both displayed a look of surprise when they saw the girls had indeed unravelled the secret to get the painting out of there. Roger instantly asked how they managed to achieve the impossible, and was informed by Naomi they simply hacked it away. She made it a point to say Laura actually helped with something, although she was standing to the side, pretending to hear nothing of their conversation while absorbing every word and sound from it.

The atmosphere around them was tensing, a noose tightening around the neck of the condemned, giving the illusion of a chance to escape while carrying the grim reality of inevitable fatality. They were all tired, beaten, scarred, and in a constant nagging pain they had learned to ignore at this stage. A few screams sounded in the distance, of either joy or suffering; the two had blended into an indistinguishable lump which grew bigger with every second it spent coursing through the streets of the town. This too, was something they had learned to ignore.

"All things considered, this new world order isn't too bad." Roger declared with the sombre air of someone made privy to the roots of tragedy. "I'm getting used to it. As a matter of fact, I quite like it." he titled his head to the side and gave a few nods to his companions. Laura threw up in her mouth a little.

"You can admit we're in deep shit, you know. Nothing wrong with that. We're gonna either drown in it or shovel our way out... but no way we're getting used to... this." Jerry waved his arm around to demonstrate the calm desolation around them. "We're cut off from the outside, and we'll need it to survive at some point. Nah, Roger, this new world order can kiss my ass. It killed Kathleen, Roger, and you know it." he instantly regretted the words which came out of his mouth.

"Don't you think I know all this?!" he snapped in the blink of an eye. "Belief in a better tomorrow, and the powers of the cosmos, are the only things capable of saving us now!" a few tears came flowing out. "I... I know... chances are nothing can save us. We're not enlightened enough to deserve salvation. Or at least, you're not. Ah!" he pounded his fist on his own thigh. "If only I had forcefully dragged you to my classes and made you listen to me, we might have had a chance." he closed his eyes and shook his head from side to side, then bowing it in shame, realizing his failure as a herald of the true knowledge of the universe.

"Don't blame yourself Roger." Naomi was doing her best to improve his morale. "It's better when you find someone else to blame. Personally, I blame Billy the Third for drawing up that painting. Felt like that was the start of it all. It really is his fault, and if I *ever* see him again... well... I'll remind him of that fact." the practicality of her reasoning resonated with Roger.

"You're right... It really is Billy's fault, isn't it? And old man Vinter, God bless his soul, is also an ignoramus of dangerous proportions. When this is all over I'll write detailed reports about them to the police."

"Hah!" Laura couldn't handle it anymore and felt the intense need to smash them with a mocking laughter. It was too long since the last time she denigrated anybody. "When you're done pitying each other and blaming anyone but your own idiot selves, let's actually do what we came here to do." through her torrent of insults a bit of truth did find its way to the surface.

"We're waiting for Tim to come back, but if you're in such a hurry to get back to the hell you crawled from, please, the way is open." Naomi decided it was once again time to bite back.

Laura still wasn't accustomed to it and responded with a dejected silence and a one-hundred and eighty-degree pivot. She pretended to examine the sky and avoided eye contact with the rest of them. Naomi turned back to her friends. "I hate to say it guys, but she's right. We can't wait here all night, and God knows what's become of Tim and if he'll ever be back, never mind in time."

"Hey! Guys! Over here!" Officer Tim's voice sounded some fifty meters down the street, and soon he emerged from the shadows along with the military troupe he was guiding with immense sense pride. "I told you I'd... find a solution!"

"You told us you'd find the workers *and* supplies to seal the place off." Roger sounded unimpressed as ever. "I'm unimpressed with your performance here, Tim."

"Is this man a rebel?" brigadier-general Grundy asked with a paradoxically alarming politeness.

"Only if a single digit IQ score can be considered rebellious." Laura answered in Officer Tim's stead.

"Is she a rebel too?" Grundy seemed to ignore her answer entirely, only focusing on the information the good officer was able to provide him with.

"I barely know her, but no, brigadier-general, there are no rebels. We don't believe in scum like that around here." he had seldom taken the time to think how good of a job he was doing policing the town, largely because it always moved him to tears. The great policeman in the sky would be proud of him.

"That's too bad. If you ever need them shot, officially declare to me their rebellious attitude. I will then be legally obligated to destroy them." he gave the officer a complicit wink.

"I... don't think local laws work like that. Then again, I'm no lawyer, so you might be right. I'll keep it in mind." he smiled at the brigadier-general, elated at the amount of trust he was being afforded. The idea of enlisting in the army even flashed in his mind, until he realized the town would be unlikely to survive without him keeping his watchful vigil over it.

"And what the hell is wrong with this painting?!" he pointed to the vibrant liquid spurting and flowing out of it. "And what the hell is that dead body doing there?! I've never seen this amount of ineptitude in my entire life!" he shook his head in disgust, at nobody in particular.

Officer Tim felt like he was about to lose his favour from the big boss. "Settle down, Darling!" poor choice of words, but he felt he had no other option but to go through with it now. At least it stunned Grundy enough to buy a moment of silence. "These are all... part of the solution. There's more to it. Come, we'll show you the secret underground tunnels and the... thing that settled there. It's quite a sight." he tried to make it sound like a touristic adventure.

"You get one chance, officer. I'm liking you less and less. If I'm not satisfied, me and my soldiers are leaving the country and letting our command wipe you out. That is..." he gave a good look around him. "If you don't wipe yourselves off the map first." there was no sarcasm in his tone. He was considering a very real possibility.

"One chance will be enough. A real officer doesn't need more." he rubbed the badge still attached to his weathered shirt, the last part of him he was prepared to lose, even if faced with the end of the universe. "Follow me."

"You two, with me. The rest of you, stand guard with these... suspicious citizens. Chat them up, gain their friendship, find out what kind of music they like, and be prepared to betray them at any moment." he never did acquire the habit of lowering his voice while speaking. The suspicious citizens looked at him with raised eyebrows, wondering if they were dealing with a scheme within a scheme, or utter foolishness in its purest form. When he noticed how close he was to everyone, the brigadier-general cleared his throat, and motioned for Officer Tim to march onward and lead the way, which he did.

As they passed through the darkened rooms of the factory, the officer tried to depict the situation as he best understood it, noting the painting and the body outside were fundamental to the eradication of evil. He also noted the methods employed here ought to be subjected to scientific study for the betterment of police forces across the world. It was all duly noted. They had barely approached the grate leading to the slope into the tunnels when they already found their senses assaulted by the sickening and unnatural heat emanating from within, the ghostly scorching sensation tingling under their skin. Grundy ordered for one of the soldiers to hand his spare gas mask to the officer while taking out a brand-new replacement for his own from his leather satchel. About as protected as they could ever hope to be, the little troupe trudged onward, opening the grate and carefully sliding their way inside. "And over here, you'll find the entrance to the secret tunnel, gentlemen." Tim was still trying to maintain the spirit of the excursion alive. Not to mention it was, after all, an adventure they were on. Little did he know, people generally prefer the sorts of adventures they can observe from a safe distance.
Walking in steady and certain steps, the group followed the reliable rope which still laid there towards increasingly painful sensations, grating on their nerves in spite of their precautionary measures. Neither the soldiers nor their leader showed any inkling of fear nor uncertainty, braving the unknown with the familiarity they could brew a cup of tea with. The tunnels were more hostile, oppressive and nauseating than the last time to the officer had graced them, but he decided to make no mention of it, in hopes of not ruining the town's reputation any further.
After a few minutes of walking through a disorienting segment of time and space, they finally arrived at the well, still standing there in all of its rotten glory. Officer Tim approached the edge, pointed his flashlight to its depth, and saw the same pair of abyssal eyes staring back at him. The middle finger was still extended. It was good to know stability prevailed in this underground domain. This meant rules existed, and rules must be followed. A terrifying familiarity suddenly struck the officer, and unwittingly he yelled out: "*You!*". A voice came out from within the well, loud enough to rumble the stomachs of all in the room: "YOU". Grundy approached and took a peek inside, and in the manliest way possible jumped back far enough to land into the arms of one of his surprised men.

"Who the hell are you holding prisoner down there? The king of all terrorists?" he questioned Tim like an angry school teacher might question the recidivist miscreant of the class.
"I'm fairly certain he lives down there. Of his own volition. We don't tolerate this sort of forceful behaviour in Hollow Crest. We think he's the source of the problem." if he had to be honest with himself, Officer Tim had to admit he had a suspicion of who the man at the bottom of the well was, but still didn't really understand why this was the source of the problem. Maybe he was never meant to. These things happen. He simply rolled with it. The alternative would have been actually admitting to himself he didn't really understand the situation at all, something unacceptable for an officer of the law.
"Who is he? Have you interrogated him? Why haven't you-"
"Sir, you better have a look-" one of his men dared interrupt him for the foolish sake of conveying important information.
"What is this insubordination?! Can't you see we're having a civil conversation?" this truly was his idea of civilized discourse.

"Sir, it's important! Our Geiger counters-" he motioned to the machine in his palm.

"You haven't turned those annoying things off yet?!" he was genuinely surprised people preferred the sound of Geiger counters to a bit of harmless radiation poisoning.

"Sir, as per your orders before the mission, we did. But I decided to turn it on down here, and look! We're bathing in radiation here! Sir!" the soldier was obviously panicked, his mind sounding the red alert at every corner.

"A third arm never hurt anyone. You'll live." with one motion of the hand he ordered him to stand guard. Both soldiers refused to listen and ran back out of the room following the rope. "I'm taking away all your rations from this day on!" he yelled at his deserters as their footsteps grew fainter and fainter. "Do you see the sorts of cowards they sent me in here with?" he incredulously asked of the officer who still remained by the well. After taking a deep and nauseating breath to regain his composure, he suggested "Why don't you try talking with it?"

"Excellent idea, brigadier-general." being Grundy's right-hand man brought Officer Tim to a seventh heaven he had no idea even existed. How all of the bullies from his school days would have been jealous of him. He could still see all their faces. His memory was painfully good, and sometimes he hated that. He poked his head into the well. "Who are you?"

"WHO ARE YOU...?" the response came a second later in a low, grating voice.

"I'm a police officer and right-hand man to brigadier-general Grundy, Timothy Krestin!"

"TIMOTHY KRESTIN..."

"That's me! I regret to inform you I must place you under arrest for squatting and refusal to provide proper identification. Please come out of the well with your hands up, and I promise not to shoot!"

"SHOOT..."

"No, I'm not going to shoot! Look, I don't want to come down there, so please don't make me!"

"MAKE... ME..."

"Fine, I can't make you, for now." he remembered to have read in an interrogation manual asking the same question over and over again could yield beneficial results. "Who... are... you?"

"...YOU..."

"Are you a criminal? Are you evil?"

"YOU... EVIL..."

"How dare you! I'm an officer of the law and-"

"You're talking to a goddamned echo!" Grundy finally jumped in after snapping out from the shock of witnessing the peak of local law enforcement. In the process, he blew wide open Officer Tim's perception of the situation.

"You're just... my echo?" Tim asked the thing in the well.

"MY... ECHO..."

"You're just... our echo."

"OUR...ECHO..."

In that singular moment the officer would remember for the rest of his life, he finally understood why the evil could take root here: it was a reflection of all the worst in them, all the worst found in any human being, even those capable of suppressing it. The potential for the destructive drive human nature can instill in us, it lives inside as long as we do, no matter where we choose to hide it. And what better way to bring it out onto the surface than the most destructive, regressive, yet simultaneously-progressive advancement humanity has ever achieved: nuclear science. It seemed inevitable

He thought about General Krestin's journal, and knew he would have to admit to himself, sooner or later, the burden which lineage placed on his shoulders. He didn't know the man in question, though he did remember stories about how his great-grandfather disappeared without a trace, offering little insight into the kind of man he was. In his mind though, there was no doubt. He played a hand in what happened here, and the overwhelming sense of familiarity wrapping around him when looking at the figure was proof enough for an aspiring detective such as himself. It was only fitting his bloodline would end up here and now. Whose else? The sequence of thoughts played through Tim's mind at the speed of light, while the brigadier-general stood a few steps away, holding his masked face in the palm of his hand, tremendously disappointed at the whole situation.

"We have to bring the painting and the body down here, throw them down the well, then seal the whole place up to the grate, blow the factory up sky-high, and scorch the entire neighbourhood it's in." he was now the one dictating outrageous terms to the army man.

"A little extreme, no?"

"You were planning on blowing the whole town up anyways. *That's* extreme." he had a good point.

"The point doesn't stand, we're talking about your methods, not mine." but not for Grundy.

"We've both seen the source of this now. If we can put an end to it, maybe the town can recover and come back to normal... one day. Maybe we can live in total secrecy while the rest of the world pretends we never even existed. This is my town, and if I can save it, along with myself, by blowing up a neighbourhood soaked in nuclear radiation, the blood of slaughtered cows and, as far as I can tell, the root of all modern evil, which might also be by pure coincidence my great-grandfather, then I think I'll do it! Now let's get out of here, get in touch with your command and convince them to do the right thing! That's an order!" he let himself get carried away just a little too much.

"I will relay your idea to my commander. But only if you apologize sincerely to me for your insolence. This is no way for anyone to talk to me, except for my superior, which you're not. Well? I'm waiting." he crossed his arms and nervously tapped his foot.

"I'm... sorry... brigadier-general." he squeezed through his gritted teeth, excited at the prospect of actually being the hero he always dreamt himself as.

A few minutes later, both men emerged back up from the grate. Officer Tim quickly ran to the three childhood friends and Laura, standing a bit to the side, and excitedly shared his discovery and appraisal of the situation.

"We already figured it out, Tim. Or at least, something like that. But great work doing it on your own, we're all proud of you." Roger still hated the fact he had to spend so much of his time traversing the town and hiding from the officer. Even worse, Tim seemed to understand more than him. It was exceptionally annoying.

"Don't listen to him, Tim." Naomi saw the importance of not picking any more fights with people. This could wait until the end of the ordeal. "We didn't figure it all out, it was all you."

"It was all me." the officer reaffirmed.

"And we sure as hell didn't know you were a Krestin." Jerry added, almost forgotten in this conversation.

"I thought Officer was your first name." Roger tried to make fun of him, but failed to realize this was the type of insult which implicitly backfired on its maker.

Meanwhile, Grundy was on the military field radio, having a discussion with his upper chain of command. Contrary to what Tim expected, the brigadier-general put all of his efforts into making an argument in favour of the town's preservation, even if under permanent quarantine. He posited the phenomenon found here could be studied for immeasurable scientific and military gains, and throwing it away would be an inexcusable waste of potential, worthy of condemning an innocent to death, specifically by firing squad, for some reason. He raised his voice where appropriate, lowered it when the situation demanded it, and the arguments kept on flowing through the radio like a revolving waterfall. Little did his superiors know, Grundy was captain of his school's debate team when he was twelve years old, an experience he was now putting to full use. They never stood a chance. In its entirety, the process took about an hour, during which everyone kept huddling closer and closer, understanding the implications of the conversation based on Grundy's end of it. When he finally put the receiver down, he turned to address everyone who had gathered around him.

"I have good news, and bad news. Which do you all want first?" he looked over the faces of the people who had entrusted their lives to him. Each one of them told a story, held secrets and ambitions, even if they were as idiotic as Roger's. He too, had the right to live.

"Both at the same time." Jerry's suggestion was sarcastic.

"We have explosives and it's all we're getting." the brigadier-general never was good at detecting it.

"What about the cement trucks? Couldn't they at least spare fifty or so?" the disappointment in Tim's voice was almost contagious.

"I tried, believe me." Grundy admitted regretfully. "But they were needed to cover up a biological warfare lab where... it's not important, don't worry about it. Long story short, everyone inside the bubble my soldiers put in place can't leave this town until further orders. This also includes my men and I. Even if they had the spare trucks, they wouldn't have allowed them in." he pointed to a duffle bag next to one of his soldiers while smiling with the conviction of a man with a plan. "But we do have explosives!"

Chapter 34

The small troupe of soldiers was running around like a horde of worker ants, planting and priming the explosives on all the load-bearing columns, under the silent direction of their brigadier-general. Their final moment of respite before the big show, the all-or-nothing gambit which would either save everyone who was left, or do absolutely nothing for anyone. It wasn't their fault they ended up with such a risky and uncertain hand to play with; none of them ever had experience dealing with this sort of thing, even though Roger did often imagine himself facing a nemesis only he could stop. Unfortunately, daydreaming is no substitute for experience. All things considered, they had managed to accomplish more than most who didn't get swept up by the current, not running away from the fight, and for the most part at least, not content with sitting and waiting for the end to claim its due. Not content with attempting to secure their own comfort and survival in hopes of weathering the storm. They were trying to stop it, and for this they all deserved statues dedicated to their courage in the face of the inexplicable... needless to say, no statues would ever be erected in their honour. As a matter of fact, they were destined to become an erased footnote in the official annals of human history, like most heroes before and after them.

"So you think the well-dweller is your great-grandpa?" Jerry asked Timothy in a weary tone, indicating he was more than willing to accept the shortest answer possible.

"You see, the journal we found was signed by him, and the last entry sort of matches up with his disappearance." he gave his audience a pause, allowing them to try and piece the chain of logic together. They waited in silence, and he was forced to continue. "He was an honourable man, venerated to the point where he was brought in to a top, top secret experiment just to witness it. They probably assumed he'd take it as a glorious gift. I've come to the conclusion they found his body, and interred him at the site of their little nuclear experiment as an ultimate sign of honour. The well... was his grave." he made it sound like more of a campfire story than a biographical fact. "Also, my granduncle Clint disappeared without a trace back in his day as well, but I doubt he has anything to do with it." giving them the complete picture felt necessary.

"Runs in the family, huh? All right, let's assume sounds logical. How does that help us?" Jerry almost blacked out from tiredness while listening to the long explanation.

"How... does that help us?" Timothy was a little dumbfounded at the question, having been taken by surprise.

"Yeah Timmy, what do we do with this knowledge?" Roger was starting to assume a mockingly familiar air with the officer.

"Well... at least we know... who it is? I suppose it's better to know than... not know?" he was having quite a bit of trouble defining the significance of his discovery.

"What we really know, Officer Timothy *Krestin*," Naomi made the pronunciation of the name sting like a barb. "Is whose duty it is to go back down there and put an end to it. Your family… involuntarily contributed to starting this in a very roundabout way, and it's up to you to clear the Krestin name while we cheer you on." she was about as tired as Jerry and wasn't keen on taking any more trips below the surface. Up here the air wasn't as full of radiation, at least.

"Haha! Can't argue with that." Roger was ecstatic seeing the good officer paint himself into a corner.

"Did you actually think there was a chance I would allow you, civilians, to risk your lives while us military men are here?" Timothy was offended at the mere thought of it. "You guys just, have a nap, we'll be back soon."

"Gladly." the three childhood friends announced in unison, and stepped off to sit together on the nearest bench they could find. Laura watched them go for a bit, and then reluctantly joined them, much to their dismay.

"Are we prepared, brigadier-general Salazar Darling Grundy?" Officer Tim shot a heroic look of anticipation at his newfound boss.

"Don't ever call me by my first name again. And even less by my second name. Apologize right now, that's an order." there were few things he hated more in this life.

"I apologize, sir. Are we ready?" he was getting quite good at delivering truthful-sounding apologies, especially when he didn't really mean them. He would have made a stellar politician.

"We certainly are. And make your apology sound more truthful next time, it was as fake as my wife's breasts." Grundy saw through it, though.

"You don't have a wife, sir. You're thinking of your stripper." and one Grundy's men saw through him as well.

"It's a figure of speech, and whoever tells me it isn't will get a Court-Martial." he eyed his underlings for any signs of resistance or rebellion. He was satisfied to be back in control. "Are we ready, men?"

"We done placed all but one charge on the weight-bearin' columns. This final one right here," the soldier held it in his hand and felt its weight. "we kept for the well. Tell your gramps I'm sorry. He was a real hero." he turned to Timothy with this final request of his.

"You should apologize to him on my behalf when you carry the charge down there." At the final second before committing to the plunge into the precipice, Timothy started feeling a bit of doubt in himself. Like everyone who had been down there, he had a negative desire to return. What if he were to fail? What would people think of him then?

"It's your gramps, not mine. You better do it." the soldier thrust the explosive charge into Timothy's hand, not even giving him the time to refuse the request. At this point, he felt he was too macho to back out. "Hail Satan!" the soldier added with jovial emphasis. Timothy simply nodded in response.

"All right men, let's move out! I want two on the painting, two on the body, and three of you to stand guard outside. Officer Krestin will lead the way with the charge in hand. I will direct the operation from up here. The tunnels are too cramped to make for a headquarters." no matter how it sounded, an order was an order, and they had no choice but to follow it, the good soldiers they were.

In only a few seconds the brigadier-general's orders were being fulfilled, and Timothy was leading the final charge into the Big Cow and the rotten depths concealed beneath it. This wasn't the first time he had been down there, and as a matter of fact, he more or less remembered the path to take by heart at this point. Nevertheless, he felt something was bound to be different, something was bound to go wrong at one turn or another. It felt like a fool's hope to assume they would be allowed to simply blow the place up and seal the thing in without having to put up some sort of final struggle. This wasn't the way life usually went; a dying organism resists and lashes out until the last possible moment, and here it was dawning closer and closer… in theory, at least. The soldiers behind him didn't seem keen on talking with him, largely concentrating on keeping their fears hidden as deep as possible, to be unburdened at a later, more opportune time. Timothy opened the grate, began descending, and motioned for the soldiers to follow right behind him, which they did. Once they had reached the bottom of the slope, Tim's worries came to fruition, as a pleading voice came out from the painting, directed at the two men carrying it.

"Don't... kill." the man depicted on the painting seemed to beg them. "Don't kill us. We're a wonder. We're impossible. We're more important than any number of people. You've never seen anything like us." his voice was slowly moving on from pleading into indignation. "You army men birthed us. Assume your responsibility. Let your children live."

"I'm going home." Declared one of the soldiers holding the painting before letting go of it.

"Me too. Have a nice evening." his partner added before setting the painting down on the ground and following his friend.

"Guess I'll be carrying this, too." Timothy carelessly grabbed the frame wherever it was closest, almost like he was willing to crush the thing in the palm of his hand. The liquid spewing from it burned him, but just a little bit; he was shielded by the mantle of holy duty.

"Timothy...You're not going to kill me, are you?" there was a sense of worry in the voice, but it somehow seemed a little feigned to the officer.

"Of course not, gramps. I know you're immortal. I'm just going to bury you under tons of rubble and make sure nobody digs you up again. I'm a considerate great-grandkid. Now shut it, we're not far away now." his tone was even and authoritative, even commanding to a certain extent.

The soldiers behind him kept following, but he could feel their resolve slipping away, only waiting for the body to come back to life before sprinting back up to the surface. He didn't blame them. He too, would have loved to have been able to ignore this whole proceeding. The brigadier-general should have been the one down here with him. Then again, Tim thought it might have been a risky waste of an excellent commander. They were following along the rope which had served as their sturdy guiding light in this netherworld, and only a few steps away from the room with the well, one of the soldiers could no longer contain himself and let slip a manly yelp when he felt the body beginning to jitter. His partner slightly soiled himself, but managed to retain his outward composure a little better. Timothy already knew what was coming.

"I'm alive." the body announced with little interest. "I've made everything whole. I've brought everyone together. Fusion. Happiness as one." these soldiers were made of sturdier stuff than the last ones, and were still carrying the body towards the well. "Can't you see all I've done for humanity? If the greater good is what you seek, the greater good is what I offer. No more divide, no more tearing between us, all happy as one, giant sea of people. Atoms ripped apart and fused together again."

"We don't want to be happy as one. We want to be happy as many." Timothy thought it wise to argue against the speaking, headless, radioactive dead body. "What would you know anyway? You've been dead for ages. Jazz has gone out of style, it's all terrible rap and electronic farts these days."

"I was born from the greatest advancement of this civilization. I am the frontier of human knowledge. You won't see as much as I offer in twenty lifetimes. I know what humanity needs. I know how you need to live." with these words the body suddenly became a little more than jittery, its arm smacking one of the soldiers in the knee hard enough to make it buckle momentarily. They were almost at the well now.

"And I know how you need to die." Timothy was proud of what he thought was a badass one-liner to send off a being of pure evil with.

On these words, he threw the painting down the well, and heard a guttural scream of indignation rippling out from within. "Quick, throw it in!" he turned to the soldiers, but it was too late. One of them lay still on the floor, while the other one was nowhere to be found. Before him the blackened radioactive body was standing upright, piercing his mind's eye with a heart coveting forcefulness and violence. An abominable aberration of the human anatomy. The trained officer wasted no time in drawing his firearm and unloading three shots into the body's torso, and two in its leg. "Ow! You prick!" it cried out as it lunged at him with uncontrollable anger. Timothy took the opportunity to swiftly step off to his side, pivoting around as his opponent lunged past him, first giving him a hard kick to push him to the edge of the well, and then a shove with his shoulder to send him careening down to the depths. "I'm fucking… James Bond!" he declared out-loud to the dweller in the well, his vessels gushing with macho energy.

After his adrenaline settled down just a little notch, he glanced at the motionless soldier on the floor, and turned him over, revealing a hole in his chest the size of a football. He took the soldier's pulse. There was nothing to be done anymore, another life lost to the eternal darkness of mankind. He himself started to feel a little sick, and remembered how much radiation he had been absorbing all this time. He had to move fast before he turned into a glowstick and passed out. He took out the explosive device, and only now realized nobody had explained to him how to use it.

* * *

"Think we're ever going back to anything remotely normal?" Naomi wondered out-loud, half-awaiting a response, half-awaiting being completely ignored.

"Not sure I remember what normal feels like." Jerry wasn't too excited with any prospects at this point.

"It might take years of practice, meditation, rigorous self-care and spiritual guidance, but if what we're doing works, we will, one day, get back to normal, and that's a fact." Roger really did see this as an indisputable fact.

"No. We're not." Laura's answers sure were concise and full of hope. The others mostly accepted her presence and ignored her ideas.

"You're a ray of sunshine today, glad you're with us in these difficult times." Jerry gave her a courteous nod.

"Nowhere else I'd rather be. What's taking them so long?" she really was doing her best to spoil the mood for everyone.

Just as she asked, the two soldiers who had been carrying the painting burst out of the factory in shame and panic, attempting to explain to their commander the horror they had just been through. They all sat on the bench and listened from a distance, witnessing the brigadier-general's disappointment in the men he had hand-picked. There they were, the best of the best. Shortly after, another one ran out, and he kept screaming about his friend having been murdered by the lifeless body which wasn't so lifeless anymore. Grundy was now fuming from his eyes, nose and ears, his face red from his own ineptitude as a leader. He made a mental note to delegate recruitment to someone else from now on. He had humiliated himself in his own eyes. He thought for a moment, and concluded he was unwilling to leave the good officer down there to do the Lord's work all by himself. After all, he didn't cower away like his own men. There was only one thing left to do. He turned to the civilians sitting on the bench, watching the whole scene unfold.

"One of you has to go down there to help him out! That's an order!" he assumed the air of the all-powerful despot, seeing no other local figure of authority capable of challenging him.

"We're not soldiers, in case you forgot." Laura was the first to spring into an act of defiance, as was her style. "We don't follow your orders or anyone else's."

"I'm using my authority as the sole remaining figure of authority to not only remind you about the current state of Martial Law, but to also put in place an obligatory conscription starting right now. From this moment on, you're all my conscripts until Martial Law is lifted. By me." he was dead serious and doing his best to get the point across without any unnecessary malice.

"Can he even do that?" Jerry asked of his fellow friends and Laura.

"They can't, but they will." Roger correctly reasoned.

"They're the ones with the guns and the soldiers and the backup artillery waiting to wipe the town out. We kind of have to do whatever they tell us." Naomi truthfully remarked on the situation. "So, which one of us will be going down there? It won't be me." she turned to her friends with an air of defeat, just waiting for the whole thing to come to its end.

"My ankle isn't hurting *too* bad right now, so I will do it." Roger was ready to fight for the opportunity of being a hero with either Jerry or Laura, but neither of them offered much resistance. As a matter of fact, Jerry even shook his hand and gave him a proud look, while Laura didn't even comment with something offensive, the most which could be expected out of her. "I will help out our Timmy and bring him home safe and sound." he turned to address the brigadier-general. "Please provide me with weapons and protection adequate for a conscript of my importance. I'm going into battle, but I'm not doing it naked."

"Fair enough." Grundy agreed. "Although, going into battle naked can be quite liberating." he turned to the remaining ones among his troupe. "Give him a sidearm, a gas mask, and the field manual for arming explosives." he quickly glanced at Roger from the side. "I'm afraid body protection is out of the question. We have nothing that fits you."

"The cosmos fits and protects me."

* * *

Despite his skin burning and boiling, his eyeballs feeling like they're about to melt, his nose catching fire with every inhalation, and an annoying song from his teenage days stuck in his head, Timothy didn't lose focus for a second while examining the explosive device he was handed. It didn't look like anything he had seen in the movies, being essentially a block of putty wrapped in a dark green film. There was also a small bag attached to it, with three tiny metal rods with wires protruding from them, a small circuit board, as well as an object the officer guessed was a remote detonator. He had at least one element of it down. He was staring at the materials he had to work with, without making progress, long and hard enough not to hear Roger sneak up on him. He took a seat on the floor with the officer, rubbing his ankle which began trying to tear away from his body as soon as he descended into this place.

"Should I tell the others you've decided to live down here too?" Roger poked Timothy with the baseball bat he had resolved to keep carrying until the end of days.

The officer slowly turned his head to him and craned his neck, articulating his words with ghastly effort. "Do you know... how to use this?"

"Do I look like a terrorist?!" he was just about ready to leave the officer down here, having taken massive offence to his insinuations.

"You're... under arrest." his long-forgotten backlog of duties as a police officer was beginning to play in the back of his mind.

"Say, Timmy, good friend..." Roger had a million-dollar idea. "If I show you how to use this, will you give me your lawman's word all my former and future crimes will be pardoned?" he was trying to sound as cordial and amicable as possible.

"Former crimes... yeah... future crimes... no." forming words was increasingly difficult. A pain in the depths of his gut forced him to physically fold.

"Agreed. No refunds." he shook the officer's limp hand as he took the explosive device from it. "See, all you need to do is..." after briefly studying the field manual, he proceeded to plug the three metal rods into the brick in careless fashion, and connected the wires to the circuit board as best he knew. "See? Easy and simple. You've really taken a bad a deal here, but I did say no refunds. I'm surprised you couldn't figure it out, seeing as how you're a police officer. Hey. Wake up!" the officer seemed to have fallen asleep on his knees. A thin stream of blood flowed down his neck from his nose. "I'm not wiping that for you!" a second later he used a piece of Timothy's own shirt to wipe it off. "Let's go, we're all set, I need you to help me walk out of here, my ankle is getting worse by the minute!" still no response.

Roger then noticed a sound coming from inside the well, and though he was inspired to be reasonable by his heroic intentions, his sense of curiosity got the best of him, and he leaned on it to peer over the edge, into the seemingly bottomless chasm below. There wasn't enough light to pierce through the thick veil of darkness, but Roger thought he saw darkened hands slowly clawing their way up, pressured to the surface by the smile of brutality behind them. "I hope you're ready for a thousand years of solitude, because...by the powers of the cosmos, eat shit!" Roger's one-liner in the face of all-encompassing evil was about as good as Timothy's. They had more in common than either of them imagined. He placed the charge at the base of the well, said a quick prayer to his deities in hopes he armed it properly, and began to limp back to the exit while leaning on his trusty bat, his gun precariously positioned in his trousers, and the detonator held dangerously in his other hand. He was just about to leave the room when he remembered he had forgotten something, but he couldn't quite put his finger on what. "Timmy!" he exclaimed after a few seconds of digging his memory. He was still slumped on his knees, unable to move, though Roger suspected he was at least partially unwilling and just being difficult for the sake of it. In truth, he was merely judging another by his own standard.

This marked the moment Roger understood where he fit in the grand plan, finally confirming his hypothesis of having been reserved the most important role to play in this cosmic drama, the linchpin which held the whole construct together. Without him, the explosive wouldn't have been armed, and without him, the other hero wouldn't make it out alive. In his eyes, if hero A saved hero B, logically hero A would be the more important one, and that's who he was. He briefly did consider how leaving Timothy down in the depths would play out, but decided against it, concluding it would make people think of him as a lazy kind of person, which he certainly wasn't.

With the decision now having been made, he faced the problem of barely being able to walk on his own, let alone carry someone who couldn't muster the good grace of not falling asleep at the doorstep to the human civilization's greatest problem. This was the moment. He knew it, he could feel it. All of his preparation came down to this. He assumed the most experimental and secretive meditative position he had ever worked on, a stance he had been perfecting since adolescence, only reserved for the direst of circumstances, never to be used again. Despite his bulk, he managed to contort himself into perhaps the least comfortable arrangement of limbs ever imagined, and began to chant his mantra in a language he had invented himself.

At first, not much happened, and he could even hear the hands from the well crawling closer and closer, threatening to spill through onto the surface. He closed his eyes, focused even harder, and chanted twice as loud. Timothy was sadly sleeping through the whole performance; he would have unironically loved it without ever admitting it. Then, the miracle happened. Roger felt not only all pain, but all sensation leave his Earthly body, and had a feeling he was floating up through the air, inches off the ground. He looked down, and saw himself sitting in his meditative position, and panicked. An out-of-body experience wasn't at all what he was going for, and he had no idea how to get back down. He assumed he'd just have to wait for it to end, and so he floated there for a minute, then two, and then relief washed over him as he saw two familiar figures entering the room. Jerry and Grundy had finally ventured down here too, followed by a soldier whose lack of enthusiasm was palpable even through his gas mask. The sense of failure at having taken too long and having generally failed to fulfill his role in the cosmic play were minor details now that Roger was hanging on to dear life by a thread, at the mercy of others. After Jerry and Grundy were finished marvelling at the level of ineptitude they were witnessing, they finally found it in themselves to drag the two men out of there. Roger seemed to be frozen stiff in his position, which thankfully made him easier to carry. After a few minutes of hauling later and some clever teamwork to push the unconscious men up the slope, they were finally out of the underground radioactive slosh pit.

With a bit less urgency, they dragged them outside, into the fresh air, and Roger was still floating above himself, observing it all from a strange vantage point which didn't give him much of new perspective on anything. He was starting to feel impatient about returning to his body, and already began to wonder what he would do if forced to spend the remainder of his life in this hollow state. Would they preserve him in acrylic? Donate his body to science? Feed him to the sharks? The possibilities were endless, and their consideration kept him occupied until he slipped back into his corporeal form without even noticing it. He woke up just in time to see the fireworks go off. He glanced at Officer Tim, still asleep and positively glowing like a fluorescent lamp. Things weren't looking great, and he decided to keep his distance from him. He walked over to where his friends, Laura, Grundy, and the soldiers stood, joining them in saying a final goodbye to the place.

The brigadier-general held the remote control in his hand, and explained it would activate the explosive near the well. His soldiers had the other remotes for the explosives planted on the factory. They all took a deep breath, Grundy yelled out "In Her Majesty the Queen's name!" and pressed on the button. There was a slight and barely audible rumble from deep within the earth, the tremor from it vibrating in their guts. The soldiers were given the order to activate their remotes as well, and so they did, the shockwaves from the blasts roaring through the air and inspiring an all-consuming terror.

The whole place stood still for a moment, and then began the creaking and cracking, the slipping and sliding of concrete and metal, rubbing against each other, scratching and crashing at an astonishingly slow pace. Just as the walls, columns and ceilings began to slide in on each other, a dirtied figure was visible at the main doors, and it sounded like it yelled at them "Tis I, Sher-" before it was crushed underneath a sliding cascade of rubble. Grundy attempted to inquire about it, but everyone else denied having seen it, and so he too, ultimately denied having seen it.

The factory fell inwards on itself and an unnatural screech was discharged upon the land, imbibing it with an enduring radioactive miasma. The ground began to slowly collapse on itself, and a sinkhole methodically formed at the exact centre of it all. Rays of multicoloured light and splashes of unidentified liquids shot out from the earth as it chewed and digested through the hardened flesh of Man's structures, through countless years of toil, tears and bloodshed. They all watched the spectacle with bathed breath, except for Timothy, who was still sleeping through it all, bound to never have any kind of memory of what might perhaps be the most important moment in his life. Once every peace of man-made material had fallen into the sinkhole, it began to stop its movement, slowing its expansion, and ultimately moulded in the form of a giant crater, reminiscent of a massive explosion, the kind the human civilization has become far too proficient in creating. Now *that's* a fitting monument to mankind.

In a split second after the whole thing was over, the air started to feel lighter and more pleasant, and the darkness around them seemed to have receded ever-so-slightly. Morning was already on the way. The cacophony of suffering which had permeated the town, to the point everyone had become accustomed to is as a background noise, was also receding further and further away. Soon, even the great mass of people causing havoc through the city began to lose steam, as its members fell unconscious into the streets, bound to never have any memory of how they got swept up by the general current, opening themselves to making the same mistake in the future. A sense of calm and peace was returning bit by bit, and though it is unknown how long such a thing can last, they felt they buried the evil deep enough for the time being, walling it off from the human condition... but only temporarily. Such is our lot: to bring about our own counter-productive destruction time and time again because we cannot help being the imperfect and tremendously fallible creatures that we are. The day would come again, and they all knew it.

Grundy went back to his radio and began to inform his command about the success of the operation and its interesting consequences. He returned to the three childhood friends, Laura, and the sleeping Timothy, with an enthusiastic announcement. His commanders agreed to let the town keep on existing as long as it was erased from the pages of all maps and history books, and its people could go on living as long as they never left and subjected themselves to continuous study and analysis in hopes of unravelling the truth behind the event and its consequences. Essentially, they would be living under a half-metaphorical dome, receiving supplies on the sly in the dead of night, and remain unrecognized citizens of the illusory free world. The few people with relatives living outside of town were given the choice to either have them brought into the town as well, on a permanent basis, or feigning their own demise. Surprisingly enough, most of them chose the latter without batting an eye. "Exciting stuff, isn't it?" Grundy asked earnestly from his small group of listeners. Timothy was still sleeping and glowing through it all.

Chapter 35

The first few weeks after the incident were difficult for everyone, but in time, things returned back to a very relative sort of normalcy. The town's complete isolation made it turn its focus entirely on local industries, and there was a noticeable rise in agricultural practice to compensate for the lack of imported products. They were even in the process of building a new and improved slaughterhouse next to where the Big Cow had once stood, to accommodate the need for a local meat production. Some lessons are never learned. Many people sought out work in new sectors, and many others were getting used to a reality where their former education didn't hold much value anymore. The town needed more people who could work with their hands rather than their brains, and ultimately, it's what it would get, for better and worse.

Jerry still hadn't decided on what to do with his life now that his security guard job at the Big Cow was a thing of the past, and so he spent his time as Roger's assistant, who not only kept his Loose Brain Dojo open, but saw it thrive more than ever before, especially after he had his foot amputated when he was told the recovery time for his ankle might take years, if not decades. In times of exceptional crisis people lose their aversion to fringe beliefs and practices. It was a relaxing job, and consisted largely of chastising Roger's students when they followed his instructions incorrectly and filling up his bottle of water. He didn't mind. A bit of calm life was something he definitely needed at this stage.

Naomi also went back to her painting studio, teaching kids whose parents forced them to take extracurricular activities so they'd get out of the house more often. They were still just as lacking in talent as they were before the crisis, and she found it very easy to slip back into her old habits. As a matter of fact, none of the three childhood friends saw their lives change all that much; they were already outsiders and, in their own ways, recluses.

The only aspect of their lives which did change for them was the fact they were all living together in the same apartment building, in the forgotten part of town which escaped the chaos and destruction the rest of it saw. For their services rendered to The People, they were awarded rent-free dwellings until the end of time. Not too bad of a deal, all things considered.

Occasionally, men in hazmat suits and strapped with protective gear from head to toe would swoop in to pick a few people up, bringing them back only a few days later. They didn't seem worse for wear, but swore not to discuss what had been done to them under penalty of death. They understandably always chose silence in the face of all temptations to spill the truth. From time to time, teams of scientists with strange apparatuses as well as excavators would be seen at the mount where the sinkhole still remained, evidently trying to penetrate the mystery hidden to them under who-knows how many layers of dirt, steel and concrete. They would get to it one day, but hopefully, not too soon.

Officer Timothy Krestin did finally wake up from his sleeping beauty impersonation, only to find himself in a sealed observation chamber with strange men and women in white coats all around him. Sarah was among them, absolved from her crimes on the basis of insanity, now secretly working on her Nobel prize in radiobiology, which she would never get. Tim had apparently absorbed such a large dose of radiation without dying, the government decided he would best serve them as a lab rat for the foreseeable future. Gratitude comes in many forms, especially nonexistent ones.

Laura took up residence in her ruined library, dedicating her existence towards its restoration to former glory. Her crazed manners and misunderstood drive towards the archaic drove people away at first, but in time they warmed up to her as a necessary monolith to the evils of knowledge. Jerry made a habit of coming by to help with the doomed project, first out of pity, then out of love. It was a complicated affair, which naturally meant it was of interest to people who had nothing to do with it. He was far beyond being bothered by it.

Jerry spent most of his evenings sitting on the rooftop with his friends, looking on in the distance as again and again people tried to break free through the cordon around town, sneaking about this way and that, only to be either captured, or sometimes outright shot. Not a single person ever made it through, and the numerous attempts to dig tunnels were quickly dissuaded with some hasty kidnappings from which none returned. Nevertheless, they kept on trying and trying, hurling themselves headfirst into a brick wall in blind pursuit of their own selfish ideas of freedom. It's simply what people were doing at this stage. They watched on with amusement, knowing that same senseless determination was bound to unearth all they buried and continue the cycle anew. They tried to think of the future, but always found themselves terrified by their own thoughts, and so they didn't. They agreed the present always had a lot more to offer anyways. A bird which sneaked past the cordon flew overhead, and dropped its load on Roger's shoulder. He knowingly smiled at it. These things happen.

9 781777 861902